SPACE
TAXIS

~

A&H Frosh

ISBN: 1916212688

ISBN-13: 9781-9162126-8-8

Typeset in **Garamond**

www.BurtonMayersBooks.com

DEDICATION

To Rachel, an amazing wife and mother.

To Janie

Happy reading

Adam

Harriet

~ CONTENTS ~

Acknowledgments

ACKNOWLEDGMENTS

A special thank you to Rachel Joyce. Without your input,
Space Taxis would never have ventured into the world.
Thank you to Andy Headland who drew the figure on the
front cover of this edition.   Thank you to all our friends
who helped critique the manuscripts.
We will be forever grateful.

A&H Frosh

A FREE RIDE

August 16th, 1977, Brooklyn.

Mike Redolfo pulls up his yellow Checker cab. The man hailing him looks like he's been at a costume party or some kind of military convention. He's impossibly thin, looks almost seven feet tall, and is wearing a dark uniform with so many buckles around his waist that he must be uncomfortable in the afternoon heat.

"Where're you going, buddy?" he says through the open cab window.

His passenger stares at a cluster of bullet holes in the rear door before curling up his long frame to settle into the back of the cab.

"Just drive."

As the cabbie pulls out, he checks his rear-view mirror and sees his passenger's wide, unblinking eyes fix on him. Redolfo's seen more than his fair share of weirdos in his time, but something about the guy's stare is making him nervous.

"Turn right."

They take a right turn down Euclid Avenue. "This alright for you?"

The man doesn't respond.

They pass the Church of the Blessed Sacrament where the choir, bedecked in white robes, has assembled in front of the building. As they sing the priest raises a smile to heaven.

"Turn left," the man commands. They travel along Fulton Street, the sunlight flickering through the steel canopy of the elevated railway track. "Now right. Stop here." He exits the checker, closes the door and heads towards a parking lot that's crowded with cars, but devoid of people. An unmanned graffiti-covered hut guards the entrance.

"Hey, buddy! You gotta pay for that ride!" Redolfo shouts before he too jumps out of the vehicle and gives chase.

The man strides into the parking lot and disappears from sight between two lines of parked cars. Redolfo soon reaches the lines of cars to find they end at a brick wall and the man is nowhere to be seen. He drops to the floor and looks underneath the surrounding vehicles. "What the hell?" he mutters as he uses his cap to dust off his shirt. His passenger seems to have vanished into thin air.

As he returns to his cab, he hears a female voice calling over his intercom, "Mike! Mike! Come in, Mike. Mallinson says you've got to get your ass back here. He's not happy. Seems serious."

~

Redolfo enters the cab office and tilts his cap to the young radio operator. She smiles back at him, her lips bright red with lipstick. His corpulent boss, Mallinson, is in his usual position at his desk, which Redolfo always thinks would look classy were it not for the explosion of paperwork covering every inch of it. Mallinson points to the seat opposite him. As Redolfo sits, his boss jabs at a paper with his pen.

"So, what is it this time?" says the cabbie, "I've already had the goddamn craziest day and—"

"We've had enough of your crazy days, Redolfo. I've told you before, this is a business, not a charity. And remember that guy you bust up? He's pressed charges. You think you can treat the company like some sort of vigilante outfit? It's gonna be splashed all over town. It's something new every week with you, and this is the last straw."

Redolfo tries not to stare at his boss's blubbery jowls. "So, I should've just done nothing and let the woman get knifed?"

Mallinson ignores the comment. "And it's not just that. Those bullet holes in your cab - why're they still there? It looks bad, Redolfo. You think that cab belongs to you? It's the company's."

Redolfo's proud of the bullet holes in the back door. He'd used his Checker as a shield to protect two innocent pedestrians from a gang shootout. He's always good at sensing trouble and his quick reactions saved their lives, but even so, it was a moment of pure instinct that even he couldn't explain. The bullet holes are like a trophy to him. He has no intention of getting them repaired.

Mallinson's fierce look softens. "Listen, Mike. I know you mean well, and the customers like you, but you're a liability for the company. I've recommended the commission suspend your cab licence, at least until you pull yourself together. It's out of my hands now."

Redolfo feels like he's been kicked in the guts. He can barely pay the rent for his apartment as it is. Without a job, he'll probably end up on the streets. He looks around the office with its greying paint and cracked glass partitions. It may be a ramshackle outfit, but he loves it. It's his home.

"So that's it, Mallinson? Ten years of service. I've worked my butt off for this company, just like my pa did. This place would've been nothing without him. What do you think firing me will do to him?"

"Hey Todd, give the guy a break," the radio-control girl protests, her over-sized beads rattling around her neck.

Mallinson silences the trembling girl and her beads with a glare.

"Okay, I get it, Mallinson. I'm outta here. I'm the best goddamn driver you've got, and you know it."

Mallinson gestures to him to hand over the keys. "We're taking that bullet-ridden junk-heap. Another driver's going to need it."

Redolfo ignores the demand, adjusts his cap and leaves the office. He returns to his cab, ignoring the parking attendant who has begun to write a ticket.

"Oh no, you don't!" Mallinson bellows, as his rounded form fills the doorway. "Give me the keys, Redolfo! That cab's ours."

Pretending not to hear him, Redolfo starts up the engine and speeds off.

~

Redolfo pulls up the Checker at Brooklyn's Ferry District. His father, Alfonso, sometimes took him there when he was a kid. He'd told him how it had once been an important cargo port. The place now looks like a disused wasteland, but it's still a great place to view lower Manhattan.

He opens the glove box, pulls out a bottle of whiskey and takes a large swig. He loves this skyline, carved from the tallest buildings in the world. There's no better place in the world to watch the stars roll behind the skyscrapers until morning.

As the liquor begins to pervade his mind, he traces the outlines of the buildings with his eyes. When he was younger, he watched the construction of the World Trade Centre's twin towers with fascination as they rose from the ground to dominate the skyline.

He turns on the radio.

"Police in Memphis, Tennessee are reporting that Elvis Presley died this afternoon at the age of forty-two at his Memphis mansion, possibly of a heart attack…"

Redolfo takes another big swig from his bottle. "As if this hell-hole day couldn't get any worse! The King, man? No, this can't be right. I know you're not dead…I can feel it!"

"…this is the last song he performed live…"

Are you lonesome tonight?...

Tears roll down Redolfo's cheeks. He joins the singing...

His mind wanders. He sees Mrs. Moeller, his fourth-grade teacher, shaking her head as she says to his mother, "I'm sorry, Mrs. Redolfo, but unless your son changes his attitude, I don't think he'll ever make anything of himself."

His eyes cloud over. Emerging through the haze, an intense beam of bright light forces him to cover his eyes. He sees his mother shouting at his father, "Alfonso, tell that good-for-nothing son of yours how you worked your ass off so we could have a roof over our heads - and this is how he repays us?"

The song changes...

The light surrounding his cab intensifies, forcing him to shield his eyes with his hands. The vehicle begins to shake. "Man, I've got cab-spin! Goddamn cops! Why can't you just leave me alone?"

The ground falls away as it becomes clear the Checker's lifting into the air. He leans out of the window and peers up towards the source of light. Through the brightness, he can see what looks like sliding doors opening to reveal a gaping hole in a panelled metal structure directly above him. "Damn cops. What's this, some kind of tow-truck?"

From the radio, the opening chorus of *We're Moving Out Today* echoes in his head just as everything turns black.

A NATION IN TROUBLE

Prague 1944

The weekend is approaching, and the hairdressing salon is
bursting with people. Above the din of the hair dryers and
the animated chatter, Marianna Kravová hears her name
being called from all directions around the shop floor. She
rushes past the line of silver hair dryer domes, each
occupied by a woman wearing a blue hairdresser's gown
and with a magazine on her lap.

"Marianna, can you get another can of hairspray?"

"Marianna, can you tidy the rollers away?"

"Marianna, Mrs Horáková needs a coffee."

Thankful for a break from hours of washing hair,
Marianna retreats to the kitchen at the rear of the salon
and fills an old pan with water. She lights the gas hob
carefully with a match and spoons ground chicory from a
jar into the pan. It feels like an age to her since real coffee
was available. Even the German customers can't access it.
The chicory substitute is better than nothing, and at least
the people of Prague can still get milk and sugar in the
shops.

As she sieves the brewed chicory into the cup, she
hears her name being called again from the shop floor. She
scuttles out with the cup on a saucer in one hand and a jug
of milk in the other.

Mrs Horáková is a regular at the salon. Marianna has
heard that her businessman husband has been working

with the Nazis since the occupation and has become very wealthy. As Marianna approaches, she hears her talking loudly to the blonde hairdresser standing behind her, who is paused with scissors in hand.

"Sorry for the delay, Mrs Horáková," Marianna says. "Would you like m—".

Ignoring her, Mrs Horáková continues talking to the hairdresser who is weaving rollers into her hair. "My husband says that Moravec is a real ladies' man. He's a great role model for our young men, too, helping them to understand how much the Germans are doing for us."

The hairdresser pulls a hair pin from her mouth to fix a roller into place.

"Moravec was right all along. The problems between our countries were all down to the Jews and their greed. They infected our nation. With the Germans' help, we can clean up our country."

Marianna purses her lips. With the slightest tilt of her hand, the cup slides off the saucer she is holding and lands on the customer's lap. The hot liquid scalds through the woman's gown.

"Oh, Mrs Horáková, I'm so sorry, I—"

"You stupid girl!"

Marianna stands frozen to the spot. *What on Earth have I done?* – the words scream inside her head as she tries to take control of her thoughts.

"Let me sort this out, Marianna. Go home now," the floor supervisor orders as she rushes toward the scene with a towel. "I'm so sorry Mrs Horáková. It will never happen again."

Shaking, Marianna grabs her coat from the back. As she walks through the salon to the shop door, she notices Mrs Horáková looking at her with narrowed eyes.

~

The burning chill of the winter air fills Dominik Kominsky's throat as he walks along the cobbled streets of Czechoslovakia's thousand-year-old capital city. He never tires of its breath-taking beauty. As he heads towards Old Town Square, he considers how different life was before the invasion. So many streets are now off-limits. The grand, neoclassical Petschek Palace, once the proud centre of banking and finance, is now the Gestapo headquarters, where countless people sent for interrogation are never seen again.

Huge swastika flags now hang from all the city's important buildings. Kominsky tries not to stare at the black-uniformed SS patrol guards that colonise the city like swarms of invading ants.

He passes the astronomical clock in Old Town Square, with the now-familiar sight of Jewish men, women and children, lined up ready for transport out of the city. All of them, even the children, have been forced to wear the yellow star that contrasts unnaturally against their grey and brown overcoats. Parents are holding their children close while trying to conceal the fearful trembling of their own lips and hands.

He returns to his house and shakes the snow from his boots. Soft arms wrap around him and he breathes in the familiar rose scent of his lover, Marianna.

"Let me take off your coat. You're freezing! Come inside and warm up. There's hot soup on the stove."

"You're home early!" Kominsky says as he looks at the warm, caring contours of his lover's face. Her eyes, once so bright and animated, are nowadays filled with sorrow. Right now, however, she looks frightened. He kisses her cheek and runs his hand through the soft chestnut hair that tumbles elegantly off her shoulders. She is wearing her blue-grey dress with the high neckline that buttons from top to bottom. He knows this is her favourite, because it enhances her slender frame and narrow waist. Her pregnancy is not showing yet.

"Has something happened today?"

"No, I'm okay. I've just had a stressful morning."

They sit down at the little dinner table where Marianna has set out steaming bowls of soup onto a floral tablecloth. Kominsky gently smooths down its frayed threads. As they begin eating, the silence is broken only by the clinking of spoons against bowls. She's clearly struggling to swallow her food.

He's thankful that since the invasion, he's managed to keep her Jewish identity secret. Marianna was a trained chemist working in Škoda Pilsen, manufacturing munitions for the Czech army. Her birth name was Miriam Manaková, a name that identified her as a Jew. Marianna was her choice of first name and she had said she preferred it to Miriam anyway. When the Germans invaded Czechoslovakia, they quickly took possession of the company. With news reaching Czechoslovakia of the worrying treatment of Jews in Hitler's Germany, Marianna decided to flee and hide in Prague. Kominsky's skills in forging documents helped her to take on a new identity as a hairdresser's assistant. So far, no one seems to suspect her true identity. They have, however, reluctantly decided not to marry for fear of drawing unnecessary attention. They know that with every passing day, the chance of their deception being exposed increases. However good his forgeries are, they don't match any centrally held records.

Marianna leaves the table and walks to the mantelpiece. She picks up a photograph of her mother who was taken away to a work camp by the Germans almost a year ago. They both doubt they will ever see her again.

She once told him how her parents had always kept a Jewish household. Kominsky is in no way religious himself, but he knows her lack of observance makes her feel guilty.

"Dominik, life at the salon is getting worse."

"I knew something was worrying you. What's happened?"

"It's the customers…more and more of them are sympathising with the Germans. They are blaming the Jews for everything."

With train after train taking whole families of Jews away, Kominsky fears what will happen if her true identity is discovered. He thinks her pregnancy has helped her find an inner strength. He loves her so much, but he admires her even more.

"Marianna..." he says as he places his spoon into the now empty bowl. "I spoke to my German client today. It seems he trusts me enough to tell me things so long as I manage his accounts well. I found out where they are taking them."

"Is it to Stutthof…like…?" Marianna replies, still staring at the picture.

"Auschwitz."

Marianna winces. "What will happen to them there?"

"He says that those not selected for hard labour are either gassed or shot like dogs into giant pits."

Marianna turns pale. Still clutching the photo, she stares vacantly at her mother's image.

"Marianna, we have to leave. Today."

She slumps into an armchair, beads of sweat appearing on her forehead.

Kominsky brings her a glass of water and a damp cloth for her face. "We're going to be met by a communist resistance fighter dressed as an official's chauffeur. There are stories of a diplomat in the Swedish embassy in Budapest who is helping Jews. We must find him."

Marianna places a hand on her brow and squeezes her eyes shut. "How'll we possibly get away with that? That's ridiculous. How many roadblocks are there between here and Hungary? We'll be discovered."

A series of loud knocks on the front door makes them both jump.

"Open the door! Geheime Staatspolizei - Gestapo. Open the door!"

Kominsky's heart is pounding in his chest. He knows these men will not hesitate to break into the house if they refuse to comply. He walks to the door and with his hand on the latch, turns and sees Marianna's terrified face steel into one of false confidence.

Another threatening knock. He holds his breath as he pulls open the door. Standing in the doorway are three men - two armed guards and a grinning Gestapo officer wearing a visor hat with its silver eagle insignia. His skin is pale and stony, his eyes a piercing green.

"Good day to you all." Kominsky says, while trying his level best to keep his nerve. "Welcome inside. How can I help you?"

"Herr Kominsky, I presume," the officer replies to him with a wry smile. "And you must be the Jewess, Fräulein Manaková?"

A MEAN HANGOVER

Muffled voices, flickering lights and a searing pain fill Redolfo's head as he regains consciousness. He tries to focus, realising with alarm that both his hands and ankles are bound to a hard metal chair. His instincts scream at him to break free and run as he pulls in vain at the metal restraints.

As his mind-fog dissipates, he can make out a room with what look like television screens built into metal-panelled walls, each displaying unfamiliar symbols. All around him he hears sounds that remind him of the electronic ping-pong game that the guys in the office hooked up to Mallinson's TV set and spend all their free time on.

A group of uniformed figures gather around him. As his sight improves further, he can see they aren't like people he has ever seen before. "Where am I? Who are you? Let me go. Goddamn cops!"

The figures around him are talking, but it appears to be in an unrecognisable language. "Iss eerr seo an fear is meean linn..."

Redolfo struggles in his shackles, "What the hell are you saying? Where am I?"

A figure in a shimmering body suit approaches him. It appears female, but in no way human. She's about half his height with black slanted eyes, crowned by a mass of grey head-swirls that resemble exposed brain. She produces a small round bead and attaches it quickly to the skin behind his right ear lobe.

He hears himself shriek with panicked confusion. Amongst the indecipherable chattering, he hears one figure shout, "Stop screaming, human!"

Redolfo's stunned into silence.

"It seems you can understand us now. The language decoder is working," says another female-looking figure with bright amber eyes as she waves a flashing wand-like probe near him. She's taller than the first and more upright in stature. Within the fog of confusion and inebriation, he finds her curiously attractive-looking. A dark uniform made of a ribbed metallic fabric clings closely to her slender figure. The hair under her military cap has a greenish hue and her skin is grey and slightly speckled. She turns towards a distinguished-looking male figure, tall and sturdy. He looks more recognisably human, save for the unusual, but somehow flattering, shallow skin-ridges that run from his temples to his cheeks. He's wearing a midnight-blue uniform with multiple emblems and a cap, giving the impression that he's senior to the others in the room.

"Just checking him again, Deputy Chief Vernikell," says the amber-eyed female as she waves the wand near Redolfo's face. The device makes a chirruping sound. "He's passed the infection screen. I'll move on to the DNA profile now." She looks puzzled. "I don't quite understand this, sir."

Vernikell steps towards her. A frown appears on his hardened face. "Understand what exactly, Officer Dowola? Is he or isn't he the renegade?"

"The scanner is showing his bio-signature is not an exact match."

"So, we shall have to let him go then," Vernikell says, resignedly.

"Sorry, sir. We thought he was our suspect because his readings do show some key genetic similarities detected by our long-range scanners, confirmed later by close proximity scanning by our field-agent. He's actually human but seems to have some weird berrantine DNA sequences that don't make sense. He also is a little..."

"A little what?"

"Intoxicated."

Vernikell concludes, "So he's genetically similar in some ways to the renegade, but not close enough? In that case, the scanners led us to a false trail, and we can't convict him of anything."

An angry Redolfo replies. "Convict me of what? Are any of you schlomos in costume gonna actually talk to me and explain all this?"

Vernikell looks at Redolfo directly. "It appears the language decoder doesn't recognise that word you just said...Mr..."

"Redolfo."

"Mr. Redolfo, you are now in the Department of Central Law Enforcement of the capital city of Catuvell on planet Vost. My name is Ariael Vernikell and I am Deputy Chief of Staff at *Vost Intelligence Agency Service*, known as VIAS. I am well aware you will be confused and frightened by all this. Your species has barely ventured into space, let alone grasped the fact that there are life forms that exist outside of your world, some more advanced than your own."

"I don't know what kind of jokers you are kidnapping me to this crazy *Lost in Space* set. You think this is funny? What's next - is Robbie the goddamn Robot gonna walk in here?"

"Although we do use robotic technology to perform a number of tasks, I'm afraid that we don't use androids in VIAS."

A soft buzzing sound cuts through the repetitive electronic noises that fill the room. Its source is made clear as a metallic sphere the size of a beach-ball floats into the room and suspends above Vernikell's head. A panel folds down from the underside of the sphere, revealing a screen that descends to the Deputy Chief's eye level. Vernikell taps at the screen with his fingers.

"Oh, boy. This ain't no costume-party, is it? This is all goddamn real! What the hell do you want from me?"

Vernikell waves his hand and the screen ascends back into the sphere. He continues his explanation, "We have given you a language decoder that automatically translates speech in two ways. We have set it up for your tongue on Earth. It also allows you to read in our language by way of stimulating the language centre of your brain. I apologise for not giving you the decoder earlier as we thought you wouldn't need it.

"We thought we had located a renegade hiding on Earth. We clearly have made an error and we apologise for this. You are therefore free to go."

The mechanical restraints release from Redolfo's wrists and ankles.

"Okay, Agent Vertical, kind of nice you apologising and all that and a great alien thing or whatever you've got going on here - but I have a life to rebuild and I need you to take me home now."

Another small, greyish female official steps forwards.

"You'll need around 25,300 varins if you want to take a transporter back to Earth," she says.

"Okay, so give me the money and I'll be on my way."

"Oh no, sir," she says. "I'm sorry, sir, but there's no policy on Vost that entitles you to a government grant to fund your fare home. There's never been a bursary for that."

As the remaining liquor swirls within Redolfo's head, his strange captors seemingly morph into the officious bank managers, cops and traffic patrolmen who'd dogged his whole adult life. "You can't be serious! What am I expected to do? You abduct me like some bunch of space-head amateurs and now you say I can't get back! So, what does your goddamn policy say I should do?"

Vernikell replies, "Well, you could in theory get a job. There's a Vost government work rehabilitation scheme that may accommodate your needs. It was modified recently after a similar felon-retrieval from Earth was made in error. It took months to find her a job, though. They are continually trying to improve the scheme, but frustratingly, there's insufficient motivation to invest political time, money or effort into it."

"Son of a bitch, alien ass!" Redolfo is on his feet and swings a right hook into the Deputy Chief of Staff's face.

Vernikell staggers backwards and Redolfo is restrained by two hefty guards.

"We can't have this. Take him to the cells, now!" Vernikell pulls out a handkerchief to stem the flow of blood from his lower lip.

UNEXPECTED CALLERS

Still seated in the armchair, Marianna feels the strength drain from her legs as the officer and his two guards enter the room.

The officer gestures to his men to search the house. One storms into the back room and the other sprints upstairs.

"Officer, please have a drink whilst your men conduct their search," Kominsky says with an air of confidence that takes Marianna by surprise. Her lover has been so careful to keep them both out of the spotlight, but how can he save them from this situation now their secret was uncovered?

The officer turns towards him with a smile that looks anything but friendly. "That will not be necessary. This will all be over very quickly."

"No, I insist. Come with me to the kitchen. I've been keeping a fine bottle of amaro for a special occasion."

To Marianna's astonishment, she sees that her lover has aroused the officer's interest, who curiously agrees to the request.

Now alone in the front room, Marianna glances to the open front door and then back towards the kitchen. Should I run? What about Dominik? Before she can make any sense of the situation, three more men enter the house. Two of them look like German army guards and the taller of the three is wearing a military chauffeur's uniform with a small emblem on his hat. She realises these must be Kominsky's friends as the taller man places his finger to his lips as an indication for her to remain silent. One of his men produces a bludgeon and tiptoes upstairs. The other man pulls out a dagger from his pocket and darts to the back room.

Marianna hears a crack followed by a heavy thud from the floor above.

The Gestapo officer emerges from the kitchen, a glass of amaro in his hand. "What was that noise?" he says as he walks into the room. He looks surprised to see the tall man. "Wer bist du?"

"I am your chauffeur," the man replies, pulling out a blade that he plunges into the officer's neck. The officer grabs at the wound as blood spurts from between his fingers. He fixes a confused stare at the chauffeur and collapses to the floor, convulsing. Marianna watches in horror as she sees his visor hat momentarily sail like a little boat in the widening pool of blood.

One of the chauffeur's men returns from the back room, displaying his blood-soaked dagger. His other man reappears from upstairs, tapping his bludgeon against the palm of his hand.

"Meet Otto and his men from the Resistance," says Kominsky as he returns from the kitchen, his drink raised as if in celebration. He finishes his amaro with a sharp tilt of the glass.

"Enchanted," Otto says to Marianna, raising his cap. "We need to leave here immediately."

"Gather what you need to, and quickly," Kominsky says to his lover.

Marianna looks at her trembling hands. She steps over the dead Gestapo officer and runs upstairs, where she sees the lifeless body of the bludgeoned German guard. Fighting back a surge of nausea, she fills a bag with toiletries and spare clothes. She returns downstairs to see Otto's two men have left the house. Kominsky is holding a briefcase and Otto is leisurely swinging a car key on a string.

As they exit the house, a burgundy and black car awaits them. Otto opens a back door and gestures for her to climb inside. Shaking her head with resignation, she says to Otto, "You know we'll never get away with this."

"Why the sad face?" the chauffeur replies with a warm smile, "We'll be fine. This is a classic Fiat 521. It will make the journey, no problem."

TROUBLE A LONG WAY AWAY

Schneiderian Defence Agency (SDA) laboratory, Catuvell City, Planet Vost.

Zanusso checks and rechecks the 3D diagrams as they hover and rotate in front of him. His two support staff tap furiously at their consoles. An expression of calm satisfaction settles on his rounded face with its over-sized eyes that, to the amusement of his staff, always appear disproportionately large for his small grey head.

He is immensely proud of his senior position in the SDA. He glances up at the imposing portrait of its founder, Talamat Schneider that presides over the spacious laboratory, fitted with the most advanced equipment available on the planet. The consoles flicker with streams of code and algorithms.

It's clearly a family thing, he thinks, recalling the ground-breaking achievements of Talamat's daughter, Temeria, who now directs the SDA. Zanusso respects only a handful of scientists. To him, Temeria was the jewel in the crown of scientific creativity - her work had changed the face of Vost by making it possible for objects such as vehicles and even buildings to float in the air.

Zanusso is acutely aware of how envious Vost's own *Governmental Science Division* is of the SDA's technology. It angers him that the government appropriates the rights to so many interesting designs developed by private industries, including some of his own.

He knows, however, the importance of keeping these thoughts to himself. The imposition of the new *Planetary Interest and Securities Act* means the media are never allowed to discuss such political issues openly.

He rotates the hologram that in turn rotates the actual ten-foot long hardware that dominates the centre of the laboratory. He reflects how he designed his pet creation, the *Neuron 86G Synaptic*, to have the general appearance of the archaic artillery that the invading settlers used when fighting the original inhabitants of Vost, six generations ago. These settlers travelled to Vost in hundreds of vessels and occupied the planet with devastating force.

His thoughts are interrupted by a voice calling out from behind him. "Zanusso, you will regret this - and it won't just be you who suffers but everyone you love."

The scientist shifts his blinking gaze from the projection desk and turns towards the source of the noise. He fixes a bulgy-eyed stare on the three subjects, each shackled at their wrists and ankles. They are standing, contained within a shimmering force field on the other side of the laboratory. They each have a nametag on their white gowns: Boca, Dozor and Vestbo. He knows them as the ultimate of their criminal class - intelligent, agile and strong. He cannot help but feel intimidated by them, despite their incapacitation.

He answers, "Once we are done with you, you can complain to the *Schneiderian Defence Agency Customer Relations Department*—" He hesitates. The *Neuron 86G Synaptic* is designed to render its target under the control of its operator. As a scientist, he believes his work will ultimately improve the quality of life for the people of Vost. However, the compromises he has to make lead him to be complicit with government actions that go against his own beliefs on the rights of the individual. But he now has a job to do. Compartmentalising his ethical views, he orders one of the laboratory assistants to lower the force-field and power up the machine.

The hardware begins to glow a pulsing green and the delivery-end rotates towards the prisoners who start pulling frantically against their shackles. Smoothly and accurately, the device aims at the first subject and a beam of green light shines into his face. Within seconds, the device swivels and targets the other two prisoners in turn. All three subjects are staring blankly, their eyes now glowing green.

Zanusso takes a deep breath and moves to inspect the prisoners, but halts when he hears a commotion on the other side of the door. Shouts are followed by loud weapons fire. Zanusso recognises the voice of his friend, the SDA Security Chief. He hears him scream. The scientist is gripped by a cold dread when he realises the subsequent fizzing noise is the sound of his friend being vaporised behind the door.

~

Sarokis has always felt intimidated by Cern Tannis. This formidable, muscular being is unlike anyone else he had seen on Vost. Tall, with dark, angular eyes, a long face, pointed ears, and impressive antlers, Tannis resembles a bipedal animal more than a planetary citizen.

Sarokis considers his own lithe physique - that of a seasoned mercenary. Tannis is something different. People cannot help but be humbled by the arcane strength that radiates from him like the blinding rays from the desert sun.

The mission has gone well so far. The security system of the planet's most important scientific agency has crumbled within moments. Whilst working for the SDA as an outsourced security contractor, Sarokis had made it his business to learn as much as he could about its defence systems. It was so easy to manipulate the personnel department to employ two other sleeper agents. Now the planned attack is underway, he and his men have no trouble in vaporising five security guards and shutting down the building's grid-protection fence.

He taps the button on his wrist comms, signalling to Tannis to commence the next phase of the operation.

~

Tannis has concealed himself outside the perimeter fence of the SDA compound, while Sarokis and his agents carry out their mission within the building. He knows the SDA is protected by a deadly security barrier in the form of a grid of hidden maser cannons, enough to slice through anyone whose DNA profile the system fails to recognise.

Tannis' transmitter flashes, indicating that the shield has been deactivated. As he approaches the outer gates, three armed guards look distrustfully at the imposing, although unarmed, form of the stag-like figure.

"Stop there!" shouts a guard as he raises his weapon.

Tannis gives him a solid stare. The intruder's eyes have turned bright red.

"What's going on?" shouts another guard, whilst hastily raising his own weapon.

"It's okay. I know this man," says the first guard, whose face contorts before he discharges his weapon into the chests of his two colleagues. Tannis seizes the weapon from the mesmerised sentry, firing it directly into the man's face. The decapitated body slumps to the ground.

With a gesture of Tannis' hand, the outer gates slide open. He races unimpeded towards the grand three-story high entranceway. Ahead of him is the main reception desk. At its centre stands the four-foot high metallic emblem of the company - the *Orb of Vost*, with its characteristic shield. He dodges a slew of blue tracer fire coming from three guards who have taken cover behind the desk.

Sitting at the desk is a young, bespectacled receptionist. Pale-faced, she appears frozen to the spot, motionless save for the quivering of her jaw. All around her, the air ignites with blue jets of plasma crossfire as the guards take turns peering up to shoot, blocking any safe path to the lobby.

Tannis leaps behind the main pillar. Now shielded at least for a few moments from the onslaught, he lowers his weapon. He raises his left hand, his eyes fiery red. The *Orb of Vost* judders and rolls off its pedestal with a thud, picks up speed and flies off the desk and launches directly into two of the guards, toppling them like dominoes. It rises again and accelerates towards the third, knocking him to the ground.

~

The receptionist sees the antlered intruder bound towards her. In a frozen state of fear, her eyes fix on a wheel on the buckle of its belt. Out of the corner of her eye, she notices the guards have recovered their composure and are aiming their rifles. The beast's eyes are bright red. The guards pull at their triggers, but their rifles are dead.

One guard jumps on to the desk and takes a big swing at the assailant with the heavy butt of his rifle. The beast grabs his wrist, twisting it with a sharp movement that sends the weapon hurtling to the floor. Without releasing the guard, it delivers a knee-strike into the man's ribs. A tug of the arm and the receptionist can hear the crack of a shoulder dislocating.

As the man collapses, another appears. The monster strikes him with the palm of its hand, slamming the guard's head against the wall. The body slides lifelessly to the floor. The girl stares transfixed at a rosette of blood on the panel where the head had cracked on impact.

The final defender turns to run. With one stride, the creature catches him and effortlessly snaps his neck. It turns back towards the first guard who lies dead, choked on the blood that had filled his throat.

The receptionist, trembling in her chair, starts to sob. She watches as the beast lifts the *Orb of Vost* from the floor and walks with it towards her. She sees its dark eyes and powerful shoulders, aware of the thud of each of its steps. Her thoughts wander. *Why did I have to argue with mom yesterday?* The creature rises to its full height and lifts the orb like an executioner's axe, its eyes boring into her small frame. *Why didn't I let Pogg kiss me? He's a nice boy*. A pause. She hears the sound of its breathing, heavy from the action of the battle. Its eyes, merciless and narrowed, seem to lay on her forever.

It drops the Orb back onto its pedestal. A small adjustment to the right, back a little, and the *Orb of Vost's* shield faces forwards once more. The beast turns its back to the frozen receptionist. It walks out through the back door, the girl left whimpering in her seat.

~

Tannis can soon identify Sarokis' whereabouts from the sounds of plasma rifle fire. The building klaxon is disturbingly loud, and the corridor lights are now flashing a red warning, confirming the security breach. He bounds down the walkway to the mercenary's position.

~

Sarokis is busily engaged in furious crossfire with two SDA security staff. His sleeper agents have been vaporised and he has found himself alone and cornered. He shouts to Tannis in the hope that his boss has made it as far as the other side of the door, "Tannis, if you're there, I could do with some help right now!"

~

Tannis hears Sarokis' call from behind the security door. He focuses his mind. The door begins to move - slowly at first, with the screech of reluctant metal scraping against metal. Finally, it yields, and a flurry of plasma streaks burst through the aperture as the guards focus their fire at the doorway. Sarokis fires a volley to distract the guards. Tannis uses this opportunity to slide into the room. With eyes burning red, he focuses his gaze on a metal container that elevates and launches towards one of the guards. The guard is propelled at speed and smashes against the wall, his neck broken by the force of the impact. The container reverses and propels towards another guard, knocking him to the floor. Sarokis delivers a plasma blast that rips open the man's chest.

The door to the laboratory slides open, revealing a frantic Zanusso tapping at an array of touch controls. The attackers can now see their objective - the *Neuron 86G Synaptic*. The weapon rotates and points towards Tannis. As the weapon begins to glow green, Sarokis aims his plasma rifle at the scientist's head.

"Step away from the controls, Zanusso!"

The terrified scientist raises his hands in surrender and the Neuron 86G Synaptic deactivates. Sarokis binds Zanusso's wrists behind his back with a cable tie and releases the restraints from the prisoners. Staring into their glowing eyes, he says, "From now on, you will completely and exclusively obey the commands of Tannis or myself." He turns to his boss. "The mission is now complete. The *Neuron 86G Synaptic*, Zanusso and the prisoners are yours. The prisoners are fully under your control to command as you please, even unto their deaths."

"VIAS will be here in moments. We have to leave," Tannis replies, his voice, deep and authorative.

THINGS YOU CAN'T SEE

A mist. His mother shouting at his father. Mallinson's sitting gloomy-faced at his desk with an untouched mug of coffee. Elvis is lying in his coffin...did he just wink at him? Ridiculous. The mist clears a little to reveal a woodland. In a small clearing stands a majestic stag eating the buds off a bush. The animal has seen him. It stares at him. It moves a little closer. Something about that stag! What is it? A deafening screech. The stag is now hard against his face with eyes burning red flames.

Redolfo wakes with a start. His head is pounding. "What the devil?"

"Some breakfast for you, human," says a voice from behind the padded door. A bowl of food is slid through a small hatch. Redolfo's stomach growls as he realises he cannot remember when he last ate. He looks around at the featureless walls of what's clearly a prison cell, grabs the bowl and inspects its writhing tentacled contents. He drops it, retching.

The voice outside continues, "Get yourself ready. The chief wants to speak to you."

Minutes later, the door opens, and two burly prison warders walk him to a grey-walled interview room, so spartan and simple, it wouldn't be out of place in an episode from Starsky and Hutch. He sees Vernikell sitting at a metallic desk and feels guilty when he sees his swollen lower lip. Sitting next to Vernikell is the grey sleek female with speckled skin, greenish hair and attractive amber eyes who scanned Redolfo on his arrival. She's wearing a flattering version of what he now recognises as the VIAS uniform.

Vernikell looks neutrally at him. "Mr. Redolfo, I trust you had a comfortable night. This is Officer Dowola, my second-in-command, who today will act as our *Divisional Workforce and Employment* representative at VIAS. She has some news for you which will be of interest."

Redolfo, feeling hungover and famished, sits down in the interview chair. "Look, Chief, I'm sorry I hit you. My life's not exactly going well...and I've lost my job and—"

Vernikell interrupts. "Mr. Redolfo, we all here recognise that your life has just been turned upside-down and we shall do all we can to rehabilitate you on Vost. However, I am not tolerant of violence or any other form of disruptive behaviour. While you reside on our world, you are expected to behave as well as any other citizen. If your conduct here is seen to be in any way subversive or inappropriate, believe me, Mr. Redolfo, you will not be given any preferential treatment. In any case, Officer Dowola will fill you in."

The officer begins. "Good morning, Mr. Redolfo. We do understand you will be rather unhappy about your unexpected arrival on Vost, and on behalf of VIAS, I apologise for this. You are also understandably upset that due to the regulations and restrictions within the service, we are unable to repatriate you to your planet. However, we feel that we have a duty of care towards you and we would like to achieve a speedy resolution to all this. As luck would have it, we have found a job that may suit you. However, I shall be honest - we do have some...serious reservations."

"Okay, then." replies Redolfo. "So, tell me about my great luck."

The amber-eyed official continues. "There have been precedents in the history of VIAS where species from other planets, including humans from Earth, have been abducted and later integrated into Vost society. The *Vost Government Work Rehabilitation Service* was set up over three generations ago to rehabilitate felons and malefactors into normal society."

"Hey, I'm no felon! If anything, you're the criminals, going 'round kidnapping innocent folks."

"No, of course you're not a felon, Mr. Redolfo. After the first human was brought here from planet Earth almost thirty years ago, this scheme was broadened to find work for aliens who find themselves facing a new life on Vost. A number of companies use this scheme as an alternative source of personnel."

"Well if it's anything like the companies where I come from, it's always the two-bit, no-hope outfits that rely on the extra government money," Redolfo says.

Vernikell replies, "Well, it seems that our two planets are more alike than I realised, Mr. Redolfo. However, I would strongly advise you not to, as we say on Vost...*blow on the fur to reveal the defects*...A human I know tried to explain something about a gift-horse but the language decoder wasn't able to process this human idiom."

"Cut to the chase, Chief. What's this job?"

"It happens to be a job in a taxi firm. Although you will be familiar with this type of employment, we have concerns that you, being used to driving on flat roads, will have trouble adapting to driving in the three dimensions of space, as is the requirement on this planet. There will need to be a period of intensive training and your licence will only be issued to you subject to your developing the necessary competencies to drive."

"Okay, Chief. Fair enough. How hard can that be? I was the best goddamn driver in our fleet." Redolfo pauses and mutters under his breath, "That goddamn Mallinson knew that."

Officer Dowola continues, "The executive board has agreed to provide you with 20 varins. That should support you for a short while, hopefully until you start earning your own wage. You will need to agree your own wage settlement with the company. Sadly, this gift payment does not reflect the average daily income for this level of semi-skilled labour in Catuvell that tends to be lower than the sum you've just been given."

"So, with a daily income like that, it'll take me about fifty years before I can get my ticket home."

"Not at all, sir. It would be thirty at most, if you keep your living expenses within sensible limits," Officer Dowola replies.

"So, it appears you have a second chance in life, Mr. Redolfo." Vernikell replies with a wry smile. "Whatever happened to your job on Earth, don't let it go the same way here."

~

The rusted and oil-stained cargo transporter descends towards Vermilion Boulevard in Catuvell, landing in a space at the back yard of an industrial building. Redolfo exits from the passenger side. Two heavy doors scrape open on the roof of the transporter to reveal a mechanical arm that offloads Redolfo's yellow Checker cab. In the yard, there are large piles of scrapped transporters with twisted and crumpled panels. The yard brings back childhood memories to Redolfo when his father took him to scrap yards in Brooklyn to find parts for his old 1950s Checker. His father was proud of his old cab - he always referred to it as a *vintage model*. His father told him how the customers loved to ride in a well-kept classic.

"There yer go, sunshine!" shouts the transporter driver. The language decoder has given the driver something approximating a London cockney accent.

The driver's pointed face and dark, oil-soaked skin blends perfectly with the greasy panels of his cargo transporter. "Go rand the side. I'm told they're expectin' yer. Best a luck in yer new job guvna." The driver gives out a loud, mocking and partially toothless laugh as he returns to his transporter and speeds off into the air.

Redolfo looks upwards to see there is one gigantic sun and two bright moons in the sky. Vehicles of various shapes and colours run criss-crossed paths in the sky. Some are box-shaped and functional in appearance, others more rounded with glass panels. Occasionally a huge tank-like vehicle joins the lines.

He walks to the front of the shabby building that rises up harmoniously from the surrounding scrapped metal. He raises an eyebrow when he sees its garish and poorly maintained frontage. The broken sign above the entrance reads *Lucky Day Cabs*.

ALWAYS EXPECT THE UNEXPECTED

The Fiat, along with its driver and two passengers in the back seat, starts its journey out of Prague.

Marianna studies her lover's face - the strong, dark features and eyes that show both levity and sorrow at the same time. Although not particularly tall, her lover holds his posture well, giving him a reassuringly dignified air.

"I know you're worried, Marianna, but let's think of nicer things. I'd prefer to think about the happy times we'll share in Budapest. You'll be safer there and so will our baby."

"If we ever get there," Marianna sighs, but quickly realises how negative she must sound. Trying to appear more hopeful she says, "I do believe in you, Dominik, and I know if anyone can pull this off, you can."

He had told her how his business contacts had described a thriving Jewish community that is, at least to some degree, protected by the country's Regent. They had also talked of a Swedish diplomat, Raoul Wallenberg, who is helping to place Jews into safe houses and is giving them Swedish Citizenship.

Kominsky smiles at her, "I've heard that Budapest has hot spas, so magical, they can heal the sick. And they say the view of Pest from Buda Castle is beautiful. There's an Opera House, too. Maybe we could see Die Fledermaus again."

Despite her outward expression of confidence, she cannot help but feel he is describing a perfect life that they both know could never be. They continue the journey in silence.

The car turns a corner. Ahead of them is a military checkpoint.

"They just want to check our papers," Otto says.

"But they're looking for us!" Marianna whispers angrily to her lover.

"Marianna, don't worry, I know what I'm doing. In any case, they probably don't know we're on the run yet."

Otto drives the Fiat to the back of the line of waiting vehicles. "Whatever happens, this won't take very long," he says chuckling to his passengers. "One thing I will say for these Germans is that they are very efficient."

After what feels like an age to Marianna, they are, as Otto had predicted, at the front of the line within minutes. A German officer approaches the car. He appears just past middle age with a grey moustache but in good shape and looking formidable in his uniform. Marianna notices three young soldiers in front of the sentry box, shuffling on their feet in an attempt to stamp out the cold. One of them exhales a puff of smoke as he extinguishes his cigarette under his black boot. In her fear, she feels as if the world is moving in slow motion.

Kominsky winds down his window.

The officer addresses him, "Guten Abend, Herr..."

"Kominsky, and this is my fiancée Marianna Kravová."

"Enchanted. Nice morning for it. I feel Prague has never been so clean."

"Indeed, officer."

"You are each required to show your papers to me."

Kominsky unbuckles his leather briefcase, pulls out three documents and hands them to the officer who studies them carefully. The officer frowns as he reads and rereads the contents. Marianna resists holding tightly to her hair as she sees him momentarily raise his eyebrows and begin to puff out his cheeks. Her heart pounds hard into her chest and she feels her lungs compress to the point of suffocation.

The officer holds the papers up to the sky to check for watermarking and says, "Herr Kominsky, I am now advancing in years and have learnt that there are only a few advantages that come with this state of being."

The three soldiers at the sentry box look on in aggressive curiosity. They walk quickly towards the scene. Marianna tries not to let her terror show.

The officer continues, "I was an accountant by trade before I joined the army and I am revered for my attention to detail in all things printed. I have made it my duty to scrutinise documents to the highest level."

The young German soldiers, each gripping their rifles, now surround the car. Marianna can see the colour has drained from her lover's face.

"Your papers seem to be in reasonable order. These are very good...so good, I find it hard to believe they are genuine."

Marianna gasps as the officer reaches for his revolver in his waist holster and the young soldiers raise their rifles. She sees Kominsky stare straight into the officer's eyes.

"I think you may be mistaken, Officer," Kominsky says to him, with an unexpected air of command.

Marianna glances at the officer and looks back at Kominsky. To her astonishment, her lover's eyes have turned a fiery red. The officer slowly withdraws his hand from his revolver. His head tilts and his brow furrows as if he has become confused and troubled. He shakes his head as if trying to remember something. The soldiers train their weapons on Kominsky.

"I'm sorry, Herr Kominsky, I must have been mistaken," the officer says. "Of course...yes...you are Dominik...I remember you well. Please accept my apologies."

The soldiers look suspicious. Reluctantly, they lower their weapons.

"Here, take back your papers," says the officer. "You should be on your way." The officer waves to the soldiers, indicating for them to raise the barrier.

As Otto drives the Fiat through the roadblock, Marianna looks back. The officer is rubbing his head as if confused. She stares at her lover whose eyes have returned to their normal colour.

"Dominik...what on earth just happened? Why did he say he knew you? And what happened to your eyes?" She begins to feel light-headed and realises she's hyperventilating. What has he kept from her after all this time? Does she even know who he is?

Kominsky looks heartbroken. He does not reply. His eyes are now overflowing with tears.

The Fiat continues its journey out of the city.

REHABILITATION

"Welcome to *Lucky Day Cabs*."

A rotund, almost spherical alien is sitting behind a chipped, painted desk. He has a big head with large, oval, sad eyes, and a rather bored expression. The whole scene seems to Redolfo to be strangely familiar. Despite the cabbie's unannounced appearance in the office, the alien's eyes remain fixed on an untidy pile of paperwork. *Does nothing ever change?*

Behind another desk sits a smaller, thinner version of the first alien who smiles warmly at him.

Without looking up, the larger alien begins, "My name is Baranak Squintt." The language decoder has interpreted his voice with a slight Eastern European accent. "I'm the owner of the company." With his eyes still fixed on his paperwork, he nods towards the smaller alien and says, "This is my brother, Glyrian."

Redolfo looks around the room. The style of the room is surprisingly similar to his old workplace, but if anything, this is in a worse state of repair. It always amazes Redolfo how companies like this can survive the neglect.

In an adjacent room, two females tap lazily at control panels. One of them is dressed in bohemian-looking clothing. She has a wistful, distracted look with dishevelled dark hair, tied up in what Redolfo would swear looks like underwear.

"Come on honey," she shouts into her console, "you can find him, easy. He's waiting for you at the gates. He says you can't miss him! Honestly, you do make it hard for yourself, girl!"

The other female looks like she's made more of an attempt at glamour. Her lips are of an iridescent blue and her patterned clothing adorned with a sequined wrap. She is looking at a computer screen. Both the girls seem to have similar ridges to those on Vernikell's face.

The only computer screens Redolfo's come across are small with bright green writing. There's no way Mallinson would pay for one. This one's as large as the largest television he's ever seen in the stores, but this screen is completely flat and is displaying something that resembles beautifully coloured playing cards. He remembers the way that the girls in Mallinson's office waste time when they don't actually have to work.

Squintt lifts his dark, saucer eyes to look at Redolfo, while his large head remains tilted downwards towards the desk.

Redolfo gives him a satirical smile. "Apparently, you're my ticket off this planet."

"Mr. Redolfo, please take a seat," Squintt replies, pointing to a chair.

The cabbie sits down moodily.

"Seems the *Work Rehabilitation Office* made an accurate description of you. This is a small but proud company. Can I remind you we are one of only a handful of companies in this scheme? Just remember that we don't have to take on anyone we don't want to. I won't lie — we're always in need of an extra pair of capable hands. Ever since driving became a three-dimensional skill, it's getting harder and harder to find drivers who are actually capable of handling the navigation. The problem here is that I have no idea whether you'll be up to it."

Redolfo leans forward, his interest now peaked.

"Vehicles here are now mostly driverless and run on a computerised automated grid. Those driven by a living being are now the minority. I hear from the rehab people that you're a seasoned driver on your planet and that you have experience in a taxiing service."

"Yeah, sure I do. I'm a son of a cabbie too. It's in the blood. I could take on your crazy space roads, no problem."

"This is always a huge concern for us at *Lucky Day Cabs*, Redolfo. Everyone here fancies themselves as perfect drivers. You'll first need to be assessed for driving competence and then be tested by the *Vost Driving and Licensing Agency*. The *Catuvell Taxi Transporter Commission* will then make the final judgment for your fitness to be a taxi driver. There's been too many accidents caused by drivers not properly anticipating vehicles approaching from above. These idiots think they're too smart to need to use the CEWS."

"The CEWS?"

"Yes, the *Collision Early Warning System*. It works in a similar way that air traffic control systems worked in the days before the Temeria 3D engine."

Redolfo has never had problems with awareness of traffic or anything going on around him for that matter. The memory of the bullets smacking into his cab flash in his mind. He replies, "Where I come from, the main problem comes from drivers not moving out onto roads fast enough. Slows up the whole goddamn traffic just waiting for them to decide when to move."

"Look, best I don't know the details of your driving habits, Redolfo. All I care about is having another pair of hands on the road that won't bring my company into disrepute."

The cabbie wonders where he's heard that line before. "My God. It's like I never actually left my planet. It's like all you crazy, alien sons-of-bitches are living the same goddamn life we do on Earth. Listen here, Squintt. I know

I can do this for you - and for myself. Turns out getting a job seems to be my only way off this planet - and this job seems just perfect. But tell me something. If the technology on this planet's so goddamn kick-ass, then why not just run a driverless cab service?"

"A good question, Redolfo. You can see here that the world of transport is changing. Companies like ours and drivers like you want to be are an endangered species. The new age of driverless transporters is taking hold of every area of Vost. They say they're safer than anything organic life-forms can provide behind the wheel in 3D space. Luckily for us, the public still don't yet fully trust the artificial intelligence that runs the vehicles. Here in the twisted minds of the species on Vost there's still some sort of a prestige that goes with having an actual living driver to ferry them - like it's some sort of social statement."

Squintt's oversized, round head finally rises to meet Redolfo with a stern look. "And another thing you need to remember - the government's kept this company afloat exactly *because* companies like ours join work rehabilitation programs to employ the likes of you - the misfits - the uncompetitive - the last ones to be chosen in the team line-up - you getting me, Redolfo? We simply couldn't survive without Vost government funding. By rights, *Lucky Day Cabs* shouldn't exist at all. One day, Vost will replace all vehicles with driverless transporters, as it's simpler for them to focus their endless regulatory desires elsewhere."

Redolfo scratches his head. He's sad to think his profession's becoming a dying art.

"It looks like you're actually interested in this," Squintt says to him, as if pleased to have an opportunity to expand on a pet conspiracy theory. "With driverless technology, the government can easily snoop on exactly where everyone is going and what they are all doing all of the time. I really don't know why they want all this data on us but believe me, we *are* being snooped on. So, don't give them the excuse they want, to completely eradicate living drivers." Squintt puts his round head into his spade-like hands. "And to think I'm relying on an alien I've only just met!"

"Here's your morning drink, Baranak, with extra camflora." Redolfo looks round to see that the drawling voice came from the female with the sequined shawl and iridescent lips. She's standing at the office door with a mug of steaming drink. She looks at Redolfo then at Squintt. "Well, my, my, my, look what you've got here, Baranak."

"Thank you, Diselda. This is Mike Redolfo. If he passes the licence exams, he might well be our new driver."

Diselda's eyes widen. "Hey, he's a huuuman...and kinda cute! Hey honey, you can drive me anytime, licence or not!" Squintt's sizeable eyeballs roll in their sockets. Redolfo stares open-mouthed as she projects her generous mammaries in his direction.

Diselda returns to her office. Redolfo can hear her say to her bohemian work colleague, "You'll like this one, Cam-Ell...and he's got this cute cap..."

"You'll get used to it here, Redolfo." Squintt says, breaking a rather embarrassing pause. "However, I have another problem to consider. As much as I need drivers, I don't have a spare transporter for you. It won't surprise you that this little company can't afford spanking new transporters, so we end up buying reconditioned ones from those lousy crooks and criminals at the *SPAYCEjunk* scrap yard whenever the company is flush - which isn't very often. There's always something wrong with their so-called 'reconditioned' vehicles and we end up spending fortunes putting them right. If it wasn't for my brother Glyrian, there'd be no *Lucky Day Cabs*. That brother of mine seems to be able to fix up just about anything those verminous scrap yard scumbags throw at us."

"Hey Squintt, I've got my own cab, just round the back in your yard. Why don't you just make it fly with your magic engine thing?"

Squintt stands up from his chair. Something about his rounded frame makes him appear like he's not actually risen at all.

"Come, Redolfo. Come with Glyrian and me to the yard."

Redolfo and Glyrian follow the slow-stepping form of Baranak Squintt. They study each other as they exit the back of the office. The yellow cab stands out from the rusted scrapped transporter chassis fragments scattered across the yard.

Glyrian stares at the Checker, shakes his head and shrugs.

The bigger brother looks with his sad eyes at the cab. "Glyrian, are you sure?" Turning towards Redolfo, he says, "Look, I really don't—"

"Don't what?" Redolfo interjects. "I used to have a job on Earth, with a life - yeah, a crap life - but at least I had a life - with a yellow cab that may not look much to you but can handle the roads better than any other super-hot road-can in Brooklyn. Now this cab is all I have with me on this crazy mother of a planet!"

Squintt looks at Glyrian again. The mechanic's expression turns pensive and he takes another look at the yellow vehicle. He inspects the underside then lifts the hood. An agonising minute goes by. Glyrian looks back at his brother and nods.

"Are you sure?" Squintt asks.

Glyrian smiles.

The more spherical brother looks the Checker up and down again. "So, how good *are* your driving skills, Redolfo?"

Redolfo gazes up at the network of aerial traffic. "I won't lie to you, Squintt. I don't know anyone who can outclass me in Brooklyn or anywhere else in New York. I don't know why, but I seem to know what people are going to do on the road - it's like I anticipate them. I seem to know where I am at all times in relation to everyone else

- like some sort of instinct. Hell, it's got me out of plenty of scrapes. Brooklyn can be a dangerous place and that's both on and off the road. You need these skills sometimes just to survive."

Squintt looks from the Checker and back to Redolfo. "Somehow...I don't know why...but I believe you. Look, we might just be able to convert this heap of junk into something useful after all. I get an inkling my brother wants to take this on as a personal project. Why do I have the feeling this is going to cost me? Do you all use this type of primitive vehicle on Earth? Not sure about the colour. But we can change that—"

"No, you goddamn won't change the colour! This is a genuine 1970-manufactured Brooklyn Checker cab and it can outclass anything in the city. I should know. I get people to their destinations fast - like it's a challenge that they should all be at the right place at the right time."

Squintt nods his large head approvingly. "I like your spirit, Redolfo. There'll, however, be no work started on your vehicle until I see that licence paper in your hot hands."

Glyrian taps his brother on the shoulder. The larger Squintt gives his characteristic eye roll. "Okay! Okay! Your cab will be ready tomorrow. That'll be your driving practice vehicle."

Glyrian's eyes light up. The larger Squintt produces an electronic tablet device, and hands it to Redolfo.

"This device will give you all the tuition you'll need for learning the code of driving in 3D space on Vost. Because we have a world government, the same rules apply for any region on the planet. I suggest you read this carefully this evening."

Redolfo looks at it and frowns.

Squintt jabs a fat finger at the screen, "Look, it functions just like one of your human books, but you switch it on here and you tap the screen to turn the pages." Redolfo taps at the screen of the tablet and chuckles.

"I see you're a quick learner, Redolfo. You'll need all your skills and wits to get to grips with all this - fast - or you'll quickly find yourself out of a job. Hmm...I've been meaning to ask - did the rehabilitation scheme give you any money to live on?"

"They gave me 20 varins, whatever that means."

"Good. I'd suggest you stay at the ground-level Raut Hostel on Rautival Precinct. Return here at 10 am."

"I gotta question for you, Squintt."

"What's that, Redolfo?"

"Why doesn't your bro' ever say anything?"

"Because he can't. He hasn't spoken a word in over ten years."

FALLOUT

Department of Vost Investigative Civilian Enforcement (DEVICE) - *Catuvell Division*

Deputy Chief of Staff Vernikell waits patiently for the other twelve intelligence committee board members to shuffle into their seats around the highly polished, rectangular table. He always thought the boardroom was impressive. He studies the light panelled walls, upon which hang several images of past directors dressed in ceremonial robes.

He stands to address the committee, "Board members, I thank you all for coming. In the absence of the Chief-of-Staff, General Hostian, I'm assuming the role of acting Chair. I would like to take the opportunity to remind you that you have all signed the Official Secrets Directive. Therefore, you are legally bound not to divulge any information discussed at this meeting? Do you all understand and confirm your agreement to these terms?"

All the members nod and mutter in agreement and wave their signed documents.

"You'll have all read the report, if not heard the endless media coverage that crime in Catuvell, as well as in most of the other major cities on Vost, is at an all-time high. As you are all aware, we send out press releases explaining how rising figures reflect improvements in reporting of crime. However, even our greatest spin doctors won't be able to save us from the reality for much longer. We risk losing control of law and order in Catuvell altogether."

The boardroom resounds with groans and whispers.

"It's hardly surprising when Hostian keeps cutting our budget!" a grumpy board member calls out.

"I will have some order at this meeting," Vernikell replies. "If any of you want to discuss the political merits of the decisions made by the General, then I recommend you address him yourself."

Vernikell sighs. Why is it that so many committee members seem to be more interested in their hobby-horses than the crisis at hand? He continues, "Gangland warfare on our streets is on the rise and worryingly, criminals are starting to use military grade weaponry. We need to start demonstrating that we are winning the war against crime. The public are increasingly calling for elected law enforcement commissioners. Vost will not tolerate failure of the processes in this department. We do not want to end up as government scapegoats and replaced by faceless bureaucrats with their algorithms."

The levels of chatter and noise rise.

Vernikell raises his voice, "Look, can you all stop talking at once! The recent incident at the *Schneiderian Defence Agency* gives the impression that we can't keep our own house in order. I have therefore called this extraordinary meeting of the board. Agent Rimikk, your report on the attack, please."

Senesul Rimikk - sturdy, tall, close-cropped hair, with pinkish-brown skin and the appearance of never having been hugged in his childhood - stands up and gives the boardroom members a humourless stare that quickly silences the room. He reads from his electronic clipboard. "The attack on the SDA was both coordinated and carefully planned. It seems to have been perpetrated by high level organised criminals. We still cannot fully fathom how the SDA's extensive defences were penetrated. I'd like to reassure you, however, that the stolen *Neuron 86G*

Synaptic mind-control weapon cannot be used by the perpetrators, as the operational code has been deactivated remotely."

"Thank you," Vernikell says, "Please let me introduce Professor Capell Parchi, who represents the scientific steering group for the development of the weapon."

Rimikk returns to his seat.

Vernikell continues, "Please Professor, if you would be so kind as to explain the history of the project."

The old and sinewy professor rises slowly from his seat while rubbing away the pain and stiffness of his bent-up lower back. He clears his throat and speaks with a thin, aging voice, "Thank you, Mr. Chairman. The *Neuron 86G Synaptic* mind-control weapon was developed by Cashall Zanusso for the SDA. It was funded as part of a top-secret collaborative project with the Vost Government Science Division in the effort to tackle the rising tide of crime on the planet. Zanusso demonstrated on intelligent animal models that the weapon could control their primitive minds at a very basic level. There was considerable resistance on ethical grounds from the few senior scientific members of the board involved on the project. The steering group, however, convinced the government to use emergency state powers to suspend the otherwise inviolable rules of the Convention of Trinova on experimenting on prisoners without their consent. The first sentient life-form trials went ahead."

Vernikell frowns. Vost may be rigidly bureaucratic but it is not above serving its own interests.

Parchi continues, "The initial tests met with variable success. The first prisoner never recovered his mental faculties and would therefore not submit to mind control. The second did submit, on a fairly high instructional level, but frustratingly died of a seemingly unrelated infectious disease. Zanusso reprogrammed the weapon and used it on three of Vost's most infamous criminals taken from the highest security penitentiaries. These three prisoners are now in the hands of the perpetrators. They were supposed to function on the whims of the state and certainly not fall into the hands of organised crime-lords. Under likely full mind-control from unknown subversive forces, they now pose a significant danger." Parchi bows and gratefully returns to his seat.

For the first time since the meeting started, the board members appear concerned.

Rimikk rises. "We know two sleeper agents were trained to pose as scientists in the SDA. They were both killed by the security staff. They have now been identified as berrantine males with little or no academic qualifications and no criminal record. The personnel officers at the SDA are baffled as to how their government-approved vetting processes failed to identify the sleeper-agent's fictitious work-experience claims when they applied for their scientific roles. These sleeper agents have left behind distraught families who have no idea as to why they would be involved in such activities. Their partners have told us, however, that they were spending a lot of time socialising with mystery friends, raising suspicions on a personal level.

"The surveillance systems within the building and grounds were deactivated by the sleeper agents, so there is, unfortunately, no video footage of the perpetrators. The only surviving witness seems to be the main hall receptionist, who can't seem to remember much of the incident."

Rimikk shuffles awkwardly and says, "When the investigatory team put her under pressure, she did say she couldn't be sure, but had a vague memory of an antlered creature with super-strength who seemed to be able to move things without touching them. She also remembered something about a wheel but couldn't be pressed for any more details on this. The investigating team found no illegal hallucinogenic drugs in her system. She does have a medical record of a depressive illness and was taking prescription medications at the time. The drug she was taking, Cimetrogan, is a fairly standard antidepressant and is considered fairly safe. According to the pharmaceutical literature, Cimetrogan can, in rare instances, cause hallucinogenic side effects. The investigating team have concluded that any further interrogation or brain-probing at this time could cause her irreparable harm. They can't explain why she remembers so little of the event and have suggested that she may be suffering from some form of psychosis, or simply that the sheer terror from the event has wiped or altered her memory. They propose to re-interrogate her in a few weeks' time in case she recovers any further memories." Rimikk returns to his seat.

The board members begin talking nervously with one another. Vernikell hushes them. "I must thank the Baroness Ner-all, from the VIAS Central Species Anthropological Research and Equalities Board, who is here to give us some insight as to what this witness statement could mean."

"What does the Equalities Board have to do with this?" a board member calls across the table. "This is a security matter - not a time to discuss diversity!"

"You will be quiet!" Vernikell barks. "If anyone speaks out of turn again, they will be made to leave."

The boardroom is now silent.

The Baroness rises. Vernikell studies her long, slightly greying hair, positioned in magnificent layered braids piled high on her head, complimenting the formality of her burgundy dress and the stateliness of her jewellery. He notices how the fine lines of her face seem to enhance her timeless beauty. She speaks with an elegant and educated voice.

"Thank you, Deputy Chief of Staff, and thank you to the board for inviting me. As you are all aware, there are many species that inhabit Vost and this gives our planet the wonderful diversity and richness of culture we enjoy today. If - and that is a big if - we can believe a word this receptionist is saying, then we may be dealing with a species that has both telepathic and telekinetic capabilities. We are all well aware that our ancestors outlawed the use of these powers on our planet. What some of you may not know is that they also developed viral-airborne, gene-splicing techniques to suppress and permanently deactivate the gene sequences that gave some species their mind-powers. This technique also had a vertical transmission effect, in that it was passed to the offspring and to subsequent offspring and so on. You know that all visitors to Vost have, for years, been expected to submit themselves to an 'infection screen', which is, in fact, an inoculation of the virus, deactivating any telepathic abilities.

"I would add that while there are always reports in the lesser levels of the media of beings using telepathic and telekinetic activity, there have never been any confirmed cases. Even if there was any truth behind these rumours, their abilities would be so attenuated as to render them of little concern. That is possibly until now.

"Although there are doubts about the reliability of the witness, we must take the report of an antlered attacker seriously. There are several species on Vost that lived a primitive life before the first settlers arrived from other planets. The technologically advanced newcomers easily subjugated these comparatively primitive species. We read tales of these species to our children - we all have the books. One of several of these subjugated species are known as terannians. They have antlers. Because of their private and insular nature, very little is known about them. Despite this, they are an occasional figure in children's tales and myths and therefore represent prime material for delusional conspiracy theories."

Vernikell rises. "Thank you, Baroness. I agree this all sounds rather far-fetched. There are no terannians reported or registered in the monitored areas of the planet. As far as we know, all of them live on a reservation, west of Briganti, which was granted to them by the early settlers in a legally binding contract. They have their own jurisdiction and VIAS has no legal authority in their lands. They are a reserved species and therefore little is known about them.

"I have deputised agent Rimikk to meet the terannians, assuming they allow him access to their reservation. We concluded that the presence of more than one ambassador would appear as a threat, so Agent Rimikk has agreed to approach them alone.

"Unless there are any further questions, I am closing the meeting. Meanwhile, you all know your jobs." He watches the board members filter out of the room. Only he and the Baroness remain.

She approaches Vernikell. "I'm so glad to have been able to see you again, Ariael. It's been a long time."

Vernikell feels a softening he has not experienced for years. "You look lovelier than I ever remember, Febryalla. How is the Baron? Is he looking after you well?"

"Darryan will always be Darryan - as officious as he is efficient. But yes, he is well."

"You know it could have been different..."

The Baroness looks at him with sadness in her eyes. "I know, Ariael..."

"Febryalla..."

"Ariael, I too sometimes think of what could have been. As you know, my family gave me no choice...The Ner-all family is just too proud. I was born to continue the Ner-all tradition and that, I'm afraid, had to take precedence over my personal desires. Darryan has never once harmed me."

"But unless he's dramatically changed over the years, he can't make you happy either."

The Baroness gives Vernikell a warm and gentle smile. "I have just the thing for your lip."

A MODIFICATION

A mist. A woodland. Green scrub.

Come to us, Great Shining Lord
Come dance with us
Dance with us

The woodland is now dense with trees. A clearing. He is running. Why is he running? Exhilaration! He can feel energy surging through him like a raging fire.

Great Hornéd One,
The Life beneath the Giant Sun,
Guardian of the call of Spring,
Spirit of the Wind.

"What the hell!" Redolfo wakes with a start. "Son-of-a-bitch. What's with these weird dreams?"

Redolfo looks around his hostel room. Even by his standards, it is in a filthy state. It's not much different to the seedy motel rooms he's seen the addicts use in Kojak. He looks at an array of switches on a panel. He hits one.

"Hello. Reception here. Can I help you?"

"Redolfo here. Look, I may be new to this goddamn planet, but I do expect my room to be in a state that can actually maintain life. This place is a disgrace. Please get your cleaners here."

"I'm sorry, sir. A cleaner is on her way to your block."

He enters the miniscule *en suite* bathroom. The mirror is smeared and blackened with dirt. He stares at his reflection. Something's not right. The veins on his face are

51

standing out and pulsating. His eyes are red. Blood starts to pour from his left eye, then his right one, then from his left ear. The head he sees in the mirror swells. He sees himself scream and the eyes of his reflection burst open in a spray of blood and jelly. Redolfo springs backwards with his head in his hands. He writhes shrieking on his bed.

A knock at the door. "Hello, sir. Are you okay in there? I heard you weren't happy with your room. You've been screaming." The door is opened. The cleaner appears, a female with a scalloped appearance to her skin. There are rags tied up like a brace of rabbits around her belt. She stares at a helpless Redolfo lying on the bed.

"Are you okay, sir?"

Redolfo gets up and darts back to the bathroom. He looks in the mirror and sees his appearance has returned to its original state. "Just sort out my room, will you?" he snaps.

~

Redolfo finds the walk back to Vermilion Boulevard refreshing and calming after his traumatic experience with the mirror. The continuous lines of airborne traffic weave between and around the densely packed ground-based and floating skyscrapers whose glass and metal structures glimmer from the light of the planet's giant sun. He passes under the worn-out *Lucky Day Cabs* sign and enters the building.

"Well hello, handsome!" Redolfo is greeted playfully by Diselda. Cam-Ell looks up from her computer screen.

"Hi Diselda. Hi Cam-Ell."

"Awww, you remember our names!" Diselda says with a smile. The girls blush at each other.

Squintt appears. "Thank you, girls. You can go back to your work now. Remember I need those accounts by lunchtime."

"Too late, Baranak. They're already done, so we're taking a break now anyway."

Squintt turns to Redolfo and shrugs in resignation. The cabbie chuckles at how the girls always seem to be two steps ahead of their boss.

Squintt changes the subject. "I trust you had a good night's sleep at the hostel."

"Hell, no! Like some goddamn hobo spiked my drink. Had me some weird dreams. I'll never eat there again."

Ignoring the comment, Squintt replies, "Glyrian's worked non-stop through the night. Your cab is just about ready. You owe him one."

"He sure seems to love his mechanic work. Can't wait to see it."

They exit round the back. Flashes of a welding arc light up the interior of the repair shed. He sees a yellow vehicle.

"Now that's what I call a cool transformation!" Redolfo cries in amazement.

He can see that without a doubt it is a Checker - his Checker - but this one looks cooler. Updated. Sturdier. The *Lucky Day Cabs* logo adorns all four doors and the hood. A helmeted head appears from behind the cab and the visor lifts to reveal a beaming Glyrian whose eyes look more bloodshot than they were the day before.

"Let me take you on a tour of your new cab, Redolfo," says the older Squintt. They step forwards towards the vehicle. "Mind the spilt sealant there. You'll see the vehicle now has a perimeter reinforcement cradle - Vost regulations I'm afraid. She's also completely airtight and even has an oxygen supply that'll equip it for journeys to Arianrhod and Cerridwen, the Vost moons, should you ever need to do such a journey." Squintt waves a chubby finger skyward.

"What do these do?" Redolfo points to the array of gadgetry attached to the chassis and roof.

"This is your 3D satellite navigation antenna and decoder. This is the antenna for the Temeria engine, the thing that makes vehicles and even buildings suspend in air."

"How exactly does that work?"

"You think I know, Redolfo? But they say that it works by receiving something called a *Telleron semi-particle wave*. That genius scientist, Temeria Schneider changed everything on our planet with this technology. I've absolutely no idea what these waves are, but we're told that they're safe."

"So where do these waves come from?" asks Redolfo, scratching his head.

"I heard they come from transmitters - three of them - so they cover the whole planet. No one knows where they are."

"So, who pays for all this technology?" asks the cabbie as he takes a closer look at the exterior gadgetry. "Sounds like it's gonna cost me. They already took my blood from me for my cab licence so they can repair the terrible roads in Brooklyn."

"Don't worry, you'll pay your fair share in licence fees. They say all 3D-emitting technology is a gift from our government to the people. But never accept generosity on Vost at face-value, Redolfo. One day soon, I'm sure that a superpower on your world will use technology to run a satellite navigation system for all your vehicles and mobile communication devices. That's what happened here. Believe me, it appears to be a gift, but it means the government knows where we are at all times. I'm sure they could simply stop and control any vehicle they wish to. I gather Earth doesn't have a world government as we do, but I suspect that'll come."

Redolfo takes off his cap and scratches his head. He starts laughing. "Hot damn, Glyrian. You kept the bullet holes in the door! You knew I wanted that."

Squintt opens the driver's door and points out the additions to the dashboard. "This is your CEWS device...and please don't think you're too smart to need it, Redolfo. This one is your *varin* fare-collector. It gets updated—"

He's interrupted as something rises from the cab roof with a noisy hiss.

To Redolfo's surprise, he sees that the cab's roof medallion has been replaced with a large, shiny hand. It begins waving up and down. The palm of the hand carries the *Lucky Day Cabs* emblem. Underneath it is another emblem that is more familiar to him...the New York City Seal.

"What the hell is this?"

"Ah. Yes. This, Redolfo, is the emblem of our company. All our vehicles have it. Glyrian added the seal of your Earth city to make you feel more at home."

"He thinks a waving hand brings the company good luck." Redolfo and Squintt look round to see that was the voice of Diselda. She and Cam-Ell are giggling.

"Nice ride, Mike!" says Cam-ell. "Gonna show me your gadgets sometime soon?"

"Look, girls, I need to get Redolfo up to speed with his cab, and you two are going to put him off!" Squintt barks at them.

"Awww, come on Baranak. We just wanna get to know our new guy."

"Okay, okay," Squintt concedes. "You're all in time to see the addition Glyrian thought you'd appreciate the most, Redolfo." He points to a gadget on the dash. The four of them gather round. A touch of the button. The music of Fleetwood Mac cuts in...

...Don't stop...

The girls are dancing. "Hey, we love your sounds, Mike!" says Cam-Ell.

Redolfo takes off his cap. "Now, how in Hell's name did you do that?"

"Hyperspace probe radio, Redolfo. It would normally take about two-hundred years for radio waves to reach Vost from Earth. Glyrian thought you'd want to hear the events happening on Earth now, so he fitted this long-distance radio grabber system. It was designed for the security service to spy on dissidents hiding on other planets. Just don't ask how he's come by it."

Squintt gyrates his abundant torso to the music. "Hey Redolfo, this isn't half bad."

Glyrian's smile beams broader than ever. Eventually, Squintt switches off the radio.

"Aww, Baranak, you spoil-sport," says Diselda. Cam-Ell nods in agreement. Redolfo notices how she has tied her hair with underwear made of a more alluring chiffon than yesterday.

Squintt gives them a glare. "Now you both have work to do, and heaven knows if you've missed any business."

"See you later, Honeybunch," Diselda says to the cabbie.

The girls smile as they turn to leave. Redolfo observes, with fascination, how they return to the office with an exaggerated sway of their backsides. Squintt rolls his eyes at his chuckling new employee.

A LOT TO EXPLAIN

"Dominik, tell me what's going on."

Kominsky covers his face with his hands. The Fiat bounces as they pass over a series of pot holes in the road.

"Please, speak to me. Tell me what just happened."

"I really didn't want to have to ever tell you—"

"Tell me what, Dominik?"

"There is something...important I have kept from you all these years."

"You're scaring me. Please tell me what's going on."

Kominsky's eyes are moist with tears. "I always worried that if I told you...it would eventually come between us...I never wanted anything to get in the way of our love. I always secretly wanted you to know, but I couldn't dare risk ruining everything."

"Well, it's too late for that now. What did you do to that officer?"

"Marianna, since we first met at that dance, I felt something I've never felt before for anyone, anywhere. I can't bear the thought of losing you."

Her gaze softens, but her voice remains stern, "Tell me Dominik. For God's sake, what is it?"

"I come from a very long way away. Further than you could imagine. I was not brought up in Prague...I am not even from this planet."

"Dominik, why are you talking such nonsense?"

"Look at me, Marianna."

She sees his face begin to change slightly. His skin becomes more lined and textured with soft ridges to his cheeks. His eyes widen slightly. Marianna gasps. He quickly returns to the appearance she had only ever known him to have.

"Dominik...that's not even your name is it?"

"It is now, as far as I'm concerned. What I really am doesn't matter. What matters is that I love you. You are carrying our child and I want to live the rest of my life with you."

"My God! What will the child look like? A creature like you? And what is your real name anyway?"

"Please, Marianna. Our child will look human. I have seen to that."

"I asked you a question. What is your real name?"

"My birth name is Kandan Mikkrian. I'm of a people known as the berrantines from a planet called Vost, from another stellar system, more advanced, but in many ways similar to Earth. I'm not an accountant. I'm a dissident from my planet."

Marianna starts to tremble.

"I'm a geneticist. I discovered a way to give people mind powers so they can control objects and, sometimes, the thoughts of people and animals."

"You're talking nonsense," she says, her face flushed.

"Your species has not yet unlocked the genetic code of life, but that will almost certainly come soon. Some species on my planet have a natural telepathic ability, but it was outlawed on Vost decades ago. The government devised a way of suppressing their abilities. My research was on a way to counteract this suppression using genetic engineering techniques.

"Look, I'm no fool and I'm a scientist myself. I've even read stories about creatures from other worlds with extra sensory powers. But it's all fiction."

Kominsky wipes his eyes. "The authorities found out what I was doing and wanted me to hand over the technology to their military. I fled and took a transporter to Earth where I've been hiding from the authorities ever since. I never expected to fall head-over-heels in love with a human girl."

CAMPAIGN RISING

A secret Location in Catuvell City, Planet Vost.

"For the last time, no one can hear you. Quit your screaming," Sarokis says to the Zanusso, whose bulging eyes have swollen further within their sockets. The little scientist is shackled upright to a metal frame. "Your happy days at the SDA are over. Tell us the weapon code so you can die an easy death. It's your choice." Sarokis sees his prisoner's small hands tremble within the sleeves of his laboratory coat.

The shaking captive replies, "I won't tell you, because I can't tell you. The *Neuron 86G-Synaptic* was designed to only be used by a handful of Vost officials. The code will have been changed remotely, so the weapon is now useless."

Sarokis throws a switch and electrifies the metal frame for a full ten seconds. Zanusso convulses, his back arches before slumping back against the frame.

"Please stop it! I can't help you." Zanusso pleads between sniffles. His whimpering is silenced by the appearance of the antlered form of Tannis.

"You will tell me, Zanusso!" Tannis says, staring at the scientist with flame-red eyes. Zanusso's eyeballs begin to swell and the veins of his face stand out like curled stems of ivy. Saliva pours out from between quivering lips.

Tannis' eyes darken to their original state. Zanusso slumps back down on the metal frame. There is a pool of urine at its base.

"He is telling the truth," Tannis says. "The weapon code has been deactivated remotely. I should have accounted for this eventuality."

"Not everything is lost, Tannis. We still have full control of the three assassins."

"Yes, although we now have VIAS on high alert. However, I do not doubt that we shall get what we want, even without the mind-control weapon. Sarokis, our plans have only just commenced." He stares at Zanusso's body, now draped off the metal frame like a coat on a clothes hook. "I shall keep you alive, for now. Your skills are going to be important to me."

He turns to his mercenary. "I have another task for you, Sarokis..."

AN UPGRADED RIDE

Lucky Day Cabs, Catuvell City, Planet Vost.

"Okay, Redolfo." Says Squintt. "You've read the manual - all seven-hundred pages of it - I bet. Ha ha! Let's see what you're made of. I see you've already met Timbrell Marskell."

Redolfo looks at his passenger, stony-faced with a bulky proboscis projecting between two slit-like green eyes that give him a permanent, sneering expression. To add to the effect, his horizontal forehead ridges enhance a natural affectation of disdain.

"Marskell, make sure he doesn't go out of control. I've chosen you because I know you won't take any nonsense from him."

Redolfo stares transfixed at his boss' waddling gait as Squintt makes as hasty a retreat as he can from the repair shed.

"You've gotta be kidding me." Redolfo's passenger jibes. "You really intend to ferry the public around in this piece of crap?"

Redolfo smiles at him and tilts his cap.

Glyrian has cleared a path for the Checker at the exit of the shed. Outside in the yard a line-up of the two Squintt brothers and two waving office girls. A flick of the switch of his hyperspace probe radio - a jingle:

Music radio 77 - WABC

"What on Vost is that?" spits Marskell.

Redolfo puts the Checker into gear. The shed fills with multicoloured vapour.

"Okay, Glyrian." Redolfo says aloud. "Let's see what this baby can do."

The radio continues:

... *Rubberband Man*...

Redolfo feels the cab moving.

"Holy Moly! This thing really is lifting off the ground."

The Checker rises five feet into the air and travels forwards out of the shed. Marskell shuffles uncomfortably in his seat. The girls are cheering. Redolfo can see in his rear-view mirror that Glyrian is smiling broadly, and the larger Squintt has his head in his hands.

~

Squintt looks up and shouts to Redolfo. "Now keep within ten blocks of here. Take it easy and get used to the controls. Don't travel beyond the municipal velocity limits. Remember, if you get caught speeding, you'll be banned from driving." The Checker rises within plumes of red, blue, yellow and green vapour billowing out from a whining Temeria engine.

Squintt watches nervously as the cab wobbles from side to side, then begins to list. "Glyrian, why is it doing this?"

His brother looks puzzled.

Redolfo leans out of his window and shouts down to them, "Don't worry, I'm just pulling some fun here!"

Within moments, the Checker has straightened up and spun off into the distance.

~

"This ride is bitchin', Marsky!" Redolfo exclaims as the Checker rises at a near vertical tilt, whizzing past the reflective windows of the World Bank of Carnona. He takes the Temeria engine offline.

"What the...!" shouts Marskell. The cab goes into free-fall. "What in the gods' names are you doing?"

"Yay-hey!" Shouts Redolfo as the cab twists into a barrel spin. Marskell holds onto the ceiling. The green hue

63

of his skin turns pale. The World Bank of Carnona, then the ground, then the sky, spin in and out of view at least three times in quick succession. Redolfo reaches out. A flick of the switch and the Temeria is back online. The cab straightens out.

"How could you have known that would work, Redolfo?" You could have killed us both!"

"I just knew. Hey lighten up, Marsky! We're okay."

"Now just cool it, or I'll make sure you never drive on Vost again." Marskell's natural green hue returns.

Redolfo takes the cab for a more sedate run between the great commerce buildings at the east side of Catuvell.

Avoiding the worst of the traffic congestion, he takes a lower path to hover over Catuvell Park. The park is dominated by a gigantic floating, metallic statue of a severe-looking man in military regalia. Redolfo reckons it to be about three-hundred feet tall. "What's that, Marsky?"

His passenger replies with a grunt.

Redolfo can see children of various species on what look like the space hoppers that the kids use in Brooklyn, except these ones hover in the air. They look up and wave, clearly taking an interest in the rather unusual, antiquated appearance of his yellow transporter.

Redolfo waves back at them. Kids have always been fun.

~

Squintt, his brother and the two office girls have waited anxiously at the yard. The returning Checker emerges from behind the giant and somewhat rusted, happy face sign of the Walshram's Canisters factory and hovers over the Lucky Day Cabs building. Redolfo peers out of the window and calls out, "Hey Squintt, your office looks even more derelict from up here!" The cab then takes a curved course into the yard and settles with a perfect doughnut, raising just the correct amount of yard-dust in the process, close up to where his boss and his brother are standing.

"He seems to have outstanding driving skills for a human bound to two-dimensional roads on his planet," observes Squintt to his brother. Glyrian nods.

Marskell and Redolfo emerge from the cab. Redolfo stands with his hands in his pockets.

"He's a maniac!" shouts Marskell to Squintt.

"I expected that. But did he handle the cab well?"

"Oh, he can handle it alright," Marskell replies tersely, "but he needs to control his crazy behaviour."

The girls run towards the cabbie. "Good job, Mike!" Cam-Ell squeals, jumping up and down and clapping.

"I knew you could do it," says a smiling Diselda, planting a kiss on his cheek.

"Hey, Marsky," says Redolfo, "I just wanted to see what she can do. Look, I know how to drive carefully. I've been doing it for years. This is my cab and I know how it handles - even in the air. Even on this planet."

Marskell returns to his own lime green and purple taxi-transporter and lowers the window. "Don't say I didn't warn you, Squintt! Surely the company's not this hard up for drivers." His transporter taxi fires up. A hiss announces the rising of the Lucky Day Cabs waving hand on his roof. Marskell spits out the window. A grey, angry vapour emerges from the Temeria exhaust system and he is in the air. Moments later, with a final, defiant wave of his cab's roof hand, he has disappeared behind the eternally happy face signage of the Walshram's Canisters factory.

"Well, he seemed happy," Redolfo says.

"I am doing this against my better judgement, Redolfo," Squintt says as he passes a folder to his new employee.

Redolfo opens the folder and studies the documents contained within it. "My licence! What the hell! That's my picture! It's been stamped! How on Earth...?"

"But you're not on Earth, Redolfo. Just don't ask any more questions. There are things about this company that you'll just have to accept. I assure you those documents are fully legitimate and official. You have your first job tomorrow at 08:30 at Faolán 23. You're taking a girl to school. Remember this, Redolfo - the clients often like to talk, so you'd better sound like they're all your long-lost brothers and sisters, or you'll find yourself sweeping up the crap from the Eohipp racing stables, where you'll eventually expire from the stench - that, by the way, is the worst job on Vost - so don't screw up!"

Squintt whispers to his brother. "Let's hope, for his sake, he can retain his licence long enough to earn his fare home."

A FRANKLY IMPOSSIBLE JOURNEY

The Fiat 521 makes its clattering way along 5. května towards the city limits.

Over thirty minutes pass and Marianna can hardly bring herself to look at Kominsky. She can't help but feel his love is genuine, but how is she to cope with this betrayal? So he's not from Earth! What even is he? Her thoughts are interrupted by Otto, who utters his first words to them since the incident at the road blockade.

"The Germans even interfered with the side of the road we drive on. We were perfectly happy driving on the left. Going back to driving on the right side should be the first priority once the Communist Party takes over and all German blood has been wiped from our nation."

Kominsky's face flushes. "So, despite the theft, torture and mass murder of innocent people at the hands of the German government, you think that the *roads* should be made a priority?!"

Marianna grabs his arm. "Don't antagonise him, Mikkrian. We need this man to help us."

"Marianna, that's no longer my name. My world changed forever the day I met you. I will always be your Dominik."

She glares at him.

Otto smiles and begins singing a Czechoslovakian Communist Party song, his head swinging from side to side:

Hey, hey, eastern sun
And the man yanked handcuffs
Under the banner of Lenin,
Rumbling beneath the ground, hey
Rumbling beneath the ground, hey
The whole earth rumbles!
Hey, hey, the world is no longer on edge
And one breathes freely
Under the banner of Lenin

Kominsky holds his hand to his forehead and emits a deep sigh.

"We're approaching the city's south-east roadblock." Otto says, his jolly demeanour turning more serious. "You must have your papers ready." He stops the Fiat at the gates.

There are about fifteen soldiers with two SS officers. Kominsky winds down his window.

A sour-faced officer who looks like he's in his early sixties addresses him, "Guten Abend. Ihre Unterlagen bitte." He takes the documents from Kominsky, and studies them carefully. "Why are you travelling out of Prague, Herr Kominsky, Fräulein Kravová?"

"Guten Abend, Offizier. I'm visiting my office in Budapest. I need to make sure my Hungarian manager is not cooking the books."

"Indeed, you do, Herr Kominsky. Our Hungarian friends often claim themselves as our allies but their real intentions are as inscrutable as their language. As you know, many accountants in Hungary are Jews. I also know that many Czechoslovakian Jews are fleeing to Hungary."

He stares at Marianna. She shivers.

"So, tell me, Herr Kominsky," the officer studies the interior of the Fiat, then glances suspiciously at Otto, "what are your real intentions?"

"You can see, officer, my documents do confirm my business interests in Budapest. They even have the official seal."

"Why do I feel you are taking us for fools? Get out of the car, all of you!" Ten soldiers surround the Fiat. "Put your hands on the roof of the vehicle."

The soldiers open the doors and yank all three of them out of the car by their wrists. "Place your faces onto the vehicle!" He shouts.

The soldiers open the boot and inspect the contents of the suitcases. "Not much to show for a man who is looking after a business interest in Hungary, Herr Kominsky. You are all under arrest."

Kominsky's eyes begin to flame red. He turns to look at the officer.

The officer screams, "I said place your face..." He stops shouting, pauses and begins stroking his hirsute chin as if trying to remember something important. "We grew up together...when we were children, we used to roll down that steep hill ...we laughed so much...I remember laughing because you fell into a ditch...how could I have forgotten this, Dominik? I remember us laughing at that boy with the protruding ears."

The soldiers are now aiming their rifles at the three detainees.

"Halt!" the officer shouts with an out-stretched hand.

Another officer appears, "Demelhuber! Was machst du da?"

"I know this man," Officer Demelhuber replies to his colleague. He then raises his pistol and discharges it into his colleague's face, spraying the other soldiers with skull and brain fragments. The soldiers then train their rifles on Demelhuber.

Another soldier shouts, "Was ist hier los, Leutnant Demelhuber?" Demelhuber stares open-mouthed into space. He answers by discharging a bullet from his pistol into the soldier's neck. The remaining soldiers return fire and Demelhuber's body falls to the floor, peppered with bullet holes. Marianna lets out a scream as the headless body of the officer shot by Demelhuber rises up and discharges several rifle rounds into two of his living colleagues.

Kominsky's eyes are now scorching red. His arms are outstretched. The seven remaining soldiers frantically fire at the headless torso until their cartridges are spent. The bullet-ridden corpse slumps to the ground.

Kominsky makes a brief gesture with his right hand that sends the mutilated body of Demelhuber hurtling into the remaining soldiers, toppling them. Kominsky's eyes darken. He collapses to the ground, his face drained of colour.

Marianna sees Otto stare at her in panic as the surviving soldiers recover and start to reload their weapons. She seizes Demelhuber's pistol and fires several rounds into their heads. Otto pulls out his own handgun. Between them, they shoot and kill all the remaining soldiers.

Otto casts a glance at Marianna who with rapid, shallow breaths, stares horrified at her lifeless victims. He nods his head in respect.

"Help me lift your man back into the car," he says, grasping the unconscious Kominsky under the arms. Between them, they manage to drag him into the back of the Fiat. Otto picks up the now blood-spattered documents from the ground and returns them to their folder.

"Get us out of here!" Marianna shouts from the back of the car. The driver hits the accelerator and the Fiat makes a hasty exit from the roadblock.

~

The journey takes them to a long country road. Marianna repeatedly checks Kominsky is still breathing. Half an hour passes and he opens his eyes.

"Welcome back, Mr. Kominsky!" says Otto, who's been watching him in the rear-view mirror.

Kominsky groans.

Otto continues, "Well, how did you do that? I once read about this type of power."

Kominsky does not reply.

Marianna dabs at the drops of blood emerging from Kominsky's bloodshot eyes and his left nostril. His skin is a pale-grey colour, his breathing rapid. It's clear to her that his powers drain him.

Kominsky stares into space.

Otto starts singing, his head swaying from side to side, his expression jolly:

Roll out the barrel.
We'll have a barrel of fun.
Roll out the barrel.
We've got the blues on the run.
Zing! Boom! Tar-rar-rel
Ring out a song of good cheer!
Now's the time to roll the barrel
For the gang's all here.

"Otto, just shut up!" Marianna shouts.

A NEW CAREER

Catuvell City, Planet Vost

08:28. The Checker rises gently towards its destination, the apartments at Faolán 23. The Faolán building is suspended proudly above the city in a reasonably affluent residential area. It looks to Redolfo like a floating New York skyscraper that's spiked with landing piers. Diselda told the cabbie that it's become a fashionable residence for politicians and diplomats. The cab alights onto one of the piers.

As he approaches the building, he stops to peer over the railings, curious to see the view from such a building. He instantly realises what a bad idea that was. On reaching the apartment, he knocks on the front door and waits with his hands pushed into his pockets. The door opens, revealing an adult female who acknowledges him without smiling. He tips his cap to her. She looks as if she's taken care of her appearance. The skin on her face is pinkish with soft circlets and is capped with light hair, tied up at the back. Without any further formalities, she turns and calls out. "Gethsemona! Your driver's here. Come along now!"

Silence.

"Gethsemona, your taxi's waiting for you! Come here, now!"

"Okay, okay, hold on!" an irritated voice replies from inside the apartment.

Silence.

She looks briefly at Redolfo, her head trembling in exasperation.

Redolfo reflects back to when he was a kid getting ready for school.

Michael, your father's waiting to take you to school. Alfonso, tell that boy of yours to hurry up!

Arrivo, mamma! says a little Redolfo, zipping down the stairs. Hell, how life was so much easier in them days.

Gethsemona appears after an awkward wait. She has similar contouring and skin colour to the adult female who's clearly her mother, but the daughter is a smaller, more urchin-like version with a green, two-piece uniform, round wire spectacles, little blonde plaits, and a school satchel. She walks straight past Redolfo and outside to the cab. Without saying a word, she opens the rear car door, shuffles herself inside and straps herself in using Glyrian's safety-belt modification.

Redolfo tips his cap again to the mother as he says, "Ma'am," and returns to his cab. "Okay, Gethsemona, I have to get you to your school safely, and on time - so no problem, young lady."

The Checker leaves the landing pier in a cloud of multi-coloured vapour. Five minutes go by and Redolfo has his route worked out. The ride is smooth.

Gethsemona sits in silence, arms folded, not once showing any emotion. Eventually, she says, "What kind of a weirdo taxi is this?"

"Hell, Gethsemona! You sit saying nothing for five minutes and then come out with that line. Look, this is my first pickup job and I'm counting on you to make it a happy one. Are we okay with that?"

Gethsemona resumes her silence, continuing to sit with her arms folded. Fifteen minutes pass and the Checker hovers gently over the school landing area. Redolfo can see the area is full of parked transporters. The place is teeming with children of various species, each carrying their regulation satchels and green uniforms.

Gethsemona leans forwards and whispers into his ear. "Look, park over there." Redolfo sees her pointing to the extreme end of the parking lot.

"What the...?" He replies.

"Look, I don't want anyone to see I've been in this stupid cab."

Redolfo grunts. He moves the Checker and settles it down gently. "Is this far enough away for you?"

Gethsemona steps out of the cab. She does not reply.

"Same place at four o'clock!" Redolfo calls to her.

Without looking back, she trots down the path towards the school, her plaits swinging as she steps. The cab rises off its space, the roof hand with its NYC emblem waving merrily.

"Hi, Handsome!" Mike can hear Diselda's voice coming from the cab radio.

"Hi, Diselda. What's up?"

"There's another job for you. A pickup from Ronat 17. He says he wants to get to the Catuvell City Council. He's waiting for you, Hun."

A few moments later, he arrives at his second pickup point. Waiting for him is a creature that resembles a giant humanoid insect with iridescent compound eyes and antennae. The creature speaks to him, its shiny head jerking from side to side, and with quick movements of its thin, segmented, hairy legs, "Rekkakka rackkaka X82 Y32 Z7, rekkacka 12 Rekkakkka"

Redolfo taps his language decoder under his right ear. "Hey, Diselda, are you there?"

"Hi, Hun."

"You hearing this?"

"Rekkkaka kakara"

"Sorry, Hun—no idea what he's saying. Looks like he's too alien even for the language decoder."

FRONTIER

Briganti Mountains, Planet Vost.

The backpack's strap is beginning to chafe. Agent Rimikk checks the position of the supergiant sun and maps it to the positions of the moons. Arianrhod, red from her rich iron content is emerging on the horizon, while Cerridwen proudly radiates her sea of grey-blue reflections. There are no roads or even paths to the reservation, a challenge welcomed by the seasoned explorer.

It suits the agent that Vernikell ordered that he travel alone, having argued that more than one visitor might appear threatening to the terannians. In truth, Rimikk prefers his own company anyway.

He's pleased that the government is honouring an old, but unsigned agreement with the terannians that transporters do not travel west of the city of Briganti, leaving their reservation in peace. This gives him an ideal opportunity to exercise his fieldwork skills.

The journey north-west from Briganti, however, is in no way easy. The city's situated at the foot of the eastern side of the Brigantian Rocks, a wild and fairly unexplored mountain range. He was briefed that Briganti is a small city that grew out of an ancient trading post, situated conveniently on waterways that would have been a vital mode of transport for the original inhabitants of the planet. The tallest mountain, Uchdryd, elevates to over 18,000 feet, and stands as a dramatic, sugar-coated backdrop to the city, separating it from the terannian reservation.

He checks out his map. He's calculated a ravine path, based on satellite elevation data. Being a seasoned climber and known by his colleagues to be as hard as nails, it's no surprise he was Vernikell's first choice for this mission. From his fieldwork experience, Rimikk knows he's largely, but not completely, immune to the effects of the rarefied atmospheres at high altitude. Unusually for him, however, he's been feeling weak and muzzy headed on this particular hike and is needing to take frequent breaks.

He reflects how Vernikell was worried about the diplomatic issues that this mission entails. Rimikk's not a man for engaging in small talk. However, given so little is known of the terannians, his boss could not decide whether this was an issue or an asset in this situation.

He finds the mountainous ascent fairly straightforward. The agent's face is buried within his fur hood and he hears little in the way of sound besides the crunching of his boots on the snow and the creaking of the upright palisades of tall trees in the light, but ice-cold breeze. The stillness is broken by the occasional movement of snow liberated off the high branches by the scurrying of small tree-dwelling creatures. Happy he has reached the highest point of his journey, he begins to survey the mountainous contours on the horizon with his optical magnifiers. There are, so far, no signs of civilization. The descent path follows a clear, blue reflective stream that he considers is likely to be the main source of water for the terannian reservation. The trees are becoming more densely arranged than at the higher levels. He feels the burning of chilled air in his nostrils as the wind picks up.

Rimikk notices an odd sensation arise within his body - something unusual. Something in his past, maybe? No, something ancient - much older than anything he has ever known. He shakes the feeling off. He is not a man for fanciful notions. He always scoffs at people in his trekking parties with overly romantic views - how they feel closer to nature in the mountains and how it connects them to the old ways.

There are very few people beyond Vernikell for whom he has any time or respect. Then again, even his boss spends too much time philosophising in his own peculiar way. What use are philosophy and romantic notions for the Deputy-Chief of Staff of VIAS when he has a whole planet to protect?

Rimikk's reflections are interrupted by deep vibrations - so deep, he cannot triangulate its source. He recognises them as the low-frequency growls of heavy-pelted, bull-like giant auriachs. These powerful creatures have been banished from the Cornovi mountain range ever since the influential farmers' lobby convinced the Vost government that they are responsible for transmitting numerous diseases into their livestock. The slaughter began despite considerable protests from animal rights campaigners desperately citing the lack of hard evidence for the farmers' claims. Ignoring the pleas of the campaigners, the government commissioned a mass slaughter of giant auriachs in the area, well before the evidence became conclusive either way. Most voters don't care much for auriachs anyway.

Despite their herbivorous diet and generally shy nature, they weigh about 600 pounds, are faster than most bipedal beings, and are known to flatten or maul hikers if they think their calves are under threat. Rimikk recognises this may well be just such a situation and stands absolutely still, maser weapon at the ready. He stares to his left, towards a small cluster of boulders. He looks behind him and sees a clump of scrub bushes near a tree. Too many possibilities. The uncertainty fills the seasoned agent with a rare surge of panic.

Out of the corner of his eye, he spots the slightest movement of foliage, and with lightning reflexes, discharges his weapon into the point of the movement, releasing a plume of super-heated vapour. He feels a sharp impact against his back and the world erupts into a shower of sparks as he realises he has been launched high into the air. He lands tumbling into the deep snow.

He composes himself and looks up to see the thick-hide faces of three giant auriachs glaring down at him with luminous eyes and with steam jetting from their nostrils. He reaches for his weapon and realises it must have been knocked out of his grasp when he was thrown. A surge of pain pulses through him as an auriach sinks its serrated incisors, evolved from millions of years of stripping tree-bark, into his chest. He's lifted and tossed a few feet along the ground. Another huge auriach lowers its head towards his ear as the growl resonates through his whole body. He closes his eyes, defeated, awaiting the final blow.

The growling eases. He opens his eyes to see the auriachs are now looking downstream. They walk away. They are gone. He hears the wind whistle a long note through the trees as, despite the constricting chest pain, he again feels the sense of something ancient.

A warm trickle of blood begins to run from his chest. He realises, to his relief, that he is not fatally wounded, as he sees through his torn clothing that although his chest wall has sustained deep lacerations, his lungs have not been punctured. He scrambles awkwardly to his feet. He rubs his eyes and focuses on what seems to be a bipedal figure standing about a hundred feet away from him. It is antlered, with pointed ears, a long face and dark eyes. Wrapped over its shoulders is a dark grey cloak held in place with a metallic clasp. The creature stands motionless, watching Rimikk in silence.

The musical note of the wind rises slightly in pitch. The wounded agent staggers towards the creature, blood dripping on the snow. Weakening, he collapses.

ALL THAT'S LEFT TO DO THE JOB

The car stops. Marianna sees Kominsky wake with a start. He shakes his head as if to regather his thoughts.

"We have arrived at the safe house - in the village of Zakřany," says an excited Otto, almost singing the welcome news to his passengers. "This is where we'll stay for the night. We're doing well. We're halfway to Budapest now."

"Marianna," Kominsky says to her, "I know how hard this is for you to take in right now - but we are safe and that's more important than anything else."

She looks downcast at her tummy. Kominsky kisses her cheek.

"I can't wait to see their faces when they hear what you can do, Mr. Kominsky," says Otto.

Kominsky looks directly at the driver. His flash red. "You will say nothing to anyone about what you have seen."

Otto nods his head.

As they step out of the vehicle, a man appears from inside the house. His jolly personality matches that of their driver. "Let me help you with those," he smiles. "Just follow me. My name is Ignác. My wife, Gertruda has prepared a bed and a hot meal for you."

They enter the little cottage and are greeted by a plump, middle-aged lady and her two prettily dressed daughters. Gertruda gives each of her guests a suffocating hug. She steps back to look at Marianna, "Oh my word, Ignác. Look how beautiful she is - and with such lovely hair! Please, please come inside." She adjusts the rag in her own hair and reties her apron.

Moments later, the guests are each tucking into a bowl of hot potato knedle, washed down with a glass of potent schnapps.

"This is Ignác's homemade brew," says Gertruda, smiling at her guests, "and he's been torturing me with this lethal drink for twenty years! Now that liquor's no longer available in the stores, I guess I have to be thankful to the old goat that we actually have a drink to digest our food with."

"Gertruda, thank you so much for looking after us," says a grateful Marianna.

"It's a pleasure to have you here." Gertruda replies, "I would love to hear all about you both. Marianna, where are you from?"

Marianna swallows down a dumpling and replies, "I'm from Prague."

"Otto tells me you're Jewish. Are your family still alive?"

"Yes, I'm Jewish, but I've never been observant." Her eyes begin to moisten as she remembers her parents' strong religious beliefs. "I'm an only child. My father died about ten years ago and my mother was taken by the Germans."

Gertruda shakes her head and smiles warmly, "I'm so sorry, dear. The world has become such a dreadful place. Do you know what's happened to her?"

"The only word I've had was a brief postcard from her saying she was being sent to the Stutthof concentration camp. I've heard nothing since." Marianna says wiping her eyes with the back of her hand. "There are rumours that no one comes out of there alive."

Gertruda hands her a handkerchief. "How have you managed to survive?"

Marianna places a hand on her tummy. Not only have the Germans stripped her of her life and family, but her lover, Dominik, has dealt her a blow she's not sure she can recover from. Has he betrayed her? What even is he? Is he really just trying to protect her? She decides not to think about it. Somehow, she finds it comforting to confide in these strangers who've risked their own lives to help them. She's never been able to talk candidly about her life to anyone other than Dominik and it is a relief to have the chance to tell her story. She continues, "When the Germans arrived, we were forced to wear the yellow star at all times. We couldn't even enter most shops or public buildings. I lived with a Christian friend in a nearby house and hid my Jewish background. When I met Dominik, he was able to forge documents and give me a false identity."

"My poor dear. Were you ever able to see your mother?"

"My visits to her were rare. I had to be so careful. German soldiers came regularly to Jewish houses to take anything they could find of value such as jewellery, silver or furs. When they found nothing further of value to steal, they took away the people's pets. My mother wept bitterly after they took away her little dog."

Gertruda reaches out and touches her hand.

Marianna has told this story to Dominik before. He knows it well. He has said that of all the anti-Jewish laws enforced in the city, to confiscate people's pets is among the cruellest acts inflicted on the Jews of Prague. He told her that the more he learns about the collective behaviour of humanity, the more he despairs of it. She realises now exactly what he'd meant by that.

She continues, "Even before the deportations started, many Jews were evicted from their houses to make room for German soldiers. Food was scarce and Jewish households went hungry. One day, there was a loud knock on my mother's door. As you'd expect, she became very nervous. She opened the door to find a young German soldier insisting on being allowed in. He said his name was Wilfried. He handed her a small bundle that contained some bread, a roundel of cheese and an apple. He started shouting at her saying he was intending to commandeer her property, but all the while pointing to the thin walls of the house as if to say, *everyone next door can hear this and will tell the authorities unless he makes it sound realistic.*

"I used to meet my mother in secret and met Wilfried a number of times. He told me how ashamed he was of what had happened to his country. He said he was doing what he could for the Jews in the area. He left as many food parcels as he could without making it appear obvious what he was up to. I always feared for him that his charity would one day land him in serious trouble."

"What happened to him?" asks Gertruda.

"After my mother was deported, I never heard about him again."

"Otto," Ignác says, breaking an awkward silence as he pours the driver another shot of schnapps, "I've heard from the Communist Party that since King Michael switched sides, most of Romania is finally liberated from the Nazis."

Otto takes no time to down his drink. "Yes, my friend. My sources from the Party say that over a hundred and sixty-thousand Romanian troops were slaughtered by the Soviet army in Stalingrad. I've also heard rumours that even after Romania turned against Germany, the Soviets rounded up over a hundred and fifty-thousand Romanian troops and made them march all the way to detention camps in the Soviet Union. My contact at the KSČ told me that fifty thousand of them perished on the way. It wasn't just Stalingrad that destroyed the Romanian army!"

"A tragic consequence of making the wrong friend," Ignác replies with a sigh.

"Ignác, our comrades have stockpiled a good supply of guns. We do have a number of pipe bombs too, but we never seem to have a chance to test them as they make so much noise and we'd have the Germans all over us within seconds. We have no idea if they are even going to work."

"Maybe I can help you," Marianna says to the surprise of her hosts.

Ignác smiles and replies, "That's very kind of you, but—"

"Actually, she can help you, Ignác," Kominsky replies.

"I used to work for Škoda Pilsen before the Germans invaded. I used to help manufacture munitions." Both Otto and Ignác pull up their chairs to speak to her directly. "Look, the most common cause of failure for pipe bombs to detonate is the gas bleed out of the ignition port—"

~

"She's beautiful *and* clever. I can see why you are so in love with her," Gertruda says to Kominsky as she dries the dishes.

Marianna's soft voice continues in the background, "...If there's insufficient oxidizer..."

"I am so grateful for your hospitality, Gertruda."

"I hope you two know what you're doing. You know how dangerous it is to travel to Hungary."

Kominsky swigs back the rest of his schnapps.

"I know what will cheer us up," Ignác says, ending his intense conversation with Marianna. He produces an accordion and begins the evening's entertainment with a polka. He, Otto and the two daughters begin:

The goose flew, flew from above.
A sportsman came upon her, shot her in the side
Shot her in the side...

The lovers look at each other. As if Otto's travelling songs weren't punishment enough! However, Marianna realises that they are being looked after with kindness and, for the time being at least, are probably safe. They join in with the singing as best they can before retiring to bed.

~

The next morning, the three travellers give their farewell thanks and are back on the road. Otto takes a country road route to avoid the roadblocks at the city of Brno.

"Dominik," Marianna whispers to him, "do you think Otto told them about your abilities?"

"No, he didn't," he whispers back.

"How do you know that?"

"I can tell. It's part of what I can do."

"I guess I could never get away with lying to you, Dominik."

"You have never lied to me, my beautiful Marianna. It's part of why I have fallen so deeply in love with you."

For the first time since he revealed his past to her, he can see her face soften with just a hint of the adoration he has seen so many times before. To him, she has never looked so lovely.

"My friends," says Otto, breaking the spell, "we are soon approaching the point where I have to leave you."

"What?" shouts Kominsky. "You agreed to take us to Budapest."

"I am sorry, Mr. Kominsky. After you both went to sleep, I had a long talk with Ignác. I'm needed to help the Slovakian resistance. There's a planned uprising in the mountains against German forces where communist soldiers are joining Slovak army dissidents. The Soviet army is making a push southward through Poland. This is an important step towards the liberation of Slovakia."

Kominsky's disappointment is obvious.

"You shouldn't underestimate yourself," Otto continues. "You have a power like I have never seen before. I have confidence in you."

Marianna growls at Otto. "You've seen what it does to Dominik. It'll kill him."

Kominsky replies, "Since I've lived on Earth I've never, until now, needed to use my power in this way. I do sometimes use it for reading people and anticipating them. The only other time I've used it in a physical way was when I was escaping from my planet's government retrieval agents. It does exhaust me - it requires a lot of energy to produce enough power to have an effect on people's thoughts or on physical objects. That energy must be replaced and sometimes it can take some time to recover. I don't think the telepathy gene is suited to my species. Berrantines never evolved with this ability."

"Can it actually harm you?" says Marianna.

"I really don't know. I'm the first berrantine to ever carry the genetic code."

~

There are no further checkpoints despite several hours of driving. They pass several convoys of German soldiers in troop carriers, who often smile and wave at the three travellers. The Fiat seems to be the only civilian vehicle on the road. Otto has been boring his passengers with continued talk about how well the Italian saloon negotiates the hills. All appears to go to plan until they make the approach to Modřice.

Five cadets are standing at a blockade. They train their rifles at the approaching vehicle. "Oh, my word," cries Marianna, "they are children - just young boys! They look about fourteen."

"Yes," says Otto, "Germany needs every man and boy they can spare to keep Slovakia under German domination. It should be like candy from a baby for you, Mr. Kominsky."

"Dominik, don't you even think about hurting those boys," Marianna glares at him.

The young soldier indicates for them to exit the vehicle. Once out of the Fiat, he addresses them nervously, "Wer sind Sie? Ihre Unterlagen, bitte."

Kominsky produces the folder of stained documents. The young soldier looks at the documents and then to the three travellers. "Seid ihr alle Juden? Ihr sieht alle aus wie Juden."

Kominsky fights the urge to use his powers. "No, sir. Of course, we're not Jews. As you can see, we're off to Budapest to sort out some business interests."

The cadet kicks the gravel with his boot and lights a cigarette. Otto reaches carefully for his pistol. After an agonising minute, the cadet finishes his third puff. Looking distrustfully at Kominsky, he aims his gun and says, "Ich glaube Ihnen nicht."

Kominsky's eyes start to burn red. The child soldiers gasp. Otto pulls out his pistol. Marianna grabs his wrist.

"Don't you dare, Otto! They're just children."

"There's no other way," he replies.

She turns to her lover. "Dominik, can you make them forget we were ever here?"

"I don't know. I can try."

The boys collapse to the ground, unconscious.

"This will not turn out well," Otto explains to them, as they drive off. "If they remember this when they awake, there will be a column of military on us with no hesitation to shoot to kill."

~

Within a short time, Otto announces, "We're approaching Bratislava. This is where I shall leave you. I need to make my way to the Eastern Carpathian Mountains and join the rebels with the Slovakian Army."

"I don't know how we could ever repay you," Marianna says to him. "You have risked everything and saved our lives."

"It's been a pleasure to have met you, Miss Kravová and a pleasure to have worked with you, Mr. Kominsky. I'll never forget this."

"You have helped us so much, Otto. We couldn't have made it this far without you. We will always be grateful," replies Kominsky, "but I'm afraid you'll have to forget what you saw."

Marianna sees her lover's eyes flash red. "You'd better not have wiped what I told him about the bombs."

Kominsky smiles cheekily, his eyes twinkling.

"Good luck, and please stay safe," Marianna says to Otto.

Otto steps out of the Fiat and takes his backpack. "Farewell, comrades," he says. Moments later he is gone.

~

Back in Modřice, the young German soldiers regain consciousness. They look confusedly at each other.

"What just happened?" asks a cadet.

The leader gets to his feet and replies, "I don't know. That man seemed to have some form of strange power. I'll inform the Kommandant."

SUPPORTING THE UNDERDOG

Alfonso Redolfo feeds another log onto the campfire. He gives his young son a mournful look. "Mio caro figlio - my dear son."

"Yes, papà?"

"You know I appreciate you giving up your time with your friends to be with me. I don't get much time off, you know. We've so many bills to pay."

There is a slight chill in the evening air and the light from the campfire reflects a warm orange glow onto the surrounding trees. The fresh log starts to pop as it succumbs to the flames.

"I like it when we spend time together, Michael. I just don't understand why you like camping in the woods so much. It's the third time this year."

The awkward silence is broken only by the crackling of the fire.

"I like our time together too, papà." The young Michael Redolfo is clearly upset. His eyes are welling over.

"Look, I know mamma is overprotective—"

"Overprotective! Papà, she never lets me out. I'm always grounded when my friends are out having fun. It's just not fair!"

"You are our only child, Michael, and that makes you precious to us. Life has not always been easy. You know, mamma will do anything for you, as long as she thinks you're safe. We both just want what's best for you. Michael, don't run off. Michael! Come back here!"

Redolfo awakes from his memories to find himself behind the wheel of his Checker. He fires up the engine. The hyperspace probe radio cuts in to the sound of Bohemian Rhapsody.

"Okay," he says to himself, "time for my last job of the day." He returns to the school and finds a landing platform at the far end of the parking lot as instructed by Gethsemona. The school bell rings, and a sea of children emerge smiling, running and shouting with excitement. After what seems too long a time, most of the children have left in their transporters and there's still no sign of Redolfo's passenger. Eventually, the little figure of Gethsemona emerges at the school end of a now empty parking lot. She walks towards him, her arms folded. He jumps out of the cab and opens the back door for her. "Nice day?" he says. She gets into the Checker and straps herself in without answering. "Okay," he continues, "I'm not one for talking much either."

The novelty of soaring high in the sky is starting to wear off, so Redolfo takes a route where he can hover just above the ground.

He recalls Squintt explaining that because Catuvell had originally developed at ground level, most of the interesting views and architecture are best viewed from low down.

He sees the imposing metallic statue that Marskell chose not to explain to him. *Boy, that dude was angry!* Redolfo had later asked Squintt about it, who said that the floating statue is of Impriat Vandtner, the symbolic leader of the conquering people of Vost. He said that the three-hundred-foot high monolith depicts Vandtner as a planetary hero in full military regalia. The statue dominates the view of the city's central park in its position suspended over two-hundred feet in the air.

He takes the Checker higher for the next stretch of his journey. He remembers his new boss saying that the upper reaches of the city mainly consist of office blocks and industrial units suspended above the ground. They are positioned at staggered intervals in order to maximise the amount of light reaching the ground-level buildings. The sky-buildings are subject to tight planning regulations and all the important ground-level municipal buildings and the wealthiest residential areas are free of buildings above them.

The highest levels are largely taken up by less attractive industrial units, where the rent is cheaper. Squintt says that the economic experts initially thought that the higher-level buildings would be the most sought-after. The markets however proved differently due to the ongoing concerns of many property-owners that a building without solid foundations is at risk of a catastrophic fail.

Despite this, Squintt explained, the skies are becoming an investment haven for property developers and entrepreneurs and some fashionable residential sky-blocks are emerging. In truth, no one really knows what the future holds for the planet since Temeria Schneider's invention of the ground-breaking engine that has changed the planet's soul with levitated buildings and transporters.

The *Lucky Day Cabs* boss was unable to resist giving Redolfo his opinion that the endless, centralised legislation from the world government stifles much of the planet's innovators. Now only state-run institutions and large corporations have the ability to negotiate the complex legal requirements necessary for investment and development in buildings. He told the cabbie it is a great time to be a lawyer on Vost. Law is one industry that seems recession proof in any place in the universe, Redolfo thinks.

The night is closing in and Catuvell is bathed by the serene red and blue hues of Arianrhod and Cerridwen, the colours that Redolfo now associates with the planet itself.

Catuvell Main Square is beautifully aglow with lights, ready and welcoming for the city revellers and socialites.

"This is kinda pretty, don't you think?" he says to Gethsemona. He shakes his head and says to himself, "How I miss Manhattan." His silent passenger seems unimpressed by the view. "Well, I think it's cool. Anyway, don't fret. I'll get you home on time."

Something stirs in him as he studies the street ahead. "Hey, do you see anything wrong up ahead? I've got a funny feeling that someone needs our help. I'm gonna take a closer look."

Gethsemona winds down the window and looks out. She shrugs and winds the window back up.

Redolfo moves the cab closer. "Yeah, I knew it. It's a fight!" He lands the Checker at the end of the street where he can get a closer view. Gethsemona squints through her wire-frame lenses. The cabbie leans out of his window and is gripped by an intense sense of unease. The feeling intensifies - it's as if he is being observed. "What the...?" he says to himself.

His thoughts are interrupted by the sounds of shouting and clanging of metal against metal appearing to come from directly in front of him. About fifty yards ahead, two huge figures, about ten feet tall, are attacking three humanoids, two of which are male and the other female. The giant beings seem hefty but quick-footed despite their size. Their faces are the size of beach balls with skin of thick hide, their eyes dark and menacing. One is wielding a curved blade and the other is swinging a heavy chain. Redolfo watches as a swipe of the chain sends one of the humanoid males hurtling across the ground in a spray of blood. He rolls over a few times until he ends face up.

The female - mamma mia! She has a toned, athletic build, with long, fiery-red curly hair with blue-streaks, held in place with a patterned headband. She is dressed in what Redolfo considers to be like the outfit of a warrior in a

Raquel Welch movie. He observes, with fascination, how she is wielding two hooked swords with impressive skill.

The third figure, a male who looks far too slight and vulnerable to put up any effective fight against these large brutes, is kneeling and seemingly focusing on something. His lips move as if he's praying.

"What the hell!" exclaims Redolfo.

The injured male is still on the ground and is nursing his head. Redolfo again senses the intense feeling of uneasiness that he's being watched.

The female is now left alone to face the two giants. Redolfo gasps as he sees her twist into a triple-spin, her swords whirling like windmill blades from her outstretched arms. With three dexterous steps, she lands a deep cut into the arm of one of the oversized attackers who then, with blood erupting out of a sizable laceration, manages to punch her out of the way. She staggers backwards but with an elegant twist is able to remain on her feet.

In the meantime, her friend maintains his priestly praying-position. "That's it!" Redolfo shouts as he fires up the Checker, filling the air with its coloured vapour. The waving hand rises with a determined hiss. With the Temeria engine whining from the energy demand, he throws the cab into a tight spin, landing a direct hit into the two large aliens, knocking them sideways with a skill that impresses even himself. He rearranges his cap and sees in his wing mirror that his taxi has taken a sizable rear panel dent from the impact. "Oh, Glyrian, I'm sorry but I know you can fix it." he says out loud. He leans out the window and shouts to the three humanoids, "Get the hell inside, now!"

The flame-headed fighter stares narrow-eyed at the yellow Checker with its waving roof hand. She shouts to her praying friend, "Danysus, get up now and help me with Amitaab." Danysus stands up and seems to slap at his own thigh in frustration. He helps her to carry the wounded Amitaab into the cab.

"Hell, I know someone's watching us," Redolfo mutters half to himself and half to Gethsemona. "Quickly!" he shouts to the three fighters, "It looks like your oversized friends are recovering." He exits the cab and holds the rear door open for them. "Gethsemona, goddamn move the hell up!"

Danysus dives into the cab with a bleeding, semiconscious Amitaab and with Gethsemona now squashed up in the back. The warrior-girl sprints round to the passenger seat, her twin swords tucked under her right arm. Redolfo slams the Temeria engine into full throttle to make the cab rise quickly. Within seconds, the two hefty aliens, now seemingly recovered, reach the Checker and grab hold of the front bumper. Redolfo curses - the cab tilts down at the front as the weighty aliens pull against the force of the vehicle's Temeria engine. The air fills with frantic plumes of coloured vapour.

Redolfo feels disoriented and his breathing is rapid - he no longer senses he's being watched. "Goddamn it!" he shouts as he realises he's beginning to panic.

Without uttering a word, the warrior girl opens her door and climbs effortlessly onto the window frame and then onto the hood of the Checker. She takes a low swing with one of her hooked swords whilst skilfully maintaining her balance on the tilting cab. As her weapon swings upwards, Redolfo can see it has taken an alien hand with it that then flies off and lands with a thud and with a smear of blood on the window of a parked transporter.

With only one of the oversized attackers now holding onto the bumper, the cab begins to rise, but still in a tilted position. In the back of the cab, the shaking body of Amitaab slumps onto a horrified and now blood-spattered Gethsemona.

The warrior-girl leaps back from the roof of the cab and athletically slips into the passenger seat, shutting the door behind her. She places her twin swords into an embroidered bag and smiles at a stunned Redolfo. "Okay, move us out!" she orders.

At about thirty feet off the ground, the cab levels out. Two seconds later, Redolfo can hear the splatting sound of a large alien hitting the ground. The remaining, one-handed alien launches his chain-whip up at the rising cab, hitting Gethsemona's window with a loud crack but causing no damage.

~

Concealed within the shadows below, a figure observes the cab as it rises and makes its way out of the precinct.

~

Redolfo regains some of his senses. "Oh no. Gethsemona! Are you okay? Hell, what's your mom going to say?"

"Hey, I'm okay. Yes! That was awesome!"

He looks into his rear-view mirror to see Gethsemona's excited but blood-spattered face emerge from under Amitaab's armpit.

"I'll just tell my Mom how a boy cut himself at school and splashed me - so don't worry. That was so cool!"

Redolfo shakes his head in disbelief. He looks at the warrior-girl in the passenger seat and notices her high cheekbones, quartz-blue eyes and perfect nose.

"I'm Redolfo. Mike Redolfo. Pleased to meet you."

"I'm Caryalla. This is my friend, Danysus and this is..."

"Amitaab, at your service!" The injured male has now opened his eyes, leaned forwards and grabbed Redolfo's right shoulder into a jarring and excited shake. "My gratitude to you, Mike Redolfo!" he says with an unexpectedly loud voice, his long black hair draped over the protesting face of Gethsemona. "We definitely owe you one, humanio."

"So, what the hell was going on out there? Those two were busting you up bad."

"We had them on the run," interrupts a seemingly unimpressed Caryalla. "I would've finished them off if you hadn't appeared."

"Yeah, you can handle yourself alright, girl. Where did you learn to fight like that?" he replies, looking around out of every window of the cab with nervous concern. "Even so, those dudes almost ripped you guys a new one - and if it wasn't for you, lady, they would've trashed my goddamn cab." Pointing at Danysus, Redolfo continues, "So what was this wise guy doing while Amitaab was getting his butt kicked? Looked darn well like he was praying."

"I wasn't praying."

"Then what the hell were you doing?"

"I'm Danysus," he replies, with a voice, softer and deeper than expected for his thin frame. "I was using telepathy to change their mind about figh—"

"And a fat lot of good that did!" retorts Caryalla.

"They were just too stupid to react to a mind storm...well, it usually works."

"More like we're still waiting to see this legendary ability actually do something," Caryalla replies.

"What were those big guys you were fighting?" asks Redolfo, putting an end to the squabble.

"You must be new here," Danysus replies. "They were corattians."

"Those cratt'ns were huge!"

"Yes - just not a lot going on in their dense brains. They're not all bad as a species. Most are law-abiding citizens but some, like these two, get involved in gangs."

"So, what was with this fight? I had a bad feeling about those guys."

Danysus provides the answer, "We were passing by a shop and saw those two running off. They'd threatened the staff and ran off with the takings. There's no good law enforcement around here, so we ran after them. Trouble is, the fight got dirty. It was like they were actually trying to kill us."

This reminds Redolfo of a time when he witnessed a carjacking while working in a notoriously dangerous part of Brooklyn. Two men armed with handguns had stopped a car driven by a man with his daughter in the passenger seat. Within an instant, they'd shot the driver, dead. Redolfo pulled the girl out of her car and into his own cab. He wonders whatever had happened to the poor girl. Did the cops ever find the gunmen? So much crime in Brooklyn went unsolved. The police were usually too overwhelmed with the sheer numbers of murders to be able to investigate every one of them. Hell, they never even ask the right questions. Do they even want to know?

"Beeeeep!" The loud klaxon of an overhead transporter gives a proximity warning. Amitaab opens the window and shouts up, "Hey bozo-man, we just survived an epic fight and you almost kill us!"

Redolfo feels another surge of panic and disorientation.

"Sorry, but that was definitely your fault, Mike. Are you sure you're up to driving this thing?" says Caryalla, her expression surly.

Redolfo punches the on-switch of the CEWS device. It's the first time since he has been driving that he has felt the need to use the high-tech early warning collision system. The head-up windscreen display bursts into life and he stares intently at the array of lights and images. He tightens his grip on the steering wheel.

"Hey, that's not fair!" Gethsemona shouts at Caryalla from the back of the cab whilst she struggles to push a floppy Amitaab into a sitting position. "Get this *thing* off me!" She then glares at Caryalla. "Mike was driving really well until you losers showed up. He's got a skill, actually. The least you can do is to thank him for saving you all. Anyway, I bet that near miss was your fault. I reckon you're putting him off, what with your painted face and fancy outfit."

Caryalla looks at an astonished Redolfo and with a mocking tone says, "Hey, Mike. Looks like you've got a little lady fan."

Gethsemona blushes pink.

"Looks like we owe you one, Mike," says a now recovering Amitaab. "Hey, there's a bar called Opprobrium at the edge of the Great Square. Get yourself a transporter ride there this evening and we'll meet you there. Buying a drink's the least we can do for our cool humanio."

"Yeah. I'd like that. I could do with the company. I've got a lot of catching up to do with this crazy planet of yours, so I got a lotta questions. I was taken here just three days ago, managed to get myself a job, and now I get caught up in some weird street-battle thing you've got going on here."

"Hey, man. No problem! Like, answering questions is my thing!" says Amitaab with an animated voice.

"Don't be ridiculous," says Caryalla. "What do *you* know? You can barely remember what street you live on half the time."

Danysus cuts in. "Mike, thankfully, I'll be there to tell you what you need to know." Redolfo sees Danysus' large reflective eyes peer at him in the rear-view mirror.

Another klaxon. This time, an automated, driverless transporter sets off a proximity alert. Redolfo curses. "I just don't know what's wrong," he says, "I've been in full control of this cab up until this point. I need some time to work this out. You've gotta get to where you're heading and I've gotta get Gethsemona back to her folks."

"Okay, just drop us all off here, Mike." says Danysus. "We all live together on this precinct in the Henwas building. We'll see you this evening."

"Just one thing before you all go," says Redolfo, "did any of you feel we were being watched earlier on the precinct?"

The three look at each other and shrug.

"I don't know why, but I just sensed something...I'm usually right about stuff like that."

Redolfo alights the cab with a bump onto the landing pier and the three get out. Gethsemona takes the opportunity to stick her tongue out at the back of a disembarking Caryalla.

"You think I don't know what you're doing, child."

Redolfo watches the three leave. He takes a deep breath and slumps back in his seat. Within seconds, his anxieties have gone.

"You okay, Mike?" says Gethsemona. "What happened to you? Your driving went to pieces."

"I don't know, Hun. But I feel absolutely fine now. I really don't get it."

The cab rises. He punches the off-switch of the CEWS and the head-up light display on the windscreen disappears.

"What was I thinking using this crazy device anyway?"

"I bet it was her." says Gethsemona, resentfully.

MAN, MYTH AND MAGIC

Schönfelder enters the library to find Heinrich Himmler seemingly lost in his thoughts whilst dipping into a bowl of sweets. Himmler pauses guiltily from his dietary vice, quickly dons his rounded pince-nez spectacles and brushes the sugar off his moustache. "Ah. Guten Tag, Herr Obersturmbannführer. It's been a while."

"Yes, indeed, Herr Reichsführer," Schönfelder replies.

Schönfelder hesitates before asking after the health of Himmler's family. It's no secret that Himmler's busy position and lifestyle has strained his relationship with his wife, Margarete, to breaking point. To make matters worse, Margarete is repeatedly arguing with many high-ranking SS officers' wives who don't take kindly to her controlling, superior personality. For the last five years the young secretary, Hedwig Potthast, has been Himmler's mistress and has just given birth.

Schönfelder continues, "I must congratulate you on the birth of your daughter. You must be very proud."

"Thank you," Himmler replies. "However, right now, I have other matters on my mind. The loss of Paris has angered the Führer. It seems that the commander of our garrison deliberately disobeyed the Führer's explicit orders to hold the city at all costs, even if it meant levelling it to the ground. Instead, he chose to hand over Paris to our enemies without firing a single shot."

Schönfelder pauses and looks down at his nails before replying, "I heard that you ordered the deaths of many hundreds of prisoners in our POW camps. Our army officers are not happy."

Himmler, apparently ignoring the comment, continues, "You will be interested to hear the Führer has now placed me in charge of the Volkssturm."

Schönfelder winces. "So, we're recruiting even more boys now?"

"The Führer believes about six million soldiers can be recruited this way."

The box jawed Obersturmbannführer gives Himmler a satirical smile, "Indeed, Reichsführer, especially as some of them are as young as twelve. I suspect you could fill the ranks of the Volkssturm very quickly."

Himmler maintains a look of composure on his thin face.

Schönfelder studies the black SS flag with the double-lightning bolt that is draped behind Himmler. "I have always admired the insignia you designed for the Schutzstaffel. How exactly did you come by this idea? They are Scandinavian runic symbols, no?"

"They are the ancient symbols of our indigenous Germanic people," Himmler replies, tersely. "It symbolises how we are the descendants of the Teutonic Knights of the Order of Brothers of the German House of Saint Mary in Jerusalem. The SS is a natural and spiritual continuation of this Holy Order. It is a reaffirmation of our German racial superiority."

"Absolutely, Reichsführer. Your knowledge of mysticism and the occult is well known."

Himmler appears momentarily lost in thought. He looks down at his papers. "I know what you are about to say, Obersturmbannführer. I too have heard of these reports about an unarmed man who has managed to penetrate our roadblocks, killing several officers and soldiers."

"Have you heard the report from one young recruit who managed to survive an encounter with the man?" Schönfelder replies.

"Yes, I have. It seems a flight of fancy, but the young soldier really believes this man has some form of supernatural power over others. Do you have any more details of this encounter?"

"Yes, Reichsführer." Schönfelder unclips his leather document case and takes out the typed report. "The man is known as Dominik Kominsky and he's travelling with a woman whose documents have identified her as Marianna Kravová, almost certainly a Jew. A third man, the driver of their vehicle, is presented as Obrecht Hrabe although this is probably a false name. They claim they are making their way towards Budapest. The soldier gives an account of how Kominsky was somehow able to control their minds and thereby escape their interrogations."

"It appears that this man seemed quite prepared to kill the officers and soldiers at the Prague road control, but let the young soldiers live to tell this strange tale," says Himmler scratching at his chin. "This man has a weakness. Obersturmbannführer, I have a new task for the Volkssturm. Make sure he and his two consorts are apprehended. Take a column of armed men and two armoured assault vehicles with you."

"Heil, Hitler!"

"Heil, Hitler!"

THE DIATRIBE

I just don't get it, Redolfo thinks as he peers out of the window of the driverless transporter. I don't know why I lost it back there. I've never felt so uncertain about everything and anything...crazy, but I actually kinda enjoyed it...and by the time those guys left the cab, I felt back to normal again.

He sits back in his seat and continues with his thoughts. Hell, this is one dull way to ride - like being in some sort of high-tech cable car. Next time I'll call a favour and get old Marsky to take me - even if he is a miserable sucker.

"Opprobrium Bar, Central Square." squawks the transporter cabin tannoy with an officious, female voice. "Please remain still for five seconds." A beep from the overhead retinal scanner and Redolfo's payment has been withdrawn directly from his bank account. "Your payment has been successful. Please have a most excellent day."

Maybe Squintt's right - this government loves having all this data on us. What if the President here went crazy? We could all be toast. Hell, who is the president? Is there even a goddamn president?

Redolfo adjusts his cap and exits the transporter. The squat, white-rendered building with its hanging sign looks out of place compared to the modern glass-clad office blocks either side of it. It looks strangely like an old-world British pub he'd once seen on TV. Yet another of the many places he'd never been able to afford to visit. He can hear chatter and laughter emanating from the first-floor window. Adorning the front entrance is a welcoming light display that says, Opprobrium Bar - come upstairs and escape a telling off. Redolfo smiles in amusement as he climbs the stairwell. He swings open the double doors to see a wood-panelled bar heaving with a wide array of aliens, many humanoid and some less so, chatting, drinking and eating small chunks of food from little round bowls.

The background music is slow and disharmonious. The musician is a grey-brown, hunched-up alien with a shrivelled face. He's perched on a large beanbag, looking almost asleep whilst lazily plucking a primitive stringed instrument. Redolfo, feeling very at home, reflects on how the best bars must be the same on any planet.

He looks around at the groups of drinkers. He welcomes the fact that his usual ability to get the measure of the people around him is working as it does on Earth. He could tell, somehow know, if a crowd was content or agitated, or if a fight was about to break out. It was not a truly unique ability, but it was his skill - a skill that had kept him out of danger for years in the harsh world of the Brooklyn inner city. In this bar, however, he senses nothing but fun and enjoyment, with many of the clientele clearly relieved to have escaped work. Several customers are becoming loud and animated as the liquor pervades their heads. Is it even liquor?

"Hi, Mike." Redolfo looks around and sees Amitaab, who's thrust a stone cup with a fizzing drink into his hand. "You can't come to this bar without first trying its signature drink - A right old telling off. Take a sip." Redolfo sniffs it, gingerly.

"Is it safe?"

Amitaab contorts his face into a square-mouthed, wide-eyed expression and, tilting his head, says, "Safe? Of course it isn't safe! You don't come to this bar to be safe."

"So why didn't ya say!" Redolfo takes a big swig and smiles, "Thanks, man. That ain't half bad."

Amitaab performs a twirl to finish in an open-armed theatrical pose, "I knew you'd like it, Mike. Come and meet the owner." He grabs Redolfo's wrist and leads him to the bar.

Amitaab points to a figure behind the bar - human, male, stout, with silver-white hair and matching beard, heavy jaw line and glasses and probably in his seventies. The barman gives Redolfo a big smile and a firm handshake and says with a British accent, "Good evening to you, sir. John Moorshead, owner of Opprobrium. I hope you like my bar."

"Mike Redolfo. Pleased to meet you. I love this bar. You're the first human I've seen for some time. I guess that explains why this joint reminds me of home."

"New York? Downtown Manhattan? You have a soft accent, Mike," inquires the silver-bearded proprietor.

"You got me, chief," Redolfo says with an exaggerated Brooklyn accent. "You thought good but I'm Brooklyn through and through - but my folks always wanted me to talk right." He raises his stone cup to the barman, "Excellent juice by the way."

"Thank you," Moorshead says with a smile, "I assume you were abducted, as most humans here were."

"Yeah. Three days ago. This has been one hell of a story. I still can't get my head around it. They said they thought I was some kind of badass scientist who escaped from this planet some forty years ago, so they abducted me and scanned me. They said I matched a bit, but not quite, so they let me go."

Moorshead smiles at him warmly. "It's been a while since I've spoken to another human. You remind me of a dear friend of mine from long ago." He looks like he wants to say something further, but instead looks around at the growing crowd of impatient customers and says, "It's so busy here at the moment. Are you going to be here when the bar closes?"

"Sure. Hell, it's not as if I've got any other plans."

"Excellent. Looking forward to it."

Amitaab points Redolfo to a table near the centre of the bar, "We're sitting over there."

Caryalla and Danysus are waving to him. As Redolfo approaches the table, he senses something again. A change. What is it? Calmness? Peace? It's as if he's released from the concerns of the people around him. He mulls over how people have always accused him of being a moody son-of-a-bitch, as if he's always seeing the sinister side of them. But folks have sinister thoughts - well maybe not all, but a heck of a lot of them do. They have stresses. Boy, do they have stresses! It's not their fault. Was it his fault for picking up on it? What is it with this place, though? He's never felt so free. Is this the place he's meant to be? Somewhere where he doesn't feel the need to shoulder the burdens of others?

"Hey, Mike, did you manage to drive home safely?" Caryalla taunts him in her surly way.

Redolfo looks at her. Alien. Female. Almost human looking. Stunning, and at the same time, unfathomable. Redolfo reflects how he has never found difficulty in starting relationships. What was hard was making them last, but then again, maybe he'd never wanted them to. His mind wanders further. He's in his apartment in Brooklyn, last year. His girlfriend, Lillian, is waving a letter with red-inked writing. Redolfo's slouched on a threadbare sofa surrounded by empty beer bottles. There's a half-drunk bottle in his hand. The radio's blaring music.

Lillian's looking angry, "Jeez, Mike. I know you know what I'm gonna say, but I'm gonna say it anyway."

"Like I didn't know this was coming," Redolfo slurs.

...more than a feeling...

"This is the third month in a row you ain't paid the rent. I swear to you, if we're evicted, I'll go home to my mom, 'cos the way I see it, even she's less of a drunk than you."

"So, what're you sticking around here for?"

Lillian screams, "Mike, what in Hell's name's gotten into you? It's like you've just shut off from me, and your mom thinks nothing's ever good enough for you. I hate her, Mike. I hate her for making you like this. I swear I know nothing about you, but you know everything about me. I can't bear it. It's like I can't ever keep a secret from you. But worst of it all is you know my problems, but you just don't give a crap! You just wanna drink and do your stinking cab work. Is there nothing else you wanna do with your miserable life? You don't even wanna make love anymore".

Redolfo's reflections are interrupted. "Hey, quit daydreaming, Mike!" says Danysus, "come and join us."

Redolfo sits opposite Caryalla and tries not to stare.

"So, you've met John Moorshead?" she says to him.

"Yeah," says Amitaab, flattening down his long black hair from various angles, "like it's this great huuuman party!"

Redolfo looks around. "I'd appreciate if you guys could tell me a bit more about this whacky planet. Actually, tell me about yourselves first. I had a weird ass feeling we were being watched earlier. You guys in some kind trouble?" He sees Amitaab picking off the label of his drink bottle.

"No, Mike, I don't think so," says Danysus. "We three grew up together. We even live together. We were brought up in the West City Orphanage."

"Just as well I was always there to protect you two," Caryalla jibes, tapping at her glass expectantly, indicating Danysus should buy the next round of drinks. She looks at Redolfo, and, rolling her eyes, sighs, "They were always such needy kids."

~

Caryalla hasn't talked about the orphanage in a long time. She looks at her childhood friends and reminisces. She remembers a much smaller Amitaab and Danysus playing with a toy transporter. An older orphan, berrantine, snatched the object from them and swiped it hard against Danysus' head, smashing the toy into pieces. Amitaab was paralyzed with fear and Danysus looked devastated. Although she'd never spoken to them before, she became enraged at the unfair treatment and landed a firm fist into the berrantine's jaw, sending him crashing to the ground. She smiles nostalgically at the memory. She never likes to show anyone her softer side. To this day, she believes no one has ever seen it.

Danysus interrupts her thoughts as he says to Redolfo, "Of course, we've all had to make our own way in life, but we've always looked out for each other. I work in administration, but these days I usually just work from our apartment with cloud-link technology. Amitaab's officially an events organiser but most of his money comes from entertaining holidaymakers in Catuvell. It's a pretty historic place, so a lot of tourists come by. Amitaab's got a great way with the kids." Danysus laughs. "You can guess what he's like on the job."

Caryalla sees that Redolfo is transfixed by Amitaab making some sort of architectural shape with some drink mats.

"So, what do you do when you're not kicking alien ass, Caryalla?"

Caryalla smiles. "I make stuff - little things. Trinkets. I sell them to shops and market traders."

"You mean like that little shield?" Redolfo points towards the small silver object on her belt with its intricate, interlocking curves, linked by three individually patterned swirls.

"Nah. I'm good, but I couldn't make anything quite that intricate."

"It's beautiful. Where did you get it? I'm sure I've seen something like that back home on Earth."

Caryalla takes a short pause before answering, "It was apparently in my baby-basket when I was found." She looks down at the little shield. It is her only clue about her parents' identity.

"Okay, then. Another question. Where'd you learn to fight like that? Reminds me of this crazy movie I saw a while back. A guy swinging two sticks on a chain beats off a load of dudes. I've seen some movies with sword-fighting, but nothing like your two swords."

"I was taught to use them by the leader of a group I used to be involved with."

"What, you mean a gang?" Redolfo stares at her wide-eyed. "I guess that's a thing here too."

Caryalla begins to feel uncomfortable, "Yeah… I fell in with the wrong crowd. That's all behind me now, though."

"Where I come from, you can't just leave something like that. We have real gang problems back there. It ain't safe at all – not enough cops to deal with it."

"It's the same here, Mike," Caryalla sighs.

Redolfo pauses and looks straight into her eyes. "Sounds to me like this boss guy was your lover. Am I right?"

Caryalla becomes even more ill at ease. "Yes."

"So, he just let you go?"

"No," Caryalla replies as she stands up. "Another drink?"

"Not until you tell me what happened."

Caryalla rolls her eyes and sits back down. "Well, he challenged me to a duel. He said if I lost and survived, I'd have to stay. If I won, I'd be free to go. He was the strongest of us all. No one, including me, thought I'd live. But I won. That's it. Can we talk about something else?"

Redolfo gives her an imploring look, "Hey, you can't stop the story there! How did you beat him?"

"Hey, it's a long story, Mike," she replies, "You've got better things to do."

"Hell, I'm not going anywhere, and I've got all evening."

"C'mon, Caryalla," Amitaab says, twisting on his seat with excitement. "After all these years, you've never told us this story."

"Alright, alright!" Caryalla rolls her eyes again, "The plan was to meet in the Cornovi mountains and hunt each other down in the forest."

~

Caryalla's story is interrupted by raised voices from a crowd at the far end of the bar. At the centre of the commotion, Redolfo spots a small figure, less than three-feet tall, with small legs, long arms, and an extended, almost stretched-out neck at the end of which is an imp-like face. The creature is perched on the edge of a table and is being shouted at by a group of much larger aliens with whom he's been playing some form of card game.

"That's H'droma," chuckles Danysus, "he's a kitchawan. He's one of those annoying types who're just good at everything. I'd stay clear if I were you. You'd have to be at the top of your game to beat him at anything."

"Hell, I learned my lesson with gambling," says Redolfo. "Problem was, I was darn well good at it, especially in games when you had to bluff. It was all too easy to read people."

"Hooooooo yooooooooow!" shouts a beaming Amitaab. "You must've made your fortune with that kinda skill."

"People would always get upset or get mad, so it wasn't worth it. Either way, I figured there're better ways of making a living. I was never cut out to be a gambler." He looks at Caryalla who smiles at him. Hot damn! What is it about this girl? He says to her, "So, don't think I forgot. What happened up on that mountain?"

"My story can keep, Mike." she replies with a smile. "There's a lot you need to know about this place. Danysus, tell him about all the species on Vost. You can start with the ones in the bar now."

Danysus turns his head on his slender, sinewy neck to address Redolfo, who sees his own image, widened and inverted, in his friend's dark, reflective eyes.

"Okay, Mike. The basics. The population of Vost is made up mostly of three species. The berrantines, such as Amitaab..."

Amitaab generates an over-dramatized facial expression to display himself as the example of his species.

"...the garryans, such as those in that group there," he says, pointing towards a group of scaly, humanoid beings leaning against the bar with large reflective eyes like those of Danysus himself and seemingly engaged in conspiratorial chatter, "...and the kyanagis. Berrantines are usually in some kind of service industry or other, but there are some that turn to gambling and criminality. Garryans are of reptilian lineage and are of an ancient order. They're said to be descended from one of the original people of Vost, but their heritage has been largely lost to history. They're also known for their intelligence and cunning."

"As if!" interjects a mocking Caryalla, rolling her eyes.

"I take it that you're a garryan, Danysus," says a chuckling Redolfo.

"Indeed, I am. Garryans usually work as professional people, but often serve in the military and the intelligence services. Some of us have limited telepathic powers," he winks, "but we tend to keep that a secret."

"Well, I've never been convinced you have any telepathic powers," Caryalla says.

"As I've said before, Caryalla, my abilities centre on reducing the will of individuals to fight. It just happened to be at its most effective when you were working late one day and weren't around to see it. That corattian ran away like a big baby."

Caryalla's eyes are rolling again.

"Whaddya mean? You mean controlling folk with your mind?" asks Redolfo.

"Yeah, controlling objects and people's thoughts using the power of the mind. According to the government, telepathy and telekinesis no longer exist on Vost. They reckon they somehow managed to wipe them out with some kind of hi-tech virus. Mind powers have actually been outlawed. It makes you wonder why they need such a law if they're so sure telepathy can't even function here anymore."

"Have you seen anyone else able to use it?"

"Well, no, but everyone's got stories about it."

"Don't believe his nonsense, Mike." says Caryalla, looking irritated by the conversation.

Redolfo sees Amitaab copying the waving hand actions of the diminutive form of H'droma who's clearly getting the better of the two larger aliens at his game. It seems Amitaab is easily distractible.

Danysus continues, undeterred by Caryalla's scorn, "Either the government's got no idea what's really going on or they're hiding something.

"Anyway, the kyanagis, are covered in fur. There's a bunch of them over there." Danysus points to a table with a group of what look more like pets in leather and cloth outfits than actual sentient bar clientele. "They may look cute, but don't let that fool you. They're as smart and as quick-witted as garryans, but most of them become engineers and healers." He scans the room for further examples. "The epeiryans are probably spawned from the most poisonous depths of the planet. If you see tentacles, that's usually them."

He points out an individual standing at the bar, dressed in loose black clothing that seems to Redolfo to be designed to hide some of their tentacled anatomy. He's instantly reminded of the hideous food in the VIAS prison cell.

Danysus continues, "I'm certain they come from the murky recesses of the poisonous sulphur-bogs in the caverns of Smerta. I swear they've always got one tentacle that you don't see, doing something you wish it weren't. They're not particularly friendly and I wouldn't trust them even to clear eohipp crap."

"Another of those, sir?"

Redolfo looks up to see a waitress with a very low cut, black top and a long red skirt with a split. The skirt has been tied over her left leg to reveal most of her right thigh. Her hair's tied up to the side. So, this is John Moorshead's choice of bar staff uniform? Redolfo muses, ordering another round of drinks from her.

"You'll remember the corattians, too," says Danysus, pointing to a group of three hulking aliens that remind the cabbie of 1950s B-movie badass sea-creature aliens. Their heads almost reach the ceiling of the bar.

"I couldn't forget 'em if I wanted to," he replies, remembering their encounter with the two violent corattians on the precinct.

"Tell him about the drug trade." Caryalla says to Danysus.

"Yes, indeed. Most of the interest of the villains and scoundrels of Vost's underworld centres on varins and the sale and distribution of peyate, a highly addictive, recreational drug that's costly and hard to manufacture—"

"But allows the user to briefly live a life that's better than the crap reality on Vost!" cuts in the loud voice of a beaming Amitaab, who has now managed to prise his gaze away from H'droma's antics. Amitaab is waving his hands in the air to animate the point.

"One random question," says Redolfo, "who's the big boss on the planet - the king pin?"

"At the moment, it's General Hostian," says Danysus. "He's taken on a caretaker presidency, as President Cassiana is said to be ill. She's not expected to return to office, so it's likely there'll be elections set for next year."

"Another thing that's been bugging me. It's a crazy question, but why do you think the days and years here are the same as that on my planet? You've got two moons here, and a sun that's a lot bigger than ours."

Amitaab is now on his feet. "Well that's because only planets with that configuration can support the development of carbon-based, organic life!" He waves his hands alternately up and down with the excitement of his own knowledge.

"How on Vost would you know that?" Caryalla says to him, with a shocked look.

"You know me, full of useless information," replies Amitaab.

Redolfo smiles. *I love these guys.*

Renewed shouts come from H'droma's table. "You damned cheat. Give me that money back!"

Redolfo can see that whatever game H'droma was playing, he'd clearly wiped the floor with the other aliens. One of them takes a swipe at H'droma, who jumps clear of the incoming fist. He returns the gesture with a sharp slap across the alien's face, toppling him over. "Takez that for insultingz my motherez and zat for insultingz the game and that for sayingz I cheatedz." H'droma jumps up and down on the alien's chest. "Okayz who'z is nextz in linez to takez on ze great H'droma?"

The floored alien jumps back on his feet and picks up a chair while others in the crowd are holding him back.

"Now this is looking like a familiar scene." Redolfo says as the skirmish extends across the tables. Within seconds, dozens of the bar customers are involved in a punch-up. Redolfo can see H'droma picking off anyone coming near him with leaps and slaps. "He's quite a handy dude for such a little guy," Redolfo says to Danysus. He turns to see Danysus is no longer sitting next to him but is kneeling and reciting some form of incantation with movements of his fingers.

Redolfo watches as Caryalla grabs an angry looking berrantine by the wrist. With an almost bored expression on her face, she sends him spinning to the ground with an effortless movement of her other hand. Amitaab is relaxed with his feet on the table looking determined to finish his drink before getting involved in any fighting.

The scene becomes more chaotic. An alien launches himself at Redolfo, who responds by landing a punch squarely into his attacker's face. He floors a second alien. Just as he is about to take on a third, he feels a sharp blow to the back of his neck. The world turns black.

THE INCURABLE STATE

"It's been a very long time since we did anything like this, Febryalla," Vernikell says to the Baroness, as he pours some more Coritan wine into her glass.

The Baroness puts on her spectacles as she struggles to focus on the small writing of the menu in the candle-lit interior of the Greffen Berrantine Restaurant. "It seems I've reached the age where nothing works as well as it used to," she says placing the menu back onto the white-clothed table. "You choose a dessert for me, Ariael."

The soft background music echoes through the restaurant's decorative arches. Vernikell studies her beautifully constructed face, adorned by her dark braids that she has piled so elegantly in layers high above her head. *At least the Baron has looked after her from a jewellery point of view*, he muses, watching as the perfectly cut gems of her necklace scatter the candlelight into multi-coloured rays. "Well, from where I'm sitting, you look more wonderful than I can ever remember." He notices she has not been fully able to suppress a smile.

"Have you heard from Agent Rimikk?" the Baroness asks him.

"No, not a word from him since he landed in Briganti - but he's not the sort of man who reports in much anyway, and he'd be irritated if he thought I was checking up on him. If he doesn't check in by tomorrow morning, I'll contact him. His tracer was indicating he's making progress through the mountains."

"He does make me laugh, Ariael. He's so serious about everything."

Vernikell smiles at her. "He is, but he's so very capable and reliable. I'd pit him against a dozen of the other agents for ability and efficiency. I was so impressed by him when he entered the service that I made sure I was personally involved with his training."

"I bet you're proud of him – although I can't remember ever seeing him laugh," the Baroness giggles.

"He's just not that kind of guy. Can you imagine him trying to tell a joke?"

They are both giggling now.

The Baroness composes herself. "Ariael, I'm concerned that the days are going by fast and we seem no nearer to answering questions about those mysterious events at the SDA."

"Yes, so am I," replies Vernikell, "The receptionist hasn't remembered anything else about the event. If anything, her memory seems to be fading further, rather than improving, as the psychologists had predicted. The fact that we've not seen any further criminal activity that in any way relates to this incident is unnerving. Whoever they are, they certainly knew what they were doing. I still don't know how they could possibly have breached the SDA defence systems *and* overcome the building's security. I've got a bad feeling about this. VIAS is on high alert."

"We've tried to look further into the terannian element to this story," the Baroness replies, "Because they're such an isolated and secretive civilization, we know next to nothing about them. They're one of the original, ancient peoples of Vost, and as with so many of the indigenous beings, they've had their differences with other native species. One thing we do know is that they were at war with at least two other neighbouring civilisations. They've kept themselves separate from modern society so effectively, we've had almost no contact with them for over a century. As far as we can tell, there's no good reason why any of them would venture out from their reservation, let alone be involved in highly organised criminal activity."

Vernikell looks pensive. "We're starting to think that the receptionist's story may be just a fanciful delusion based partly on her terrifying experience and partly on her pre-existing mental health issues. But there's still this niggling doubt." He looks at the Baroness. "What of the notion that the perpetrator used mind-powers? Were terannians telepaths?"

She nods, "The accounts of the first settlers on the planet were full of narrow-minded ignorance, so it's hard to piece together the truth. The settlers were so superior in technology to the relatively primitive inhabitants that, mind-powers or not, there was simply no contest between them in military terms. One of the first priorities of the invading people was to combine their technological resources to rid any species of their telepathic powers. They were very effective at this. I've never personally been convinced I've seen anyone with true telepathic abilities."

"Me neither," replies Vernikell, "I've never bought into all those street acts. You know, those fakes who say they're telepaths. It's all just clever tricks." He looks warmly at his dining partner. "It's ridiculous how the government always gives out such confused messages about laws on telepathy."

The Baroness starts laughing, "Of course it is! The government can't say on one hand that telepathy doesn't happen on Vost and on the other say it's illegal. The whole law is a mockery."

They laugh together. Vernikell looks into her eyes with an expression of adoration. "Febryalla, what's the Baron up to at the moment? He spends so little time with you."

"The Baron is out on yet another business venture. No doubt he's using his status to influence people to buy into his schemes."

"He's not just trying to influence business people," Vernikell says, suppressing his anger. He knows, full well, how unscrupulously the Baron uses his family heritage to win over young impressionable females with mendacious promises of fame and money. He rankles over how the Baron would never have made it in a true meritocracy. Such privileges can easily make fantasists of people.

The waiter appears.

"May we have a few more minutes, please?" says the Baroness. The waiter bows out. She sighs and looks at Vernikell. "Ariael, there's something I have to tell you."

"Febryalla, why do get the feeling I'm not going to like this?"

"I've told you before about my medical condition."

Vernikell remembers well how when they were children, the young Febryalla had told him she had a condition that affected the tissues of her body. "I thought that just allowed you to amuse us all when we were kids. I remember the party tricks you did with your joints."

"Well, I'm afraid it does a little more than just that. It also affects the major arteries in the body as they rely on collagen for their strength and flexibility. Most people who have my condition eventually die as a result of a sudden rupture of the major artery that exits the heart."

Vernikell turns pale. "Febryalla, why did you never tell me this before? When is this likely to happen?"

"There was never any good reason or good time to tell you, Ariael. The great artery, in this situation, tends to rupture at around my age. There's not often much warning and the death is said to be quite quick, but painful."

Vernikell looks crestfallen. "Is there no treatment for this?"

"No. Frustratingly, the work that Talamat Schneider did on stem cell tissue regeneration was stopped on ethical grounds."

"Schneider? Why would he have been working on medical treatments? He was a military scientist!" Vernikell says, baffled.

"Schneider wanted to find a way of regenerating tissues for soldiers so they could be fixed up after they are wounded and then quickly placed back on the frontline."

"But that's not how battles are fought anymore," Vernikell replies, "Nowadays it's less about conventional warfare and more about dealing with peyate gangs, separatists and religious zealots killing non-believers. Our emphasis is on intelligence and targeted response rather than full-on military might." He shudders. The last actual war on the planet was over forty years ago. Since then, it seems the garryans have learnt to be a bit less superior in their attitude toward the berrantines."

"Exactly. With no current military conflict to worry about, there's been no appetite to fight the ethicists who are fundamentally resistant to stem cell research."

"But what about the medical needs of the people on Vost? Surely stem cell therapy could be used to treat a whole manner of illnesses?"

"Ariael, I wish that were the way of things. But it will never get past the *Central Council of Ethical Medical Practice*."

Vernikell despairs at the way unelected bodies have *de facto* taken over the running of the planet. Way before President Cassiana was in power, the newly founded world government became rapidly overwhelmed with the processes of running a whole planet and quickly learned that it could be effectively run on a day-to-day basis by a collection of unaccountable committees. "It continually fascinates me how the planetary-elected representatives are always subject to the fiercest of scrutiny by the media and by vociferous lobbyists, yet the faceless leaders of the unelected working groups are never held accountable for their part in generating reams of questionable legislation."

"And there you have it, Ariael. The *Central Council of Ethical Medical Practice* decided that our use of stem cells to regenerate body parts was behaving like we were gods and so all the excellent work Schneider achieved was halted."

Vernikell's sadness turns to anger. "Who are these unelected people to decide our fate? Febryalla, this government has become too big. Who are they to make such decisions? It's just not ethical." He looks around the restaurant to ensure no one is listening. "One day, the world government will split as Catuvell secedes from its grip."

"I agree with you, Ariael. I want that too. But that will sadly not be in time for me. In the meantime, we must make the most of the time we do have together. None of us know when it will be our time to go." The Baroness musters a tearful smile.

Vernikell rises from his chair and holds her closely to him.

WHEN WE ARE NOT IN CONTROL

A cool breeze flows across his face. Agent Rimikk realises he does not have the strength to move. His head is rested upon a clump of turf and his back is hard against what feels like a flat piece of stone. His chest wound has been dressed and covered in moist leaves. Is it dusk or dawn? The fading light and the gathering mist answer his question. Soft, rhythmical drumming fills the air, joining the crackling sounds of a nearby fire. Both Vost's moons, Arianrhod and Cerridwen, are visible, making halos in the mist and smoke.

He tries to focus. He can make out the movement of people around the fire. Antlers. Lots of them. Dark, angular eyes, pointed ears and long faces. Cloaks. Soft whisperings. He strains to move his head. His vision improves a little. A stone table. There is something behind it. Rimikk turns his head to see more clearly. The movement sends a searing pain through his neck and chest. He can see it now - a wheel, made completely of stone. Six spokes with a central hub, intricately carved in workmanship far superior to anything he had ever seen in his many travels. Between the spokes are carved depictions of the supergiant sun, twin moons, trees, fruit, leaves, animals and an antlered being. The rim of the wheel is encircled with a form of arcane writing he cannot decipher.

The light fades further and the drumming intensifies. The orange glow from the fire reflects on the stones and the trees around him. He can sense it again. That strange perception of an ancient order. Something almost as old as the planet itself. His sense of pain, so real to him, so much part of his life - and then there's this mysterious power he can feel. Is it some form of weapon? Is this the side effect from exposure to some form of particle wave? Such fancy notions - those beliefs shared by his trekking colleagues were always so ridiculous. But this feeling...? No. This is real. What is it that he feels?

The gentle whispering becomes more audible:

Great Hornéd One! By fire we serve, Great Ancient One! Our
rites observe.
Thee we call by the moons and seas!
By reflecting stream and gnarléd trees.
Thee we invoke near the circle of stone,
By the hoary woods, where the ancients roam.
Come to the ring where our dance is trod,
Enchanted scourge, and wand and rod!
We summon thee Cernunnos!

Another sound joins the air. Rhythmical breathing. Gasping, breathless. This is recognisable now. It is the sound of pleasure. Intense pleasure.

By spectre of moonlights, on tree-dense hill,
When the spirited wood is hushed and still,
We speak to thee with song and prayer,
As the moons bewitch our hallowed lair.
The Great One claims with hunter's stride,
The Vost Goddess, his celestial bride.
In amber flame from the force divide,
By nature's will, her lover inside,
Of bloodroot, aspen and mousebane take,
By woodland sprites and fresh mandrake

We summon thee Cernunnos!

The sounds of pleasure become louder, more forceful. He hears softer, faster gasps from another direction - so very feminine! Rimikk feels a fullness rise within him. His own breathing matches the cadences of the surrounding life, as if he has become part of one giant being, swelling and rising, as fresh as a newborn, yet as ancient as the world itself. He can feel it filling him. He is inside it. Inside the power that drives the breaths and the very life-force of those around him.

His physical strength is now utterly drained from him. With renewed determination, he guides his hand into the high side-pocket of his jacket. He knows he will not stay conscious for long and will soon lose his chance. Why is his body not responding? Why is his arm so heavy? A summoning of will. *Come on, Rimikk!* A final gathering of strength. Yes! His hand is moving. He can feel the switch slider of the small box located in his pocket. It is his final chance. The slider clicks into position. Deep within his high side pocket, the power light on the little device starts to flash green. The night sky is now aglow with climbing embers. The woodland dancers twist and swirl their tasselled cloaks and wave their burning wands.

Come O Lord to the drummer's beat,
Our ancestor, borne of cloven feet!
Come to us who gather below,
Through blue Cerridwen's light bestow.
Come take thy strength from Nature's force,
Thy mighty hooves, we sense the source.
Come set thy power within our minds,
Our thoughts of joy and pleasure it binds.
We chant the spell that splits the rocks,
At Solstice, Sabbat, and Equinox!
We summon thee Cernunnos!

His head clouds. His thoughts fragment and descend into deep unconsciousness. The light on the small box continues to flash within his inside pocket.

A MEMORANDUM OF
UNDERSTANDING

The yellow Checker weaves its way through the Manhattan traffic - from road to road, building to building, person to person, passing unhindered like a bird through the air. A new scene. He can sense the man's confusion - or is it pain? Is it his memory or one of his own? Is it even a memory? That face, though! An emotion so strong, it hits you squarely in the gut. Like a dream, magnifying sorrow, love, rage and passion.

Redolfo wakes with a start. High rise office blocks glide past the window and he realises he's in a transporter. A figure is seated opposite him - slender, lithe, with strong, dark features and a fierce expression. From what he can tell from his growing knowledge of the planet he appears to be berrantine but different to the others he has met. Redolfo has seen more than his fair share of this type in New York. Henchmen. Usually at a high level but not the king pin. This man has killed many times and is capable of killing him now - and with no hesitation. Deadly.

The berrantine leans forwards to address him, "Good evening. I am Sarokis. You'll be wondering why I've taken you away from your friends at the bar."

Redolfo has a surge of realisation. "You were watching us at the precinct, weren't you?"

Sarokis leans back into his seat. "Indeed, I was. That is very...perceptive of you. I was well concealed and yet, for some reason, you sensed I was there. How could you tell?"

Redolfo shrugs.

Sarokis studies him again. "What kind of a being are you? How is it that a human is driving vehicles on Vost? Most of your species wouldn't be capable of such a task."

"My name is Redolfo, Mike Redolfo. What do you want from me?"

"You are clearly capable, Mr. Redolfo. We have indeed been watching you. However, you are behaving in a manner that gets you noticed. That needs to change."

"What's it to you? Who the hell are you? Let me go now, buddy and we can just forget this ever happened."

"I have been commanded by my leader to find people with certain skills."

"Skills? What goddamn skills?"

"In short, Mr. Redolfo, we need a driver - a driver who can get us out of trouble when we need them to."

"Hell, no way. This ain't the first time I've been asked to be a driver for lousy, rotten gangsters. I've never gotten into this stuff. Look, I've just arrived on this goddamn planet and I've gotta earn an honest living so I can get back to the dump I come from. Yeah, it's a primitive dump compared to here, but it's *my* goddamn primitive dump, and I don't need the likes of you making it harder for me." He leans forward towards Sarokis and looks him straight in the eye. "Sounds like the moment I get involved with you, I'll either be killed or end up doing time in some backend, alien ass penitentiary. So, count me out." He leans back in his seat, folding his arms.

The transporter weaves past the spires of a cluster of towering skyscrapers, winding through the aerial traffic with automated and clinical precision.

"Well, maybe that's where we can help you. You're working as a taxi driver on low wages, right? You are, no doubt, working on a government rehabilitation scheme. It would take you years to build up enough varins to afford the space-transporter fare to your home planet, and it's highly unlikely you'll ever make it back at all. Certainly not without the help of a...benefactor. As far as I'm aware, no human taken to Vost has ever managed to return - and that's where we may be able to assist you. You help us, and we can sort out your fare home." He gives Redolfo a humourless smile. "Not that I understand how a *human* can drive in 3D space the way you can."

"Okay, Sarokis, I'm listening. But I'm gonna need to know who exactly I'm working for. Who's your boss?"

"None of this is your concern. If it all goes to plan, you'll never need to meet my employer. As I'm sure you'll understand, he would rather remain in the shadows."

"Yep. Sounds like the way kingpins work where I come from. So, you want a driver, but what's the deal? Is it a heist? Are you a hitman? I ain't gonna have anything to do with any goddamn killing, I'll tell you that!"

"Look Mr. Redolfo, you know how these things work. If it goes well, no one will get hurt. We're after a particular object that's kept in a high security building. We need to infiltrate the building, retrieve the goods and get away safely. As far as you're concerned, you're just the driver."

"And if I refuse?"

Sarokis stares at Redolfo, his turquoise eyes as cold as ice.

"Okay, I know. Seems I don't actually have a choice anyhows," Redolfo concedes with a sad look.

"I'm glad we've reached an understanding, Mr. Redolfo. By the way, I was rather impressed by the abilities of the girl you were with."

"You damn well keep her out of this. I've agreed to your terms, Sarokis. Leave her be." Redolfo is now glaring at him.

Sarokis gives him a smile that sends a shudder through the cabbie. "I can see the picture here, Mr. Redolfo. I'm not a dishonourable man, however. I'll make this all as painless as possible for you. But if you step out of line, even for a moment, I will kill you and anyone important to you in an instant."

Redolfo has no doubt Sarokis could and would carry out such a threat. In his time as a cabbie, he'd come across some real unsavoury characters. Once he'd even been coerced to act as a courier for a package he knew to be either firearms or drugs, He'd known the boss would have been prepared to kill him if he'd declined. Even so, despite all the scrapes and threats Brooklyn life threw at him, he'd never before encountered such an unsettling character. What's with all the secrecy about his boss? He can tell Sarokis is withholding something important.

"Where shall I return you to, Mr. Redolfo?" says Sarokis, still smiling with his mouth but not his eyes. "Shall I drop you back at *Lucky Day Cabs* or perhaps you'd prefer your apartment in Rautival Precinct?"

Redolfo knows he now cannot escape Sarokis' grasp. Defeated, he says, "Take me back to my apartment."

Sarokis drops his smile, "I will ask you one final time, Mr. Redolfo. I advise you against evading my questions. How is it that you possess this driving skill?"

"The truth is I've always wondered that myself. I've always been a good driver. Somehow, I knew I could cope here - I've no idea why. I seem to be able to anticipate other drivers - some weird ass awareness. Call it instinct."

Sarokis pauses for a moment then breaks away, seemingly lost within his own thoughts. Appearing to a degree satisfied with this explanation, he replies, "We'll have a job for you tomorrow evening, so keep your language decoder switched on so I can communicate with you. I suggest you run a daytime shift, so you'll be ready for me after work."

NO QUARTER

Sepp feels his nausea intensify as Schichau drives over another large pothole on the crumbling Czechoslovakian road. He undoes another collar button on his cadet's uniform and gulps in more air.

"It's a three-point-eight-litre engine with eighty-nine horsepower, capable of fifty miles per hour." Schichau is clearly enjoying the opportunity to show off his hardware to the young Cadet. Undeterred by the fact his new recruit is leaning out of the window and groaning the happy driver continues, "Sepp, the SdKfz 222 reconnaissance vehicle is the pride of the Panzer divisions. It has a two-centimetre KwK thirty L/55 autocannon and Kurt, up in the turret, is manning the seven-point nine-millimetre MG Thirteen machine gun." Schichau thumps the ceiling of the vehicle and the gunner returns the salutation with a thump of his own.

"Stop, I need to puke!" shouts Sepp who opens the door of the slowing vehicle and jumps out to vomit on the side of the road. As he empties his stomach, he hears laughter, all at his expense, emanating from the personnel carrier behind him as well as from the riders of the motorbike column who have now all stopped to admire the spectacle. *My God, a carrier full of child soldiers*, Sepp says to himself as he briefly pauses from his retching. *Some of them look about ten!* One final stomach contraction and he manages to steady himself before returning to the vehicle.

"Feeling better?" Schichau laughs. "We'll be making contact with our target any moment - In fact, this looks like them now."

They see a Fiat 521 with wine and black colouring, just as the kommandant described to them, approaching from about half a mile away. "Okay, get ready." Schichau bangs on the ceiling twice to alert Kurt up in the turret. "I can't see why this assignment is considered so dangerous that it needs this level of military hardware." he says to the young cadet. "They've got us all out here for just *three* people!"

The Fiat pulls over to the side of the road, as if to let the column of military vehicles pass. Within moments, Kurt has the turret cannon trained on the vehicle, and about twelve of the child soldiers have spilled out of the personnel carrier, their guns readied in a scene that reminds Sepp of some of his earliest memories in his school playground.

Schichau shouts his command through his megaphone. "Dominik Kominsky - you and your party must step out of your vehicle!" They emerge from the car with their hands up.

The man looks downcast while the woman begins to shake and cry.

"There should be three of you. Where's the other?" Schichau shouts into his megaphone.

The man replies, "He is no longer with us. We are Czechoslovakian citizens with a business interest in Budapest. I have documents—"

"We know exactly who you are and you are now under arrest. You're wanted for questioning."

A DAY TO REMEMBER

Lucky Day Cabs, Catuvell City, Planet Vost.

"My poor Honey, you look like you need some relaxation," Cam-Ell says, stroking Redolfo's hair. "You don't wanna talk about it, Hun? I understand. Look, I can tell you've gotten yourself into some kinda trouble. It shows on your face. Mike, whatever's happening here – I know you're a smart guy - these things have a habit of working themselves out, you know."

Redolfo looks up at her. He studies her caring expression and sees something in her that somehow reminds him of himself.

"Here, Mike. You can have Baranak's drink. It's got extra camflora to relax you," Diselda says passing the hot beverage to him. "I wish it worked on that crotchety old boot," she says pointing to a concerned-looking Baranak Squintt, who now resembles a type of stranded sea-mammal, with his flabby jaw moving as if to speak, but not actually saying anything.

"For pity's sake, leave him alone, girls," Squintt finally manages to produce audible speech. "I'm sure the man will be perfectly fine."

He turns towards his employee, "Look, Redolfo, you've got the blues. They all get it. It's not just you. Marskell, Apperbay, Cerramain, they all went through the same thing. Look - I understand - you're light-years from home - but you're doing great. I even got a compliment from that little girl's mother - you know - the one whose daughter you took to school. Seems they're all taken in by you. They want you back tomorrow. Glyrian says the dent in your cab will be sorted in just another few minutes, so you're good to go."

Redolfo nods and finishes his drink. He stands up and walks outside. As he enters the repair yard, he feels somehow warmed by the presence of the mute engineer who, in his silence, always seems to convey an aura of positivity. Despite this, Redolfo can't help but feel the mechanic is hiding a deep-rooted sadness.

Diselda appears with a piece of tissue paper and wipes off the lipstick she left on his cheek. "There's a job for you, Mike. A guy needs to get to the hospital before 10 am. Urgent medical appointment. I'd rather you took the job than give it to that grump, Marsky."

Redolfo shuffles reluctantly to the cab and settles inside it. The Checker rises, the coloured vapours and welcoming hand-waves contrasting starkly with the low mood of the driver. The Lucky Day Cabs building disappears from his rear view as the Checker passes behind the Walshram's Canisters factory building sign. Redolfo notices rust has started to erode parts of its eternally happy face.

A few minutes later, he spots his passenger and settles the cab onto the landing pier. "Where're you going', bud? I was told Catuvell Main Hospital, right?"

"Yes please, driver." The gaunt alien croaks as he steps into the cab, filling the interior with a sour, ketotic smell. His appearance reminds him a little of Danysus, but he's even more emaciated and ill-looking than his friend.

"So, they gonna fix you up in there?"

"Yeah. I've been losing weight and the docs don't know why. They need to do some tests on me."

"Gotcha. On our way. No problem. Let's get you to them doctors." Redolfo looks into his rear-view mirror and sees his passenger's eyes are closed. "Hell, you sleep it off, man. Just another fifteen minutes and we're there."

The journey's smooth and before long, they've arrived at the hospital. Redolfo nestles the cab in the drop-off bay. "Hey, fella. Wake up, we're here. That'll be a nice round five varins for you, my friend."

The alien doesn't move.

"What the..." Redolfo gets out the cab to open the back door. He gives him a shake, "Wake up, buddy."

He closes the door and returns to the driver's seat. "Diselda, you there?"

"Yes, Hun. What's up?"

"That pickup, the one for the hospital..."

"Yeah, what about him?"

"He's dead, in the back of my goddamn cab!"

"Oh, my!" Redolfo can hear her whispering the story to Cam-Ell who then starts to giggle. He hears the voice of Cam-Ell in the background shout in a laughing voice, "Hey, Baranak, listen up. Mike's got himself a stiff in his cab!"

"So, what do I do with him?" asks an exasperated Redolfo into his comms.

"I don't really know, Mike. You should try the cops. They'll know what to do." Diselda replies.

Redolfo can hear Squintt laughing in the background, "Now that's funny. We needed a bit of cheering up."

The cabbie, singularly unamused, fires up the Checker and makes his way towards the Catuvell North Precinct 21 Law Enforcement Station. He activates the hyperspace probe radio to the sound of *Fly Robin Fly*.

His thoughts wander. In his mind, he sees, as clearly as if it is happening in front of his very eyes, his mother is crying. His father is holding her tightly to his chest.

"Alfonso, what has he done to us? Four days and no one knows anything. Not a thing."

Alfonso replies, "We've always done our best. He was so much happier when he was a bambino - but I guess they grow up their own way. Michael's always had such anger in his soul. I guess he sees things in a different way to most. You know how he has that habit of being right about people. Remember Marilyn, when he said she was stealing from you? He was just six years old but somehow he knew."

Alfonso looks stressed. "Todd called in earlier, while you were asleep. He kept saying how he had no choice but to fire Michael. You know, he looked devastated. Even so, despite all the years I worked for his company, I just can't bring myself to forgive him."

Redolfo shakes his head as if to shrug away his thoughts. He switches off the radio and alights in the law enforcement station transporter park. He locks the car doors and enters the building. Dishevelled, shouting aliens held in hi-tech hand-restraints are being guided to cells by burly Catuvell police. The waiting area is bustling with dozens of stressed-looking aliens of various species - some are cursing, some are screaming, and others are sitting, seemingly resigned in downcast silence.

Redolfo sees that there's a numbered ticketing system. He takes a ticket. It reads 3017. The number presented on the screen reads 2985. "Oh, boy!" he shouts in exasperation as he realises this is not going to be a quick process at all. He walks to the cage-protected interview booth, where a uniformed female officer is talking to an angry garryan female through a speaker system. Redolfo pushes in front of the garryan and addresses the officer, "Hey, look, sorry to interrupt, but I've got this guy who's died in my cab and—"

"I'm sorry sir," the officer barks at him through the speaker, "but you can see we're busy here - you just have to wait in line."

"Hell, but I gotta get back to work!"

The officer starts shouting, "I won't tell you again - now sit down and wait in line as everyone else has to!"

Beaten, Redolfo takes a seat. 2987. "Hell, I don't have time for this." He taps his language decoder. "Diselda, I'm in the cop shop. It's going to take some time."

"Shame, Mike. I had a pickup for you. I'm going to have to give it away to Apperbay." She changes her voice to a whisper, "You know how I look after you first."

"I do, Diselda. You know I appreciate it."

Redolfo sees a vending machine offering a selection of drinks, all unrecognisable and unappetising. He chooses one. Within a few moments, the machine has prepared something that looks nothing like its picture and smells repugnant. He certainly isn't going to try the stale offerings from the food snacks machine that if anything, looks broken anyway. Unsurprisingly, none of the others in the waiting area seem interested in the machine either.

Ninety minutes pass and Redolfo's shuffling irritably in his seat. He thinks about his dead passenger in the back of the cab. Is anyone gonna see and report it? Is he gonna be arrested on suspicion of murder? Will the body even stay upright?

The crowds have swelled to the point where there are now not nearly enough seats in the waiting area for everyone. There are angry scenes where people are pushing against each other. They have the same shortage of cops on this goddamn planet as we do in Brooklyn, he says to himself.

Another hour passes. Many of the waiting aliens have bruises or cuts. Some talk about how they have been robbed. Tales of assault are plentiful.

A distressed berrantine female is ushered in by a pair of humourless, overweight-looking officers. "Get your filthy hands off me!"

"Alright, lady, what's your husband supposed to have done to you this week?" says one as he sighs, clearly uninterested in any answer.

"I'm telling you officers, he may act real nice to you, but he ain't who you think he is! What part of he beats me up don't you understand?"

"Yeah, we get you - it's the same story every time."

"So why don't you do something about it for a change?"

Redolfo feels a heavy sense of unease. He notices several small bluish bruises on the left side of her neck. He rises to his feet and shouts, "Hey guys, haven't you seen them bruises? They don't get there by themselves, you know!"

The berrantine female looks at him quizzically, then shakes her head. "Look, Hun, I appreciate you saying this, but you really don't want to get involved. I can fight my own battles."

The officers sneer before escorting the female to an interview room. Redolfo resignedly sits back down in his seat.

The place is now heaving. More restrained felons are marched through the crowd. 3015. "Okay, now we're getting somewhere." Redolfo's now having to push people away from him to prevent himself being crushed. 3017. "Hell, that's me!" he calls out and presses through the angry sea of people. "Call this law and order?" he shouts.

The officer looks at him from behind the protected booth screen and talks into a speaker system. She looks berrantine. She is clearly not someone who is going to take any nonsense from anyone in the great throng of people. "What can I do for you, sir?"

"Look, I'm a cab driver and I had this passenger this morning who's gone and died in the back of my cab."

"Where is the deceased now?"

"He's still in my goddamn cab, outside in the vehicle park. He's been there for hours, as I've had to wait so long to see you."

"Are you sure he's dead, sir?"

"What! Of course, he's goddamned dead!"

"Well, you're going to have to get a doctor to sign off a death certificate."

"Well, where shall I drop him? I need to get back to work, pronto. I've gotta earn a living, you know."

"I'm sorry sir, but you'll have to take him to the hospital where they can certify the person is actually dead. They can handle it from there."

"Son-of-a-bitch! I was at the hospital when he died! Ma'am, you've got to take him!" Redolfo pleads.

"Next!"

The screen display now shows 3018. A towering corattian forces Redolfo out the way to get to the booth. Redolfo returns to the cab. His dead passenger has remained upright. He opens all four doors to let out the putrid aroma.

"Hi, Diselda. Cops say I have to get this stiff certified dead at the hospital, so I'm taking him back there."

"Oh, Mike. That's terrible. I'm sorry – I really thought the cops could help you."

"That's okay. I know you meant well. I just need to actually start work and earn a living."

The language decoder indicates another incoming call. "Mr. Redolfo. I trust the day is going well for you," announces the steady voice of Sarokis. "I want you to pick me up from Brenna 27 at 6 pm today. Don't be late. You have your assignment."

"Son of a bitch!" Redolfo mutters under his breath. "This day's going from bad to worse."

He picks up the pace back towards the Catuvell City Hospital. The supergiant sun is casting reflective rays off the buildings so Redolfo lowers the cab's newly fitted sun-visor. He notices a vehicle travelling in his direction from about three blocks away, far enough away that it appears as a small dot in the distance. He senses something very special about this vehicle. What is it? It's pink. Yes, it's pink. It's getting closer. What the hell! It's a Cadillac!

"Hot damn. A Fleetwood 60 Special!" he shouts out loud to himself. A closer look. The driver's window's down. Redolfo slows the Checker as the two cars approach each other. The figure in the Cadillac looks at him and waves. Redolfo waves back. The driver's wearing a flamboyant, white suit. He has lowered his shades to give Redolfo a momentary wink. The cars pass each other. "Yes, yes, yes!" Redolfo turns around and joyfully punches the dead passenger's shoulder, shouting excitedly, "It's the King! The goddamn King, man! Hot damn, I knew he'd make it. I goddamn knew it!"

~

A spirited Redolfo joins the transporter parking queue for the Emergency Admissions Unit of the hospital. A sign indicates a thirty-minute wait before he can park. The cost for parking is one varin per hour. His elated state is brought to an abrupt end. "Oh, come on!" Redolfo hits the steering wheel in frustration.

After ten minutes of seemingly fruitless waiting, he takes the cab out of the parking line and joins the line of ambulance transporters at the Emergency Admissions Unit. Within seconds, two members of the hospital security staff appear and begin waving him away.

One of them bellows at him, "This is the ambulance bay! If you don't leave now, you'll be prosecuted."

"Look. I have a guy in the back of the cab. He's pretty sick. You've gotta take him now."

A paramedic appears. Judging by the fur on his face, Redolfo reckons he must be a kyanagi, like the ones Danysus had pointed out. The furry practitioner opens the back door of the cab and examines the passenger. "I'm afraid your passenger is dead. He seems to have died some time ago, judging by the fact that he has established rigor mortis."

"Okay, so you're going to take him now? I've been with this dude all day and haven't yet earned a dime. The smell of the guy's getting to me."

"I'm sorry, sir but this is a hospital."

"So, you damn well take him then!"

"No, we can't, sir. The hospital is a place for the living, not the dead. I suggest you take him to the mortuary round the back of the hospital. The pathologist there might be able to certify his death."

Without answering, Redolfo fires up the Checker. The supergiant sun has already touched the horizon. It's 4.10 pm. He alights from the cab just outside the rear entrance to the hospital. Two hospital security staff - garryans - spot him and rush towards him.

"Look," Redolfo roars at them, "just back off! I've got a guy who's died in my cab and you two are going to help me get him to the mortuary, NOW!"

The security staff look at each other and shrug. One turns to him. "Sorry fella, the mortuary has just shut for the day."

"Hell, no! I'm running out of time." The Checker rises again.

~

"Officer Dowola, I take it we still have not made any contact with Agent Rimikk." Vernikell's obvious anxiety is making the rest of the staff of the VIAS central intelligence control room nervous.

Officer Dowola feels uncharacteristically concerned. Her deep amber eyes are enhanced by the shimmering sunlight reflected through the window. She has been at her tracking station all day with no results. She is normally able to take such matters in her stride, having been trained by the planet's sharpest experts in operational procedures. Although she never particularly agreed with their glowing assessments of her, her outstanding performances in all her aptitude parameters ensured that she was given the position of Chief of Field Operations ahead of many more experienced agents.

Despite her skills, it was Agent Rimikk who has made her job much easier than it could have been. She has never known a field agent so capable and organised. She remembers that one occasion where Rimikk led his agents to infiltrate a building thought to be a secret peyate refining factory. Crackers working for the major illegal drug outfits were becoming skilled at hacking the VIAS central computer systems. On this occasion, Officer Dowola's communications station had gone offline as the crackers had managed to embed a spoiler worm-virus into the VIAS computer network. Ten crucial minutes elapsed before the IT Security team could restore its systems. For those ten terrifying minutes, Officer Dowola was unable to guide Rimikk through the building or warn him of the likely locations of hostiles.

When the system finally came back online, she discovered that three VIAS agents had been killed in an engagement with armed factory workers. To her relief, Rimikk later reported in unharmed. She was surprised at just how relieved she had been. Not only had he survived, he had also single-handedly apprehended a number of gang members who had been recklessly firing their weapons whilst high on peyate.

She looks up at her boss, "Deputy Chief Vernikell, I'm really worried about him. He's usually so reliable. I think it was a mistake to let him go alone."

Vernikell looks awkward. "In retrospect, I do think that was my error. I really didn't want our first encounter with the terannians in generations to appear like a threat. Given they have no embassy or even an official ambassador, there's no means of contacting them except in an unsolicited way." He looks down at his desk. "I hope I won't have to live the rest of my life regretting this decision. Maybe I should have sent a party of field agents."

"He may be the most difficult person to get to know," Officer Dowola replies, trying to sound reassuring, "but he's also the most capable."

Vernikell musters a small smile. "I know how much you like him, Leiath."

Officer Dowola blushes, "Not that he's ever noticed me - or anyone else for that matter. But I know he's not really as cold and detached as he makes himself out to be."

Vernikell spends no further time on reminiscences. "In any case, the way forward is now clear. Prepare a party of ten field agents to retrieve him from the Briganti mountains. Use the RC-300 reconnaissance craft and scan each area with spectral high-definition imaging."

"Yes, sir, but doesn't that contravene—"

Vernikell's console starts to flash. He pushes the button. "Vernikell here."

"Hello, Deputy Chief, Internal Security 115 3rd allocation here," the voice in the console says. "It looks like we have a small incident at the security gates."

"What incident? Separatist activists? Can't you handle it? I'm a busy man."

"There's a human here. We've arrested him. There is a dead passenger in the back of his vehicle."

"So, send him to the local Law Enforcement Station. Why are you involving me?"

"Well, he appears to be asking for you by name. He's quite insistent."

"Don't tell me he's that human we mistakenly retrieved from Earth - Michael Redolfo, as I remember?"

"Well, that's his name, sir. What shall I do with him?"

Vernikell sighs, "Take him to the interview room. Impound his vehicle and have forensics take a look at the body. I'm on my way. Whatever's going on here needs to be resolved quickly."

~

Vernikell enters the interview room, a security statement document in his hand. He takes a seat and looks at Redolfo immobilised in restraints at the opposite side of the desk. "This seems to be rather a familiar scene, Mr. Redolfo. I must inform you this interview is being monitored, so everything you say or do will be kept on official files permanently for the sake of any future legal proceedings. Now, can you kindly tell me what you're doing turning up to VIAS Catuvell HQ with a dead body in your vehicle?"

Redolfo takes a deep breath. "Look, I don't know what it is with this goddamn planet, but this ill-looking dude books a ride this morning for a hospital appointment. He then pegs out on me in the back of my goddamn cab. I wait for hours at the cop shop and they tell me they don't want to know, so I take him to the hospital, and they tell me the hospital is for the living only and not for the dead. So, I take him to the mortuary and find that it's damn well shut. So now you tell me what I'm supposed to do with a goddamn stiff in the back of my cab?"

Vernikell stands up, walks out of the interview room and closes the door behind him. Standing outside the interview room is a perplexed Officer Dowola.

"What's happened, Chief?"

Vernikell bursts into a fit of laughter.

"You okay, Chief?"

He cannot speak for laughing and starts to hammer the wall repeatedly with his fist. He regains his control and ceases his assault on the wall. "Sorry, Leiath, but I've just heard the most ridiculous story."

"Sir!"

"It's bad what stress can do to you. It's not just Rimikk. I heard some bad news about someone who means a lot to me. I'll be alright."

He returns to the interview room. His tone once again serious, he says, "It would seem, Mr. Redolfo, that luck has not been on your side since you left Earth. I'm aware that it was due to our mistake that you find yourself on a planet that is alien to you, and I do feel we have some responsibility for your wellbeing. Forensics has taken the dead body from your vehicle for analysis. Normally, the protocol would be to confine you pending the results of the autopsy. However, under the circumstances, I'm willing to let you go. I'm acutely aware you need to earn a living here and need to get back to work. However, if forensics has even a whiff of suspicion about this incident, you'll be tried under the full force of the law."

Redolfo breathes a huge sigh of relief. "Thank you, Chief."

"One more thing, Mr. Redolfo..."

"What's that?"

"Don't ever come here like this again."

~

The Brenna building turns out to be a disused industrial facility. Redolfo thinks how ideal a place Sarokis has chosen for a meeting, being fairly free of the state's prying eyes. He reaches Zone 27. His mind wanders momentarily. That stag again! Redolfo quickly shakes it off.

He sees Sarokis waiting for him next to a dark transporter. He's wearing a black combat outfit with pouches and belts that carry a selection of knives and hand weapons. Redolfo parks up the cab and opens the window. Sarokis takes in a sniff and twists his mouth in disgust.

"Does your vehicle normally smell like this?" Sarokis looks particularly unamused.

"It's a long story."

"I've arranged a transporter for you that has no traceable licence codes. You're going to be its driver this evening. Come and meet the others."

Redolfo approaches the transporter and opens the driver's door. In the back seats sit three males, each with green-glowing eyes and armed with sophisticated-looking weaponry, greet him with icy-green stares. He can sense an emptiness within them, as if they have been drained of something - something that was previously strong within them. Not physical strength, that is for sure, but more about who they are.

Sarokis sits in the front passenger seat and laughs, "Meet Boca, Dozor and Vestbo. They'll be keeping us company during this mission."

"Do I get a weapon?"

Sarokis ignores the question. "Take us here," he commands, indicating the address on a small electronic screen.

Redolfo plugs the address into his navigation system. "That's another disused factory."

"Indeed, it is."

RECOGNISING THE SKILLS

The windowless interrogation room is as dark and dank as the dungeons of Špilberk Castle themselves. The baroque castle, now flying a swastika flag, is situated at the peak of the hilltop in Brno, rising directly over the historical centre of the town. The castle, with its infamous, vaulted, thirteenth-century dungeons, is a constant reminder to the residents of the town of the Nazi oppression of the Czechoslovakian population.

On the better side of the bars of the ancient cell sits a man in a smart military uniform. His arms are folded. There are splashes of blood on the stone floor around where the prisoner is bound to a wooden chair. The swelling of the prisoner's beaten face is showing through the fabric of the blindfold.

The man addresses the prisoner with a thin, but clear, German accent, "Welcome to Špilberk Castle, Herr Kominsky."

Kominsky does not answer.

"My name is Heinrich Luitpold Himmler. I am Reichsführer of the Schutzstaffel. You may have heard of me."

The blindfolded man gives Himmler a small nod.

"Tell me, Herr Kominsky, how can it be that we have been tracing your records in Prague and can find absolutely no mention of you before 1941?"

There is no reply. Himmler continues, "Herr Kominsky, for your information, I have given the staff orders to gouge out your eyes if you refuse to provide us with convincing answers to our questions. Do you understand this?"

Kominsky nods again.

After a further period of silence, Himmler continues, "I believe your eyes are an important aspect of your abilities. I want you to understand that I am not an unreasonable man and am genuinely interested in the skills you possess that were witnessed by a member of the Volkssturm."

Himmler stands and begins pacing. "It was because of the predictions of Karl Ernst Krafft that Der Führer's life was spared five years ago. Krafft accurately predicted the assassination attempt at the Munich beer hall and the Führer was advised to leave."

Kominsky does not respond.

After a brief pause, Himmler continues, "You may have heard of the prophecies of the French apothecary, Michel de Nostredame. You may know him by his Latinised name, Nostradamus."

"I have no idea what you're talking about," says Kominsky, his voice muffled by the traumatic swelling of his jaw.

"Nostradamus made several predictions of the second coming of the Messiah:

Through the coming of the Great Legislator.
He will raise the humble. He will vex the rebels.
His like will not appear on this Earth.
By his disciples invited to be immortal.
A man from the East will come out of his seat
He will cause his blood to rise again in the ancient urn.
He will transpire the sky, the waters and the snow.
And everyone will be struck with his rod."

"What do you want from me?" Kominsky replies, "Is this your Nazi torture technique - quoting quatrains from some madman's work?"

"No Herr Kominsky. As I said, Krafft was able to predict important events. He predicted the Third Reich would do well as long as it completed its work by 1943. The success of Operation Barbarossa, the disastrous outcome of Stalingrad and the bombing by the British of the propaganda headquarters in Berlin were all predicted by Krafft."

"So, what do you want from me?" says Kominsky, spitting out more blood.

"Perhaps we have got off on the wrong foot. I want to be able to release you. I wish to be your friend. But until you provide me with the answers I require, I cannot trust you."

"What do you want to know?"

"Tell me more about your abilities."

"I have no abilities except that I am a good accountant. If you need any help—"

"No, Herr Kominsky." Himmler interrupts. "I have no use for an accountant here."

Kominsky says nothing.

"Let me tell you a story. It is a story about the Austrian Occultist, Karl Wiligut, who declared he was the spiritual descendant of a long line of mystic teachers dating back thousands of years. He claimed that his spiritual inheritance gave him genetic memories of his ancestors."

Kominsky shuffles in his seat. Himmler sees he has the prisoner's attention.

"Are you familiar with the story of the death of Christ by St John, Herr Kominsky?"

"I don't have a religion, Reichsführer."

"Pity. You should have one. Wiligut was a worshiper of the old Germanic god, Krist. This name even to a non-believer such as you would sound familiar, no?"

Kominsky does not answer.

Himmler returns to his seat and continues, "St. John describes the actions of a soldier who used a lance on the crucified body of Jesus in order to hasten his death.

According to the apocryphal Gospel of Nicodemus, the soldier was a Roman centurion by the name of Longinus.

"In the story of Parsifal, the great knight recovered the lance from the wizard Klingsor. The lance has since been passed for a thousand years between Prague, Vienna and Nuremberg. Four years ago, Der Führer liberated the Holy Lance from the Hofmuseum in Vienna and had it placed in Nuremberg, where it now stands as a symbol of the power of the true Aryan race.

"You see, Herr Kominsky, Jesus was not a Jew at all, but a true Aryan descendant. Wiligut attests that within the lance is a great force that, if unlocked, will endow its possessor with unstoppable powers."

"I still don't see what this all has to do with me," Kominsky replies, spitting out another deposit of blood.

"Because, Herr Kominsky, I believe that it is *you* who Nostradamus has described in the second coming and it is *you* who possesses the power to unlock the forces of the Holy Lance. It is the destiny of the Aryan race to conquer the world and purge it of inferior people. Come with me to Nuremberg tomorrow morning. I have prepared a transport plane. You will be the key to unlock limitless power for the Aryan race - for the race that I know you, yourself descend from." Himmler stands and paces. He raises his voice, "It is time to claim your ancestral heritage. We are the Parsifal of our time. We can finish what he set out to achieve."

Kominsky does not reply.

"I know this may seem ridiculous to you. You may even think me insane. However, if you want to save yourself and your friend, Fräulein Kravová, then I would think seriously about complying with my request. I shall return in the morning to give you a chance to consider your answer. Think of this as a great opportunity and not a threat. Heil Hitler!"

Himmler exits the room leaving Kominsky alone in his cell.

GOOD INFORMATION ONCE YOU KNOW IT

"Sir, I have received an urgent communication from VIAS *Central Intelligence.*"

Vernikell looks up from his terminal to see Officer Dowola is looking anxious. "What's happened?"

"A government installation is under attack."

"Which installation?"

"It's in an area known as *Zone 773.*"

"Okay, but what is it?"

"Sir, it's a classified military science unit, hidden in a disused industrial facility on Rhodor. I don't know yet what it's actually used for."

He spins his chair round, "Get me Professor Capell Parchi, now!"

Officer Dowola opens a communication channel.

"Hello, Capell, Ariael Vernikell here. I'm sorry to disturb your evening but I need information, quickly."

"What is it, Ariael?" Parchi's old and tremulous voice comes over the comms.

"Do you know about a secret military installation known as *Zone 773?*"

"Yes, I do. I set it up. Why?"

"Because it's under attack. I'm receiving reports of weapon-fire exchanges between the unit's security staff and an unknown number of heavily armed attackers. The security team have already sustained casualties."

"By the gods, that's not good, not good at all," Professor Parchi responds with a foreboding voice.

"What are the attackers after?"

"Ariael, you must act quickly. That unit must not, under any circumstances, fall into enemy hands. Clearly, there's been a leak. The item they're almost certainly after is the Field Modulator Shell. In short, the Modulator Shell is a device that can shut down weapons and communications systems within about an eight-hundred-mile radius."

Vernikell bangs the desk, "Why wasn't I ever informed about such an important device?"

"I'm sorry, Ariael. It was on a need-to-know basis and at that time it was exploratory research only. We assumed that any credible threat to Vost would be likely to come from advanced species from other planets. Just the other day, we spoke about the technologically advanced and warlike bhadvians from planet Besys with their philosophy of imperial expansionism. It's likely that, in the event of an invasion, any aggressors would use destructive beam technology. The Modulator Shell is designed to render their weaponry useless. It would also block any communication devices that use particle-wave technology."

"You mean like just about every bit of military hardware technology that *we* use in our domestic, industrial and military lives?"

The tremor in Parchi's ageing voice becomes even more pronounced. "Yes, we know, and that's why we're currently working on a protective string vector lock-out that would keep our own technology functioning - but that's still in the developmental stage. I'm sorry, Ariael. I know this is not what you want to hear, but this constitutes an existential threat to our way of life."

"I'll ask again. Why was I never briefed over something this important?" Vernikell says, his voice raised.

"It started as an experimental project only, but to everyone's surprise, it became a functioning system before we had a chance to think about its security implications. Yes, you should have been briefed." Parchi replies with a small voice.

Vernikell turns to Officer Dowola, "Scramble an assault transporter with ten armed security staff and five EP7 attack drones. Back it up with a second unit. I'll take command."

"But sir," Officer Dowola replies, "you're really too high a ranking officer to be—"

"I'm sorry, Leiath, but this is too important a situation to delegate, and right now, I don't have Rimikk here to lead the team. There's just no time to find another suitable field commander."

Officer Dowola initiates the Code 2 warning alert system. The klaxon pierces the air throughout the VIAS security building. Her authoritative voice resonates over the security staff comms systems, "Code 2, Code 2. This is not a drill. I repeat, this is not a drill. Security teams one, three and seven, take your positions in transporter bay seven, immediately."

Parchi continues, "I can tell you more once you're on your way."

Vernikell makes his way to the emergency access lift. He presents his right eye to the iris scanner for access priority.

"Agent Vernikell. Identity confirmed," announces the soft feminine voice of the security system. Within seconds, the lift appears. He descends seven floors into the transporter bay and enters the weaponry room. A severe looking garryan quartermaster hands him two large carriers, one with a combat suit and the other with a selection of weapons. Now fully equipped, he makes his way to the transporter bay where he greets the excited maintenance crew.

The senior engineer addresses him, "She's good to go, Chief. Look after her - she's had some good upgrades." He helps Vernikell don his combat gear. "Remember sir, your suit is made of carbon-layered rubber that's impenetrable to a few, but not many maser strikes." He hands Vernikell the visor.

Vernikell glances at the PF2-36 assault transporter. He has always loved its sleek design.

The engineer gives him a quick résumé. "Okay, Chief, she's equipped with three AP-19C maser cannons at the front and three at the rear. She's armoured with a ring-cage that's mostly impervious to hand weaponry but not to particle artillery fire or repeated rounds of heavy maser cannon. There's a state-of-the-art spatial navigation system linked to the weapons delivery system. She's fantastically fast and has excellent manoeuvrability. She won't disappoint you, sir."

Vernikell gives him a final nod then steps up athletically into the cabin. He greets the dark-skinned Captain Banattar, the driver for the mission. "Good evening, Captain. I'm glad to see I have the best driver in the fleet today."

"Happy to be of service, Chief," Banattar replies, saluting him with an air of confident efficiency.

With the security team assembled and secured into their harnesses, Banattar initiates the transporter's starting sequences. With some degree of apprehension, Vernikell settles into his seat and applies his own harness. As capable a soldier as he is, he was never a great traveller. He taps his console, "Parchi, are you there? Tell me what I need to know."

The transporter bay doors open, allowing a burst of intense sunrays into the driver's cockpit. The auto-reactive windscreen filter activates. Banattar applies his driving lenses.

"I'm here, Ariael," Parchi responds over the comms. As I said, *Zone 773* was set up to develop defence systems for potential threats from other planets. It's set within the depths of a disused industrial unit known as the Rhodor Building."

Banattar's voice can be heard over the speaker system, "All crew, brace for initiation." A powerful growl emanates from the engines and the crew are pressed back into their seats as they accelerate through the transporter bay. Banattar studies the complex array of avatars and images superimposed on his CEWS display. He makes a sharp turn before swerving with precision through columns of traffic. "Eight minutes to destination, sir."

Vernikell feels wave after wave of nausea.

Parchi continues, "We used this installation for the project because it was entirely abandoned after it was contaminated with a leak of Polonium 209. Although the leak was small, the safety inspectors closed the whole unit down."

"Yes, I remember this being in the news. Angry investors are still fighting this through the courts." Vernikell replies, taking gulps of water from his canister. "Tell me more about the device they're looking for."

"It's a surprisingly small device, about three feet across, but quite heavy as it uses a shielded micro-nuclear power supply. It can be carried by two people if they are reasonably strong. Look at your console now for an image of it."

The whole crew can see the full schematic images of the Modulator Shell on their console screens. The device appears as a rectangular metallic box with an array of controls and operational mini screens.

The clear voice of Officer Dowola fills the cabin, "The science unit is defended by a maser defence-ring and a team of around ten security officers. I believe the defence systems will be vulnerable to this attack. The Rhodor building itself is a series of cubical grids in a lattice design. We understand the architect wanted it to resemble the molecular structure of graphite."

Images of the Rhodor building flash up on the crew's screens.

"*Zone 773* is set centrally within this lattice structure. As you can see, there are no straight transporter routes, but access can be made by a series of offset routes within the structure - these are highlighted on the image on your screens now."

"Approaching the unit now, sir," announces Banattar.

Vernikel addresses the crew, "Prepare your weapons. The attackers will be armed and highly dangerous. The backup team will arrive in about ten minutes."

SURELY, *SOMEONE* KNOWS?

The *Opprobrium Bar* is now closed for the night. Danysus watches as Moorshead cleans drinking vessels with his automated brushing machine. The lounge is silent save for the echoing of clinking glass and stone as each vessel is placed on a drying rack.

"I just don't get it," the barman says to Danysus and his friends, who are peering sheepishly into their cups. "How can it be that no one saw what happened to Mike? How could he have just disappeared like this?"

"I told you yesterday," replies Caryalla, "after I showed a few garryans *exactly* who they were messing with, I checked to see if he was okay, but he was nowhere to be seen."

Danysus bristles at her jibes. He always feels hurt by her belittling of his own species. He calls to the silver-haired barman, "John, please take a break and join us."

"It was a great punch-up though, don't you think?" says Amitaab, excitedly drumming the table with the palms of his hands.

Moorshead throws his drying cloth over his shoulder and strolls over to the table. He sits down. "That insufferable H'droma and his gambling caused me a big headache yesterday. I need to have a word with him. It's that sort of thing that gets bars like this closed down.

"Yeah, it was crazy," replies Amitaab, pulling a wide-mouthed face of concern.

"I do hope Mike's okay," Moorshead says, tapping at the table as if deep in thought. "I'm worried that he may be in some sort of danger. I like that man. It was a shame I couldn't spend more time speaking to him, but I was just too busy serving the customers. He reminded me of somebody I used to know when I was on Earth."

"You know, we have been coming to your bar since we were barely old enough to drink," says Danysus, "but I have never actually asked you what you used to do on your planet. Did you own a bar there too?"

Moorshead begins to laugh, "No, I didn't. Believe it or not, I was a university lecturer."

Amitaab jumps up so quickly, his chair slides away several feet from under him. "Our mother, Brighid!" he exclaims, holding his left hand to his heart. "I swear there's so much more to you than you let on, what with your mysterious human thing going on. What did you teach? I bet it was bar studies—"

"Sorry, Amitaab, I'd rather not talk about it right now. Can we get back to talking about what happened to Mike."

"Yes," replies Danysus, "he helped us when we were in trouble—"

"And stopped me from murdering two corattians," adds Caryalla.

"That would not have gone down at all well," says Danysus. "We owe it to him to look for him."

"The problem here," Moorshead replies, "is that Catuvell is a big place and as far as I'm aware, none of you can drive. Do any of you know even where to start?"

KNOWN UNKNOWNS

Banattar aligns the transporter with the entranceway to the industrial unit. "We're entering the Rhodor building, Chief," he says with a smile. He applies his 3D navigational assist visor.

Once inside the unit, Vernikell feels his stomach churn as the vehicle swerves in several directions in quick succession. *Banattar sure can drive*, he thinks, trying desperately not to dwell on how queasy he is feeling or of the dangers he is likely to face.

"Approaching *Zone 773*," the transporter captain announces.

"On visual, now," Vernikell says as he studies the scene. The area is largely obscured by smoke from weapon damage. He addresses the crew, "Apply your thermal imaging visors. We're going to land here."

Banattar sets the transporter down with precision. The exit doors rise upward with a hiss and the agents file out. Sounds of weapons fire boom out from within the smoky interior of the zone.

Vernikell activates his visor and can now see that the security defence shield of the science unit has been destroyed. *I pray we're in time*, he thinks, relieved at least to be finally standing on firm ground. The container door of the craft slides open and five attack drones exit and whirr around them. Their lobular appearance and buzzing noise always remind him of giant insects. They have proven invaluable in previous missions. He watches as his mechanical allies disappear into the heart of the installation.

He orders three team members to scale the fifty-foot support pillars so that they can view the unit from above, another three to approach towards the exposed left face of the unit and the other four to accompany him to attack from the front. He orders Banattar to stay put at the helm. Vernikell beckons his own team of four to stay hidden behind a heavy generator.

"You're surrounded by a fully armed VIAS assault team. Stand down now, or we'll shoot to kill," Vernikell's voice echoes, seemingly from every direction, as he makes his announcement through a voice-projection system. Weapons fire continues unheeded.

It's clear to Vernikell that *Zone 773* has been hastily put together. An array of bulky machinery has been interspersed with delicate instrumentation. He calculates that the machinery would provide an effective shield to both attackers and defenders and that the conflict will therefore likely be reduced to a series of skirmishes in the network of walkways. Time is not on their side. He has no choice but to split the team to ensure the whole walkway network is covered. He orders the agents to advance to their positions and to keep communications open.

Vernikell hears the distinctive sound of a pulse of weapons fire hitting metal. It sounds close. With his fragmenter rifle ready, he jogs down the walkway. As he nears the end of the path, he flinches as he comes across the bloody remains of a security guard.

"Left flank team in position," Vernikell hears over his comms. He confirms the statement by the presence of three points of light on his console map.

"Assault team in Transporter Two, what's your position?"

"There'll be about a fifteen-minute delay, sir. There was a fault in the anchor release system in the transporter bay, but we've got it just about fixed."

"I need you here now, agent!" Vernikell replies tersely, "This is not an easy operation."

"On it, sir."

Vernikell proceeds to the path to his left.

"Sky team in position, sir."

"Good, Sky team. Make sure you have our backs from up there."

He hears a scream coming from the ceiling and sees a VIAS agent fall to the ground.

"Sky team, where did that shot come from?" Vernikell shouts into his comms.

The responding agent's voice is shrill with panic, "We think it came from an area about thirty feet from your position. We're exposed here, sir!"

"Acknowledged. Stay hidden as best you can, but I will need you to keep me covered at my command.

A roar of fragmenter fire erupts around the unit.

"Left flank team here, sir. We're under heavy fire!" Vernikell checks the console and sends one of his team of four to assist them. He is now about sixty feet from the maser defence grid that protects the device. He sends one of his remaining team of three to triangulate towards it.

"Another two agents down!" Vernikell hears the terrified voices of the left flank team. His console shows that two points of light have disappeared. "We can't hold this position for long, sir!" an agent screams into his comms.

The Deputy Chief sees a frazzled chunk of metal on the ground directly in front of him. With horror, he realises it is the smoking remains of an EP7 attack drone. *Who are these people who can take down three highly trained combat agents and destroy state of the art drones so quickly?* He shrugs off a developing sense of failure. Two sky agents, two left-flank and two with him are still operational. *I can't let my agents' fear influence my own judgment.*

A much-needed message comes in on his comms, "Assault team in Transporter Two, here, sir. We're on our way."

He hears a sound. *Footsteps?* He waves back his team of two agents and turns a corner, his own silent steps like those of a hunter ready to pounce. Years of training, charging every instinctual fibre of survival within him. Cerebral, but predatory - narrowing the mind to one primary purpose - to survive and kill - all senses heightened to screaming point. He types a message into his console to Sky team, 'Cover me now.'

A burst of fragmenter fire rains down vaporising the area in front of him. He seizes his opportunity. With his weapon raised, he swings round to the far end of a machine block and sees a figure with green-glowing eyes aiming a fragmenter straight at him. Like an arrow loosed from a hunter's bow, Vernikell launches himself forward and swings his fragmenter rifle butt, knocking his opponent's weapon upwards. The green-eyed attacker fires his weapon in haste, and with a glancing hit, splinters Vernikell's visor into a shower of small fragments, exposing the agent's head completely. Vernikell lands a heavy punch squarely to the chest. He aims his own weapon. Before he is able to fire, his opponent, unfazed by the punishing blow, leaps up at him and the two are locked together, each wrestling in a desperate bid to aim their weapons. With a knee-strike to the groin, Vernikell manages to end the impasse. An elbow upper cut to the jaw sends his attacker hurtling backwards. Vernikell takes his aim and fires a series of fragmenter rounds into the assailant's chest, killing him.

"Leiath," Vernikell whispers breathlessly into the communication system, "can you see him? What can you tell me about him?"

"I have it, Chief, I can see him on screen," responds Officer Dowola, "His name is Dozor. He is one of the three captured criminals chosen to test Zanusso's mind-control device. It confirms we *are* dealing with the same group who infiltrated the SDA. It also confirms that they were able to use the mind-control weapon on all three of the test subjects while it was functional."

Now helmetless, Vernikell replies, "That means we've two highly dangerous criminals under full enemy control to deal with, as well as anyone else who's decided to join their little party." He feels reenergised. In spite of the losses, defeating Dozor has made him a little more confident about this mission.

By contrast, Officer Dowola's voice sounds concerned, "Yes, Chief, you'll still have to face Vestbo and Boca."

"Rimikk, how I wish you were here with me now", Vernikell says to himself, knowing that was exactly what his second-in-command was thinking too. He announces to the assault team, "Confirmed, one enemy down. Sky team, I'll need your help again soon, so stand by."

"Acknowledged."

Vernikell is now twenty feet from the maser grid. He hears the sounds of splitting metal, as weapons fire blasts holes in both machinery and heavy structural building girders. The air is filled with toxic smoke from vaporised metal. A frantic voice screams over the comms, "Another officer down! I'm on my own at left flank. Help me!"

Vernikell checks his console. There is only one point of light remaining at the left flank. *What should I do? Prioritise the maser grid and risk the life of my comrade, or help the officer, and jeopardise the mission? Choices where people's lives are involved are always so difficult.* He makes up his mind and orders the three agents on his team to join the left flank. He will approach the maser grid alone.

He steps cautiously towards the end junction of the walkway where it joins another path in a T-formation. *I know I'm close.* He swings round to see the maser defence grid has been destroyed. Body parts of station security staff are littered across his path.

To the right of the defence grid, Vernikell can see the Modulator Shell being carried off by two figures. One has green-glowing eyes. Another figure, tall and fierce looking, produces a portable maser weapon and fires a volley at him. The blue-traced streams of energy smack heavily into the abdominal section of his protective suit sending Vernikell into a tumble. He cries out in pain but manages to recover and returns to his feet. He inspects his suit. He has survived the hit but his charred protective gear is now useless.

"Sir, Transporter Team Two here. We have arrived."

Vernikell tries his best to keep a level-headed command, "Good. I have the target in my sights. Send five agents to assist the left flank team. The rest join me at the maser defence grid. There are two assailants here carrying the target device."

Vernikell swings round a machine block and releases a short, indiscriminate volley of fragmenter fire. He darts back behind the block. The loud slew of responding fire indicates the two targets have not progressed very far. He sends another message through his voice amplifier, "Stand down, now! You have nowhere to hide. Our reinforcements are here. Stand down now or we'll open fire."

Vernikell hears the reassuring sounds of running footsteps from his reinforcement team approaching.

"About time too!" he says to them. "Sky team, cover me now."

Another volley of fire issues from above, and the reinforced team appears from behind the machine block. Vernikell sees that the two device-carriers have disappeared into an adjacent walkway. "With me," Vernikell calls to his agents. He knows there's only one path out and feels confident now that he has them cornered. His console indicates that the hastily built *Zone*

773 actually has no platform after another 50 feet where there is nothing but a sheer drop to the units hundreds of feet below. *With unprotected precipices like this, the station designers weren't too concerned about health and safety issues here.*

"Left flank here. An assailant is down."

"I see him, sir," the excited voice of Officer Dowola can be heard in his comms. "It's Vestbo - confirmed it's Vestbo."

"Thank you, Leiath. I'm going after the two remaining assailants. They have the device. I'm in pursuit. There's no path left for them, so they've nowhere to go."

"That's good news, sir," says Officer Dowola, "Professor Parchi will be relieved."

The team of agents approach the end of the walkway. Six weapons are now pointed at the two intruders who are standing at the edge of the precipice, carrying the heavy Modulator Shell between them. Vernikell realises there are no operational attack drones.

"Stand down, now. There's nowhere to go." Vernikell says, almost sympathetically.

The assault team watches in astonishment as their targets, still holding onto the device, deliberately step off the edge. Vernikell runs forward and peers over the precipice. The attackers' plan becomes clear as he realises they have disappeared inside a black transporter that's tilted on its side with an open door-panel. The panel slides shut, the transporter straightens out and drops to the lower levels of the Industrial Unit.

Vernikell hits his comms button, "Banattar, pick us up, now. We have a transporter to capture or destroy. Transporter Team Two, return to your vehicle and follow my command. Leiath, call for a perimeter watch of the whole Industrial Unit, in case they manage to exit before we can reach them."

"Okay, sir," Officer Dowola responds.

The deep hum of the approaching assault vehicle shakes the platform. It lands near the unit's edge. The door rises with a hiss, and Vernikell, together with two other agents, jump inside. They quickly settle to their consoles and bring their maser cannons online.

Vernikell shouts into his comms, "Captain Banattar, they dropped two floors and exited directly under this platform."

"On it, sir. They can't outrun us," Banattar replies, as he swings the assault transporter into a vertical dive.

Vernikell sees the complex array of industrial cells on his screen and remembers Officer Dowola's description of the graphite-like structure. "Captain, do you have an idea where they are?"

"Yes, sir. There appears to be a series of units ahead of us that were under construction when the zone was shut down. The jungle of abandoned construction machinery will make it too dangerous for a high-speed escape and that will limit where they can go. We'll catch up with them very soon."

Vernikell feels the force of the craft performing a series of swerves and turns in quick succession. The console viewer shows the assault transporter whizzing past numerous metal support pillars at high speed, filling Vernikell with faith in his skilled driver.

"I've a visual on the transporter, sir," Banattar announces.

"Shoot and destroy," Vernikell orders, and a rapid cannonade of maser energy issues from the PF2-36 turrets with a loud spray of blue tracer pulses, igniting the smoky atmosphere with bursting strands of ionized sparks.

The little black transporter responds with a barrel roll followed by an unexpected halt, a reverse and a spin. The cannonade has missed its target. Banattar, taken by surprise, overshoots and turns into an available space between a series of coolant towers. "This driver is smart, sir," says Banattar, "he's lured us into a tight area." He frantically manoeuvres the PF2-36 around a series of partially built structures, cranes and towers.

"How is this possible, Captain?" Vernikell asks, nauseated from the tight turning of the craft. "Do they have spatial imaging technology on board?"

"Unlikely in such a small mass-production transporter, sir. I don't know how they managed that without knowing what was up ahead." Banattar's voice has lost its former confidence.

"Transporter Two, I want you to approach from above, to block a possible exit route," Vernikell orders. "Most of the fully constructed units are at the base of the lattice, so they probably won't exit that way."

~

Camouflaged perfectly within the wrought-metallic sheets and girder fragments of the disused recycling foundry - a black transporter, with three passengers and a heavy device within its miniature hold, is now fully offline and sits virtually undetectable. The roar of a passing assault transporter marks the thirty-second count before the little transporter is reactivated. It travels a silent and tortuous route out of the eastern side of the industrial unit. Within moments, it blends, unnoticed, with the endless columns of Catuvell's aerial city traffic.

A PAUSE FOR THOUGHT

Kominsky is alone within the confines of his damp cell. His face is throbbing and covered in knuckle-shaped swellings. His consciousness pervades the cell's darkness. The sturdy bars will never yield to the forces of his mind. He will not even try. He needs to conserve his strength.

He settles down into as comfortable a position as he can muster on his hard seat. He concentrates. His mind fills, then overflows. Like soft waves lapping at the shore at rising tide, his consciousness edges outwards beyond the confines of his cell, passing through the forlorn thoughts of dozens of prisoners held within the castle dungeons. Further still and his thoughts ascend like vapours, filling invisible voids, passing from soul to soul, searching, spreading, sensing. That familiar warmth. Unmistakable. It can be no one else. Gently, softly, he calls her name. Her mind is opening. She is so frightened. There is no other way.

"Marianna, Marianna. Don't be afraid." He feels her scream. "Marianna, it's me, Dominik." He can sense her mind closing. "Please, Marianna, don't shut me out. Open yourself to me."

"Dominik? What's going on?"

"Oh, Marianna, I didn't know if you were still alive." He feels his heart overflow with relief.

"I don't understand. You're here with me - and I can even see you although I know you're not really here. So, this is your power…you're all bruised! Oh, Dominik, they've tortured you!"

He can sense her rising distress. "My beautiful Marianna, I'm so sorry it has come to this. I'm so sorry I never told you the truth about myself."

"Please don't say this. To me, you are Dominik Kominsky, the love of my life and the father of my child - that will always be the case, and nothing will ever change that. I can feel you so close to me."

Now immersed within her feelings of overwhelming sadness, he struggles to keep his mind strong, "They have taken you to a dangerous place. Please tell me where you are." He senses her mind close a little.

"I am at the Terezín concentration camp."

"What's happening? How are they treating you? Have they hurt you?"

"They haven't, Dominik. I'm okay. I'm fine."

Kominsky feels her resist him. "Tell me, Marianna. I know that's not true." Despite her resistance, he can visualise her through her thoughts. Her clothes are the same ones she wore when he last set eyes on her but they are now dark with dirt. He feels her swelling tummy is now uncomfortable in her dress. There are two heartbeats, one faster than the other. He sees prisoners cramped together in the grounds. "Oh, Marianna, they're making you sleep on the floor! He sees how she rarely has a blanket to cover her. He sees the pans of offensive hot liquid she passes round to the frail and elderly prisoners and is repulsed when he realises it's their food. "You clean lice from children's' hair!"

"It can't be avoided here."

He feels her open her mind to him. She has so little strength to fight. He sees doctors and nurses having to reuse dressings and bandages. Death comes to claim so many prisoners. He sees their bodies taken away by other prisoners and buried in deep pits. He senses Marianna is trying to think of nicer things. Her mind tries to focus on prisoners entertaining the other inmates by playing musical instruments.

"People are saying it is very different here to the Auschwitz-Birkenau camps, and that while we remain here, we have a chance to live," her mind's voice says to him.

Kominsky can see how the trains arrive at the camp each week. He feels Marianna's fear as the German soldiers round up thousands of prisoners. He can sense her terror that she may be the next to be chosen for deportation to Auschwitz for extermination.

"Dominik, I know that our baby and I cannot be saved now."

He senses a surge of loss and hopelessness. He replies in the most positive manner he can muster, "Marianna, this will not be how this story ends."

"Even with your powers, you will not be able to break me out of here."

He feels movement within Marianna's tummy.

"Dominik, you gave me all of your love and have made me so happy. I cannot help but feel grateful for my great fortune. My last few years spent with you have been my happiest. You've shown me more beauty than most people see in a full lifetime. How I wish we could have had a chance to spend more time together and bring our child up in a world of peace."

"Marianna, I have to break away from you now and conserve my energy. I do have a plan to break you out of there." He feels tears of hopelessness roll down her cheeks. "I will be able to appear to you once a day, my love. If I have not been able to before the day is out, you will know that I have died."

As he leaves her mind, he can feel her break down into uncontrollable sobs.

THE TROUBLE WITH HAYSTACKS

A whirring of engines echoes through the dense canopy of trees. A momentary pause, a scan sweep and the transporter has moved on another two hundred feet. The alarm call of a predatory avian warns the nearby woodland fauna of the unwelcome intrusion of dark technology. Unperturbed, the transporter continues its search. A halt. A slight rotation. The machine leaves the area and the forest resumes its chorus of chattering and warbling from its abundant wildlife.

Within the transporter, a blip appears on the scanner. More systems come online. A positive location is confirmed. The metallic hulk looms over the tree-tops and hovers towards a small clearing. Three bonfires are identified on the ground below, each sending up plumes of smoke. The under-belly doors slide open. Two uniformed agents emerge from the hull and descend by a wire and cradle. They find their target - a figure, uniformed and lying in the snow, wrapped in thick layers of warm blankets made from tree-bark fibre.

"We have a positive ID," one agent speaks into his comms, "We've found Agent Rimikk. I repeat, we've found Agent Rimikk."

NOT BAD, BUT NOT WHAT YOU'RE USED TO

The yellow Checker moves across the Catuvell skyline, its driver moodily punching the steering wheel. The music from the hyperspace probe radio plays in the background.

His thoughts are on the liquor store. Wasn't it liquor that messed up his life in the first place? He punches the wheel again as *Afternoon Delight* plays on the radio.

There's just no way out of this hell. Choice. What goddamn choice? He hasn't been able to make a choice since the day he was born. It's as if his whole life has been cynically mapped out for him from the start.

His life in the big metropolis was crazy, but he'd always managed to avoid getting involved with organised criminals. Now here he is, assisting badass murderers in a high-level criminal racket. What just happened in that crazy factory? People died out there. People are dying in New York every day. Yeah, that's a dangerous place too. Actually, Brooklyn's probably a whole lot more dangerous than this place - but actually to be involved in it... hell, he hadn't signed up for this. His life is now fully screwed up and there is nothing he can do about it.

"How's our favourite driver?" says the soft voice of Cam-Ell over the communications console.

"Hi Cam-Ell. I was just thinking about home."

"Awww, I'm sorry, Mike. Of course, you're homesick. You're always welcome to stay at ours if ever you want to, you know that."

He gives her a sad smile. "Gee, thanks Cam-Ell. I'll be alright. I just need to be able to get my head around this place."

"You'll be fine, Mike - You're strong. Come on now, Hun, I've got a job for you. It's in Ula 1. I've sent you the coordinates. He's some kind of priest and needs a ride to Precinct 8 to a place called the *World Church of the Holy Order*. Are you anywhere close?"

"Okay, Cam-Ell, not too far. I'm on it." Redolfo hears Cam-Ell send a kiss over the console before it goes silent.

Precinct 8. The World Church of the Holy Order. What the hell is that? I bet it's like one of them phony religious outfits we see at home.

The ministerial customer's waiting. He's morbidly obese and has glistening blue-green skin. His eyes and mouthparts are largely obscured by folds of what looks like moist blubber. Redolfo lands his cab and leans out of the window. "Wait a minute, reverend. Before you get in, I've gotta do something." Redolfo nips out of the Checker and runs towards a pile of discarded wrappers and paper bags at the opposite side of the street. His customer stares at him quizzically. Redolfo returns and begins making strategic tears in the paper refuse before spreading the pieces carefully over the back seat. "There you go, reverend. You can sit down now." *Hell, I've met some slimeballs in my time, but never a real one like this. Minister or not, he's not gonna mess up my goddamn cab!*

~

The day's gone reasonably smoothly and Redolfo seems at last to be making some sort of a living.

The console activates. "Hi, Handsome." It's the voice of Diselda. "We've had a call from Dermot 6. A party of three."

"Okay, Honey, I'm on it."

"Mike, just so you know, it's a red-light district."

The Checker reaches the pickup point and settles onto the landing pier of the Dermot building. Three female aliens await him. One of them has translucent silver hair and fluttering lashes, as long as a hand's breadth. Another looks as if she would be quite at home in the oceans with what appears to be scales and gills. *Yet another reminder of that goddamn cell food.* The third looks more like the whores he'd seen on some of the shady street corners of Brooklyn, with their pouting red lips. He looks her up and down. Well, she does have the body to die for. Something's not quite right though. He looks at her legs again. Perfectly shaped - but there is definitely something wrong. Where has he seen this before? Yes, it was a poster in the doctor's surgery waiting room that used to scare him when he was a child, showing the human body without its skin - just muscles and blood vessels.

"Whatya looking at, gorgeous? Never seen a transparent girl before? Wanna try me out?" she says, her lip muscles contracting in a translucent pout.

Redolfo breaks away from his stare and shakes his head. "Sorry, ladies. Where do you wanna get to?"

The transparent girl licks her lips and leans towards him through the window, "We're off to a party in Weylin 3. Come and join us..." She whispers breathily into his ear, "Party's for suuuuuper-rich businessmen...they know how to have a good time. They'll let a sweet-looker like you in for sure." The other two passengers blow kisses at him in a provocative pose and then proceed to kiss each other. They open the cab doors. The transparent girl sits in the front passenger seat, and the other two at the back. "Got any sounds, babe?" Redolfo hits the hyperspace probe radio. The smooth sound of *Float On* fills the cabin.

Oh no, Redolfo says to himself, *this song's just going to provoke them*. The Checker rises and Redolfo charges the forward propulsion of the Temeria engine.

He feels a searching tentacle around his waist.

"Hey, Gorgeous - ever made it with an epeiryan chick?" The tentacle winds lower. Redolfo pushes it away. He becomes aware of a wet tongue stimulating his right ear and a hand is now undoing the buttons of his shirt. Redolfo cranes his head to be able to see where he's driving.

"Okay ladies, you can stop all that now."

~

"Hi Sweetie," says the voice of Cam-Ell on the console, "we're going home now, but I wanted to tell you not to forget to pick up that little girl from her school."

"No worries, Cam-Ell, I won't forget her. She was kind of moody at the start, but she seems to accept me more now."

"Well, she's made a special request for you to get there early, so you can park near the school gates. Her mom says she won't stop talking about how good a driver you are and how great your yellow cab is. Seems she's taken quite a shine to you, Mike - but then again, that's understandable," Cam-Ell giggles.

"On my way. I'm almost there already. Cam-Ell, I've actually managed to run a full day's work today. A weird day, but at least I didn't have me a stiff in my cab. Think I'm gonna celebrate in the *Opprob'm Bar* later. I made a few friends there but never got their contact details, so I'm hoping they'll be there tonight."

"Yeah, Mike, we know that bar. Run by a human guy. Pretty popular. Maybe we could all meet up there one evening."

"Sounds good to me."

Redolfo nestles the Checker at a parking platform near the school gates. The school bell rings and moments later children of various species swarm out of the building. This time, Gethsemona is at the front of the crowd. She spots the Checker and runs towards it at full tilt. Within seconds, she's opened the back door and has jumped into the cab.

"Mike, Mike, I've had the worst day today."

She seems distressed.

Gethsemona sobs, "Ginebra says my hairdo looks weird. In fact, she says everything about me is weird - and it's not just her saying it. Do you think I'm weird?"

"No, Gethsemona, I don't think that at all. Anyhows, why do you care what that girl thinks? In my world, what matters is to be proud of what you are and have confidence in yourself."

"Thanks, Mike."

"I've spent a lifetime with people telling me how to look and how to behave, by a lot of people who end up doing bad things when they get older. Anyhows, I think you're kinda cool. The way I see it, you're the coolest kid here. I bet you're smart too. Am I right?"

"I do well at school. Especially in science. Is that bad?"

"Look, I've never thought of doing anything else other than cabbing, and I guess I never put much work in at school because I always knew that was what I was gonna do. But I get the feeling you're gonna do something good with your life. I get these feelings." Redolfo smiles warmly.

"You work a lot with your feelings, don't you?"

"Yeah. Makes a lot of folks mad with me."

"That's because you can see right through them."

"What did I say, girl? You're smart *and* cool."

Gethsemona blushes pink and smiles all the way home.

A HOLY SPANNER IN THE WORKS

*Department of Vost Investigative Civilian Enforcement (*DEVICE*)—Catuvell Division*

"Order, order! Quiet please," the deep, authoritative voice of General Hostian fills the DEVICE boardroom. The noisy conversations settle. "Thank you for attending this second emergency DEVICE meeting. Considering the recent extraordinary criminal activities, I have returned to Catuvell, having had to break off an important engagement with the Mayor of Carnona.

"The remit of this meeting is to decide firstly, whether I need to impose planetary martial law, and secondly, how we are best to respond to the latest events. To start proceedings, will all the board members identify themselves? I, General Hostian will act as Chairman. To remind you all, I am currently also positioned as Acting President of Vost and as Military Commander-in-Chief of the United Vost Army. Can we go around the table in order?"

"Ariael Vernikell, DEVICE Deputy Chief of Intelligence."

"Capell Parchi, Chair at Catuvell Science Agency, and chair of seven steering groups for defence development projects."

"Febryalla Ner-all, Chair of VIAS Central Species Anthropological Research and Equalities Board."

"Most Holy Reverend, Sellibot Spaan, Chief Protector of Faith and President of the United Faiths of Vost."

"Temeria Schneider, Director of the *Schneiderian Defence Agency*."

At the far end of the boardroom, the various city representatives identify themselves,

... "Fothad Inguba, Governor of Catuvell." ... "Bedd Pryderi, Governor of Briganti." ... "Rigbadan Mabbon, Governor of Coritan." ... "Tewdrigga Trevezell, Governess of Carina." ... "Ogma Nu-all, Personal Assistant to the Acting President of Vost." ...

Hostian continues, "Thank you all for attending. Can you all please demonstrate that you have signed the *Official Secrets Directive*?"

The board members each wave their documents in the air in response.

"You'll have been briefed on the recent events at *Zone 773*. Before we proceed, I would like to say how relieved we are that Senesul Rimikk has been found alive. He is, however, seriously injured and has been transported to Catuvell Main Hospital. I understand that while he was in the Briganti Mountains, he was looked after by the terannians, who appear to have saved his life by treating his wounds with a form of primitive balm. His doctors say he is currently too ill to be debriefed. I have no further information on this.

"For the first item on the agenda I invite Professor Capell Parchi to update us on what the stolen device from *Zone 773* does and how much of a threat it poses to Vost."

Parchi rises slowly, rubbing away the stiffness of his back. He clears his throat. "*The Super-Symmetric String Field Modulator Shell* was a classified project that was commissioned and funded by the *Theoretical Science Division* of the *United Vost Army*. It was designed to protect Vost from a hypothetical invasion from hostile worlds. It functions by disrupting quantum-particle energy transmissions within about an eight-hundred-mile radius.

It's therefore capable of disarming weaponry that use quantum-particle technology and of blocking any communications that use any form of quantum waves. The second phase of *Zone 773*'s project is incomplete. It was designed to keep Vost's own military and communications hardware operational while the device was activated, therefore selectively disarming the enemy's technology only."

"Thank you, Professor," Hostian responds, gesticulating at the arthritic scientist to sit. "Now we know that the device is in enemy hands, we need to surmise what purpose this will serve them and what threat it poses to us." He addresses Parchi again, "How near are we, Professor, to developing the counter-technology to this? By the way, you don't have to rise."

A stifled titter is audible around the boardroom.

Parchi replies, "If Temeria and I were to pool our resources on this, I believe we could have a functional system in place within about a week. From what I understand, the complex string calculations were giving the science team a headache, so it has taken slightly longer than expected to complete this piece of work."

"Thank you, Professor," Hostian replies. "The next item - who is the enemy we are facing, and how did they get to know of the *Zone 773* project? Professor Schneider, I would like you to enlighten us in any way you can."

Temeria Schneider rises. Vernikell has only met her on a few occasions but always marvelled at how such a diminutive and sallow creature had made so many scientific achievements with such breath-taking efficiency. He always felt her management role at the SDA would serve to detract from her true calling - her unfathomable scientific creativity.

She begins, "Firstly, Mr. Chairman, I am pleased to confirm that the full resources of the *Schneiderian Defence Agency* are yours to use. I knew peripherally about the *Zone 773* project but was never directly involved with it. I certainly never knew how advanced it was in its development. As you can imagine, the leaders of the scientific world do tend to talk amongst themselves about many things, including their own projects. I do know that Cashall Zanusso, our senior scientist at the SDA, was aware of some elements of the project. The fact that he has been kidnapped by the enemy forces would serve as a potential source for leaks of classified information."

"Yes, indeed," Hostian replies, "we have been far too lax in our security." Temeria returns to her seat. He continues, "Deputy Deputy Chief Vernikell, I want you and Professor Schneider to head a team to strengthen the protection of all government-linked science agencies and their staff and put into place systems that ensure that knowledge of secret projects at the highest levels is not shared."

Vernikell stands, "Mr. Chairman, I was never informed of this project and therefore was never given the opportunity to advise on security systems that would have been vital to protecting such an important device." He gives a momentary glare at a shrivelled Parchi.

Parchi begins to stand but quickly gives up. He tries to clear his throat, but ends up replying with a choked voice, "I am afraid I entirely agree with Ariael's assessment of this situation. I am sorry to you, General, to Ariael and to all of you that I let my enthusiasm for this project get in the way of my considerations for the important security matters associated with it. I never wanted anything to delay the project, as it was progressing so well. I therefore offer my immediate resignation from the *Catuvell Science Agency*, and from the various steering groups I chair—"

"All in good time, Professor," Hostian cuts in, "but while there exists a substantial threat to our world, Vost simply cannot afford your resignation."

Parchi looks down, his expression contrite.

Hostian continues, "The next item is something that I, myself, as Military C-I-C of the United Vost Army will advise you of. As you are all aware, all our military forces employ weapons and communications technology that will be vulnerable to this device. While there are long-range weapons that can be launched from outside the eight-hundred-mile perimeter, it is likely they'll be subject to navigational guidance failure when they enter the Modulator shell zone. The other side of this conundrum, however, is that any enemy forces themselves will be unable to use standard weaponry and communications systems. We need to assume that there will be an attack on other science and military stations. Deputy Deputy Chief Vernikell, you have attended the meetings of the *Planetary Military Strategy Committee*. Your report, please."

Vernikell rises, "Thank you, General. We have precious little information on who the enemy is and what they actually want. They are clearly an effective and organised group and have operators with considerable skills in combat. We have, so far, no further useful information from the witness of the attack on the SDA, who initially suggested that one of the assailants is of an antlered species. Any information from Agent Rimikk, once he is well enough for debriefing, may prove helpful.

"I personally headed the assault team on *Zone 773*. As you know, the three criminals, Dozor, Boca and Vestbo were involved with the enemy operation and were under the mind-control of the gang leaders through the influence of the *Neuron 86G Synaptic* mind-control weapon. To remind you all, this weapon is no longer operational. We know from our engagement with the enemy that of the three captured criminals, only Boca survives. There was another individual spotted, a berrantine who was involved in the heist. His image can be seen on the screen."

The board members all turn towards the big screen at the far end of the room. The image displays two figures carrying the blocking device. The berrantine fires his weapon towards the camera. The criminals are then seen stepping off the edge of the precipice.

Vernikell continues, "Our records show no trace of this individual and the receptionist witness at the SDA has no recollection of him either." All eyes now return to Vernikell. "Mr. Chairman, I propose that in the absence of any further knowledge of the motives behind these attacks, we take a precautionary approach to protecting our planet's command-and-control infrastructure including important buildings."

Murmurings of assent are audible around the room.

"We have employed maser and fragmenter weapon technology routinely for over seventy years. It has proved a reliable technology and has been universally adopted by security agencies across the planet. We're now entering a situation we've never had to face before, where our primary form of weaponry can no longer be relied upon." More murmurings around the boardroom. "I therefore propose we, at least for the time being, return to old-style gunpowder-based firearms, which would be immune to the effects of the Modulator device."

Vernikell sees the Protector of Faith, Sellibot Spaan, has attracted the attentions of the boardroom members by shaking his head in scornful disapproval. Vernikell continues, now raising his voice above the chattering, "This will mean the rapid commissioning of a large number of old-style pistols and rifles and immediate commencement of training of our agents and soldiers in their use."

Hostian cuts in, "I see you look unhappy with this proposal, Most Holy Reverend Spaan. Would you like to share your concerns with us?"

The tall figure of Spaan rises. He brushes down the creases of his shimmering robes and makes a flamboyant show of dabbing at his thin lips with a silk handkerchief. His face is wan and bony and his eyes sunken into his skull. After completing these preliminaries, he begins speaking with a pious drawl that instantly irks Vernikell. "Thank you, General. As you are aware, I have been commissioned by the Vost government to oversee the protection of faith on the planet and to give moral guidance to the legislature."

Vernikell tries not to let his frustration show.

Spaan continues, "I have a number of concerns about the Deputy Chief of Staff's proposals. Firstly, we have a duty of care towards *all* people, and that includes suspected and proven criminals, our military personnel, as well as the VIAS agents on Vost." Spaan pauses, seemingly to observe that he has impressed the boardroom members with his opening moral considerations. "Old-style firearms were taken out of the arms market a long time ago for good reasons. Notwithstanding the fact they were deadly, they could not be adjusted, as our modern weapon systems can be, to detain alleged felons safely without inflicting permanent injury. In this way, when fired with any degree of accuracy at a living target, old-style firearms can only either kill or cause significant harm, and the outcome is unpredictable.

"Secondly, as you have said yourself, if the shell device is activated, then the enemy will prevent their own ability to cause harm. I also have concerns regarding the safety of our soldiers and men who have never trained in the use of such firearms. They are likely to feel out of their comfort zone, thereby rendering the use of such weaponry both dangerous, and frankly, obsolete."

Spaan sits displaying a righteous and contented smile around the boardroom, leaving an incensed Vernikell struggling hard to prevent himself from landing a huge punch squarely into the Most Holy Reverend's face. Vernikell can see Hostian reflecting on what he has heard and, frustratingly, there are nods of agreement amongst the city governors. The Baroness alone appears concerned.

"This is an interesting take on our situation, Most Holy Reverend Spaan," Hostian responds, "but I do think we need to take this point in the context of the potential crisis we are facing here."

"You said it yourself, General," replies Spaan, "it is a potential crisis only. We have absolutely no idea what they are planning. Whichever way I see it, I cannot imagine a situation where the device will be used in any significant way before the technical 'antidote' has been developed, by which time it will have been rendered useless to them anyway."

The Baroness stands and addresses the Chair, "If I may, General, I have grave concerns that in the event of a city-wide disruption of communications and weapons systems, it will prove extremely difficult to maintain law and order. I agree with the Deputy Chief of Staff's analysis that we have never been prepared for such a potential threat to our command-and-control structures. Every fibre in me is screaming out that we must have a weapons contingency, even if it means a manufacturing and training delay while printing a cache of old-style weaponry. It is a matter of a precautionary principle, and this is one of those times where I strongly advise we employ it."

Vernikell is reminded of just how little the Baron deserves such a wife.

Hostian addresses the board, "On reflection, Most Holy Reverend, the Baroness and Chief of Staff have made a robust defence of the need for reverting to the old firearms technology, at least until the control mechanisms have been developed for the shell device. The question remains if we need to declare emergency state powers. I am inclined to say that we do."

Spaan rises, his voice now shrill, "General, by the Third Amendment of the Fifth Constitution of the *United World Order of Vost*, the Chief Protector of Faith can, if they so choose, call for a forty-eight hour moratorium in the event of a state crisis, pending a decision of the *Holy Council*. This amendment was wired into the constitution over five decades ago and you are, by law, duty-bound to comply if I invoke that amendment."

"An archaic law that will need to be changed," a furious Vernikell mutters to himself out of the audible range of the board members.

THE MIND IS NOT A VESSEL TO BE FILLED, BUT A FIRE TO BE KINDLED.

Plutarch

"Dominik, is that you? I can feel you're near me. I hope you can hear me." Marianna feels his presence, but only weakly. She decides to keep talking hoping that will help him to enter her mind more easily. "So many people have become ill. They say typhus is spreading throughout the whole camp. It's horribly overcrowded - everyone's so very unhappy.

"The guards allow the Jewish musicians to sing and play music. The elders have been teaching the children history and maths. But what's the point? So many children have been taken away to Auschwitz-Birkenau. We're sure they're all going to their deaths. We all act as if it's all going to be fine, but it's not. My hair's such a terrible mess."

There is no reply. Marianna is compelled to keep talking to her lover. She feels certain he's listening somewhere within her mind. "A single letter arrived here from a prisoner deported to Auschwitz-Birkenau. It describes shaved heads and striped prison uniforms. The very mention of the name of that camp fills us with terror. The cattle trucks keep coming. They take away thousands of us. I know we'll never see each other again. Our child will never live to see the world. I miss you, my Dominik."

Kominsky's presence within in her mind is stronger now.

"Marianna, I hear you."

She can feel rather than see his image form in front of her, radiant and beautiful.

"For all its ghastly history, I never saw cruelty such as this on my planet. I'm being held prisoner by Heinrich Himmler. He's clearly lost his mind in the pursuit of the complete annihilation of all Jews. He genuinely sees them as *lesser humans.* He's obsessed by the mystical arts and is insane enough to think I'm part of some Aryan prophecy. I'm going to try to escape. I don't know whether I'll ever make it out of here alive.

"Marianna, there's something I want to ask your permission for. It's not something I've ever witnessed being performed, but theoretically, it's possible."

"What is it, my love?"

"I'd never have thought of contemplating such a thing before our fortunes changed in this way, and I would certainly never want do anything that would make you feel uncomfortable."

"Tell me what it is."

"I don't know if we'll ever be able to see each other again. This power I have, as you can see, is something that can be used for good things as well as to hurt people. I believe I'll be able to place part of myself into your mind, permanently. I'll entirely understand if you wouldn't want that."

"Dominik, what do you mean?"

"If I never make it out of here, I believe it will mean that you'll always feel a little of my presence, as if I am actually more than a memory. Something that will feel more tangible to you than just a memory of what we had."

"I'd do anything to have you with me forever. I want you to know, despite everything, you've made me happier than I've been at any time in my life."

"Marianna...I regret now that we were never able to marry—"

"No, my love. Don't say that. It really doesn't matter." She feels his heart wrench with sadness.

"It will mean you'll need to let me deeper into your mind."

"I would trust you with my heart, soul and mind." Marianna feels a gentle warmth pervade her consciousness. "Oh, I can feel you, so beautiful within me. I want you, badly. I need you inside me - inside every part of me." Her breathing quickens. She cries out, loudly, "Never, ever leave me!"

THINGS CATCH UP

Redolfo walks into the *Opprobrium Bar* and looks around for his friends. The chattering and laughter indicate the activity of the bar is back to normal. Before he finishes surveying the lounge, he's accosted by a whooping Amitaab who's flung his arms around him and is greeting him with a forceful man-hug.

"Mike, Mike, you're okay! What happened to you, man?" Amitaab says, shaking with excitement.

Danysus appears. "We've been worried about you. You just disappeared."

"I'm okay, you don't need to worry. Old Mike Redolfo knows how to look after himself," he says with a reassuring smile.

He watches H'droma snigger as another set of gullible victims try in vain to take him on at his gambling games.

"John has given him a stern talking to," says Danysus. "I think H'droma is trying to be better behaved, although his idea of good behaviour is different from most people's."

Redolfo looks around the room and spots Caryalla. He marvels at her own extraordinary brand of beauty as she leans across the bar to order a drink. She looks at him, smiles and indicates with her hand that she's taking an order for him.

Redolfo sits with Amitaab and Danysus at the table. They are soon joined by Caryalla, who's holding a tray with four cocktails. Redolfo feels that now-familiar sense of clouding and relaxation when he is with his three friends. It's as if he has been relieved of a burden he so often carries - the weight of constantly anticipating people. He wonders if this is how most people feel all the time, entirely free of such concerns. They don't know how lucky they are.

"Mike, we were worried about you," Caryalla says smiling. With her arms around his neck, she lands a soft kiss on his cheek. Redolfo's pulse quickens.

"What happened to you?" she says as she returns to her seat, "The fight was over fairly quickly, but at the end, we looked round and you were nowhere to be seen."

Redolfo glimpses Moorshead waving to him from behind the bar with a broad, silver-bearded grin of relief. "It's okay," he replies to his friends, "some bozo got his kicks taking me for a ride to the other side of Catuvell. They left me stranded. Anyhows, enough about me, Caryalla." He looks at an array of bracelets on her left wrist. "Hell! Did you make those?"

"Yes, I made them yesterday. I was thinking of selling them to the jewellery shops. Do you like them?"

"They're beautiful, Caryalla. You really are a talented lady. Seems you're great at everything you do." Redolfo studies the designs a little closer. "Who's the lady in the centre?"

"That's Brighid, the patron goddess of the orphanage where we were brought up."

"I guess she must be important to you."

"Yes, she's important to all of us."

"Our mother, Brighid!" Amitaab and Danysus shout in unison, and each place their left hands over their hearts, their heads bowed.

Caryalla continues, "Brighid represents healing, energy and care. She's said to lean over every cradle."

Redolfo adjusts his cap and smiles, "She sounds a hell of a gal. I wanted to hear the rest of your story - the one about your gang leader."

"Hey, let's get another drink," says Caryalla.

"Don't kid a kidder. You can't change the subject now."

"You mean Murtair and me?" Caryalla sighs, "I guess I'm losing this one." She takes a swig from her stone cup. "His heart was broken, and he wanted revenge. The only way out was to fight him."

"Sounds like he wanted to control you."

"Control was like an addiction for him."

"Hell, you must have been scared."

She nods. "He used to boast he'd always beat me in a duel. I've seen him easily take on several guys at once. To my knowledge, no one had ever defeated him in a fight. He'd have made mincemeat of those two corattians at the precinct."

"But I've seen what you can do with those hook things."

"Murtair favoured using a straight sword. That put me at a disadvantage with my hook swords."

"So how did you survive?"

"I was the best in our group at stealth and thought I'd be able to launch a surprise attack - the trouble was, he was an extremely skilled tracker."

"What do you mean, stealth?"

"I can step without a sound and I paint myself with blue camouflage."

"Is that what you use in your hair?" Redolfo asks.

"Yes. It comes from the isatis plant. I seem to have a connection with it. I don't know why, but it's strangely important to me."

"So, go on," Redolfo implores her. "What happened?"

"I saw a small bird jumping nervously from branch to branch, on continual alert for predators. I thought I could use the bird's instincts to warn me. I'd be able to keep near the bird by stepping silently along the woodland floor. Murtair's more noisy presence would frighten it off, so I'd know if he was close."

Redolfo notices the bar has gone silent. He looks up. The inquisitive eyes of dozens of the bar clientele are laid upon Caryalla, clearly eager to hear the rest of the story.

"Get outta here!" Redolfo shouts at them, waving them away, "This is a private conversation."

"Oh go onz Caryallaz." says a pleading H'droma jumping up and down on an adjacent table and looking like an over-animated turkey, "You'vez never agreedz to tellz us this storyz before but youz decidez to tellz zis strangerz."

"Well, H'droma does have a point," the sound of Moorshead's educated and authoritative voice cuts through the crowd. "You've never told us this story - even though Amitaab's been so persistent about it."

Caryalla looks around at the eager faces and concedes defeat. She looks back at Moorshead. "Alright John, but you owe me big time."

An array of bar chairs is quickly assembled around Caryalla's table, and the *Opprobrium Bar* audience is now in position.

Like story-time at a kindergarten, Redolfo chuckles to himself.

Caryalla continues, "The bird reached an escarpment. There was a sheer drop of a few hundred feet to a valley below."

~

As Caryalla recounts her story, she feels compelled to stare at the wall. As she speaks, the *Opprobrium Bar* and its clientele seemingly disappear into a void. A memory rises to the surface - the moments before confronting the master assassin. Is it a memory of a memory she had at the time? - something in her past? Yet it isn't in her past - certainly not a past she can recall - but there it is - as vivid as anything else she knows from her own life.

She steps gently, silently within the shadows of the trees. Her face and hair are painted blue. She is not alone. Others of her kind - ten or more - hunters - warriors, each painted and dressed for battle, as she herself is. Instead of hook swords, she wields a long spear in her right hand. A beautifully carved longbow hangs off her left shoulder. Her cloak is held in place with an intricate clasp in front of her left shoulder. This is not the Caryalla she knows - but somehow it is more than the Caryalla than she recognises. A warrior's blood pulsing through her veins. For those intense moments, she feels it is not Murtair who is the enemy, but a force far stronger, far more formidable and numerous than the one great assassin. An enemy somehow part of her own life - part of something that links her intimately to the woodland scene.

"Are you okay, Caryalla?"

She hears the sound of Redolfo's voice, and awakes, startled, from her daydream to see the confused looks on the faces of her audience. "Yes, sorry, Mike. I got carried away with my own thoughts for a moment."

She continues her story. "I noticed the woodland wildlife had gone silent. My little bird took flight. I prepared myself for an immediate attack. Murtair vaulted over some scrub and took a swipe at me with his sword. I leapt backwards, but not quickly enough to prevent him landing a deep cut into my left shoulder."

"Weez would like to seez zis cutz Caryallaz!" says an over-eager H'droma, reaching out a sinewy arm to pull down her top. Before he has a chance, Redolfo yanks on H'droma's extended arm, toppling him off his perch. H'droma lands on the floor with a tumble amid a chorus of laughter.

"Calm down, everyone, and you sit down and behave, H'droma," Moorshead's voice rises above the roaring cackles.

H'droma lifts his small body back up to the edge of the table and sits still.

"Please continue, Caryalla," says the barman once the laughter has settled.

She glances at Redolfo and, suppressing her own laughter, continues with her story. "I managed to regain my balance and parried a series of furious sweeps of Murtair's sword. I jumped onto the topmost stone of a pile of boulders. Murtair scooped up a clod of soil and threw it into my face, narrowly missing my eyes. I linked my swords to form an extended weapon. Murtair knew this manoeuvre so held his distance. I spun off the boulder, and surprised him by unlinking the swords, then sweeping his feet with one of the hooks. He toppled backwards, and I managed to land a spinning kick to his head. He staggered back, perilously close to the precipice.

"I braced myself for his retaliation. Instead, he called to me, 'It will not be you who ends my position as leader.' He sheathed his weapon and leapt over the precipice. I looked over the edge but couldn't see where he'd landed. I can't imagine how he could've survived such a fall."

"So, is he definitely dead now?" Danysus asks her.

"Well, I climbed down the precipice and after an hour of searching the rocks and the river below, I found no sign of him. I returned to the group and told the gang's second-in-command what'd happened. I was saluted by the group and allowed to leave."

"Was Murtair's body ever found?" asks Moorshead.

"Not that I've heard. Then again, I haven't had contact with the group since then."

The rest of her story is interrupted as the bar entrance door bursts open. Ten armed and uniformed VIAS security agents storm into the bar. One agent shouts, "Everyone stay where you are!" Ten plasma rifles are now aimed at Redolfo's head.

The cabbie's face has turned white. With his hands on his head, he says, "Can I help you gentlemen?"

"What's the meaning of this intrusion?" shouts a furious Moorshead, "Show me your warrant to raid my premises like this."

"Michael Redolfo, you are under arrest. You will remain calm with your hands above your head," says the leader of the security group.

"On what charge?" Moorshead demands.

"On a matter of state importance. Under article 27A section (a) of the *Cassiana World Security Act*, we do not have to give details of the charge. We also are given license to shoot to kill anyone that obstructs the arrest."

"Heyz Misterz Securityz Agent," says H'droma to the agent leader, waving an agent's plasma rifle like a maniacal, long-armed, gun-wielding chicken. "your manz should bez more carefulz than to leave heez weaponez unprotectedez."

A furious VIAS agent, now denuded of his weapon, starts demanding its return. "How on Vost did you do that?" he shouts in bewilderment.

"Give the weapon back to the agent, H'droma," Moorshead sighs, "We've enough trouble here without you doing that."

Caryalla looks on in horror, as she watches a shackled Redolfo being taken away.

THE WINDOW OF THE SOUL

"Heil, Hitler!" The damp silence of the Spilberk Castle dungeon is disrupted by the arrival of Heinrich Himmler and his accompanying guards. Kominsky's blindfold has been removed but the blood from his beaten face is making his swollen eyes sting. He can make out the rounded forms of Himmler's characteristic pince-nez spectacles and his pale skin with receding chin that in spite of his soldierly physique, gives him the very opposite appearance many would expect of a military commander. Himmler settles onto a stool.

"Herr Kominsky, I am looking forward to seeing how your night's stay with us has changed your views. A hot bath and a comfortable officer's room await your presence. I will not at this stage expect you to salute the Führer, but in time, you will learn to love him. I have something here of great symbolic value." Himmler reaches into his inside pocket and takes out a small object. "This, Herr Kominsky, is the *SS Honour Ring*. Some call it the *Death Head Ring* and is offered only to the worthiest of my Schutzstaffel officers. I am now offering this ring to you." He passes it to the prisoner through the bars.

Kominsky rubs his eyes and studies the ring as carefully as he can. There is a central skull surrounded by runes either side.

Himmler gives him a satisfied smile. "I see you're interested. It symbolises the supreme power of the Aryan race. The sig runes either side of the skull represent the power of the Sun and the conquering energy. This symbol here represents 'Got' and is the old German word for God. In effect, Herr Kominsky, it tells us that if we enclose the universe in us, we have the power to control it."

The prisoner turns his face away from him and says, "Reichsführer, I've had time to consider your kind offer. I too share your interest in the Holy Lance and would dearly love to see it used in the hands of its rightful Aryan inheritors. I believe it will hand you almost limitless power and sway the balance of power in your conflict against the allied forces."

"That pleases me, Herr Kominsky, pleases me greatly. However, I would expect that you look at me when addressing me."

"Please forgive me, Reichsführer, but the prolonged darkness has made it difficult for me to adjust to the light you have brought with you. Before you release me, I'd dearly love to know just a little of the man I am to serve. Your reputation is that you are a *kind* man, and that you insist all your family members behave in a *kind* fashion. I can see how you recognise the importance of kindness. Yes, Reichsführer, you continually strive for you and your family to be *decent*. How do you say it in your language? *Anständig*."

Himmler stares at him suspiciously.

Kominsky continues, "Your role as a chicken farmer has influenced you profoundly - you view the Third Reich as the means by which the world itself should be cultivated by your guiding hand. You've never been a particularly healthy or physically strong man and have always struggled to develop strong and lasting relationships. You were too young to prove yourself in combat in the Great War, and it's given you the need to present yourself as the consummate soldier."

Himmler's gaze is fixed on him.

"You have many crowning achievements, Reichsführer. You single-handedly raised the image and importance of your disciplined SS above that of the unreliable and rebellious ruffians of your mentor, Ernst Röhm's SA. After all, the sexualised masculinity of the SA by comparison to your soldierly SS disgusted you. It was brash and full of homosexual behaviour. I see how that wouldn't fit with your plans for a supreme Germany."

"How did you come by this information?" Himmler demands as beads of sweat gather on his forehead. His left hand is clenched.

Kominsky continues, "Yes, Reichsführer, your vision for the Third Reich has been the driving force to your success. How could Hitler not be impressed by his most loyal servant acting out his own utopian fantasies? Who better than yourself to be entrusted with the ethnic, spiritual and military purity that is the future of the Aryan people? It connects together, like a jigsaw puzzle with a Germanic empire, utterly cleansed of subhuman life, the *Untermenschen*. The rightful inheritance of the Aryan people is in the military perfection that allows them to rise up and dominate the world order."

"Reichsführer, Alles gut?" asks an agitated guard.

Himmler turns to look at them. His mouth opens and he whispers a barely audible sound. One guard moves towards him and places an ear near to the Reichsführer's trembling lips.

"Alles ist in Ordnung. Alles gut." Himmler reassures him.

"There's a problem, however," continues Kominsky, "as your notion of *kindness* and *decency* can no longer apply to the people outside of your German elite. So, you carry out Hitler's own dream - The Final Solution - *die Endlösung* - the annihilation of every man, woman and child that you consider as lesser beings compared to your world of Teutonic perfection. Hundreds of thousands of Jews, perhaps millions, have been murdered in extermination camps in your world of violence and control. However, in spite of your obsession with the arcane world of runes and twisted tales of ancient Aryan perfection, you're in many ways a practical man. I can see that you're doubting the strength of the German military to prevent the approach of the allies. The Soviet Army cannot be stopped while elements within your own forces wage miniature wars against you. It's not just Germany that you have to control. You are losing, Reichsführer. I can feel you know that too."

Blood is now seeping from the corner of Himmler's left eye. He begins to produce froth from his mouth. His whole body is shaking.

Kominsky turns to face him, his eyes glowing a furious crimson. "So now, Reichsführer, I can offer you some advice. There is still time to present yourself as a *reasonable* man to the allies. Think how well it would go down if you become *Himmler the honest broker* of the conflict. Do you think the allies will treat you kindly when you have been captured if you continue down this fantasist's path? It's time you negotiated with your enemies. As a gesture of goodwill, you should release the prisoners from the Terezín and Auschwitz concentration camps. Set up communication lines with the allies. Use Switzerland as a base if you have to." Kominsky raises his voice, "Absolutely nothing else will save you, not your runes, not your mistress or your dismissed wife, not your Aryan ancestry and certainly not Adolf Hitler!"

Himmler stands up from his stool. He points to Kominsky and with a shrill voice, shouts an order to his guards, "Ihn jetzt töten!"

A deafening roar of rapid gunfire.

Kominsky flops onto his cell floor, peppered from head to chest with bullet wounds.

~

197

From deep within the Terezín concentration camp, Marianna lets out a scream, "Dear God, no. Please God, no. Don't let this happen. Dominik!"

IT'S NOT HOW IT LOOKS

The room, spartan but now familiar, no longer represents a dream-like, or even farcical part of Redolfo's new life. He's not there as a result of a misunderstanding or mistaken identity. This time, he really does harbour a guilty secret. The sheer madness of the situation overwhelms him. Barely a few days have passed since he was abducted to another planet by aliens - the type of thing only crazy conspiracy theorists believe in. Now, he's in deep trouble because of a series of events he's had no control over.

He inspects the room for the umpteenth time. Its white walls give him nothing in particular to focus on while he awaits his interrogation. He's been sitting alone in the room for almost an hour and has had a long time to think - too long. How was he discovered? What do they know? What will happen to him? Is there a death penalty here? Would it be by firing squad, lethal injection or maybe an electric chair? Would he be allowed legal representation?

The door opens. He recognises the familiar, upright form of Deputy Chief Vernikell. He's accompanied by two females and a frail, older male. One of the females is the attractive officer he recognises from his initial interrogation. The other female is older, elegantly presented with perfect jewellery, her hair placed in beautiful layers high on her head. Her expression seems kindly. They all sit across the other side of the interview table. The four interrogators pull out their portable electronic devices and begin to scrutinise the contents. Redolfo senses confusion.

Vernikell begins, "Mr. Redolfo, this has become somewhat of a regular occurrence. This is our third meeting in the course of a week - quite remarkable considering how new you are to Vost."

Redolfo sits with his hands in his pockets.

"Let me introduce you to my colleagues. This is my second-in-command, Officer Dowola whom you may, if you were not too intoxicated at the time, recognise from your first encounter with us. This is Baroness Ner-all from VIAS *Central Species Anthropological Research and Equalities Board*. This is Professor Capell Parchi, Chair at *Catuvell Science Agency* and Chair of several steering groups for defence development projects."

"Okay, Vernikell, do I get a brief?"

"I'm afraid there is too much at stake for that," Vernikell replies. "You've been detained here as a matter of planetary security, so you'll not qualify for legal representation at this stage."

"So, what's your charge? Let's get this over with."

"First of all, Mr. Redolfo, I need to know exactly who you are."

"You goddamned know who I am!"

"Okay, let's try this from another angle. Where were you born?"

"What the hell? I was born in the Brooklyn Hospital Centre in 1945. What of it?"

"Who are your parents?"

"Where are you going with this?" Redolfo replies, beginning to feel angry.

Vernikell continues, "You may recall you were abducted because our DNA scanners suggested you may have been an escaped criminal from some years ago, who was hiding on your planet. Your DNA profile turned out to have some sequences compatible with that criminal, but the sequences were in no way a match. Furthermore, we know also that you are a human."

"Okay, so what of it?"

The Baroness answers Redolfo's question, "It appears that you have some DNA sequence fragments in common with two species that reside here on Vost. One is berrantine, and another is the species known as the terannians."

Redolfo puts his head in his hands, "This place just gets crazier by the minute. I'm just a simple Brooklyn cab driver, goddamn it. My parents are immigrants from Europe, so what's that got to do with this goddamn planet?"

"That's what we would dearly like to know, Mr. Redolfo," replies Vernikell. "We recently sent a field agent to investigate a species that are an ancient people of Vost. They are known as the terannians. They are a people who have kept themselves separate from the rest of the citizens on the planet, ever since they were subjugated by the allied invaders from other worlds about a century ago. They are so secretive a people, we know precious little about them."

Redolfo begins to relax a little as he realises the authorities seem unaware of his involvement in the heist. He replies, "This sounds like a similar story to where I come from. The white folk took the land from many native tribes who'd lived there for God-knows how long. What's left of them now live on reservations or have become interbred with the white folk. I read about this stuff at school and watched the natives getting beat up in movies. So, why are you interested in these terrapin guys?"

The baroness continues, "A witness to an attack on a science station described one of the assailants as having antlers. The only antlered species we know on this planet are the terannians. Our field agent managed to probe a sample of their DNA. The curious thing is that some of their sequences bear a striking resemblance to your own."

Redolfo takes off his cap and starts prodding his head. "Believe me, little lady, but I don't have any antlers, at least not the last time I looked."

Vernikell looks at Parchi who looks at the Baroness. Parchi sighs, "This is going nowhere, Ariael."

Vernikell places his electronic device down on the desk and says with a sigh, "I just can't imagine this man we abducted can possibly have anything to do with this. Just look at him. He's even more confused than we are. Mr. Redolfo, we cannot let you go just yet. Our field agent was injured but is reported to be making good progress, and we need to gather more information from him. I'm afraid you'll have to stay in a cell until we're happy we have you excluded as a suspect in this crime."

"Agent Vernikell, can I make one request?"

"What is that, Mr. Redolfo?"

"Can I choose the menu? The last time I dined here, the food almost ate me."

Officer Dowola lets out a small giggle.

BEYOND THIRD CLASS

Marianna can no longer feel hunger, or pain. She has even become largely immune to the intense stench that fills the almost non-existent spaces between the passengers crushed up within the heaving cattle carriage. Her camp uniform is saturated with filth. She has been stripped of just about everything in her world. Even her unborn child is to be slaughtered with her and everyone else in the freight train in the death camp of Auschwitz-Birkenau. She knows she is soon to join the hundreds of thousands of souls that have perished at the behest of the greatest evil the world has ever seen.

The floor of the carriage is covered with straw as if to symbolise how the passengers are like cattle that release waste where they stand. There is no choice but to behave like the cattle they are considered to be. Some frailer passengers lie lifeless on the floor. At least they didn't die by execution. Is that anything at all to celebrate?

The only light within the carriage issues from between the slats of the panels. The lazy clatter of the wheels on the rails reflect how slowly the train is moving towards its terrible destination. The carriage is bitterly cold, but Marianna cares nothing for this. Her greatest suffering is the separation from her soul mate and lover, Dominik Kominsky.

Earlier that morning, the Terezín bell had announced the abrupt arrival of dozens of SS personnel, waking

Marianna and the others in her section of the camp with whips and sticks. "Get up, get up! Schneller, schneller! It's time for your transfer. By order of the Reichsführer, you are to be sent away from this camp. Get up!"

Hundreds of the inmates were herded onto the cattle trucks. Some covered their heads with their hands as they tried to pray. Many screamed at being separated from their friends and relatives. Whatever privileges they enjoyed in the typhus-ridden, over-cramped conditions of the Terezín camp, they all knew those privileges had now gone, and they were about to experience something far worse.

From within the carriage, the prisoners have endured hour upon hour of suffering in the cramped conditions. Their voices are weak from starvation, illness and the sense of utter defeat. It is no secret. There have been numerous mass transports out of the camp. Why did the guards even bother lying about work-camps when everyone knew they were being taken to their deaths? The rumours of people being killed by rifle-fire in front of ready-made mass graves or through poisoning in large gas chambers were ever present.

Marianna can hear babies crying. Children are asking questions to grown-ups who are either too weak or too full of despair to answer. Would they spare the children? Of course not. She will never see her own child. Is that better than bringing up a child in this God-forsaken world? Where is God now? Marianna has never been in any way religious, but never before has she thought so much about how a kind God could let so much suffering take place on his world.

Hours upon hours. Is it days? The soul feels ebbed away, a little more with each clatter of the wheels, like the ticking of a clock that will never again be rewound.

A series of announcements shouted in German heralds the final approach of the train. Several of the male passengers place a hand over their head and begin the prayer, "Sh'ma Yisrael Adonai Eloheinu Adonai Ehad."

The door slides open and a panic surges through the carriage amidst the confusion caused by the intensity of the incoming light and the shouting of the guards. "Get out! Get out! Schneller! Schneller!" The passengers who are slow to move are forcibly pulled out by the guards. Some are placed onto stretchers. Emaciated and weak, the passengers are filed out onto the platform. Many are too broken to cry but not to scream. Twelve armed guards have trained their rifles onto the crowd. Two aim machine guns. "You will be quiet!" the Commandant orders with a threatening voice.

The crowd becomes silent, save for some scattered whimpers. "By order of the Reichsführer, we are to hand you over to your new administration." The guards raise their weapons into a salute position and file back onto the train.

"What's happening?" the crowds whisper in deep confusion.

A stream of new soldiers file onto the platform to replace the SS. They look altogether different with broader helmets, long grey coats and with brown leather breast bags strapped around their waists. The commander addresses them, "Guten Morgen, everyone, and welcome to Switzerland. You have been released to us by order of Heinrich Himmler. There is food and accommodation at an embassy building. You are to be directed there."

PEOPLE CAN CHANGE

Rimikk indicates to each of his visitors to sit down. There's one seat short, so he gestures to Officer Dowola to perch on the side of his hospital bed. As she sits, she's aware she's blushing.

"Well, how's the invalid?" Vernikell says smiling at Agent Rimikk. "I hear you came second in a fight with a giant auriach."

"Remind me not to travel alone in the Briganti mountains again," he replies, looking around the room at the concerned faces. He catches Officer Dowola's eye. She flushes again.

"It's good to have you back, sir," Officer Dowola says to him. He gives her a look she's never seen before – at least not from him. Is that a look of interest? Is it possible from this otherwise impenetrable man?

The Baroness studies Rimikk's bandages. "So, you were bitten on the chest," she says to him.

"I still don't understand how it happened. I've been scaling mountains infested with giant auriach for years. What was *really* strange, though, was my encounter with the terannians."

"Indeed, Senesul," Vernikell says to him, "now that the medics have finally agreed we can question you, we need to know everything."

"A terannian found me after the auriachs attacked me. They have some sort of power over them - the auriach pod left when the terannian arrived. But there's more than that..."

"What do you mean?" asks Vernikell.

"I don't know how to explain it. It's nothing I have ever felt before. Something not part of my usual world. Look Ariael, I've been doing this job for a long time now, and I've travelled a lot more than most in VIAS, but never have I sensed something quite...so weird."

Knowing him as she does, Officer Dowola can tell how uncomfortable Rimikk must be feeling about recounting such a strange story. He continues on an easier subject, "The medics say that the dressing they used was full of biological chemicals that are similar to modern medicines but have come from forest plants. They want me to do some field work on this."

"Well, you've got some way to go before you are up to that," Vernikell chuckles.

"You got the DNA analysis okay?" Rimikk asks.

"Yes, we did," Vernikell replies. "Turns out there were some strange similarities to the genetic coding of a human that we retrieved from planet Earth when investigating an old crime."

"Do you mean the case of the scientist who broke the telepathy suppression virus?"

Vernikell nods. "We were following a lead to find Kandan Mikkrian. We've scoured his old files but we keep coming to dead ends. Whatever he did to cover his tracks, he hid it well. Anyway, there's been no trace of him for decades.

"We now have the human in custody. He seems to have absolutely no idea about what's going on. He goes by the name of Michael Redolfo and works as a taxi driver in Catuvell under the government work rehabilitation scheme."

"Well, I can't tell you if the terannians are telepathic or not. I never saw anything that would confirm that. They do seem to be an intensely spiritual people though. They seemed to be worshipping a god called Cernunnos. Have you ever heard of him?"

"No," replies the Baroness, "we have checked that and there's no record of this god on our history database."

"Another thing," Rimikk adds, "I was either drugged or delirious from my injuries, but before I passed out, I saw a most beautiful and ornate carving of a wheel."

Vernikell looks round to the Baroness, "The receptionist at the SDA described a wheel motif on the belt of the antlered attacker! All the pieces are coming together, but I've still got no idea what they mean. What do they want? We need more information, and we need it fast."

"I'm afraid I must ask you to leave Agent Rimikk to rest now," interrupts the young medic.

Vernikell stands up and gives Rimikk a friendly tap on the shoulder, to which he responds with a faux wince.

The visitors all turn to leave, but before she can rise, Rimikk takes hold of Officer Dowola's hand. She feels her heart skip a beat.

"Leiath," he says to her, "please, just before you go..."

"What is it, sir?"

"Thank you for coming to see me," he says, smiling at her.

"All of you, out, now!" the medic ushers them out of the room.

IT'S A SMALL UNIVERSE

"So how long are you gonna to keep me here for, Agent Vernikell?" Redolfo says to the Deputy Chief. It's the second day of his imprisonment and the featureless walls of the interrogation room are beginning to make the cabbie feel queasy. Professor Parchi and Officer Dowola study their electronic tablets.

Vernikell places his tablet on the desk. "Mr. Redolfo, there has been a new development in our investigations. It comes from a somewhat surprising source that we believe is fairly close to you. Can you imagine what that may be?"

The eyes of all three interrogators are on the cabbie. After a few seconds, an increasingly nervous Redolfo shrugs, "What the hell are you talking about?"

Vernikell addresses his communication device, "Please send the Baroness in with the witnesses."

The door opens. To Redolfo's astonishment, in walks the distinctive silver-bearded form of John Moorshead. The bar proprietor takes a seat. "Morning, Mike," he says smiling.

"What the hell's going on?"

"Please send in the other witness," Vernikell calls. In walks the Baroness followed by the beautiful form of Caryalla, who's uncharacteristically wearing a style of patterned fabric clothing favoured by many Vost civilians. Redolfo stands up.

"Calm down, Mr. Redolfo." Vernikell says to him, "We have a lot to talk about."

Redolfo returns to his seat.

Once all parties have settled around the table, Vernikell introduces the interrogation team. "Can our new witnesses confirm their identities. Let us start with you." Vernikell nods to Moorshead.

"I am John Moorshead, owner of the *Opprobrium Bar* on Main Square, Catuvell. It's also my home address."

"I am Caryalla. I have no other name, having been brought up in an orphanage. I am an itinerant craft designer by trade. I live in the Henwas building at 33 Precinct." She looks directly ahead, avoiding Moorshead's concerned gaze. "Now, can you tell me why I'm here?"

Vernikell addresses everyone in the room, "It came as a surprise to all of us that the owner of the *Opprobrium Bar* should approach us as a witness in this case. He insisted that Caryalla be present. He made it a condition that this interview will not be recorded and that he will be given immunity from prosecution for any historical crimes. I have honoured this wish. If I feel, however, that a recording should be made for the sake of planetary interest, then I shall reserve our privilege to record subsequent interrogation interviews."

Caryalla is now staring at Moorshead.

"Please, Mr. Moorshead, please begin your statement," Vernikell says gesturing to him.

Moorshead begins, "From the first moment I saw Mike, I felt some form of connection with him. I know you'll think that's because there are so few humans around, but it was more than that. There was something I recognised in him. Something familiar. It didn't finally click until your stormtroopers unceremoniously retrieved him from my bar. As you know, I'm from planet Earth. You'll have it on record that I was abducted by a renegade anthropological research scientist, but that's actually not the case. Thirty-nine years ago, I came to Vost voluntarily.

I was a lecturer in anthropological research at Cardiff University in a country on Earth called Wales."

The Baroness raises her eyebrows.

"One day, a man approached me at the end of a keynote lecture I had given on Celtic Mythology. He said he had been taking a keen interest in my work and said that he had an offer of work that he felt I couldn't refuse."

"What was this man's name?" asks the Baroness.

"He said his name was Dominik Kominsky and that he'd travelled all the way from a country called Czechoslovakia to meet me. I believe you know him as Kandan Mikkrian."

Vernikell stands abruptly. The Baroness holds his arm, pulling him back to his seat. "Just let him tell the story, Ariael."

"He tried to explain to me, unconvincingly at first, that he came from another planet, a planet with a supergiant sun and two moons. A planet called Vost. On Earth, in 1938, our insights into the existence of other worlds came largely from literature and partly from Space Operas screened in cinemas. I was an avid reader of H.G. Wells' science-fiction novels, but never particularly considered the actual existence of other worlds and civilizations in any way seriously.

"Given the enormity of space, it did seem probable that life could exist outside our Earth-centric notions of self-supremacy. I also did entertain that, if other intelligent life forms did exist, they would probably resemble humans, given that the humanoid form is a tried and tested evolutionary template for biological and technological success.

"This man, Dominik Kominsky, showed that he could shift his physical form in front of my very eyes. He demonstrated this by momentarily changing into what I later learnt to be a berrantine. Being a close resemblance to humans in physical form, the transformation to berrantine was a subtle one. He also demonstrated that he had the power to move things with his mind. It was this ability that finally convinced me that he was what he said he was. I'm sure you'll understand how astounded I was to see my fountain pen rise out of my inside pocket and float gently towards my right hand. It seems to be a human characteristic to view such physical *miracles* as defining answers to the otherwise inexplicable forces we observe in our lives."

Moorshead's audience look at each other in astonishment and then gaze back at the silver-haired storyteller.

"He explained that he was a scientist working on Vost. He said that his telepathic and telekinetic abilities were something he had engineered into his own genetic code. He explained that the Vost government had outlawed any mind-control activity and that the authorities had managed to bioengineer a virus that disrupted the genetic code that allowed telepathic species to use their abilities. He therefore used Earth as a platform to study his newfound powers. He convinced me to go with him to his planet. I was excited to have such a unique opportunity to use my expertise to further such incredible science. I was going to miss my job, but I had no personal reason to stay on Earth. "

~

A memory floods into Moorshead's mind.

A group of students gather around him at the base of the lecture theatre. "Professor, I can't believe you're leaving us," says one of them, sweeping his unruly hair off his face, his round wire glasses misted from tears.

Moorshead is overcome by guilt. He knows his students enjoyed the course. His lectures were regularly packed, and the ones on Celtic mythology were standing room only. He's going to miss them terribly.

Another memory.

"It's for the best," his wife says, as her solicitor hands him the divorce papers to sign.

He stares at the document, the words blurring as the pen trembles in his hand. It probably *was* for the best. Perhaps he deserves it, he has been spending most of his time at the university. Even so, she always seems to find fault with everything he does. As an only child, and both his parents now dead, he has never felt so alone.

~

"So, what has this got to do with your being here?" asks the Baroness, interrupting Moorshead's thoughts.

"Dominik said that his work involved using the DNA of an ancient species on Vost. He said that several native species from Vost used to have this power. He particularly focused on a species known as terannians. Dominik was good with people, an asset given the insular nature of terannians." Moorshead looks directly at Redolfo. "He had a certain way about him that made people take notice of his views. He managed to convince the terannians that his research was in their own interests as it could re-establish them as a telepathically active species, despite the presence of the Vost blocking virus. He actually told me that he had sympathies with the terannians, whom he felt had been subjugated unfairly by the invaders who arrived from other worlds about a century ago."

"Dominik told me that while he'd been successful at incorporating a telepathic ability into his own DNA, his power was fairly weak and would not work at all on his home planet. He said he intended to return to Vost after he'd increased its power and rendered it immune to the blocking viruses.

"So why did he choose Earth to further his research?" the Baroness asks.

"From his studies of Earth's history, he'd noticed some strange similarities between terannian heritage on Vost and ancient Celtic history and mythology on Earth. The style of terannian art he had seen in his travels to the Briganti mountains bore an uncanny resemblance to that of the Celts. Even some of the names in both histories were identical. He travelled to my planet to explore this connection further. His investigation eventually led him to a series of archaeological finds in a country on Earth known as Britain.

"Not only was the style of art on ancient British relics similar to terannian designs, but the depictions of the Celtic gods Herne, Cernunnos and Taranis closely resembled the appearance of the terannians themselves, as they all portrayed human-stag anthropomorphism."

"You've lost me," says Vernikell, scratching the back of his head.

"He means that the terannians closely resemble ancient Earth gods with human bodies, and heads that look like a forest-animal on Earth known as a stag," explains the Baroness. "Am I right, Mr. Moorshead?"

"Indeed, you are absolutely right, Baroness," Moorshead replies. "The physical appearances of these gods were always thought to have been a mystical combination of humans and stags - animals that would have represented the spirit of the forests to the ancient Celts."

"It's kind of weird," Redolfo cuts in, "that ever since I arrived here, I've been having dream after dream about stags."

"I don't believe that your dreams are a coincidence, Mike," replies Moorhead.

Professor Parchi sits glued to the discussion, "I am astounded," he says to Moorshead. "How can this link be possible?"

"Vernikell looks at the Baroness, "Febryalla, the story Senesul told us about his time in the Briganti Mountains!"

"Yes, I remember. The ceremony Agent Rimikk recorded seemed to show that they worship a god called Cernunnos."

"That is important, and I will come back to it," Moorshead replies. "When I arrived on Vost, I immediately started to research terannian anthropology.

Although I found Vost considerably more technologically advanced than Earth, there were many similarities - surprising similarities - but I think that discussion is for another time.

"I travelled with Dominik to the Briganti mountains. As I'm sure you know, it's a hazardous journey, and neither of us were in any way seasoned explorers. I often wonder how we actually made it there and back in one piece.

"I was bowled over when I first met the terannians. They're just like the images I had seen of Celtic gods - strong and intimidating. They're not a people to engage in much conversation but I found them to be a most spiritual people, with a sacred bond to the soil and their forest. They see the act of love as a most important link to the planet, their ancestors and to the universe itself - a bit like an entryway to a form of supreme power. They reminded me of the native peoples of a large continent on Earth called America."

"That's more or less what Mr. Redolfo said earlier," adds Vernikell.

"Terannians see vegetation, trees and animals as part of a cycle of existence that connects to the sun and Vost's two moons. What was particularly notable was the fact that they worship the ancient Earth god, Cernunnos, not really as a god, but for them, as an historical terannian."

Moorshead stands and begins to pace up and down the room. As if presenting a formal lecture, he continues addressing his transfixed audience, "We discovered a young terannian male, by the name of Tannis. He was unusually strong for his age and known for both his fiery temper and for his fiercely entrenched views about terannian rights. He was angry over the plight of his people. The terannians offered up this young fellow to assist in Dominik's research because he seemed to have retained some telepathic and telekinetic ability, where no other terannian in their living memory had done so.

"Tannis displayed considerable skill and power in his ability to move rocks and other objects with his mind. Because of his wild nature, however, he was often in trouble with the disapproving terannian elders. They were concerned that Tannis said he had the ability to control minds, and, worryingly, wanted to demonstrate this skill to his people. I know the terannians feared that this angry young boy living among them would one day wield inestimable power that they couldn't contain. However, his powers did not just engender fear, but also a considerable level of patriotic pride, and many saw Tannis as a mascot or even a champion of the terannian cause. The elders worried that he would encourage extremist elements within the community.

"Dominik organised a meeting for us with Tannis and the terannian elders and explained to them that something had evolved in the boy's natural makeup that made him immune to the blocking virus. He told them that by studying Tannis, his research could restore telepathy to all species that, by evolutionary rights, should have it.

"I saw Tannis approach Dominik and gaze closely into his eyes. The boy's eyes turned a deep red, and Dominik responded with a cry of pain, sweating and shaking. Blood appeared from Dominik's mouth. I was terrified - I thought that Tannis was killing him - but after about a minute, the boy's eyes reverted to their original black colour and Dominik staggered back and spent the next quarter of an hour recovering by sitting on a rock. Tannis told the elders that he knew Dominik's intentions were honest and that he was prepared to accompany him to his laboratories.

"Tannis returned with us to Catuvell and Dominik started his work immediately. Dominik put out feelers for anyone who thought they had telepathic powers who would like to participate in research. Given the government position on this, I thought it was a risky thing to do. I guess his eagerness to continue with his work got the better of him."

"Yes, indeed, Mr. Moorshead," Vernikell explains, "This was how the authorities found out what he was up to."

"Yes, this eagerness proved costly. Anyway, while Dominik was working on further genetic techniques, he was bombarded with people who imagined themselves as telepaths. Not one of them showed any demonstrable telepathic abilities at all."

"That sounds like a familiar story," says a sighing Caryalla, looking straight at a chuckling Redolfo, recalling her frequent digs at Danysus.

Moorshead continues, "It wasn't until after we heard a knock on the door, one morning, that we found a being that did have genuine powers. At the doorstep, there was a tiny baby in a crib. Whoever had left the child had clearly not wanted to be discovered. The baby was a little girl and in fine health. Next to her was a small artefact and a note. The artefact was a beautifully crafted miniature shield, made of a metallic material and resembling the finest specimens found in Celtic archaeology."

Caryalla looks down at her own belt.

"What was in the note?" asks Parchi.

Moorshead's expression changes. His voice takes on a softer tone. "The note said, 'This child is sciath. Her name is—'"

"It was Caryalla, wasn't it?" interjects Caryalla, looking blankly at the wall ahead of her.

"Yes, my dear...It was," he replies, as his eyes become moist with tears.

"Why didn't you ever tell me about this?"

"I'm sorry, Caryalla. I always felt it was something you never really needed to know. It was bad enough that you were abandoned soon after you were born. We felt a responsibility towards you, but we were not in a position to take on the role of your carers. We were academics, not foster parents. We thought that you'd be better off being looked after by the authorities. I assumed you'd been adopted and had a proper family. I didn't know that you'd stayed at the orphanage. I apologise. I hope you can forgive me."

Caryalla takes her shield emblem in her hands and studies it as if it were the first time she'd seen it. Tears begin to well in her eyes. "So, what is *sciath*?" she asks.

The Baroness responds, "We know a little about this species. They are an ancient people, as old as the terannians themselves. We believe they were locked in a continual war with the terannians. To the shame of our planet's history, the incoming species subjugated them viciously with systematic rape and murder. There was never a reservation made for them and there are now no recorded communities in existence anywhere on Vost."

"So," says Caryalla, tersely, "tell me, John. Tell me what my telepathic ability is all about, because I've never seen it."

Moorshead, who seems choked with remorse, is for a moment unable to speak. "The Baroness is entirely correct about what she said of the sciath-terannian wars. Courtesy of Tannis, who for a young man had a large source of knowledge about his people's history, we know that sciath and terannians evolved together. An evolution of war, if you like. They were both fierce and able physical fighters, and both had significant telepathic capabilities. In accordance with the evolutionary principles described by our own Earthly scientist, Charles Darwin, sciath evolved protections against terannian mind powers. The sciath have a passive ability to block telepathy and telekinesis, thereby levelling the advantages of their powerful enemies. Both sciath and terannians had become formidable in melee combat, as they needed to fall back on their physical skills to fight each other."

"That story sounds - like opposites in both conflict and harmony. I think humans call it *yin and yang* - in a way it's almost sexual," Vernikell adds.

"That is most observant of you, Deputy Chief. To the ancients, the processes of conflict, life, death and rebirth are all tied by a spiritual bond by a higher power or purpose. Even today, there are those on Earth who worship Cernunnos. They see him as the male counterpart to the Earth goddess, Gaia. They view the seasons on Earth as symbolic expressions of that bond of Cernunnos' birth, sexual union with Gaia, and his eventual death. He is reborn in spring. Yes, Deputy Chief, the active and passive forms of their relative telepathic abilities do indeed represent the perfect *fit* of the sexual act. An intense concentration of energy and power between individuals and even nations. This is something that humanity on Earth and all other species on Vost have lost, I fear never to be regained."

Moorshead gives Caryalla a kindly smile and says to her, "You may be interested to know that the word *sciath* in an ancient Earth Celtic dialect actually means *shield*.

"Dominik's work turned out to be a success. He integrated the viral-resistant genes into his own genetic code. He became able not only to move objects with his mind but could control people by implanting false memories and even sometimes to change a person's opinion. I volunteered to be his test subject. He promised me that he returned me perfectly to my original state, but then I could never be absolutely sure that he did."

Redolfo breaks the momentary silence, "Well that's a great story, John and I'm loving the big mind-power stuff and all that, but what's this got to do with me?"

Moorshead looks at him directly, "That's because, Dominik Kominsky is almost certainly your father."

"And how would you know that?" replies Redolfo.

"I recognise those same eyes, that same smile, that same way you stand around with your hands in your pockets, even the same way you go off in a daydream. Do you remember the first conversation we ever had when you told me why you were abducted? I had my suspicions then that VIAS was still after Dominik. Your story about being mistaken for a renegade hiding on Earth fitted."

Redolfo shakes his head in disbelief. He replies, "But my father is Alfonso Redolfo. He's been part of my whole life. My mother never told me there was a different father. Anyhows, I sure as hell look nothing like those brantime guys."

"Berrantine." Vernikell corrects him.

Moorshead continues, "Mike, I really don't know what happened to Dominik after he went on the run from VIAS. He knew they were onto him, so he destroyed every trace of his work and fled to Earth. I suspect he would have returned to Czechoslovakia, but that's just a guess. It was where he first landed, and I know there was a woman he'd fallen for there. When I left Earth, something really awful was happening in Germany with the rise of Hitler's National Socialist Party."

"You missed the goddamn Second World War." replies Redolfo. "Millions of people around the world died. You missed the murder of twelve million people in concentration camps, six million of them Jews."

Moorshead's jaw drops.

"It would seem it is not only Vost that has a dark past," Vernikell says, "but we need to stay on track here. I suggest you fill Mr. Moorshead in with the details later over a drink in his bar."

"So, I'm free to go?" Redolfo asks eagerly.

"Soon. We have a crisis on our hands, and I need Mr. Moorshead's help. Given Professor Mikkrian hard-wired telepathic abilities into his genetic material, I would like to know whether this can be passed down to the children."

Moorshead responds, "Dominik always maintained it could."

All eyes are on Redolfo.

"Hell, I've never had any special powers. Are you sure you have the right man?"

"You tell *us*, Mike," says Moorshead.

Redolfo scratches his head, "I'm a good driver, so big deal. I can anticipate people on the road. Isn't that kind of normal anyway?"

"I never saw your great driving," Caryalla responds. "Unless...Unless it was me that stopped you. You kept saying while you were driving us in your crazy yellow transporter, that you didn't know what was wrong."

"Yeah, it was the only time I ever needed to activate the CEWS." Redolfo replies.

Vernikell frowns, "You should always activate your CEWS, Mr. Redolfo. Statistics show that most accidents can be prevented—"

"Do you feel you can read people generally?" Moorshead cuts in.

"Well, yeah, I think I can. It drives people crazy and gets me into trouble a lot of the time. Yeah, it's true. When Caryalla got out of the car, I was fine to drive again."

"So, it wasn't that I was making you nervous?" Caryalla winks at him.

"Okay," says Vernikell placing a cup in the centre of the table. "Let's see if you can make this move, Mr. Redolfo. Capell, can you confirm this is definitely not being recorded?"

"It's fine," Parchi responds.

"There's no way." says Redolfo, dismissing the notion with a wave of his hands, "I have absolutely no idea how to do that. I really think you've got the wrong guy."

"Focus your mind, Mike. Channel your energy into it," says Moorshead.

Feeling pretty stupid, Redolfo looks intently at the cup. Nothing. "You're all nuts!"

"Ah, we're doing this wrong. We're forgetting that we are in presence of Caryalla," Moorshead reminds them all.

"Okay," continues Vernikell, "this is all very interesting, but we must keep focus and move on from here. The question that remains is whether the attacker at the SDA was actually Tannis. I suspect that this is the case."

The Baroness adds, "The description of the wheel on the assailant's belt is compelling. Do you know anything about this wheel, Mr. Moorshead?"

"From our own Celtic mythology, the god Taranis is the personification of thunder. His images are often depicted with a wheel and thunderbolt. We believe the wheel is a symbolic representation of the Sun. It's possible that Tannis himself is named after this deity."

"One huge question remains here," replies the Baroness. "How can there possibly be such a strong link to Earth mythology?"

"Dominik and I had thought about this very question for a long time, and we believed we had worked out the answer."

There is a steady knock on the interview room door. The door is opened, and Vernikell tries his very best not to thump the table in frustration as the embodiment of the most unwelcome intrusion to the meeting enters the room.

"Good day to you all." Sellibot Spaan addresses the unfamiliar faces in the room. He adjusts his ostentatious robes and takes a seat at the interrogation end of the table.

AN HONEST BROKER

November 3rd, 1944

It is a meeting that the Swiss politician, Dr Jean-Marie Musy wouldn't in his wildest dreams have expected to have with his friend, Heinrich Himmler. He'd first met Himmler over ten years ago, when a younger Musy was a publisher for the pro-German newspaper, La Jeune Suisse. Musy was a Nazi sympathiser in his earlier life - there is no getting around that. He used to think the Jews were just too powerful and too influential to go unchecked. An answer to the Jewish question was needed and the Nazis seemed, after all, on the right track.

Even Musy cannot fully get his own head around this. What was it that changed his mind, enough for him to decide to put a stop to his beloved newspaper? Maybe it was his Catholicism that eventually brought him to realise that the Nazis are in fact a murderous group of criminals intent on world domination. He feels confident he's managed to keep his change of heart a secret from Himmler.

What is he doing here on this German military train from Breslau to Vienna with his old friend, now the Reichsführer of Nazi Germany? He, the former president of the Swiss Confederation, is now about to embark on a fool's mission to convince the world's most prolific mass murderer to halt the extermination of Jews. How can he possibly stop Himmler, a man so utterly motivated towards the creation of a Jew-free utopia, from carrying out Hitler's direct orders to implement the last phase of the Final Solution - the extermination of all the remaining Jews in Nazi concentration camps?

He reflects that it was through a series of connections within the Swiss diplomatic community that he had met a man called Reuben Hecht. Hecht, insistent and resourceful, is an active member of the paramilitary Zionist movement known as Irgun. This Jewish activist had used his influence to persuade a series of intermediaries in the American and Swiss diplomatic communities to embrace Zionism, eventually bringing him into contact with Musy himself barely two months ago. This charismatic man, the son of a shipping magnate, had organised the rescue of many Jews trapped in Nazi occupied Europe and settled them secretly within the British Mandate for Palestine. He considered that as Musy was a Roman Catholic and a fierce critic of communism, he might just be able to influence his old friend, Himmler.

Musy enters the train carriage. "Heil Hitler!" he says, addressing the Reichsführer with an extended right arm. Himmler returns the salute.

"Good morning, Jean-Marie."

"Thank you so much for agreeing to meet me, Heinrich."

"It's been a while since I've seen you. How can I be of help?" Himmler says, adjusting his pince-nez spectacles. "Your message said it was an important matter."

"Heinrich, I hope you know I speak to you as a friend. I know how much Germany is in need of medicines, supply vehicles and munitions."

Himmler looks at him suspiciously.

Musy continues, "There's talk in the diplomatic circles that Germany's war is not going well."

"Tell me what it is you want, Jean-Marie," he replies, tersely.

Musy's pulse-rate rises. He realises there is no other way but to ask the question up front. He does his best to appear to speak through concern for his friend, "Heinrich, I believe that if Germany loses the war, the allies will not take too kindly to anyone they believe has been complicit in the extermination of millions of people in death camps."

To Musy's surprise, Himmler starts to nod in agreement. "I agree, they would not take too kindly to us at all in this hypothetical eventuality. So, what do you propose?"

"I know you've ordered the extermination of the remaining eight-hundred-thousand Jews in death camps. I propose that you immediately rescind this command and allow the safe passage of Jews from the camps into Switzerland and into the care of the International Red Cross."

Musy sees Himmler is paused in thought. How ridiculous this whole idea is, the diplomat thinks, beginning to regret his involvement in Hecht's insane plan. What on earth was I thinking? Himmler must think I've completely lost my mind. How would such a man ever agree to this suggestion? He feels his chest tighten.

After a prolonged and suffocating silence, the Reichsführer stares straight into Musy's eyes and replies, "I will tell you the terms of this agreement, Jean-Marie. Firstly, you will promise to transfer five million Swiss Francs directly to our party's accounts. Secondly, you will secure an agreement with the American army that the concentration camp guards will be given the same treatment afforded to regular soldiers and therefore be subject to trial at a military court and not shot on the spot like dogs."

Musy, surprised, and feeling relieved replies, "Perhaps this can be arranged, Heinrich, but whether or not they are treated as soldiers at the point of arrest, and whether or not they wear camp uniforms or the uniforms of soldiers, they will likely be tried for war crimes."

Musy watches as the Reichsführer stares into space while muttering something inaudible. The diplomat leans forward and places his ear near Himmler's mouth. The voice is faint, but he can just make out the words, "…honest broker".

NOTHING IS EVER STRAIGHTFORWARD

"What an interesting interrogation you seem to be conducting, Deputy Deputy Chief Vernikell," Spaan drawls with a tone of extravagant irony. "I would be most interested to read the transcripts." He looks around the room. "Oh, it appears you've not been recording it. I wonder why that would be?"

The Baroness stands, "May I introduce the Most Holy Reverend, Sellibot Spaan, *Chief Protector of Faith* and President of the *United Faiths of Vost*."

Spaan acknowledges this introduction without smiling. "Please don't let me interrupt anything. I thought you may all welcome some spiritual guidance into this interrogation. You may also like to know the *Holy Council* is to meet tomorrow to discuss the ethical and spiritual implications of your proposal, Deputy Chief of Staff."

"That is enormously kind of them to put themselves out like this for the sake of the safety of the planet," Vernikell responds with barely disguised sarcasm. "Let's hope the timing of your meeting isn't incompatible with our preventing a future planetary cataclysm."

The Baroness glares at Vernikell.

Spaan continues unperturbed, "So tell me what it is that has been such a secret that you chose not to record the interrogation?"

"We have only just begun the session, Most Holy Reverend, but you are more than welcome to stay with us for the duration of the interrogation," the Baroness replies.

Spaan looks directly at Vernikell, "I am sure you had your reasons, but I would like to point out how non-recording of interrogations is contrary to the inviolable rules of the Convention of Trinova. I know you've all been here for the last twenty minutes at least. I'm sure you'll all agree that it's in the interests of Vost that this anomaly is reported to the VIAS *Council of Standards*. Of course, it would be up to them to consider whether this incident requires investigation. It would not be the first time that a mass replacement of senior staff has been instigated by the *Holy Council*."

Spaan looks at Moorshead. "Tell me sir, may I respectfully inquire as to whom you are?"

"John Moorshead, Most Holy Reverend. I am here acting as a witness for Mr. Redolfo."

"Lovely thing, just lovely," Spaan says while studying Caryalla, who winces in disgust at his leering eyes. "This seems to be a most unusual case, Deputy Chief of Staff. Let us take it from the beginning."

The tension in the room is interrupted by a klaxon. A tannoy resonates with the sound of Officer Dowola's voice, "Deputy Chief of Staff and Chief of Science, we need you in the VIAS control room urgently."

Vernikell stands, "My apologies to you all. We'll need to adjourn this interrogation for the time being. Capell, you're with me."

Spaan looks at Vernikell through narrowed eyes, "How convenient for you. Almost too convenient. Let us hope that the urgency of this call merits the interruption of this meeting."

Vernikell gives Spaan a brief nod and opens the exit door. He orders the guards to accompany the witnesses to the waiting lounge. He and Parchi proceed to the VIAS central control room, where Officer Dowola greets them.

"Thank you Leiath. You'll never know how welcome your announcement was to us all."

"I knew there'd be trouble, sir, the moment I heard that Spaan was heading to the interrogation room." She smiles at Vernikell and adds, "Our sensors picked up a sigma 5-anomaly, which could mean the modulator shell device has been activated."

Vernikell replies, "But don't such anomaly alerts happen all the time?"

"Indeed, sir," she smiles back at him, "but, given what has happened, we can't be too careful."

"Indeed, we can't."

SOMETHING CLOSE TO LIBERATION

Marianna collapses into her seat, exhausted. She's been working non-stop for sixteen hours and knows she'll not have much time to sleep. She's had a lot of time to think about her life and the lives of the people around her and still can't fathom how and why she, alongside hundreds of other prisoners, have been released into a new life of relative safety.

What on earth is Himmler playing at? Known for his mass deportations and likely murder of hundreds of thousands of *sub-humans*, he has inexplicably allowed hundreds of Jewish prisoners to escape to Switzerland. Was this Dominik's doing? Why does she have such a strong feeling this is all down to him? Why else would Himmler behave in this way? Is Germany losing the war? Is this to show what a compassionate human being Himmler is to the allies, should he and his family be arrested? That itself is a notion beyond the ridiculous.

The reality is that they are all now working in Swiss labour camps. At least they are alive and as far as anyone could tell, no longer under threat of deportation for slaughter to Auschwitz-Birkenau.

Marianna examines her fingers, swollen and blistered from the constant weaving of threads to produce fabric for the Swiss military uniforms. She has heard the stories of other workers. They speak of the Swiss labour camp authorities, who probably feel it's in their own interests that the refugees should contribute useful work for an impoverished Switzerland. Marianna understands they work closely with the Jewish organisation, ORT, to help Jewish refugees develop useful skills.

She's picked up the technique of weaving the threads quickly. In truth, Marianna welcomes the long working hours - anything to stop her focusing her mind on how she will never again feel the loving warmth of Dominik's arms. Food is always scarce. In some ways, she almost welcomes the distraction of the pains of hunger. At least she seems to have enough food for the baby. She looks down at her tummy. Her pregnancy is now obvious.

"This is what we made together, my love," she whispers to herself as she feels the sharp pang of her loss with every kick of her unborn child's little feet. "Dominik," she whispers to herself, "why is it that I can feel you so strongly when I am not occupied in my work? Are you really here within me, somewhere inside me? I know you did something to me with your mind. I know you only meant well for me. I know you wanted to make sure I wouldn't lose you forever, and I welcomed it. If you are able to hear me, I want you to know, that I wanted it and would do it again if I had the choice. Are you really here with me? You make me feel so warm inside. I feel your kindness now. I feel more than that. I feel you touching me..."

Marianna's pulse quickens as she makes a sharp gasp. At once it is over, and she breaks down into uncontrollable tears.

WHEN YOU HAVE THE WORLD IN YOUR HANDS

At least the relative comfort of the VIAS waiting lounge is preferable to the unpleasantness of the cells. Redolfo looks across to Caryalla and Moorshead and says, "John, this upside-down world is driving me crazy."

"How do you think I feel?" says Caryalla glaring at the barman. "All this time you hid my identity from me!"

Moorshead's eyes are downcast. He's looking genuinely sorry. "My dear, you have to understand I was never cut out to be your carer or guardian. At that time, we felt we had no choice but to hand you over to the orphanage. We knew your telepathic powers would never pose a threat to anyone, so no one needed to know about them. After you went to the orphanage, I didn't meet you again until you were all grown up and happened to be hanging out in my bar with your friends. I wasn't sure it was in your best interests to drag up your past. You seemed so well adjusted; I didn't want to risk that."

"Look John, I won't be angry with you forever, because I know you're a good man. I do however feel that now I finally know a little more about myself, my heritage has actually been taken away from me - and by the ancestors of so many of the people of Vost. It turns out I've a greater right to live here than they ever had."

Moorshead nods, "Yes, Mike was right to compare your ancestral history to the stories of several nations on

Earth. The desire to subjugate seems a universal constant for intelligent species throughout the universe. I suspect that one day, Vost will again be invaded by an even more advanced species, and the cycle of control and conquest will continue."

The lounge door opens and in walks Vernikell followed by Parchi, the Baroness and Officer Dowola. They all sit down.

"Look, Mr. Redolfo," says Vernikell, "I have absolutely no intention of keeping you any longer than is necessary. Before I let you go however, we do need to clear up a few things. I believe we on Vost are on the brink of something potentially quite catastrophic. Whoever is attacking our installations has appropriated an extremely powerful device that can effectively shut down much of our technology within a perimeter of several hundred miles."

Redolfo feels his gut tighten, realising that his recent mission with Sarokis may have had something to do with this.

Vernikell continues, "So far, we simply don't know what it is they are planning. We do know, however, that they are highly professional and extremely effective in how they operate. I believe that whatever they want somehow relates to Tannis, and I respectfully request that if any of you know any information that could be helpful to us that you tell us immediately. Mr. Redolfo, is there something you want to say?"

"Er...no, I was just moving to get more comfortable in this hard seat."

"Deputy Chief," says Moorshead, "is everything okay with that holy chap?"

"Don't worry too much about him," Vernikell replies, "We have a potential crisis on our hands, and that must be prioritised."

The Baroness looks first at Redolfo and then at Moorshead and says, "While Tannis represents just one man, his telepathic and telekinetic skills will make him powerful. We have no idea how powerful he is, and we desperately need more information."

Moorshead replies, "He was only a boy when I knew him. He was powerful then but I suppose he'll have grown stronger by honing his skills over the years. He's also likely to be formidable in combat, whether using weapons, or even in hand-to-hand fighting. The terannians view martial arts as part of their spiritual connection to Vost."

"Mr. Moorshead," says Vernikell, "You were about to explain why there seems to be an uncanny resemblance of terannian history to Earth's ancient Celtic mythology."

"Yes, Deputy Chief, Celtic mythology has a strong and compelling connection to this planet. I have also noticed that even the place names have links to ancient Britain. I believe that in millennia past, there was indeed a terannian called Cernunnos - a terannian whose telepathic and telekinetic abilities far exceeded those of any before him or since. You could imagine how the many generations since Cernunnos would see such a figure with god-like powers as being close to the very soul of the planet. What your field agent discovered in the Briganti Mountains was likely to have been an invocation ceremony of their ancestral champion. I also believe that Tannis himself carries some of the genetic heritage of Cernunnos, so powerful that his telepathic abilities are not fully suppressed by the viral blocker."

"So how can you possibly link this to Earth's history?" Parchi is shaking his head and frowning as if trying to fathom the enormity of what is unfolding.

Moorshead continues, "Dominik found that when using his telepathic abilities, he was able to enter the minds of others by projecting his thoughts across short distances. He tried to explain the science behind it to me, although most of it went over my head. He spoke of the theoretical possibility of using the power of the mind to scale the complexities of inter-dimensional space and thereby be able to traverse vast distances across the universe in just an instant. Frustratingly, he had insufficient time to put his theories to the test and, as you already know, he fled from Vost."

Parchi is animated. He says with his thin and aging voice, "I would have to agree that this kind of ability is theoretically possible. We utilise inter-dimensional probing technology to retrieve messages and radio signals from other planets in nearby systems in real time. If we waited for electromagnetic waves to reach us naturally, it would take hundreds or even thousands of years to receive them, and the signals would be extremely faint and difficult to pick up in detail. It seems incredible to think that nature itself may have evolved such inter-dimensional technology thousands of years before we did. It's at times like this when I miss my old friend, Zanusso. His insightful genius would have been invaluable here." Parchi's tremulous voice strengthens, "Yes, Mr. Moorshead, you are about to tell us that Cernunnos visited the people of Earth, several thousand years ago."

Moorshead looks straight back at Parchi, "Indeed, professor, he almost certainly did. He would have appeared as an antlered being to the ancient Britons as an apparition in the woodland, half stag, half man. They will have felt his power in all its glory, both physical, and of the mind. You can imagine them bowing down in reverence to such a god-like being - a creature that could wield such potent power using his mind alone. To them, he would have appeared as a god. In fact, he became one of their gods. His influence on the ancient people of Earth was to be profound."

Moorshead glares straight at Vernikell. With his voice raised, he thumps the table and says, "I believe the events that have led up to this point now confirm this theory, which was proposed by the great scientist and my best friend, Kandan Mikkrian, whom you and your establishment hounded off this planet and pursue to this very day!"

Vernikell responds, "Mr. Moorshead, I entirely understand your frustrations at the way our government's laws are enacted and I have always maintained that we are a world bound far too heavily to bureaucratic processes. A world government is as inflexible as it is subject to corruption, with decision and law-making made by the unaccountable few who grasp the levers of power. As close as I am to the top, I am not blind to the endless abuses and inefficiencies of the systems that command and control the planet. However, we now have a crisis to attend to and we all need to stay calm."

"What gives the telepath power?" All eyes are on Redolfo who has asked the question.

"I'm sorry," Moorshead answers with a frown, "what exactly do you mean?"

"I mean like a car needs gas, a sailing ship needs wind, a guy needs food..."

"That is a question I have never thought of," says Moorshead. "Professor, what do you think the answer is here?"

Parchi scratches his chin, "Well, we all derive energy from food, which ultimately is generated by the sun. However, to generate the energy required to be able to move objects through space or even negotiate inter-dimensional space using the power of thought alone, would far exceed the energy available from mere food. It is indeed a very good question, Mr. Redolfo. Why did you think of it?"

"Because I think I know the answer," he replies. "I've felt it."

"Felt what?" asks Parchi.

"I felt it as I ran through the woods."

"What do you mean?" asks Caryalla, wide-eyed with curiosity.

"Maybe it was just a dream, maybe it wasn't, but I felt it. I felt its power. I was a stag, or at least I think I was. I could feel energy from the woodland fill me. I felt so strong, so powerful - I felt I could do almost anything."

Moorshead responds, "There is a mythological idea that Cernunnos derives his energy from the spirit of the woodland."

"I know that feeling," replies Vernikell, "I'm sure I've felt it when on field work. I even mentioned it to Rimikk once who simply laughed and said something about how too many people harboured such silly ideas."

"Yes," says Caryalla, "I do know what Mike means. I'm sure I've felt that energy too."

The Baroness cuts in, "Mr. Redolfo—"

"Hey, Ma'am, please call me Mike."

"Okay, Mike," the Baroness says with a warm smile, "You have now told us about your intuition, your ability to read people and your experience with energy from the woodland. Have you ever been able to move objects with your mind, even perhaps in hindsight, now you know the truth behind your genetic make-up?"

"I've never been able to do anything like that, ma'am."

"How about being able to influence people in a way that surprised you?"

"That's kinda difficult to say, but I think no."

The Baroness stands up, " Mike, I suggest we try to get you to awaken some abilities. I'm really sorry, Caryalla, but we are going to have to ask you to leave the room. Officer Dowola will escort you to the canteen area just for ten minutes or so."

Caryalla nods and exits the room with Officer Dowola. She gives Redolfo an almost imperceptible wink as she leaves.

Gah! Redolfo remarks to himself, *how that girl gets to me.*

"Okay," the Baroness says as she gestures to Moorshead, who then reaches for his inside pocket and hands her his fountain pen. She places it on the table. She now addresses Redolfo, "Try now to concentrate. I want you to lift this pen from the table without touching it."

The cabbie slumps lazily into his seat with his hands in his pockets and stares at an unmoving fountain pen on the table.

"Sorry to disappoint you, folks. Isn't this all against your rules anyway?"

"Concentrate, man!" Moorshead shouts at him and thumps repeatedly on the table. "You've been taken to a planet against your will, you've been arrested for simply being yourself, you've found out your father is not your biological father, there's no real prospect of you ever returning to Earth - so get angry, for heaven's sake."

Redolfo's eyes begin to glaze as he descends deep into thought. His mind begins to cloud, then to whirl. Soldiers. Crowds. Yellow stars. Beatings. Shop windows are being smashed. Thousands of voices shouting, 'Sieg Heil! Sieg Heil! Sieg Heil!'. A uniformed man. His face, wracked in pain and confusion. The man is resisting it. He is strong but not strong enough. Every instinct burning to hurt him. Hurt his mind. No, destroy his mind.

~

"Oh look!" shouts a startled Baroness as she sees Redolfo's eyes have turned flame red. He is shaking and sweating.

With frightening speed, the pen has lifted from the table and spun off like a bullet to embed deeply into the wall. The table begins to shake violently, and cracks appear in the walls of the lounge. The room itself begins to move and shake on its very foundations.

"Okay Mike, you can stop now!" Moorshead shouts.

Redolfo is on his feet and screams, "Sieg Heil! Sieg Heil! Sieg Heil!" He stares at Parchi who elevates out of his seat and suspends in mid-air.

"Get Caryalla here, now!" orders Moorshead to Vernikell.

Vernikell shouts to Officer Dowola through his comms.

"You murdering sons of bitches!" Redolfo shrieks at the top of his voice and points an angry finger at a picture on the wall. The picture fragments into thousands of shattered pieces. The rumbling sounds from the shaking building structure become thunderous. Cracks appear in the ceiling and threaten to rain down lethal chunks of masonry. Parchi remains suspended in mid-air, his limbs flailing in fear. Everyone else in the room, save for a red-eyed and angry Redolfo, is holding on to the table in panic.

The door flings open, and Caryalla appears with Officer Dowola.

"What's going on?" Caryalla says in surprise as she sees, amidst the loud creaks of twisting support girders, the room crumbling into what looks like a demolition zone. "Mike!" she cries running over to him. She flings her arms around him and caresses his head. "Mike." She holds his head in her hands. "Please, don't do this. Look at me."

His eyes darken and the room stops shaking. The terrified form of Parchi is lowered back into his seat.

Redolfo's eyes moisten. "Caryalla, I'm so sorry. I felt my father's anger - his pain and his fear. I felt what he went through. I lost control."

Caryalla looks into his eyes and wipes his wet cheeks. She takes his trembling hands into her own and draws him close to hug him. "It's okay, Mike, I'm here. It's over."

THE PERSUASIVE PROCESS

"How far do you trust him?" Sarokis asks.

"Zanusso does not have the mind of ordinary people," Tannis replies as he watches the sallow scientist who is deeply engaged in calculations at the make-shift terminal. "I can only penetrate it so far. I can feel his pain as he resists me - so much pain and fear, I don't know how he can withstand it. Yet still, he defies me. I do believe he's carrying out my orders, but I can't help but feel he's hiding something."

"I'm close to finishing the modification process on the modulator shell, Lord Tannis," Zanusso's voice screeches with stress.

Tannis growls back at him, "I've already told you not to refer to me by the titles used by the occupying species. I've no interest in such foolish formalities. What I do want to know is whether we will have full control of the Ephysus Particle Transmitters."

"Sir, the modulator shell wasn't set up for blocking the antigravity technology of Temeria engines, but to block the weaponry and communicational abilities of an invading species. I can, and will, alter it, but it may be a piecemeal process."

"Tell me the instant it goes online. My patience is short and we're running out of time." Tannis turns and exits the laboratory, leaving the fearful trail of his presence in the minds of both Zanusso and Sarokis.

A NEW WORLD IN A NEW WORLD

"Try this, Mike, it's the nearest thing there is to coffee on this planet," Moorshead says, as he serves steaming hot drinks to Redolfo, Caryalla, Amitaab and Danysus in the *Opprobrium Bar*. "I'll need to open up soon for the morning trade." He sees the cabbie is looking down with his head in his hands.

"I'm worried about Vernikell," Redolfo says without looking up. "He's never gonna explain away the damage I did to the building. He's gonna be in serious trouble."

"Yes, I'm worried too," agrees Moorshead. "He's a good man. I can't see how he'll recover from this."

Redolfo looks even more troubled.

"What are you going to do now you know about your abilities?" says Caryalla, changing the subject.

"I really don't know. I lost it pretty bad back there."

Amitaab stands up and waves his hands in the air, "Well, just a moment, people! We have a powerful telepath dude right here, I mean right here, in our bar! You're one of a kind. I mean, awesome power, right?" He makes a gesture that somehow does seem to resemble power, at least in his own peculiar way. "The world is yours, Mike. See where it takes you."

Redolfo doesn't react.

"I can't believe what you told me about what happened on Earth, Mike." says Moorshead, seeing the wisdom in diverting the topic of conversation for a second time. "Of all humanity's dark past, I think this must top it all. So, the Great War, which you call the First World War, wasn't destructive enough! Let me get this right - by the end of what's known as the Second World War, in 1945, twelve million people were exterminated in concentration camps and about eighty million dead around the world including twenty million dead Russians - and all because, as you put it, Adolf Hitler was *up his own ass*!"

Redolfo looks up and replies "Yep, that's about right."

"So, why were you shouting the Nazi salute, 'Sieg Heil', in the VIAS lounge?"

"Yeah, it's kinda crazy, but it's like I remembered something. Maybe it wasn't my memory. Maybe it was my pa's. I mean my real pa. I felt as if I was in another country. I felt his fear."

Moorshead watches Caryalla looking at Redolfo with concern.

"Anyway, I need to start work. I've got to earn a living here," says the cabbie as he stands up.

"Come back here after work, Mike?" says Caryalla. "We can make things seem clearer with a special John Moorshead cocktail."

Redolfo gets up and walks to the door, his head hanging low, "Thanks for the offer, but I'm gonna be busy this evening. Got a call from a friend who needs some help." In an instant, he's gone.

"I'm worried about him," Caryalla says to Moorshead.

Danysus looks at Moorshead and then to Caryalla, "He seems to have something on his mind. Is he in some sort of trouble?"

"I've been concerned about him too," says Moorshead, "it wouldn't be a bad idea to check on him."

IT'S NOT EASY TO DO THE RIGHT THING

Hostian enters the *Central Operations Room*. It's buzzing with activity, as dozens of stressed technicians each pore over the strings of data on their screens. Officer Dowola is tapping at one of the many monitors at her control station. She raises the optical enhancement hood off her face and looks around towards him as he approaches her. "General, there's been a significant development. We've just detected an unusual broadcast."

"What do you mean, unusual?" Hostian booms.

"It lasted just a nanosecond. Our sensors only picked up on it because of its archaic carrier tag. I can't work out its source."

"Well, what is it?"

"It doesn't make any sense, Sir but I think it's important. Could I please involve Deputy Deputy Chief Vernikell?"

He shakes his head. "Officer Dowola, Ariael is currently under investigation for not only conducting an interview without recording it but also for the mysterious destruction of the VIAS waiting lounge and the damage done to the surrounding building structure. He's been taken off the case and is currently in a cell."

"I'm sorry, sir, but I don't think that's entirely wise at the moment. I'm now receiving information about a large number of terannians that have boarded hundreds of old cargo transporters from Briganti. The destination is unknown, but they are heading in the direction of Catuvell."

"There's no law against travel." Hostian replies.

"Yes, sir, but we're talking about a mass movement of the most secretive and insular people on the planet. This is the first time in over a hundred years that terannians have been known to venture out from their reservation in the Briganti mountains. I really think you should summon Deputy Deputy Chief Vernikell, Baroness Ner-all and Professor Parchi here. They've been at the forefront of the investigation and, with respect, we desperately need all the help we can get."

"Look, Leiath, off the record, I do agree with you, and I will send for them. However, Sellibot Spaan knows as much as I do about the events in the lounge and is personally heading the inquiry into it. If he gets wind of any of this, he has the power to impeach me."

"I'm sorry, sir, but under the circumstances—"

He takes out a handkerchief from one of the canisters on his bulky utility belt and wipes his brow. He takes a sharp intake of breath, "It's okay, Leiath, I know very well what's at stake. So, tell me what you think this broadcast's about?"

VICTORY IN EUROPE

May 8th, 1945

Marianna hears shouting. Excited screams of joy. She stops her weaving. The people on the factory floor are on their feet.

"Marianna! Marianna!" her gaunt friend from the factory, Sara, shouts excitedly as she runs towards her, "The Germans have surrendered. The war's over." They clutch each other, sobbing tears of joy.

Marianna looks around at the excited factory workers. They are hugging and kissing each other as if they have never been so happy. She is led out onto the street where great crowds have gathered. People are dancing in the middle of the road. Cars and trucks have stopped, and their drivers have stepped out to join the celebration.

Dominik, can you see this? The war is finally over. Just listen to everyone singing. How I miss you. If only you were here with me. Our child will arrive soon and will hopefully be born into a better world than you ever saw on Earth. How you must have despaired of humanity. How did you come to love a human when you know what we're capable of doing to one another?

"Marianna!" Sara has caught up with her outside the factory building, "You can return to Czechoslovakia. I'm so pleased for you. Your baby can be born in Prague. You'll be a free and wonderful mother."

She holds her swollen belly. "No, Sara, I have no one to go back to. Almost everyone I ever knew in Prague will be dead. I need to make a new life for myself somewhere else."

"But where will you go?"

"I don't know, Sara. Somewhere my child and I can be free. Somewhere I'll feel wanted and useful. Maybe I can get work as a chemistry technician. I never want to weave another thread ever again."

ALWAYS KNOW WHOM YOU'RE REALLY WORKING FOR

So, Alfonso Redolfo wasn't his real pa. Alfonso certainly treated him as his own son. As far as Redolfo is concerned, he's the proud son of a Brooklyn cabbie, who'd shown him nothing but love and support throughout his life. His mother never once mentioned it. Did she even know about Dominik Kominsky's abilities? Did she simply choose never to talk about it? Did she keep it a secret to protect him from becoming some sort of freak, to be laughed at and experimented on? Redolfo feels a pit open in his stomach, realising he'll never see his parents again, let alone have a chance to ask them about his family history.

He emerges from his Checker. The *Lucky Day Cabs* waving-hand emblem hisses down flat to the roof. He's parked it in the same disused industrial site where he met up with Sarokis and his deadly green-eyed minions for his first job for them. What did Sarokis want from him this time? He'd been lucky to have survived the last heist – he'd avoided being either arrested by the authorities or worse, vaporised, and only because of the intuition and guile he'd inherited from his father.

He senses the approach of Sarokis, an experience unpleasant enough in itself - but there's something more - something even more dangerous associated with this seasoned killer. Redolfo has rarely felt such a deep sense of fear in his lifetime. He's always been able to skirt trouble, even in the worst streets in Brooklyn. It's his intuition - a power he's harboured all his life, locked somewhere within him. Then again, it's not just intuition. It's a power far beyond the raw physical - the ability to move things using the mind alone. Yet, even more powerful than that, somewhere within him, he may be able to influence the way people can think. Should he use it on Sarokis? He feels somehow that this will not be the right time for that. Why does he feel so scared?

Sarokis appears. "Mr. Redolfo, thank you for coming."

"You've got another job for me, Sarokis?"

The mercenary does not answer immediately and instead eyes Redolfo suspiciously. "Remember when you asked who the boss is? Well, he wants to see you."

"What's going on, Sarokis? I've done what you've asked of me."

"I thought seeing the boss was what you wanted?" he replies with a smile that seems anything but reassuring.

Redolfo's head begins pounding. He can feel the approach of an intense presence - a being of immense strength. The footsteps are heavy yet measured. He can see him. His huge form. Muscular. Antlers. The head of a stag. The stabbing realisation that he knows exactly who the boss is.

"So, this is the human you've told me so much about." Tannis says, staring at the cabbie. "Extraordinary driving talent - I have a lot to thank you for."

He knows this is no thanking ceremony. Tannis studies him like a predator deciding which part of its kill it will devour first. Redolfo can feel his heavy breath on his shoulder.

"I know you know who I am, human - but how can that possibly be? Have we met before? I don't think so. So, tell me, how can you possibly know my identity?"

Redolfo does all he can to resist the urge to panic.

"You see, the problem is that you're not a man to be quiet for long. You have an unfortunate habit of getting noticed - and that's not a good thing - when all the while I want you *not* to be noticed."

Redolfo's jaw begins trembling as he realises, he can no longer conceal his terror from this being. "What do you want from me? I've served you well."

Tannis leers down towards the shaking cabbie. "So, this is your idea of serving me? You were arrested and interrogated by VIAS only to be released days later. You see, human, this is of a particular concern for me."

He feels Tannis' eyes burn into him. "Look, I never told them anything about the heist." He feels his head pound even harder. Tannis' eyes are now glowing red.

Redolfo feels the intrusion into his mind, a force so powerful, he can't stop it. He hears himself scream, "Please, stop this! Please, I can't take it!"

~

Sarokis watches Redolfo rise into the air. The cabbie's arms are flung backwards, and his face and body contorted in pain. Blood begins pouring from Redolfo's mouth and ears. Sarokis has witnessed such interrogations before. Tannis' methods are cruel, but effective. In his experience, no one has ever yet survived this level of deep intrusion.

~

Through the pain, Redolfo sees a mist clear to reveal a woodland - the image he has seen before. It somehow calms him, and amid the sound of his own screams, he sees soft plumes rise from the mossy ground, like vapours. A glow. No. A light - intensifying. A figure appears within the brightness. Ancient. A being, somehow part of the woodland itself - part of more than that, much more - part of life itself. The source of life's power, enhancing it, in spite of the unending struggle. The vessel that fills its lungs with every intake of its breath. Pulsing. Healing. Nourishing. So fragile yet nurturing the precious strands within its immense grasp. The cycle of death and rebirth, unstoppable yet volatile and brittle. This doesn't make sense.

Redolfo is on the ground. The pain has gone. He realises he has dropped from a height and has hit his head. He can feel blood is pouring from his scalp. He rubs his eyes. He hears shouting. What is this? His eyes begin to focus. His friends! Amitaab is struggling to hold Sarokis in an arm-lock while Danysus is whacking the killer with a staff. Oh, no! Caryalla is fighting Tannis! He can hear the sound of the air being cut with the sharp swings of the blades of her twin hook swords, but despite his great size, Tannis is dodging the cuts with almost supernatural dexterity. Tannis strikes and delivers a glancing blow to Caryalla's cheek, but she manages to recover instantly, snarling at the formidable warrior.

"Tannis!" Redolfo shouts, "Leave them alone. It's me you want."

"You are sciath!" Tannis bellows at Caryalla. Tannis takes a step backwards. "Just like the old days. Now we engage in battle again. I see how you have the power of the ancients within you."

Tannis turns to Redolfo, "Son of Mikkrian, we are related, it would seem. You carry a piece of me within you. Out of deference to your father, I shall let you go. However, I warn you that next time we meet, you will become my mortal enemy."

He turns back towards Caryalla, "Our battle has just begun, sciath!"

Amitaab releases Sarokis from his arm-lock and pats at his shoulder. "Hey fella, no hard feelings here - all cool, you know what I mean?" and confirms his point with a few thrusts of his hip.

Danysus retracts his staff with a spin that would be the envy of any baton-master at a military parade.

"Not bad, Danysus. For a serious guy, you sure handle yourself well," the cabbie says, smiling at his friend.

"Let's get out of here before big antler-dude changes his mind!" Amitaab shouts to his friends.

The four of them run to the cab, jump inside and slam the doors shut. A hiss heralds the rise of the ever-friendly *Lucky Day Cabs* waving hand. With a whine of the Temeria engine, the Checker is airborne.

Redolfo looks in his rear-view mirror and sees Tannis watching them with suspicion as the cab joins the evening Catuvell traffic.

IS THERE ACTUALLY ANYTHING LEFT TO LOSE?

"Marianna, your hands!" Sara cries with a gasp.

Marianna is reading a newspaper and Sara can see how sore and blistered her friend's overworked fingers have become.

Marianna places the newspaper down on her now heavily pregnant belly. Sara can see her expression is upbeat.

"Look," Marianna says, "This article says that President Truman's taking a soft line on European Jews entering America. He's concerned that tens of thousands of Jews won't have homes or a family to go back to. He's also worried they're now facing fierce antisemitism in countries all over Eastern Europe. He's expected to announce a directive later in the year. This is my calling, Sara, I'm going to travel to America."

"But will they let you in? Marianna, it sounds like President Truman hasn't actually issued his directive yet."

"Sara, my child will be born soon. I am grateful to the Swiss for sparing me from death, but I have to think of my child's future. Surely there'll be opportunities in a country with a history of welcoming refugees. I'm leaving tomorrow."

Sara looks at her, imploringly. "I wish I could come with you, but I've promised Benjamin I'll emigrate with him to Palestine. He says he wants to help set up a nation that keeps us safe. Please come with us."

Marianna looks at Sara's thin face and her unruly dark hair - she's pretty in her own way, although worn out from the hardship of her life in successive labour camps. Marianna smiles. "Sara, you need to make this work with Benjamin. I have to make my own life work. I've lost so much. I need something that's entirely of my own choosing."

Sara looks sad. "I understand. I'll miss you terribly. I can't believe you're going to travel when you can give birth at any moment."

"Neither can I, Sara."

THE PENNY FINALLY DROPS

"Why do I feel certain I'll regret this, Ariael?" Hostian's voice fills the *Central Operations Room.*

"General, I'm certain that something fairly catastrophic has been planned and I know you feel the same way." Vernikell replies. "I entirely agree with you that this broadcast probably refers to an address of some kind. So far, the investigation team have come up with nothing out of the ordinary - and how does this link to the mass movement of terannians towards the capital?"

"Sir!" Officer Dowola calls to Vernikell, "We've received a communication from Mr. Michael Redolfo. He wants to talk to you urgently. Shall I tell him you're busy?"

Vernikell makes an exasperated expression, "Has this man been sent to torment me? As much as I want to say I'm busy, he may have something important to say."

"On your comms, sir."

"Hello, Chief? Mike Redolfo here. We gotta talk. I've met Tannis. I know what he wants."

"Okay, Mr. Redolfo. This is not a fully secure line. I see you're at the *Opprobrium Bar.* A transporter will be with you in thirty minutes. Wait outside for me."

"Make it quicker, Chief. There's no time to lose."

~

Redolfo exits the *Opprobrium Bar* and waits near its entrance. In the square, the night is illuminated by a spectacular array of animated advertisements. From the other side of the planet, the gigantic sun sends rays that bounce around Vost's strong magnetic field into cascades of greens, reds, pinks and blues - giving the already dazzling square a backdrop of almost overwhelming colour. Redolfo is reminded of the wonderful array of colours that adorn much of Manhattan. How he misses the skyline.

The square's unusually quiet for this time of the evening. Where there are often crowds of young night time love-seekers off to the various bars and restaurants, this evening, there are just a few couples and solo figures crossing the precinct. Redolfo's intuition is alerted. Trouble. He can't quite pinpoint it but he senses it. He runs to an adjacent street where the lighting is particularly poor and immediately regrets making that decision. He can see the giant form of a corattian who has noticed him - and recognised him. The hulking alien is missing a hand. It bounds towards him.

"Okay, buddy that's far enough. You'd better back off or you may find you'll lose the other hand."

Undeterred, the corattian continues its charge towards him.

"You think I haven't had to deal with big badass wise guys like you before?" Redolfo says as he swings a strong straight punch squarely into the giant alien's abdomen. He feels his fist sink into the blubbery protection of the creature's thick hide and realises his blow has not had the impact he had wanted. A back swipe to Redolfo's head sends him spinning into the air. He lands heavily onto the concreted ground.

Redolfo staggers back onto his feet, dusts off his cap and places it back on his head. The corattian charges towards him.

"That's enough!" Redolfo shouts, holding up the palm of his right hand. His eyes are now a fiery red.

The over-sized alien stops in his tracks. It begins to tremble, and its massive, blubbery head starts to swell. The alien makes a deep, gurgling noise and its eyes seem to bulge out of their sockets.

"Well glory be!" Redolfo can hear Amitaab's excited voice.

"Now that is impressive, Mike," says Danysus, as he emerges into the alley.

"This goddamn cratt'n attacked me!" Redolfo growls as he makes crushing gestures with his hand.

Blood starts to pour from the giant alien's mouth then from both eyes and ears. Its eyeballs begin to pulsate, and the giant blood vessels of its head swell to bursting point.

Redolfo hears the voice of Danysus, "Mike, that's enough!"

"Oh man! His head's gonna explode!" shouts Amitaab, pirouetting with a mixture of excitement and anxiety.

Caryalla appears on the scene, "Hey Mike," she says marvelling at him, "you're in control of your powers - now you must be in control of yourself."

Redolfo's eyes darken and the corattian collapses to the ground.

Amitaab rushes over to inspect the blubbery foe. "He's breathing, man. He's okay. He's gonna wake up soon and he won't be happy!"

Caryalla rushes over to Redolfo, "You okay, Mike?"

"Hey, I'm okay - I feel good. Really good," Redolfo replies with a triumphant smile. "I coulda killed that son-of-a-bitch, but when I saw you all, I realised it weren't right. I'm not going to lose who I am."

Redolfo hears the approach of his transporter. Moorshead arrives and studies the telepathic handiwork.

"John," Redolfo says, "would you mind coming with me to the cop shop? I kinda feel you could be useful."

"Of course, dear boy!" the scholar replies and returns to lock up the bar.

The transporter alights outside the *Opprobrium Bar*. A door opens and Vernikell steps out. He sees the gigantic form of the semiconscious corattian on the ground. "What have you been doing?" he asks Redolfo.

"Look, Chief, that dude's a killer. I don't have time to explain that right now because we've got something far more important to discuss."

"What is it with you, Mr. Redolfo?" Vernikell says with his hand clasped to his forehead. "Why do I see you as the problem and the solution tied together in a bundle?"

"Can I talk to you in the transporter, Chief?" Redolfo says to Vernikell. They all settle into the vehicle.

The cabbie stares at the striking, dark-skinned driver with a frown. The driver in turn stares back at him. Vernikell looks at this unexpected interaction and says, "Is everything okay, Mr. Redolfo? This is Captain Banattar. Have you two met before?"

Redolfo shakes his head, breaks off his stare and turns to Vernikell, "Chief, I met with Tannis and I think I know what he wants."

"How did you get to meet him?"

"It's a long story, Chief, but he's been threatening me."

Vernikell stares suspiciously at Redolfo. He punches the seat in front of him. "It was you, wasn't it?"

Banattar turns back in his seat.

"What was me, Chief?" asks Redolfo trying to look innocent.

Vernikell shouts, "You were the driver, weren't you! The only person I know who could outwit the best trained driver in the VIAS fleet."

Banattar raises the palm of his hand in salute. "So, I've finally met you. It was me you managed to escape from at *Zone 773*. My full respect to you, sir! I've never met anyone with such driving skill."

"He forced you to do it, didn't he?" Vernikell says to Redolfo. "And now the safety of the whole of Vost is under threat. Do you have any idea at all what it was you helped them to steal?"

The cabbie looks downcast with shame.

"Well you just helped Tannis acquire a device that can effectively shut down most of the technology we use on this planet!" Vernikell shouts at him.

"I had no choice, Chief. An assassin dude called Sarokis gave me no choice but to work for him. How was I to know what he was up to? But this is making sense now."

"What do you mean making sense?" Vernikell is glaring at him.

"Tannis is one angry son-of-a-bitch who uses powerful telepathy and can handle himself in combat like no one I've ever seen. He darn well near killed me just with his mind. He worked out I'd seen you and wanted to know if I'd grassed on him."

"Grassed?" asks Vernikell.

"He means informed, Deputy Chief," says Moorshead helping Vernikell out with the limitations of the language decoder. Vernikell nods.

Redolfo continues, "Tannis is angry with the world for the way his people have been treated. The way he sees it, being forced to live on a reservation is beneath their dignity. He's mad that he's the only one of them with any real mind-powers. He's mad that his people were forced to give up their land, their telepathy and their freedom to live as they used to. He believes they all should be allowed to be free to be at war with other folk as they had been for thousands of years."

"So, what's this got to do with everything that's going on?" Vernikell asks him.

Redolfo looks at Vernikell with a serious expression, "Chief, did you know there's a whole bunch of terannians on their way towards the capital."

Vernikell looks surprised, "How do you know that? That's classified information. So why is this happening?"

"Because they're going to war with you. It's clear now, that once they trash your technology, you'll be stripped of your military advantage. They'll easily overcome your army, because compared to them, your guys are poorly trained in hand-to-hand combat. Chief, they're about to end a hundred years of occupation."

Vernikell's jaw drops open. He opens his comms, "General, can you pass me over to Capell Parchi, right now!"

"Parchi here, Ariael."

"You knew Zanusso better than anyone. Did he have a hand in developing the Modulator Shell?"

"Only in the original schematics, but he was not involved with the developmental engineering side of it."

"Capell, I think that the strange message we have been puzzling over has come from Zanusso. I think he's still alive."

He activates his comms again. "Leiath."

"Yes, Deputy Chief," the voice of Officer Dowola replies.

"That encrypted message is almost certainly an address of a floating building...maybe one with dignitaries residing either in it or in a building below it."

"Okay, that's helpful, I have the head of decryption with me now. He's just running an algorithm as we speak."

"Hurry Leiath, please."

"Sir! We think we've found it. It does indeed look like an address. It's the Faolán building. You are right. It is the residence of many politicians and visiting city governors."

Redolfo looks at Vernikell in horror. "You have to evacuate the Faolán building and any of the buildings beneath it, right now, Chief."

Vernikell hits the comms button again, "Capell, could Zanusso modify the modulator shell to block anti-gravity engines?"

"Perhaps, Ariael. It is theoretically possible but would take a genius to achieve that. If Zanusso *is* alive, Tannis could be controlling his mind against his will. He's about the only individual on the planet capable of carrying out such a feat."

"Chief," Redolfo says to Vernikell, "you've also gotta evacuate everyone in the City Central Park."

The Deputy Chief of Staff looks at him quizzically, but within moments his expression changes as he quickly realises what the cabbie is predicting. "Leiath!"

"Yes, Deputy Chief."

"Organise a patrol to the Faolán building and another to Catuvell Central Park, immediately. The park must be completely evacuated. There isn't a moment to lose"

"Certainly, but whatever for?"

Redolfo interrupts the conversation, "Please, Chief, I need a favour. I need you to drop me at *Lucky Day Cabs*. There's someone in the Faolán building that means a lot to me, and I've got to make sure she and her family are safe."

Vernikell gives him a nod and continues his conversation with Officer Dowola.

Redolfo turns to Moorshead, "John. I saw him."

"You saw who, Mike? What are you talking about?"

"It was while Tannis was busting my ass - the most powerful son-of-a-bitch I ever saw. It was Cernunnos."

Moorshead stares in wonder, "I guess his blood does flow through your veins."

"Yeah, and also through the veins of Tannis. It was like Cernunnos knew we were fighting. For just a moment, I felt his power was mine."

Moorshead turns towards Vernikell, "Deputy Chief, of the many things I studied in my university days, I do have quite an understanding of combat and war strategy of the ancient Celts on Earth. I feel those skills will be needed now."

Vernikell nods, "Yes, indeed. You're with me."

WHEN YOU THINK THERE'S NOTHING LEFT TO GIVE

It's the first time Marianna has felt so nauseated since the early days of her pregnancy. The small American cruise ship she's boarded is in desperate need of an overhaul. She was told by the ferry operator that it had been used in the last few years mostly to transport troops and supplies in the war effort. The ship is swaying heavily at its moorings and Marianna concludes she is not a natural seafarer.

She struggles with the weight of her bag. She'd managed to create a pretty carrier bag out of embroidery remnants at the labour camp. It's not particularly heavy, but Marianna becomes quickly exhausted as her swollen belly restricts her breathing.

"Buongiorno Bella. Can I help you?"

Marianna looks around to see an attractive young cabin worker rush over to help her.

"Thank you, sir," says Marianna, grateful for the help. She notices he is slightly awkward and is blushing under his woollen hat, his hands are in his pockets. "It's been a while since I met a true gentleman."

The crewmember swings her bag over his shoulder and takes her by the hand to lead her into the ship. "I can help you to your berth, signora," he says with an Italian American accent.

Marianna studies the tanned features of her helper. His face is kind and his eyes sparkle with youthful energy.

"I hope you like our ship," he says to her. "It's been my home for the last few years. You must excuse me, but I've been working mainly with military supplies and am not used to seeing beautiful ladies."

Marianna gives him a sad smile. Feeling now so swollen and so close to giving birth to her child, she feels anything but beautiful. In almost any other life or situation, she would have blushed heavily at the compliment. What had become of her life? She decides she would try her hardest not to dwell on what she had lost.

"I see you're proud of your ship, sir."

"Yes, she's served us better than we could have ever hoped for," he replies.

Marianna can see that the young man was about to say something else but decides not to. "What is it, sir?"

"I have done my time here, signora. I want to seek a new life. I intend to get off at the port when we arrive and go back to my home city."

"Where is your home city?"

"It's New York, signora. My family moved there from Italy when I was thirteen."

"Well, that's where I'm heading. By the way, I didn't catch your name."

The cabin worker is now visibly blushing. "My name is Redolfo, signora, but you can call me Alfonso."

'I SIMPLY CAN'T BUILD MY HOPES ON A FOUNDATION OF CONFUSION, MISERY AND DEATH...I THINK...PEACE AND TRANQUILLITY WILL RETURN AGAIN.' - *ANNE FRANK*

"Come on, lil' lady," Redolfo says to his Checker as he speeds towards the Faolán building, "I know you've never once let me down, but I need you now more than ever." The yellow cab makes a determined dash as it kicks out frantic plumes of pink, yellow and green vapours from the Temeria exhaust system.

He approaches Catuvell Central Park. The giant statue of Impriat Vandtner floats imperiously and in Redolfo's mind, now threateningly, over the city's public green area. Vernikell's team have wasted no time at all in starting to evacuate the area, as official vehicles are ushering hundreds of people out of the park.

Redolfo's prediction is right. The great statue begins to move. Of course, Tannis would have wanted the city's proudest symbol of subjugation of his people to be the first thing to drop out of the sky. The gigantic Impriat Vandtner, complete with full military regalia, begins to topple, rotate and plunge head-first into a humiliating dive. Redolfo can hear screams from the terrified people below as they run in various directions. The statue lands with a deafening force as it fractures into several large fragments, kicking up a gigantic wave of dust, soil and chunks of metal. The park is now covered by huge pieces of broken statue, but as far as he can tell, no one was caught up in it.

He checks his console. At this speed, he can reach the Faolán Building in just under five minutes. A series of proximity klaxons erupt angrily from numerous vehicles as the Checker weaves perilously in and out of the lines of heavy aerial traffic. Redolfo ignores them.

He can see his mother's saddened face. How she would have suffered during the war years. Until now, he'd not given that much thought. She never talked about it so no one ever really thought it an issue. What had happened that had made her not want to talk ever about his real father? He thinks back to the freak show theory - she'd clearly protected him. She'd once told him she'd survived a Nazi-controlled labour camp and that she'd found out that her own mother had died in one. He never thought to ask any more about it. How he wishes he could ask her now. He was always too wrapped up with his own ridiculous problems. How kids never seem to think to ask their parents about their past until they are older, by which time it is often too late. How he misses his parents. A million questions he would like to ask them.

The Faolán building is now visible in the distance. It's intact and still suspended in the air, for now.

Nearer and nearer, the building comes into full view. To Redolfo, it appears as a huge hulk of concrete, pitted with glowing rectangular windows in regular clusters and spiked with dozens of landing piers, like a giant suspended hedgehog. Directly beneath the building, Redolfo can see what looks like an industrial site. At least if the building falls, there are no residences below to be destroyed.

He hopes he's worrying for nothing. The building is full of dignitaries. It would be a demonstration to the world of Tannis' willingness to do anything to achieve his goal, even if it means targeting a large residential block. This will be just the first building to drop. The city will be ruined and Tannis will take control of the planet unopposed.

What about his own cab? Hell, he hadn't thought of that. He could drop like a stone out of the sky with the building and everyone in it. He tries to put this thought out of his mind.

He can see that Vernikell had acted fast here too. A small fleet of VIAS cargo transporters are alighting on some of the landing piers. Without warning, all the lights in the building turn off. The structure starts to list. The Checker begins to lose height. Some of the newly arrived cargo transporters begin to slip off the piers.

"Almost there, almost there!" he shouts, as he twists the Checker onto the landing pier, now at a slant from the tilt of the building. The cab lands with a hard jolt. He jumps out and runs to the apartment. "Gethsemona!" he screams, as he dashes straight towards the door, forcing it open with his shoulder. The terrified family are huddled together in the hallway. "Come with me, now."

The building tilts further. The boom of concrete scraping against concrete warns that the building is starting to fall apart. "Son of a bitch, Tannis, there are thousands of people here!" he shouts.

The ceiling splits open and lethal chunks of rubble shower onto the hallway floor. Redolfo holds out a hand, his eyes are fiery red. The rubble stops falling, remaining suspended in mid-air. "Go!" he shouts to the family. "Get in the cab."

Redolfo watches the little figure of Gethsemona, who, with a determined stride, leads her terrified parents out of the apartment. They look up at the suspended rubble above them in fear and amazement. Once they are clear, Redolfo lowers his hand, and heavy lumps of concrete cascade to the cracking floor in a plume of dust. The building jolts sharply, and Gethsemona and her parents lose their balance. They fall, rolling several times and slide off the side of the building.

"No!" Redolfo shouts, and leaps towards the Checker on the now perilously steep walkway. As he reaches the cab door, the Checker too tilts off the pier. He falls with it, still holding onto the driver's door handle. "Hell!" he shouts. He manages to fling open the door and scramble into the driver's seat. The cab falls with a nauseating spin amidst threatening boulders of plummeting concrete and metal girders. Redolfo holds out his hand. His eyes are blazing. The rubble begins to organise into a more orderly orbit around him.

~

Gethsemona is in freefall. At the back of her mind, she has always wondered what would happen if the building one day dropped out of the sky. Why was Mike there? She saw what he could do. She recalls the stories of telepathic people. He had stopped the ceiling collapsing on them. Where is he now? He had tried to save them. He was the coolest person she had ever met.

The rubble starts to spin around her. Why is it doing that? That's not how things fall. Mom and Dad! They are all falling together, inside a tunnel of twisting debris! How can this be? They will reach the ground at any moment now - and that would be the end.

A break appears in the rubble. She can see the Catuvell city lights. What is that? Mike's cab! He's saving us! The cab doors are open and Gethsemona feels a force dragging her towards it. In an instant Gethsemona is pulled into the front passenger seat and her parents the back seat of the Checker. The doors slam shut by themselves.

"Belt up, everyone. We're in for a rough ride," orders Redolfo, as he spins the Checker out of the line of falling rubble. To his relief, the Temeria engine starts to whine as the power returns.

"Finally!" he shouts, punching the air. The cab levels out and exits in an exultant cloud of multi-coloured vapour. The roof hand waves with renewed vigour.

"God damn it, Tannis!" Redolfo screams as the Faolán building collapses in a massive plume of smoke and dust onto the industrial estate below. "You've taken so many innocent lives. I'll kill you, you son-of-a-bitch!"

Piercing red eyes penetrate a dense mist within Redolfo's mind as he hears the growling voice of Tannis probe his head, "I'll be waiting for you, human!"

"How did you do all that, Mike? I saw what you did," says Gethsemona.

"It's a long story," he replies, "but right now I'm taking you all to my apartment. It's at ground level, and you'll be safe there. The planet's in danger, and I need to help the dudes in power." He can see Gethsemona's parents in his rear-view mirror. He knows they will not be capable of speech for the time being.

Redolfo hits the comms, "Squintt, Squintt, wake up! I'm gonna need Glyrian's help."

"What is it, Redolfo? I'm trying to relax in a foamy bath. It had better be important."

Redolfo tries to block the image forming in his head of the naked, spherical form of Squintt in his bath. "I've got a job for him. I want you both to meet me at *Lucky Day Cabs* - the future of your planet's at stake and I need him there right now!"

ONE MUST STILL HAVE CHAOS IN ONESELF TO BE ABLE TO GIVE BIRTH TO A DANCING STAR - *FRIEDRICH NIETZSCHE*

"Aww, look, Mrs. Redolfo, it's a beautiful baby boy, yes, a boy - and *how* is it a boy!" the stout midwife squeals with delight, as she makes her final check on the infant. "Seven pounds and four ounces. Do you wanna rest a while before I call your husband?"

"Please," says an exhausted Marianna, "let me hold him. I want to have a little time alone with my son."

The midwife places the little bundle into the proud mother's arms and walks out of the birthing room. Tears flow from Marianna's eyes as she holds him. "My dear little child, I cannot begin to tell you how much I needed you to come into my world. I know you will help me to heal from my loss. How Dominik would have been proud of you. Somehow, I can feel his pride. Maybe I'm crazy, but I can feel that. My little one, I'll do everything in my power to make sure you have a good life - a life where no one will say you are inferior because of the circumstances of your birth - a life where you'll never have to be in constant fear for your life because of who, or what, you are. To me, you'll be the most precious thing that exists, but to the outside world, you'll be a normal boy, then a normal man who will never be judged for being different in any way. I'll see to that, little one. If there's anything I'll make sure in this life, it is that you'll be part of this world and not a victim of it, as I and my family were made to suffer as victims."

Marianna dries her eyes and rings the bedside bell. The beaming midwife returns to the room. "Hey, darling, how's it going? Isn't he beautiful?"

"Yes, thank you. He certainly is. Thank you for being there for me." Marianna replies.

"Hey, that's no problem, sugar. So, you want your fella in here, right?"

Marianna nods. The midwife exits and returns with a man whose smile extends from ear to ear.

"Would you take a look at that," he says in wonder. "Mamma mia, look what you have there!"

"It's a baby boy, Alfonso."

"Oh yes, I can see that, amore mia, he's just perfect!"

"Alfonso," Marianna says to him, "I'm so grateful to you. I'll be the best wife. But I understand if...we have only just—"

"Marianna, no," he stops her short, "Let me tell you something - we Italian men always know the perfect woman when we meet them - it's one of our many great skills. If you're happy to stay with me in America and be my *donna perfetta*, you'll make me the happiest man alive."

"Okay," she says smiling at him, "so what shall we name him?"

"Well," he replies, "my father was called Michele, so how would you feel about naming him after my father?"

"Yes, we could call him Michael. It's a good name and would fit into New York really well."

"Okay, amore mia. Michael Redolfo it is. I feel it has a good ring about it."

THINGS THAT JUST HAVE TO BE DONE

Redolfo lands the Checker in the repair yard of *Lucky Day Cabs*. He's greeted by the rotund form of Baranak Squintt and by the smaller but similarly shaped brother. The larger one has clearly applied some kind of scent after his bath that reminds Redolfo of bathroom cleaner.

"Hey, Squintt," says Redolfo to the portlier brother, "I could swear you've gained some weight."

"Enough of your cheek, Redolfo," Squintt replies, "What's so important that you brought us here at this late hour?"

"Look, Squintt, I know you're going to find this hard to believe right now, but this goddamn planet's going belly-up."

Squintt's blubbery jowls begin to quiver.

Redolfo turns towards the silent brother, "Man, Glyrian, you might be a guy who doesn't say anything, but it looks like your planet can't do without you right now. I'm gonna need your help, and I need it fast."

A PREPARATION FOR WAR

"Why are you so sure the battle will be fought here?" Moorshead asks Vernikell.

Vernikell looks across the grassy field with his optical magnifiers and studies the woodland edge for signs of activity. "By observing the last known movements of the terannian forces, the strategic unit at VIAS has advised we prepare ourselves at this place for battle." He lowers his magnifier and looks at the silver-haired scholar, "Maybe the real reason is that Leiath Dowola believes it to be true, and that's a good enough reason for me."

"Are you even sure that a battle is inevitable?"

"They've ignored all our attempts at communication," Vernikell replies as he surveys the field again. "It's like some sort of dream, Mr. Moorshead. It would seem the technological advances we've made on this planet have now brought us to a disadvantage. It's abundantly clear we've lost the ability to live without technology and we now face a foe that has the war skills of the ancients hardwired into its makeup. I can't see how we'll survive this. It's unclear what the terannians have planned for us but I suspect it won't be any nicer than our treatment of them after they were subjugated."

"Maybe, Chief," Moorshead replies, "but right now, we have a battle to fight and now you have to think and act like a military general rather than an intelligence officer."

Vernikell looks pensive, "Yes, you're right. It was a surprise that General Hostian was so willing to hand over the task to me. I guess it reflects our shortcomings as a military force. We have slept for too long in the comfort of our world government, thinking that we're surrounded by nothing but allies and have never felt the need to prepare for a potential war. Mr. Moorshead, I fear we are sunk."

"Look Chief, consider what you've achieved here," says Moorshead, gesturing towards the battlefield. On our planet, the Celtic tribes around the world were easily and swiftly dealt with by the armies of the Roman Empire. Luckily for us, I am well versed in the writings of Publius Flavius Vegetius Renatus..."

Vernikell lets out a sigh.

Moorshead shrugs, "Okay, okay...Vegetius, for short. He was a Roman military historian who wrote down many of the battle tactics of the invincible Roman army."

"But we don't have the weapons used by the Roman army, let alone the training discipline of their troops."

"I agree, but given the authoritarian history of Vost, you do have a huge stockpile of crowd-control items. Take another look at your infantry."

Vernikell focuses his optical magnifiers on his army. To him, they appear as disorderly and poorly trained regiments equipped with riot shields, electrical shock sticks and assault batons.

Moorshead continues, "At least their shields resemble those used by Roman soldiers and their body armour and helmets are a great improvement on the Roman design."

Vernikell focusses his magnifier on the horse-like steeds shuffling amongst the ranks of his troops. He has positioned these mounted *Eohipp Crowd-Control Units* to support the infantry on each side in order to prevent the terannians from outflanking his army. The infantry reserves behind the front rank are ready to take care of any terannians that penetrate the lines.

Vernikell nods, "Yes, it's all impressive. But with barely a day to drill your military procedures into the soldiers, I cannot see how this will work."

"It will work, because the soldiers fighting for you are fighting for their way of life."

Vernikell cannot hide his gloomy thoughts. "Well, so far, all our hardware is operational. Unbelievably, the terannians remain undetectable within the woodlands - almost as if they are part of the woodland itself."

"I agree. Until we know exactly what the terannians are planning, we cannot justify carpet-blasting the woodlands, however tempting that may be," Moorshead adds, trying to hide his own worry.

"Well, the maser cannons are in place atop the towers, the EP7 attack drones are buzzing overhead in their hundreds and our comms are currently working normally," Vernikell adds.

"Sadly, they will be shut down just when you need them most, Chief."

As if to cue, the display on his comms goes blank. Vernikell's heart sinks as he also sees the array of control lights on the maser cannons fade away. The drones drop out of the sky like a metal hailstorm.

"Curse that Spaan! He's left us completely exposed while he hides himself away in his holy sanctuary," Vernikell shouts, gripping the sword at his hilt.

"Well, well, well," says Moorshead as he observes the forest edge with his field telescope. "Seems your intel was accurate. Look what's arrived."

Over the space of the next few minutes, the pair watch as the terannians form a formidable line of infantry at the forest edge, the line of antlers appearing as an intimidating combination of force and nature. They are each carrying an assortment of long weapons and a colourful, round shield looking large enough to block a charging auriach. At the centre of each shield is a wheel emblem with a central metallic boss. Another line forms behind them. To their flanks, dozens of chariots appear, each controlled by a terannian warrior and pulled by a sturdy eohipp, decorated in an intricately embroidered cloth. Vernikell realises with dread the impossibility of his task as two more terannian regiments appear.

He looks away from his optical magnifiers and sees Moorshead focus his eyeglass. In spite of his obvious fear, the scholar seems to be marvelling at the emerging spectacle.

"I can't help but notice how similar their bows, long swords, spears and shields are to the archaeological equivalents found in the British Isles," he says to Vernikell. "Cernunnos' influence on the Ancient Britons was profound."

A regiment of archers, five layers deep, emerges behind the terannian infantry lines.

"Reporting for duty, Deputy Chief of Staff," a female voice announces behind Vernikell. He recognises this voice well. He smiles as he turns towards the owner of the voice. "Oriana!" he yells, as he sees the aging, but upright figure of his old martial arts training instructor. Her hair, once bright and blonde, is now silver-grey and tied up for battle. She is wearing the shimmering blue and black uniform of the *Catuvell Martial Arts School* that he remembers so clearly from his youth. Behind her are about fifty of her students, standing in formation with the school's signature *claiomh* swords slung across their backs. *How young and fresh-faced they are! Is this how I used to look?* Vernikell thinks as he feels his throat begin to close with emotion. He looks down at his own sword at his side. He had looked after it over the years, never thinking he would ever need to use it.

"This is no time to choke up, soldier!" Oriana says with a smile. "I know you think I'm not what I used to be, but I can promise you there's life left in the old eohipp fighter you remember - I can still teach those terannians a lesson on how it's done."

"They are so young, Oriana - men and women in the prime of their lives. You run a martial arts school, not a military academy. This is no place for civilian volunteers. Send them away."

"I never invited them, Ariael - they came to me as I was preparing myself for battle. You won't be able to stop them. They've dedicated their training to defending themselves and their loved ones, and now they've chosen to use their skills to defend our way of life. I taught you how to fight, Ariael, and now my sword and the swords of my students are yours to command."

Vernikell knows when he has been beaten. With a voice more tremulous than he would like, he says, "Oriana, position your fighters behind the last line of infantrymen. My signal for your advance will be three waves of my flag."

The aging instructor gives Vernikell a nod, and signals to her students to take their positions.

"Oriana," Vernikell calls.

She turns back to look at him.

"Thank you."

She gives him an almost imperceptible smile before leading her students to the battlefield.

"It is time." Moorshead announces to the Deputy Chief.

Vernikell sees the terannian lines advance towards his troops. He raises a single red flag. In the space of about fifteen seconds, his front two infantry lines have achieved the desired Roman military formation of the *tortoise*. His troops in the front and sides have interlocked their shields, while the soldiers in the back lines have placed their shields over their heads to form a protective shell structure of transparent riot shields.

"*Testudo!*" announces Moorshead to Vernikell. "One of two manoeuvres we had any time to practice - and look how quickly your troops have acquired the skills! They should be impenetrable under that shield formation."

"Not bad!" Vernikell says, nodding in surprise.

For a terrifying few minutes, the terannians release hundreds of arrows that soar high into the air and then rain down heavily on the *testudo* of interlocking riot shields. A second wave, and another clatter of arrows is deflected harmlessly by the impenetrable shield-wall. The terannian military drums boom across the battlefield as their lines of infantry advance.

"Riflemen!" Vernikell commands from behind the *testudo*. Hidden within the ground vegetation are a dozen troops armed with historic firearm weapons. Frustratingly for the Deputy Chief, there were only five old-style gunpowder weapons available from the military museum that were operational. The other seven were the personal belongings of some of the agents that were collectors of historical weapons. The draconian Vost firearms regulations meant that ammunition was almost non-existent and barely enough for one single salvo. The riflemen aim their weapons at the approaching terannian infantry line. "Fire!" Vernikell shouts his command and deafening reports from the ancient firearms fill the battlefield. Several warriors from the terannian line are felled, but their overall advance is barely affected.

Vernikell looks worriedly at Moorshead. Spaan, through his bloody-minded interference, has placed the future of the planet in peril. How easy it would have been to manufacture significant numbers of gunpowder weapons and ammunition to shift the battle advantage in their favour. The interfering priest had prevented his troops from having a meaningful way of defending themselves.

"With your permission, sir," says Moorshead.

Vernikell nods and the silver-haired historian produces an animal horn, places it to his lips, and creates a loud single note as an instruction for the troops to break the *testudo* and to commence the next formation. Rather more clumsily this time, but still with reasonable order, the front Vost army line assumes several wedge formations with one soldier at the front and the others in increasingly wide layers forming triangles of infantry units.

Moorshead had previously explained to Vernikell that by using this formation, the terannians would be at a disadvantage, as they would be forced into restricted positions that would make wielding their long weapons difficult.

A second sound of the horn resonates across the field and the wedge of fearful troops advance into the approaching terannian lines. Vernikell clutches his optical glasses. Some of his soldiers are muttering prayers, while some are vomiting as they march. This was the moment Vernikell feared the most, and with good reason. How will they fare in hand to hand combat against such natural fighters? The odds were not good, and his troops knew it.

The points of the wedges of the infantry troops make contact with the terannian front lines. At first, the terannians are wrong-footed by the surprise of the orderliness of the attack. Their lines are quickly split into fragments, and, as Moorshead predicted, the antlered warriors are forced to clamber around each other, being unable to wield their long weapons at such close range. They begin awkwardly jabbing their spears against a firm line of riot shields. The Vost army soldiers are now able to utilise their comparatively short stun sticks effectively, felling several of their antlered foe. With only a poor availability of sharp implements, they finish off the fallen by bludgeoning them with their batons and piercing body parts followed by frantic stabs with their daggers. The soldiers' relief at their initial success instantly evaporates, as the next terannian line advances.

Moorshead sounds two blasts of the horn and activates a line of corattian mercenaries, who stand several feet taller than all the other soldiers on the field. With a low, burbling war cry, these tank-like warriors tear into the second wave with a series of blows from their chain whips.

Vernikell watches grimly as terannian blood sprays across the field under the ferocity of the attack.

The success of the corattian attack is, however, short lived. Vernikell despairs as he sees his front-line troops are too shaken to be able to reform into another wedge. He observes, with some suspicion, that the third terannian line has halted its advance. The tactic now makes sense - within a blink of an eye, he sees their line split apart to allow a wave of charioteers to enter the fray. The corattians are taken by surprise by the speed of the attack. Vernikell sees the despair on the faces of his infantrymen as they witness the terannians on their fast mounts use their javelins to pierce their mighty corattian allies, who collapse to the ground in pools of blood.

The rhythmical clatter of terannian sword on shield intensifies. The orderliness of Vernikell's assault has completely broken, and with horror, he sees more lines of terannian infantry march forward. With his heart heavy in his chest, he raises his red flag and waves it three times. It is now the turn of the *Catuvell Martial Arts School* members to engage the enemy. He sees Oriana lead her students with her *claiomh* sword raised high in the air. She shouts her order and her students respond by unsheathing their own swords before running headlong into the oncoming line of warriors. Vernikell cannot bear to contemplate how this will end. He knows their training is about individual self-defence and not military tactics. His throat tightens as he marvels at the bravery of Oriana's students. It is a credit to her leadership.

Oriana's sword is swift and deadly as she takes on and slays two terannians with dexterous cuts of her blade. This spurs on her students who then break into individual mêlées with their terannian adversaries. In spite of the strength of their assault, they are soon each engaged against waves of more warriors.

Vernikell points his flags towards his mounted cavalry who then charge around either flank of the terannian regiments. Realising there is no way to give any further command, he takes a pistol from his holster and runs into the thick of battle. The cries from fatally wounded troops begin to swell his gut with guilt. He fires all his rounds in quick succession and begins slicing at enemy soldiers with his sword as he encounters them. One down. Two. He feels the slippery mixture of blood and sweat on the sword hilt and tightens his grip. He lifts an abandoned javelin and with a strength he never knew he had, advances further into the maelstrom of attackers. He dodges the thrust of a large spear and drives his javelin through an advancing terannian's neck. He is knocked backwards by a blow from a shield but manages to make a fatal counterthrust with his javelin into his assailant's abdomen.

The world becomes less defined, the patterns of the battle blur as he charges again and again. More of his troops lie slaughtered on the ground. The raw, acrid scent of their blood fills his throat. The grassy ground is now a sea of red. He knows it is only a matter of time before he himself will be fatally run through and his army completely destroyed, with Vost yielding completely to terannian control. Maybe they all deserved it. Maybe this was fair recompense for the injustices endured by a species utterly humiliated by berrantine and garryan domination.

Through the fog of battle, Vernikell becomes aware that he is now surrounded by a group of enraged terannian warriors. As they thrust their spears at him, the movements of their antlers sway like the branches of leafless trees in the wind - as if part of the woodland they emerged from - as if the forest itself has sent its emissaries to destroy its intruders. The terannian war-cries made all the more menacing by their crimson and blue war paint and piercing reflections from their dark eyes.

Vernikell realises there is now no escaping death. He makes one final thrust with his javelin towards the terannian directly in front of him, who easily parries his attack and pushes Vernikell to the ground with a spear jab directly into his protective vest. Although the vest is not penetrated, he falls, winded and unable to recover to his feet. His assailant raises his spear, ready to drive a fatal blow through Vernikell's neck.

A new noise intrudes into the battlefield amongst the cries, shrieks and clangs of metal. The terannian stops in his tracks. The delay gives Vernikell a chance to focus. The enemy warriors peer to see its source.

He hears it again - a sound like a vintage vehicle klaxon. His attacker walks away.

Vernikell gets back onto his feet. As he catches his breath, he can now see the battle has eased, as the terannians have pulled back and regrouped. They appear to have taken a moment to survey a new development to the battle scene. A different sound - this time perhaps more familiar - historical. He recognises it - the sound of an internal combustion engine! A yellow road vehicle adorned with an array of lethal-looking spikes is racing towards the battlefield. Poised on its roof, Vernikell can recognise the seated form of Caryalla, now in warrior clothing, with skin and hair streaked with blue paint. Next to her is the curious spectacle of a small kitchawan, barely more than two feet tall and expertly juggling a series of knives. On the roof behind them, a mechanical hand gestures with an intimidating wave. There are two figures in the back seat, and the driver is none other than Michael Redolfo.

"Now that's one item of technology that can actually work in this crazy world!" Vernikell shouts aloud, now almost laughing at the bizarre appearance of this unexpected ally.

He sees Redolfo accelerate the Checker towards the column of terannian chariots. With considerable driving skill, he has clipped the wheels of several of the wooden war-vehicles with his spike attachments as he passes behind the terannian infantry line. One by one, the entire line of chariots collapse, and the charioteers are flung violently in various directions.

To his astonishment, Vernikell sees a line of six terannian foot soldiers collapse to the ground. The small kitchawan has jumped on their backs and has slashed their necks in rapid succession.

Amid the sounds of the kitchawan's cackling laugh, Vernikell sees Caryalla jump off the roof of the cab and make a fierce inroad into a line of antlered infantryman, her twin hook swords slicing skilfully into her objective.

The back doors of the vehicle open, and a slender, almost gaunt garryan male joins Caryalla in the skirmish, swinging and jabbing his staff into the faces of terannian warriors.

"For Brighid!" a long-haired berrantine shouts his battle cry, as he too emerges from the vehicle and enters the fray with his sword held high.

These brief moments of relief soon disappear as Vernikell observes that three more lines of terannian infantry have replaced the broken chariot regiment. As they advance, their arcane chants and the deafening rhythm of blades against shields drain him of hope.

~

Redolfo hits the reverse gear of the Checker, and tears into the advancing terannians with a doughnut spin, the waving roof hand further taunting the incoming assailants. Blood sprays across the cab windows as the blades slice mercilessly into the advancing terannian troops. The cabbie winces as he hears the agonised cries of the felled warriors.

"Why is this HAPPENING? Why am I having to do this terrible thing?" he shouts aloud, thumping the steering wheel with a mixture of frustration, bewilderment, anger and guilt. Before he has any more time to reflect further on this, more terannians have surrounded the cab and have raised their spears to jab at him through the window.

"Son-of-a-bitch! You leave my goddamn cab alone!" he shouts and revs the engine to make his escape. He can hear the wheels spin, but the Checker does not move.

"You bust my goddamn tires!" he shouts as he swings open the doors and jumps out of the immobilised cab. In an instant, he is face to face with three fierce fighters, aiming their spears at him. Before he can make any real sense of his predicament, he sees that one of the terannians has been felled by a sword-cut through the neck and realises it was Amitaab who had delivered the fatal blow. The eccentric berrantine performs a small, and unexpected, jig that momentarily transfixes the other warriors. A sudden dance-like twirl, his long black hair twisting in an enigmatic display and Amitaab has thrust a series of dexterous cuts through their hearts in rapid succession. They drop to the floor. Speechless, Redolfo tilts his cap to him, and a smiling Amitaab re-joins the battle.

Terannian riders on gigantic steeds, formidable and seemingly unstoppable, advance towards Redolfo with frightening speed. The ground shakes around him as they gallop. His eyes burn red. A wave of his hand sends the steeds hurtling to the gound, their riders fatally crushed under their weight. A further column of infantry appears to replace them. They release a shower of javelins. Another turn of his hand sends the javelins back towards their throwers with deadly effect.

"This is where it ends, human," Redolfo can hear Tannis' angry roar within his mind. Redolfo looks up and sees Tannis is staring directly at him from a point of high ground. The mighty terannian keeps his gaze firmly fixed on Redolfo, while he effortlessly runs a sword through the chest of a Vost soldier and kicks the lifeless body down the slope. Tannis stamps hard against the ground. A shock wave tears up a deep ridge that reaches Redolfo and sends him flying.

WHEN YOU'RE NOT SURE WHAT IT IS YOU'RE DISSECTING

Musy calls the waitress to the table and orders two coffees. He puts his newspaper down on the table.

"Something of interest, Jean-Marie?" says the Irgun activist, Reuben Hecht, as he rises from his seat to peer at a highlighted article.

"Yes, it's about the capture of the Carpathian town, Dukla, by the Soviet army. It was a costly and bloody battle for the Slovenians, but they fought hard with the help of expertly designed pipe bombs designed by communist forces. I marvel at their ingenuity. "

Musy smiles at him, "Reuben, even now, I haven't a clue how you achieved what you wanted."

"It's what you achieved, Jean-Marie," Reuben replies, diplomatically. "It was you who negotiated with Himmler, not I."

"I know you will be critical of my past affiliations, but we all can be charged with harbouring stupid views in our past. Your own history of activism begs many questions too."

Hecht smiles, unrepentantly.

Musy cannot help but smile back. He continues with a more serious tone, "In April, I travelled with my father to the Buchenwald concentration camp to liberate a family of Jews. The conditions we saw there were truly appalling. Prisoners were being evacuated in their thousands under

Hitler's orders and sent on *death marches* towards camps across Germany."

Hecht's smile drops. "I know that thousands of prisoners are dying on these marches from starvation, exposure and exhaustion. Hundreds of those who collapse or lag behind are shot dead."

Musy stares down at the pink tablecloth and says, "What I just don't get, is how Himmler bought into our story. How did I actually convince him he'd appear favourable to the victorious allies by liberating Jews and keeping the camps open for when the soldiers arrived? He knew the war was likely to be lost - but having coordinated the systematic murder of twelve million people, it's inconceivable to anyone that he'd somehow receive a more lenient treatment."

"I do agree, Jean-Marie, it doesn't make much sense at all. It did seem a hopeless project from the start, but that's all we could do at the time." Hecht stares at a stylised painting of a First World War soldier on the wall. After a pause, he then looks back at Musy and replies, "Maybe there was some other force at work that we don't know about."

"In the end," Musy continues, "Himmler actually countermanded Hitler's orders to shut the camps and exterminate the remaining Jews." He smiles, "I am told Hitler actually declared his 'loyal Heinrich' expelled from all offices of state and even stated that point in his will."

The waitress appears with their coffee.

"Jean-Marie, I know what's troubling you," says Hecht as their coffee is served.

Musy looks warily at him. "What do you mean?"

"I know you feel you've betrayed us by allowing the concentration camp guards to have escaped justice."

Musy puts down his coffee, "You're among the most intelligent and perceptive of men, Reuben. You are right."

"The truth is, you may well have lost the deal completely with Himmler if you hadn't agreed to that condition. You made a deal with a bad man for the sake of the greater good. In the midst of this awful tragedy at least a few people have been spared that otherwise would not have been."

Hecht's endorsement does not lift Musy's lowered mood. The Swiss diplomat stares into the depths of his coffee.

"Jean-Marie - tell me - how many Jews do you think were actually saved by Himmler's interventions?"

Musy looks up at him, "It's difficult to count numbers in this way, but I know there were twelve-hundred released from Terezín, seventeen hundred Jews spared deportation from Hungary to Bergen-Belsen and the remaining people imprisoned in the Budapest ghetto were spared extermination. Himmler invited the allies into the camps without a shot being fired. I don't think the number of people spared by his suspension of concentration camp exterminations can really be accurately calculated."

Hecht looks warmly at his Swiss negotiating partner, "Diplomacy is all about compromise, Jean-Marie. You know that - and remind me of the fate of the five-million Swiss Francs promised to Himmler in the negotiation."

Musy breaks a smile, "He received none of it."

MAYBE IT NEVER REALLY ENDS WELL

Redolfo lands heavily onto his left shoulder and for a moment lays incapacitated with pain. Realising Tannis is now directly targeting him, he manages to scramble back onto his feet and charge into the thick of the fighting, his eyes burning red. As he runs, a path opens within the sea of terannians who, one after the other, clutch at their throats, choke and collapse. With a path now cleared, he can see Danysus and Amitaab are back to back, surrounded by chanting terannian fighters. They are only just managing to fend off the cruel probing of numerous terannian spear jabs, and Redolfo can see his friends are now in trouble.

A burly terannian pushes to the front of the attacking circle of warriors. Using great strength, he swings his javelin and knocks the staff out of Danysus' hands. A quick jab sends the javelin through the garryan's abdomen. Danysus collapses, his large, reflective eyes blinking in pain as he clutches at the bleeding wound.

Redolfo's eyes redden. The javelin lifts out from the garryan's bleeding tissues and plunges into the necks of three of the attacking terannians in quick succession. Amitaab delivers a fatal strike to the remaining two attackers with a shout of, "Take that as a gift from Our mother, Brighid!" and waves his sword in triumph. He nods to Redolfo, in acknowledgement that his telekinetic power has, for now, saved their lives.

Danysus is unable to move while blood continues to pour from the wound. Amitaab rushes to kneel next to him and strokes his head. "Be strong, my friend. We've been through so much together. You can get through this." He looks imploringly at Redolfo who responds by pointing a finger at Danysus' wound. Danysus cries out in pain as the blood coagulates and chars through the fabric of his jacket. The bleeding has stopped, but he looks pale and weak. The garryan reaches out his hand and Amitaab holds it.

"Don't leave me, man!"

For an almost imperceptible moment, Danysus' reflective eyes flash red. Amitaab screams and jerks backwards, clasping his hands to his face.

"Amitaab!" Redolfo shouts. At once, the terannians are upon them, but Amitaab seems to have recovered and slices at the wall of shields and spears that have formed around him. Redolfo sweeps his hand through the air. A series of loud cracking sounds comes from the column of antlered warriors who collapse to the ground like skittles. They are unable to get back up on their feet and instead clutch at their now misshaped legs.

~

Vernikell's troop numbers are rapidly depleting. He manages to take down a terannian by shocking him in the neck with a stun stick, then cracking open his skull with his baton. He takes a step back to view the scene. Exhausted and breathing heavily from fighting, he watches as Caryalla ploughs through a column of terannian fighters with a series of swings and thrusts from her hook swords. He is taken aback by her grace and power.

He can now see the path cleared by Redolfo and his friends but becomes disheartened by the seemingly endless numbers of fresh terannian reserves entering the battle. Their numbers are now overwhelming, and he begins to fear for Caryalla who is now completely surrounded by enemy soldiers.

~

Caryalla feels a surge of strength course through her - just the one remaining sciath fighting an ancient war against an army of terannian warriors.

Outnumbered, but bursting with desire to engage with the enemy - she now understands who she is. Trained as a street fighter, but now using her skills on a battlefield. The cycle of birth, love, spirituality and death - now all making sense to her, like the final piece in a puzzle, as she drives her swords into the onslaught of attackers.

As the energy surges within her, in her mind she is fighting alongside an army of sciath - brave, flame-haired warriors, each painted in the blue dye of the isatis plant. While she has entered this battle with her twin hook swords, she sees herself holding her long bow steadily in her left hand as she releases a series of sharp darts from the taut string with her right. She feels the release of her arrows freeing the core of the planet, as if liberating Vost from the suffocating dominance of generations of spiritless people. How the planet has yearned for the long-awaited return of her children. The Vost goddess is smiling.

The haemorrhaging bodies of the fallen warriors slain by Caryalla's fierce attack now make fighting precarious. More lines of fresh terannian soldiers arrive to replace their colleagues. She is surrounded by enemy soldiers.

"Get out of there!" she hears Redolfo shout to her with panic in his voice.

With a delicate foothold onto a surprised terannian's belt, she steps onto the warrior's shoulders, and flips out of the throng of antlered attackers.

She now can see Redolfo himself, surrounded by dozens of angry terannians who leap directly onto him, with brandished weaponry.

"Mike!" Caryalla yells in terror, and spins round to help him, but thinks better of it as she realises her presence will negate any telekinetic power he could use for self-defence. Before she can make up her mind, she sees a flash of brilliant light arise from within the mass of the attacking terannians. The light explodes with a spray of terannian body parts. Caryalla can see, and feel, the expanding ring of energy, with Redolfo at its centre. The energy dissipates and Redolfo returns to his feet, seemingly unharmed, but rubbing his sore shoulder.

"Tannis, you son of a bitch, I'm ready for you!" she hears Redolfo shout, as he repositions his cap.

As if in answer to Redolfo's cry, the monstrous form of Tannis appears, leaping forward and landing in front of the cabbie with a resonating thud. He launches a palm strike that Redolfo manages to duck. The terannian then launches a front kick which makes contact with Redolfo's flank, sending him spinning off and toppling back a number of steps before falling to the ground. Caryalla can see Redolfo is hurt. She makes to run to help, but then hears the firm shout of Amitaab, "Caryalla, no! You must leave him to fight this. You can't save him and you'll only get yourself killed."

Caryalla stops in her tracks. "No!" she shouts in frustration. She begins to run again, but stops herself, as she can now see that Redolfo has managed to sit upright, his eyes burning red. Tannis' eyes are now as red as her friend's, and she realises they are facing each other in telepathic combat.

~

Redolfo can feel that now familiar surge of energy. Through the flames he sees him - the glow of the ultimate expression of nature's force - the presence of mighty Cernunnos himself. He knows that Tannis can sense this too. They equally feel it - the precious and ancient power residing within them both. Their anger combines - both wielding nature's inestimable and mysterious energy. They see each other as children - their respective problems - worried parents – relationships - conflicts. Terannian rituals, angry words shouted by a young Tannis to his weary parents. A moody young Redolfo in fights at school. Tannis hurting his friends in a series of angry exchanges. Redolfo's mother, a young Marianna Kravová, staring out of the window. Deep, deep love as she looks into Dominik Kominsky's eyes. German trucks with taunting words shouted through megaphones, telling the Jews of Prague where they are not allowed to go. Tannis locked in endless, heated arguments with terannian elders with talk of revolution. A young female terannian shouting at Tannis in frustration. Large crowds gathered on the streets shouting to the passing German army cavalcades, "Sieg Heil! Sieg Heil! Sieg Heil!" Tannis' and Redolfo's lives now fully exposed to each other, a lifetime of memories, mutually experienced, mutually lived.

The strain intensifies and Redolfo redoubles his efforts to overpower the crushing force of Tannis' mind. He can feel his own power surge, but this is countered by the mind-strength of his terannian adversary. Through the vice-like grip, he can feel Tannis' pain, his anger, his overbearing sense of patriotism. Redolfo knows that before long his own mind will break, and he will be no longer able to resist the warrior. Tannis will destroy each and every one of the defenders of the planet. He knows Tannis can sense this too. He knows he is unable to compete with a terannian, who has lived a lifetime wielding and honing the power of the ancients. Redolfo's mind begins to slide. "I'm sorry, mamma!" he screams.

The relief comes like the sudden lifting of a dead weight. Redolfo opens his eyes to see Tannis is on the ground, hurt with a deep cut sliced into his shoulder. Tannis springs back onto his feet, but by this time, he is facing the onslaught of a furious Caryalla and Amitaab. Even in his injured state, Tannis shows his formidable mastery of the martial arts. Amitaab receives a punch to the chest that sends him tumbling. Tannis grabs Caryalla by the wrists, and to Redolfo's horror, he sees her hook swords clatter onto a small heap of rocks.

"This is where your life ends, sciath, and then I shall end the life of your precious human friend."

Caryalla cries out in pain as Tannis twists her arm. He places his other hand around her neck, ready to break it in one swift movement. A pause - Tannis looks down at the spear head that has exited his chest wall. Blood begins to pour out from the exit wound, forming a red puddle on the ground. His great strength begins to leave him, and Caryalla pushes herself free. Tannis turns to see that it was Vernikell who had run him through.

Vernikell withdraws the spear from the sinewy wound with an audible scrape against the terannian's ribs. Tannis collapses to the ground. It's clear to Redolfo from the softening of Tannis' expression that the warrior knows he is soon to die.

A mist has gathered. Within the haze, Redolfo sees the outline of hundreds of terannian soldiers that have formed back into ranks. The antlered warriors look at each other in confusion, as if they have unexpectedly found themselves in a place they don't recognise. They lower their weapons.

Tannis beckons Vernikell to come forward. His breathing is now shallow and gurgling and he struggles to compose himself to speak. "You did well today, berrantine, much better than I had thought you capable. The terannians have lost this battle, but our struggle goes on." Blood wells up in his mouth. "Before I die, I want a promise from you."

Redolfo takes off his cap, while Caryalla places her left fist over her heart in deep respect for the greatest warrior she has ever encountered. Even Amitaab's eyes, normally so full of energy and life, now seem dulled with a mournful sadness.

Vernikell looks at the hulk of expiring terannian and feels somewhere within himself a pang of sympathy. "What is it you want, Tannis?"

"I want you to pledge that my people will not be persecuted or punished for this. They were under my mind-command and therefore not acting under their own volition." Tannis looks imploringly at the VIAS agent and grabs him by the throat with a weak grasp. "Promise me!"

Vernikell releases Tannis' grip. He gives the dying terannian a sympathetic look and then his answer: "Under the laws of Vost, they will be treated as soldiers acting under authority, and from what I have seen today, under duress."

Satisfied with Vernikell's words, Tannis turns to Caryalla. "You have fought well, sciath, and live up to your name. Your people are now a shadow of what they were. They would certainly be proud of you."

Tannis is rapidly losing blood. He points a weak hand towards Redolfo. "Son of Mikkrian, you have acquired great power. You have my experiences and memories within you and I know that you have sympathy for the plight of my people. I saw how your mother suffered from subjugation by enemies, perhaps even more destructive than those my ancestors had to face. I bow to your mother and to all the millions of humans that lived and died under such oppression."

Redolfo replies with tears welling in his eyes, "Goddamn it, Tannis! Why did you have to deal with this in such a goddamn crazy way? There are better ways. We could have worked something out. We are brothers. We could have looked after each other. Hell, I've found a goddamn relative on this planet and now I'm losing him! Why didn't you just talk to me instead of kicking my ass? It didn't have to end this way."

Tannis' voice becomes weaker. He replies, "Son of Mikkrian, my people and my heritage are everything to me. I know you know this. I always believed diplomacy would have ended with empty berrantine promises and lies, just as I believe your people were lied to about the labour camps that were really death camps. It is now too late for me but I know that with time, your powers will increase. I hope that you will use them wisely and not recklessly, as I have done, to protect those in need of liberation.

"You carry the spirit of Cernunnos within you. He will want you to ensure the gift given to us all, the energy that resides within both Vost and Earth, is preserved, honoured and revered, and not abused - as I now know has also been the case on Earth."

The terannian warrior raises a weak hand to point at the finely carved wheel on his hide belt. He utters an inaudible whisper as his now grey eyes remain fixed on Redolfo. The cabbie kneels down and places his ear to Tannis' mouth. He can just make out the words, "Take it, for it is now yours."

Tannis lays lifeless on the ground.

~

Vernikell looks down at Tannis then casts his eyes towards the battlefield. The mist has lifted and the terannian warriors have returned to the forest. Lifeless, blood-soaked bodies in black uniforms are scattered throughout the area. Interspersed between the dead VIAS agents lay the bodies of slain terannians. Vernikell falls to his knees, winded as he sees that within this dark sea of the deceased, occasional bodies in bright blue and black uniforms appear like delicate flowers within a meadow. Not one of them is left standing.

Vernikell's comms beeps. His maser weapon lights up. "We are back on-line," he announces. He answers his comms.

"Is that Deputy Chief, Vernikell?" asks an unfamiliar voice through the device.

"Yes, who is this?"

"This is Professor Cashall Zanusso. I have been freed," the thin voice announces. "Are you all okay?"

"The war is over, Professor, but many have died today," Vernikell replies.

"Did you receive my coded warning? Were you in time to save the residents of the Faolán building?"

Vernikell pauses and looks to the ground in sorrow. With grief in his voice, he replies, "I'm sorry, professor. We understood your message, but were sadly not in time to save them."

There is a pause before Zanusso answers with a weary voice, "I'm sorry, sir. With Tannis constantly on my back, I was only able to send a warning about one single address. Was anyone hurt after the fall of the statue of Impriat Vandtner?"

"No, professor. I am pleased to say that we had warning from another source that the statue would collapse. I'll explain all about that later."

"May I ask what's happened to Tannis?"

"I can confirm he is now dead. Professor, you don't need to worry about your involvement with all this. I know you were coerced into doing what you did. You would have had no choice. I've witnessed the power Tannis wielded."

"Thank you, sir. He originally intended to make every building and every vehicle drop out of the sky in one single moment but changed his mind after the collapse of the Faolán building. I have no idea why this made him change his mind."

Vernikell looks down at Tannis. The pool of blood around him has grown larger. "Perhaps there was some goodness in him after all. Anyway, professor, I have a favour to ask you, and it's a considerable one. I guess you're in dire need of a rest now, but I desperately need you to work on something for me - there may not be much time left."

~

Tannis lies still. The light has now faded, but his mighty form casts two shadows derived from the beams of light from Vost's two moons, Arianrhod and Cerridwen.

IT'S THAT RARE KIND OF OCCASION

The Checker passes over the giant advertisement board with the perpetually happy, face of the Walshram's Canisters marketing creation. Redolfo notices how rust has now eroded the corner of the right eye.

The cab still bristles with metal spikes from Glyrian's assault-vehicle conversion. The two back tires are flat. The hyperspace probe radio is blaring.

He checks out the landing area in the *Lucky Day Cabs* repair yard below. "Time to take off the scary spikes and start work again," he says to himself. He sees the yard is full of people. "What the hell?"

As he approaches, he can see the *Lucky Day Cabs* staff are waving to him - but it's not just them - Caryalla and Amitaab are there too. He sighs inwardly as he reflects how Danysus didn't survive the battle. "What is Amitaab doing?" he chuckles, as he sees the eccentric berrantine perform spin-jumps with excitement. "What the...?" he shouts out loud, as he sees Vernikell, Officer Dowola, Parchi and the Baroness have joined the welcoming committee. "And John too!" he cries, as he sees Moorshead in the gathering.

The battle-Checker settles gently in the landing-space in a cloud of coloured vapour, and the *Lucky Day Cabs* waving hand lowers to the roof with a hiss. Redolfo exits the cab. Caryalla breaks into a run and leaps up to fling her arms around him, landing a drawn-out and passionate kiss squarely on his lips. A roar of applause emits from the crowd as the two embrace.

"Awww come on, honey!" Cam-Ell shouts, "Put her down - you should be saving that for me. And anyway, we have a party to start!"

"Yes, Redolfo," Squintt senior says with belly-bouncing laughter, "this is a party day. I'll give you a day's takings so you don't need to work, but remember, I want you back in the air tomorrow, hangover or not - Redolfo, you must put her down!"

Caryalla reluctantly breaks free from the smiling cabbie.

Diselda runs to Redolfo and gives him a big hug. "Your cab looks so cool now!"

Amitaab runs towards him and cries, "I love you, man! You're the best!" before giving him a sentimental, teary-eyed, man-hugging embrace.

Redolfo's smile breaks away. "Dany—"

" Mike," Amitaab replies, "There's something I need to tell you."

Redolfo eyes him suspiciously.

"Danysus did something strange just before he died. That crazy garryan put himself in my head! Look, I know it's super weird, but he's there."

"Look, we're all grieving, but this is ridiculous," Caryalla says. "I miss him too, but this is the kind of nonsense he used to talk about all the time."

"I'm not kidding. I know it's him because I can't stand his ordered mind. I don't know if I can live like this."

The cabbie moves towards his friend and peers closely into his eyes. For a moment, he sees his own reflection in eyes that appear much bigger than Amitaab's. "Well, hi there, Danysus! Good to see you again, buddy."

"It is good to see you, too, Mike," replies Amitaab. "I hope you like my solution." The berrantine starts slapping at his own head. "You crazy mirror-eyed garryan! Get out of my head and find someone else to torture!"

"Our mother Brighid! Danysus, looks like you were telling the truth," says Caryalla, her eyes moist with tears. "It was me dampening your powers. You were right all along. I'm sorry I doubted you, old friend."

Redolfo leaves his friends talking and approaches Vernikell. Shaking his hand, he says, "You're a true leader, Chief."

"And you are a fine specimen of humanity, Mr. Redolfo." Vernikell replies with a warm smile. "I'm pleased to have been the one to have welcomed you to Vost. You've served our planet well."

The Baroness smiles at Redolfo, "Coming from Ariael, that's a big compliment."

"Thank you, ma'am."

"No, Mike, thank *you*. Without you, we'd probably not have survived."

"I've brought a fine keg of rum punch - or the nearest I can get to it!" adds Moorshead amid cheers from the partygoers.

Redolfo looks around at everyone. His eyes are at the point of overflowing.

"Is everything okay, Mike?"

He sees it was the Baroness who'd noticed how he's feeling. "Yes," he replies, "I was just thinking how, throughout my life, I've never really fitted in. Maybe I was supposed to be here all along."

"Maybe, indeed, Mike," the Baroness replies, with a beaming and elegant smile. "It has been an honour to have you here."

"Okay!" announces Moorshead to Redolfo, "You, my boy, and the Deputy Chief—"

"Hey, call me Ariael," Vernikell cuts in.

"Okay, then, call me John," he says with a warm smile. "Mike and Ariael, you two should be the first to test my latest brew." He passes brimming cups to his test subjects, "Now, it should be drunk in one go."

The two drink-testers comply instantly. After an enthusiastic test-swallow, there is a worrying pause. They both turn a shade of purple, then red, then both start to splutter in agreement, "Yes, that's good!" they croak, while coughing and guarding their throats.

"Hey Johnez, thesez iz ze best you'vez madez yet!" says a voice appearing from Amitaab's direction. H'droma, by some sleight of hand, has already helped himself to a large glass of the liquor, while perched on Amitaab's shoulders, and using the eccentric berrantine's head as a table. Amitaab points at H'droma and shrugs in resignation.

"You crazy kitchawan!" Moorshead replies with a chuckle.

Now satisfied with the initial responses to his beverage, Moorshead serves it out to the rest of the party.

"I love the car conversion," Moorshead says to Redolfo, as he gulps his drink, seemingly immune to the potency of his own alcoholic invention.

Redolfo studies the drink in his own glass and swills it gently in the cup. "John," he says.

"What is it, my boy?" Moorshead replies.

"What is it with the crazy names of your bar and your cocktails? Why is that drink called the *Right Old Telling Off*?"

Moorshead strokes his silver-white beard and smiles, "Remember I said that my wife left me? Well, it was probably a blessing that I should end up living on my own. I'm not exactly an easy person to live with, what with my various eccentricities. She kept on telling me off for just about everything. I guess the name of the bar and the drinks are a reflection of my former life. Anyway, let me ask you about your cab conversion."

"What do you wanna know, John? Glyrian did a cool job, huh?"

"He did a splendid job. You may not realise it, but you have actually added a Celtic touch - it's a popular historical belief, but it probably never really actually happened."

"What belief was that, Mr. Moorshead?" asks the Baroness, overhearing the conversation.

"There was an historic queen named Boudicca, who was queen of the Iceni tribe of Celts. She fought very well against the might of the invading Roman army. The Roman historians described her as having scythes on the wheel hubs of her chariot. Sadly, up until the time I left Earth, there was never any archaeological evidence to support this idea."

"If it wasn't true, then why did the Romans describe it that way?" the Baroness asks.

"We don't really know, Baroness, but it may have been because people like to embellish their stories," Moorshead chuckles as he takes a swig of his drink.

Redolfo leaves the history scholars to chat and joins the portly cab company owner. "Hey, Squintt, I gotta ask you something."

"What is it, Redolfo?" He says, studying the cocktail with some trepidation. "Do you think this is safe to drink?"

"Safe?" Redolfo replies with a broad grin, "Of course it isn't safe!"

Squintt takes a tentative sip and shakes his head in disapproval.

The cab driver chuckles and says, "What your brother can do is just amazing, and he seems to put so much joy into everything he does."

"Yes, he does, Redolfo. So where's this going?"

"So, tell me why he hasn't spoken a word for such a long time."

"Ah, you see, Redolfo, my brother and I are of a species called essechewyns. While we're a successful species on Vost, with some skills in business and engineering, we do seem to have evolved a flaw in our make-up."

"What do you mean a flaw?"

"You see, we have a tendency to bond strongly to our partners and make partners for life."

"Okay, so that's a good thing, right?"

Squintt looks at him with a serious expression, "Yes, it is, except for when that bond is broken, it affects essechewyns at a very deep level, and some of us do not survive the separation. If we do survive, we often lose something of ourselves. Ten years ago, Glyrian's partner died of a terminal illness. From then on, he lost the power of speech."

Redolfo looks horrified, "I'm so sorry."

"It's okay, Redolfo, but at least you know why, despite my irresistible looks and charm, I have chosen not to engage in a relationship," he says drumming his sizable belly, and performing a distinctly unprovocative wiggle.

"Hey, Squintt, come on man!" says a despairing Redolfo, "I know there's a perfect partner for you out there. You've got to sometimes take some risks in your life."

"Ha ha, Redolfo. I'm not a one for risks. My business—"

"Wait up!" shouts Redolfo, "I can see something."

The various conversations are paused, as everyone looks up and tries to see what Redolfo is referring to. A pink speck in the distance. A transporter. A similar but grander design to Redolfo's Checker. It approaches.

"It's him!" shouts Redolfo, "It's the *King*! Can't you see it's a Cadillac, John?" Moorshead pulls out his eyeglass, "It doesn't look like any Cadillac I ever saw. To begin with, it's pink, for heaven's sake! Anyway, Vost doesn't have a king." Moorshead replies.

As the Cadillac passes overhead, the driver's window lowers and a white-sleeved arm waves to the party-goers. The driver looks out of the window.

Redolfo gives him a big smiling wave. The cabbie shouts up to him, "Wayda go, man! Love the shades! Come back and sing for us sometime."

The driver raises a thumb of approval as the pink Cadillac continues on its trajectory towards Catuvell City centre.

Redolfo looks around at the party of bewildered faces. He shrugs. "Okay, maybe you had to be there."

He grabs Caryalla. He's never felt so alive.

"So, you wouldn't mind being my girl?" he says, beaming at her.

"Mind?" Caryalla replies, "Why would I mind? Even for a human, you're pretty sexy." She kisses him passionately.

FROM HELL'S HEART

Small, almost frail. Shivering from head to toe. Vulnerable. Why is it that Captain CJ 'Jimmie' Wells of the Royal Army Medical Corps almost feels sorry for this naked creature standing in the centre of the furnitureless, octagonal room? Is it even human? Does it actually have its own feelings? Is it capable of suffering?

The open windows usher in the icy blast of the north-east wind, making the barren room of 31a Ulzener Strasse, Luneburg feel utterly frozen. The scene is made all the more pitiable to Wells as the only light in the room is generated from a single naked bulb.

He has had serious reservations about this medical examination. What was the purpose of treating this man in this way? He watches the figure wince as the chilled winds bite through his wretched frame like invisible whips. Is it because he is now the custodian of this daemon that he harbours some sense of responsibility towards it?

Wells had served his community for years as a country doctor in Oxfordshire, England, and before that, was a dental practitioner. Now in his mid-fifties, he has found himself faced with a task of a very different sort, one he feels not in the least qualified to perform.

The prisoner has been categorised as high risk for a potential suicide. So much is at stake. Wells knows it is essential to keep this man alive in order to bear witness to the countless atrocities committed by the German authorities. The world needs him to admit to and answer for his crimes. The tragically high numbers of willing conspirators need to be identified.

Treating the prisoner in this way is not, however, in Wells' opinion, a sensible way of going about an interrogation. This man, responsible for the deaths of millions of innocents, now stands before him, about to submit himself for a medical examination. Perhaps those in authority have allowed emotions to cloud their judgment. *However terrible the actions of those held in our care, we are their guardians - as we are also the guardians of the search for truth.*

To one side of the prisoner stands Company Sergeant Major Austin. To the other stands Colonel Murphy, Second Army Chief of Intelligence, the architect of this interrogation. A single sentry has been posted outside the room.

Wells addresses the prisoner, "Can I confirm, once more, that you are not ex-sergeant Heinrich Hitzinger of the Armoured Company, as you said you were when you were captured and you are in fact, Heinrich Himmler, previous chicken farmer and former Reichsführer of the Schutzstaffel."

The naked man nods in humble assent.

"I'm sorry, Colonel," Wells says to Murphy, "I need you to leave. I would like to examine him alone."

Clearly unhappy with this demand, the Colonel leaves the room. Wells indicates to Austin that he can stay. The doctor throws a blanket over Himmler and closes the windows. Wells does his utmost to conduct the examination in as professional a manner as possible.

He starts at Himmler's hands - delicate and slender. He notices his fingernails have been clipped to neat little points. He lifts the arms to inspect the armpits. He examines the buttock cleft and realises that he cannot - will not - examine Himmler's rectum. Wells was aware that many captured SS officers had been found hiding poison in their rectums, but a *per anal* examination seemed a degradation too far. He was not going to treat this man as less than human - if he did so, wouldn't he be just like the very war criminals who the allies were now trying to hold to account?

He calls Austin over to shine a light into the prisoner's mouth. His dental training alerts him to the possibility of poison being hidden somewhere within the mouth cavity. Himmler meekly complies with this examination. Wells sees some gold and a few amalgam fillings. *Now what is that little blue object in the groove of Himmler's left cheek?* He tries not to let his panic show as he realises this is a little capsule of poison, and that Himmler could kill himself quickly by simply biting on it. With as much natural grace as he can muster, he tries to disguise the discovery of the capsule by repeating the examination of Himmler's hands, arms and face. He begins to regret not taking Austin's controversial advice to first knock him out with a sandbag.

Wells seizes an opportunity to remove the capsule and jabs a finger into the prisoner's mouth. He realises Himmler has seen through his deception as the prisoner bites him. He yanks his finger away and at once detects the bitter almond scent of cyanide.

Himmler's face turns a purplish hue as he contorts in pain, his neck veins standing out like a network of drainpipes. As he crashes to the floor his glasses skid to the ground. Wells commences cardiac resuscitation and calls out in vain for a cardiac stimulant.

The horrified dentist soon realises that Himmler is beyond resuscitation. He looks at the corpse and then at Austin, "My God. He has done it on me. He has beaten us!"

WELL NOW IT SEEMS OBVIOUS

Caryalla exits the *Opprobrium Bar* to see the Checker, parked illegally just at the foot of the bar stairway. It's been restored to its pre-battle appearance. Redolfo gets out of the cab and opens the passenger door for her. Her hair is set loose in red and blue curls. She smiles as the cabbie gasps when she descends the steps in her figure-hugging black outfit. She knows she looks good. Before she enters the cab, she puts her arms around Redolfo's waist, and pulls him towards her for a hungry kiss.

Once inside the Checker, Redolfo finds his key and places it in the ignition. He looks at her and says, "Wow, girl, you look amazing."

"Thank you, Mike, you're not so bad yourself. It was fun today at your cab company."

"Yeah. *Lucky Day Cabs* may be falling apart at the seams, but I'm feeling it's my home now."

She studies the chiselled lines of his face. What is it about this human that allows her to display tender feelings so openly, feelings that she had made sure no one could ever see? Was this really such a bad thing? Perhaps this is what she was always looking for.

"Mike,"

"Yeah?"

"It seems like my life has changed an awful lot since I met you."

Redolfo looks at her quizzically.

"The stuff that John has told me about my past...I did somehow...know it anyway. Does that sound crazy to you?"

"Nothing sounds crazy any more. Actually, it kinda makes sense. If I can remember things that happened to my father, then why shouldn't you feel something for your folks? After all you've got a gift too."

"It's like I came face to face with my ancestors. I feel them - I have felt them fight alongside me. Mike, I want to find out more about what happened to my people. I don't even know if there are any left. I could be the last one. I could do with your help."

"Hell, of course! But where do we start? Let's ask John. I guess he's the one to ask. Maybe we could speak to the Baroness, too."

Caryalla sees Redolfo staring, deep in thought. "What is it, Mike?"

"I was just thinking about my mom."

Caryalla gazes at him as she strokes the back of his head. She has never known parents and regrets not being able to have experienced the familial love that Redolfo was feeling now. "What about her, Mike? I would love to know more about your family."

"I was thinking about how, for as long as I can remember, she would spend hours simply staring out of the window. I think I know now why she did it. I can feel his presence within her."

"His presence? Whose presence do you mean?"

"My pa. I mean my blood pa, Dominik Kominsky. I can feel he somehow placed part of himself in her head. I seem to know he died at the hands of the Nazis. That poor lady never got over him. In all the time she stared out of the window, he was there with her."

He pauses, seemingly in silent reflection. "Anyways, I've got to get Gethsemona to school tomorrow. She needs picking up from her parents' temporary apartment.

A lot of her friends lived in the Faolán building and never made it out."

"That girl has spirit! I like her. Listen, Mike, it's been such a tragedy for so many people. But if it weren't for you, a lot more people would have died."

"But it's not just that. I've been thinking about my life back on Earth. It's my home and it's what I'm used to."

"I guess it must be so hard being here in a place so alien to you."

"It is, Caryalla, but Earth was also a hard place for me to fit in. I realise now why I was always second-guessing people, and I know that got on a lot of people's nerves. I was always angry at the world. In a strange way, I feel less angry about stuff. The way you block my mind powers is a relief to me. I'm so happy that I don't know what it is you're thinking - and that's crazy, isn't it?"

Caryalla laughs, "If you say so, Mike. I know a lot of people who would dream of being able to know what I'm thinking. But can you really not tell what's on my mind?" Caryalla stares into his eyes.

"Right!" he says, and in a flash, Redolfo has fired up the Checker and a large plume of frantic, multi-coloured vapour surrounds the cab. The *Lucky Day Cabs* hand begins waving energetically. "Okay, your place or mine?"

The cab rises and, within an instant, they are greeted by the deafening blast of a proximity klaxon. Redolfo flinches.

"What do you think you're doing, you crazy alien!" shouts the driver from the passing vehicle.

Redolfo hits the CEWS and the head up display screen bursts into life.

"Has anyone ever said to you how much you put them off their driving?" Redolfo asks her.

Caryalla starts laughing, "Not quite in this way, Mike."

The Checker makes an unsteady exit out from Catuvell Main Square.

"You sure you don't want me to drive?"

SEIZING THE OPPORTUNITY
WHEN YOU CAN

Baroness Ner-all enters the Central Operation Room. "Ariael, is everything okay? I had a message you wanted to see me."

"Oh, yes, Febryalla. Welcome. Leiath and I have spent most of our time today discussing the memorial service to honour our brave dead. The *Holy Council* has permitted some members of VIAS to read out tributes to the deceased."

"I'm so sorry, Ariael. We lost so many brave souls. I know how dear many of them were to you."

"We were also discussing the possible whereabouts of Sarokis and Boca. There's simply no trace of them, having left almost no useful clues at all at their make-shift control room where Professor Zanusso was held captive. Anyway, I must meet with you in *Operations Room 2*. There's something I need to show you. Please follow me."

Vernikell leads the Baroness and Officer Dowola through the short passageway to the operations room. As they enter the room, they can see Parchi is engaged in an animated discussion with a smaller male, dressed in a white coat, with a rounded head and blinking eyes, seemingly too large for their sockets.

"Oh salutations, Febryalla," says Parchi. "Please may I introduce my old friend, Cashall Zanusso."

"Oh, my!" says the Baroness, "I've heard so much about you. I understand that you prevented what could have been a full shutdown of every anti-gravity engine in Catuvell."

Parchi interjects with an energetic croak, "Cashall was subjected to a sustained onslaught of telepathic mind-probing—"

"Yes indeed, Baroness," Zanusso interrupts with his squeaky voice, "it is a pleasure to meet you. Likewise, Deputy Deputy Chief Vernikell speaks very highly of you."

Vernikell addresses Officer Dowola, "Can I confirm we have a few minutes to discuss this without impacting on your work in the operation room?"

"Yes, sir, it's fine."

Vernikell studies Officer Dowola's face, "Are you okay, Leiath? You look worn out. I guess the events of the last week have taken their toll on all of us."

The second-in-command's expression is evasive, "Oh, no sir, it's fine."

"Leiath!" Vernikell replies suspiciously. "I know you too well. What's troubling you?"

"Well, if you have to know, it's Agent Rimikk."

"Ah, yes, I hear Senesul has been making good progress. Is everything okay?"

Officer Dowola blushes, "Yes, he's quite recovered."

"So, what has that to do with you looking tired?"

Shuffling from one foot to the other, she says, "Something changed within him after his experience in the Briganti mountains with the terannians."

"Oh," says Vernikell, cheekily, "what do you mean?"

"Well, he is quite demanding of my attention. Neither of us slept."

The Baroness, Vernikell and Parchi are unable to suppress their laughter.

"Please, everyone, take a seat," says Vernikell, trying to limit his officer's embarrassment. "Febryalla, Professor

Zanusso has something to show you that I'm certain will be of interest to you."

"Well, I'm intrigued, Ariael. What can it be?"

Zanusso appears with a box-shaped package, wrapped in a colourfully patterned silky paper and adorned with a bow. It's clearly heavy by the way Zanusso is carrying it.

"I still don't get why you wanted this wrapped," Zanusso says to Vernikell, shaking his head as he places the package on a desk in front of the Baroness.

"Please open it, Febryalla," says Vernikell.

The Baroness pulls at the decorative bows and carefully unwraps the paper to reveal a clear tank filled with a bubbling liquid. Within the tank is a tubular structure, swaying in the bubbles. It appears to be made of living tissue, with overlying blood vessels and numerous blind-ending branches.

"Is this what I think it is?" she asks Zanusso.

"If you're thinking this is the Talamat Schneiderian, stem-cell engineered replica of the major blood vessel of the outflow of your heart, using modified gene-splicing collagen enhancements, then you'll be thinking correctly."

The Baroness looks at a beaming Vernikell.

Vernikell explains, "Zanusso reopened the stem cell tissue regeneration project. We are still technically using emergency state powers, so we have taken advantage of the temporary relaxation of the rules - although we are officially standing down from them in eight days' time."

The Baroness is speechless.

"Febryalla, this has been made using your own tissues, so there is no chance of rejection. It's tough enough to last more than your lifetime. You'll be the first person on Vost with your condition to be fitted with a replacement vessel." He gives her a loving smile. "Don't you see? Once this has been implanted, you will not die from a sudden rupture of the vessel. You said yourself, you've reached the age where this tends to happen. Febryalla, I don't want to lose you."

All eyes are on the Baroness. Her eyes have welled up and she is weeping floods of tears.

"Febryalla, what's wrong?" says Vernikell.

"I'm sorry, Ariael," she sobs, "no one has ever been so kind, considerate and caring towards me, least of all my husband. You've made me so happy - I can't seem to stop crying."

Vernikell hands her a handkerchief. He holds her by the tops of her arms and kisses her head. He addresses Zanusso, "Professor, do we have a surgery date in mind?"

"Yes, sir. If it suits the Baroness, it has been set for seven days' time. The surgeon and anaesthetist have made themselves available for the procedure."

BAD DRESSED UP AS GOOD

The VIAS Control Centre door bursts open and Officer Dowola sees a stream of armed agents pour into the room. Their weapons train on Vernikell. "What is the meaning of this?" she shouts.

The large form of General Hostian appears through the door, followed by Sellibot Spaan, dressed in the most ostentatious robes she has seen him wear to date.

"I'm sorry, Ariael, but I can't legally countermand this order," Hostian says with an uncharacteristically small voice.

The priest explains, his voice drawling, "I, the Most Holy Reverend, Sellibot Spaan, *Chief Protector of Faith* and President of the *United Faiths of Vost*, hereby declare that the Deputy Chief of Staff at *Vost Intelligence Agency Service*, Ariael Vernikell, is to be detained by order of the *Holy Council* for crimes against the planet." He points a bony finger at Vernikell. "You have violated seventeen Rules of the *Global Court of Trinova*: you have failed to follow interrogation protocols, you have lied to a permanent member of the *Holy Council*, you have embaced and encouraged telepathy and telekinesis, you have abused emergency state laws..."

Officer Dowola clasps her hands to her mouth as the Holy Reverend reels off all seventeen of the violations.

"...and you have violated the regulations laid down by the *Ordovic Council of Ethical Medical Practice*. I do not need to remind you, Deputy Chief of Security," he adds with a sneer, "that the inevitable sentence for such violations is death by plasma vaporisation. As for your human ally, we will need to bring him in for interrogation under suspicion of using telepathy. It will be necessary to dissect his brain to further our understanding of his powers." Spaan turns, then pauses and turns back again. "Oh, I almost forgot. Your little stem cell creation is to be confiscated - on ethical grounds."

"You will pay for what you've done, Spaan! You have the blood of thousands of souls on your hands," Vernikell shouts.

Two agents restrain Vernikell with arm locks. Officer Dowola feels for her maser hand-weapon in her belt as she sees her boss being dragged towards the entranceway, but then thinks better of it.

She hears a commotion arising from outside the entranceway. Spaan cups his ear to identify the source. Heavy footsteps begin to shake the Control Room floor. A gigantic creature in dark uniform appears through the entranceway, so tall as to only be visible, up to its mid torso. It bends down low to push a huge, blubbery-jowled head through the door frame and squeezes through into the control room. Although she had only ever read about them, she recognises the creature as a Corattian Guard of the *Holy Council of Trinova*. The massive guard is quickly followed by two more of its kind. The corattians, checked by the level of the ceiling, rise almost to their full height.

"What are you doing here?" shouts a shrill Spaan.

"All kneel for the Reverential Priestess of the Palatarian Order of the Most Holy Quinternity!" the three Corratian Guards announce in unison, with deep burbling voices. Spaan looks horrified as a tall female figure appears. She is dressed in shimmering robes of purple and gold and is crowned with a metallic headpiece adorned with an array of golden orbs, fierce spikes and leaves. Her face is wounded with deep, bleeding cuts that appear to Officer

Dowola to have been deliberately crafted and treated in some way to prevent them from healing.

Spaan drops to his knees and splays his arms outward and backwards, his head bowed low. "Most Reverential Priestess, how honoured we are—"

"Silence!" Interrupts the thin but commanding voice of the Reverential Priestess. The priest remains in his awkward kneeling position. His bottom lip is quivering. The Priestess continues, "Most Holy, Sellibot Spaan, *Chief Protector of Faith*, and President of the *United Faiths of Vost*, you stand accused of abusing your position and thwarting the sublime ministerial process that safeguards the spiritual and consecrated welfare of the peoples of Vost."

Spaan stutters, "But, but Most Reverential Priestess, I was only acting for the—"

"You were facilitating the compromise and potential annihilation of the approved faiths on Vost by obstructing the government in its *Holy Defence* against the propagation of a pagan religion as determined by the 17th Ecumenical Meeting of the Council of Trevona - and as a result of this abuse of your Exalted Office, you are henceforth stripped of your title and immediately demoted to the position of *Patriarchal Penitent of the Prelatic Order of the Faith Advisory Council*." She moves her right hand as if to sever the air.

Spaan looks crestfallen, the colour completely drained from his sallow face.

A corattian guard growls at the two VIAS agents restraining Vernikell. The terrified agents release the Deputy Chief and meekly straighten out his uniform where they had manhandled him moments ago. Spaan turns his head to Vernikell with a burning glare of loathing and mutters something inaudible, but clearly hostile.

The Reverential Priestess turns her icy stare towards Vernikell. "Do not think you have got off lightly, Deputy Chief of Staff. The Council will be watching you." She makes a swift turn and then exits the control room. The three gigantic guards follow her, each struggling to squeeze back through the doorway.

"Your crimes are still crimes and you *will* answer for them," Spaan hisses at Vernikell, before he too leaves the room. He calls after the Reverential Priestess, running with his arms projected backwards.

Vernikell stares open-mouthed at Officer Dowola. "What just happened here?" he asks her.

Before she can form any meaningful answer, she hears someone approaching through the doorway, clearly out of breath. The unmistakable, bent-over figure of Capell Parchi stumbles into the control room, beckoning for a seat to recover from his tottery run.

"What is it Capell?" Vernikell asks him.

"Did it work? Parchi asks him.

"Did what work?" Vernikell replies.

Parchi responds between wheezing breaths, "I sent an urgent message to the *Holy Council*...saying that Spaan...had been responsible for the deaths...of thousands of VIAS troops and a near catastrophic outcome for Vost itself."

Vernikell and Officer Dowola place their grateful hands on his shoulders.

"Capell," Vernikell says with a smile, "you have just saved my skin. It worked perfectly."

"It's the least I can do considering I'm responsible for this fiasco."

"How did you know that your message would work?" asks Officer Dowola. "As far as I was aware, Spaan was the top rank on the *Holy Council*."

"I guess there's always someone more holy in the Council," he says with a grin.

A NEW LIFE

Redolfo rests back in the soft seat in his apartment. He's not made much of an effort to improve the interior décor and is thankful that Caryalla is not a particularly keen interior designer either. He's found much solace in her company, finding that he's at his most relaxed when she's around. He appreciates how much she excites him, as if he has a second chance to be young again. He's finding much more pleasure in the simple things life has to offer than ever before and has even taken to regular woodland walks with her. It's now clear why the forests have always meant so much to him.

On this occasion, however, he has chosen to travel alone. He rises from his seat to prepare for his trip.

~

Wrapped from head to foot in thermal clothing and wearing a large backpack, Redolfo looks back at the Briganti Mountains. He feels the mountain's energy course through him. The journey has been tough but never has he felt so close to the natural world. He descends through the forests of the ancients towards the valley of the terannian people. The path clears for him like a receding tide. He knows that he's reached his destination.

A soft wind whistles a haunting note from between the stones. The supergiant sun's rays lift columns of steam from the dewy grass. The air is crisp and the natural loud chattering of wildlife is now thrown into a muted, respectful silence. He stops at a large gravestone that's been recently carved and settled into place. It bears an inscription that he's unable to read. He knows they are terannian words. For Redolfo, however, these words are unimportant. He kneels down at the foot of the stone and produces a pouch that he carefully unties. He places his hand inside it and takes out a carved wheel.

His eyes begin to overflow. "I've so many questions I wanna ask you. So much I need to know. Why did you give this to me, Tannis? What did you want me to do with it? What the hell were you playing at?"

The wind responds for the dead terannian with a short, whistling gust. Redolfo places his right hand on the gravestone. Darkness covers the sky and the stone begins to glow a blue hue. The world fades to black. He feels a stirring within his chest as a voice arises from within the void.

"Son of Mikkrian, you call upon the shadows for advice when you know within your own heart the answers to all your questions - for we have shared our lifetimes together and you know me far better than does any other creature in this world. I shall forevermore remain a shadow - but you, Son of Mikkrian, must live on, and deliver the spirit of our mighty ancestor, Cernunnos to the people of this planet. I know that his spirit visited your own planet Earth thousands of years ago and was worshipped as a god by its ancient people. I have seen how the people of Earth have forgotten their duty to their planet and have sought instead to annihilate each other rather than to respect each other through the sacred cycles of battle, love, life and death."

"So, what do you want me to do, Tannis?"

"Son of Mikkrian, help free my people from the oppression laid down by the newcomers of this planet. Terannians should be once again able to use their mind-powers in the way they have evolved to do, for it is in their nature and no species in this world or beyond should have the right to take that from them."

Redolfo replies to the shadow, "How can I possibly help your people? I'm just one man, a simple cab driver."

"Take my wheel to my people. They will know what I have asked of you. You will know what you will need to do."

Redolfo feels the shadow of Tannis recede into the abyss. "But that's the point - I don't know what to do!" he shouts. "Tannis, don't leave me now!"

Darkness. Emptiness. Redolfo is shouting into the void.

A ripple forms within the darkness. Another figure emerges.

"Who are you?" Redolfo asks of the shadow.

"It is your father, Michael. I am Dominik Kominsky."

Redolfo stands face to face with him.

"Papà!" Redolfo calls, "I've so much to ask you."

Kominsky replies, "My son, I would spend a lifetime talking with you but I am a mere shadow and you are of living flesh. You have my spirit in you, just as I gave mine to your beautiful mother, Marianna. I know that your powers made your life difficult on Earth but I feel you have found inner peace and purpose now you are in my world."

"Papà, I don't know what Tannis wants from me."

"Michael, you do not need to worry. If I was able to save the lives of thousands by whispering thoughts into the ear of Heinrich Himmler, then you can achieve anything you turn your mind to."

Redolfo feels the shadow of his father begin to slip back into the abyss. He shrieks, "Papà, no! We have had so little time!"

His father's voice fades into the distance, "Know, my son, how proud I am of you. Know how I shall always love your mother even to the deepest caverns of the abyss. I shall wait for her."

Kominsky has gone.

Emptiness. Loss. Redolfo feels as if his soul has been ripped to shreds. Through his tears he sees a clearing. A stag. Magnificent. It looks at him and then turns away.

"Wait!" Redolfo shouts.

He sees the beast has walked to the edge of dense woodland.

"Don't go," Redolfo pleads.

The stag looks back at him and nods its great head in salute. Within a moment, it has disappeared amongst the trees.

The sky lightens.

Redolfo sits with his back against the stone. The wind stills. Light drops of rain begin to patter on the leaves around him. An hour passes and he has not moved. Grey clouds now cover the heavens, draining the scenery of its natural colour. Redolfo is soaked through as the rain picks up. He opens his hand to look again at Tannis' wheel. The beauty of the craftmanship that made the carved image of Cernunnos atop the giant sun gives him a surprising sense of warmth and belonging. Every bit as detailed as Caryalla's miniature shield, he marvels at its intricate swirls and geometric patterns.

His mind drifts through the graveyard and upwards beyond the clouds. Onward, through the vortices of space-time, the journey vast yet tiny, between the ripples that blur the boundaries of thought and substance, passing between the dimensional spaces that bridge the indivisible particles of existence, pushing the thread further and further until he is sure he has reached his destination.

"Mamma, I know this will sound crazy, but this is Michael. Mamma, I want you to know that I'm okay and that I'm eating well. It's been kinda nuts here, mamma. I hope that you and papà are okay and haven't worried about me too much..."

~ THE END ~

HISTORICAL NOTE

Although *Space Taxis* is a work of fiction, the historical context in which it is set is very real. The descriptions of the Nazi occupation of Prague are rather typical of contemporary eyewitness accounts and recorded descriptions of people's experiences.

The Prague Astronomical Clock in Old Town Square is six centuries old and is today the focal point for tourists from around the world. On the hour, hundreds of people armed with cameras gather to marvel at the clock's mechanical spectacle; the Walk of the Apostles, and symbolic moving statues, which adorn its stunning astronomical and calendar dials. In the years of the occupation, the clock often formed the backdrop to scenes of long lines of terrified Jews, all forced to wear a yellow star who were to be sent to their deaths in extermination camps such as Auschwitz and Treblinka.

In *Space Taxis*, Marianna is sent to Terezín concentration camp. This camp, known in German by the name Theresienstadt, was a former military fortress, consisting of a citadel and barracks. The inmates were primarily Czechoslovakian Jews and deported Jews from Germany, Austria, the Netherlands and Denmark. Many elderly Jews were sent there, and the Nazis presented Theresienstadt to the International Red Cross as a 'model' Jewish settlement. Almost 150,000 Jews including 15,000 children were interned into barracks designed to accommodate seven-thousand troops. As a result, many thousands died from the effects of overcrowding, hypothermia and malnutrition, and various infectious diseases such as dysentery and cholera. Eyewitness accounts describe inmates receiving regular beatings delivered by Czechoslovakian guards.

Despite the harsh conditions of the camp, the guards did allow cultural activities to take place amongst the prisoners. Children were allowed to learn mathematics, poetry and art, and artists were even allowed to hold several musical and theatrical performances.

From 1942, weekly trainloads of prisoners were taken from Theresienstadt to be later sent to their deaths in Auschwitz and Treblinka. Many were exterminated through rifle fire when they stepped off the trains. The story of Marianna's train journey reflects documented testimonies by the deported inmates at the time. They had thought that, on reaching their final destination, they would be put to their immediate deaths. The surprise of those terrified prisoners exiting the carriages of the trains to find they were in fact being released into Swiss hands on Himmler's orders is well documented.

Space Taxis offers a fictional explanation for an actual historical mystery surrounding the rather unexpected decisions made by Himmler in the final months of his life. These decisions included this sudden release to Switzerland of 1,700 deported Hungarian Jews previously destined to be exterminated in Bergen-Belsen, suspension of the annihilation of the Jews in the Budapest ghetto, and the release of 1,210 Jews from Theresienstadt to Switzerland. The accepted explanation of how the architect of the Holocaust could show such clemency towards the end of the war, is that after his meeting with the Swiss diplomat, Jean-Marie Musy, Himmler believed that the allies were winning, and therefore needed to present himself as 'decent man' in case he was ever taken prisoner. Musy did offer Himmler five million Swiss francs and a consignment of much needed trucks for the German army. How Himmler expected to convince the allies of his 'good' nature when he was responsible for the deaths of millions of people in concentration camps is not at all clear. In *Space Taxis*, we have explained this logical inconsistency and apparent character transformation through his meeting with Dominik Kominsky.

Ruben Hecht was an historical character who did, through a series of intermediaries, come directly into contact with Musy. The dialogue between the two in *Space Taxis* is our fictional interpretation of what took place, although much of what was negotiated in the story is historical fact. The subsequent meeting described between Musy and Himmler was on a German military train from Breslau to Vienna. Although the dialogue is our fictional interpretation, the meeting itself was a real historical event. Switzerland has a long history of accommodating refugees, giving asylum to many Huguenots fleeing France in the 16th century. Their skills in working with gold, watchmaking and banking ensured that Huguenots were to have a profound influence on the future Swiss economy. However, from 1933 to 1944, Switzerland only offered refugee status for those in personal danger because of their political beliefs and not as a result of their religion or ethnicity. A mere 644 qualified on this criterion. All other refugees were admitted on a permit basis.

After Hitler seized power in Germany in 1933, Jews in Germany began to flee to Switzerland. By 1938, Switzerland had accommodated over 10,000 Jews. Over 100,000 refugee soldiers were interned. Around 60,000 refugees escaping persecution by the Nazis entered Switzerland, and approximately 26,000 of them were Jews. About 20,000 Jews were refused entry despite the Swiss government officials knowing they would face immediate execution. The Swiss authorities of the time have been criticised for being complicit with the then German process of adding a red "J" stamp to the passports of Jews. The Swiss authorities at the time felt it useful to be able to discriminate Jews from the rest of the refugee population.

In 1995, the Swiss president, Kaspar Villiger, issued a public apology for this, albeit 50 years after the event. It should, however, be remembered how Switzerland was a small country in constant peril of losing its position of neutrality. Its total population was only around 4 million, and large numbers of refugees represented a serious threat to their already shattered economy. Wartime Switzerland was largely dependent on the German lines of trade and was therefore placed in a very vulnerable diplomatic position.

In *Space Taxis*, Marianna is given employment in a Swiss refugee work camp. It was commonplace that healthy refugees were given work for the benefit of Switzerland. Although laborious, it offered security without the constant threat of death, and was therefore generally welcomed by the refugees.

In *Space Taxis*, the Celtic deity, Cernunnos, makes several appearances. He represents one of the most important of the ancient Celtic gods. This horned deity appears in mythologies and belief systems throughout Europe in various forms such as goats and stags. Other examples of horned deities include the Greek gods, Pan and Dionysus, the Canaanite god, Moloch, and the Indian deity, Naigamesha. Some medieval depictions of the beliefs of the Knights Templar show their deity in the form of a goat-like creature known as Baphomet. Although there are no biblical descriptions of Satan, medieval Christianity used the pagan symbolism of a horned god to depict the various evil conditions of mankind. This proved highly influential in establishing the traditional image of Satan as bearing horns or antlers.

Other important ancient Celtic horned gods include Herne the Hunter and Taranis, the god of thunder, who is usually depicted as carrying a lightning bolt in one hand and a wheel in the other. The wheel, which is in the style of a Celtic chariot wheel, is said to represent the sun. In *Space Taxis*, we have derived both the term *terannian* and the name *Tannis* from this deity. The wheel on Tannis' belt reflects this ancient symbolism.

SPECIES ON VOST

Giant auriachs—Bull-like, herbivorous quadrupeds.
Can be dangerous if they feel their calves are in danger.
Berrantines—Human-like bipeds. Major species on
Vost.
Corattians—Hulking, tall species of great strength.
Epeiryans—Tentacled humanoids.
Garryans—Scaly humanoids with large, reflective eyes.
Major species on Vost.
Kitchawans—A species of small stature.
Kyanagis—Furry humanoids.
Sciath—An ancient species of Vost.
Terannians—An ancient species of Vost.

CHARACTERS

Earth, 1977

Mallinson—Boss of Brooklyn cab company.
Alfonso Redolfo—Retired Brooklyn cab driver,
Michael Redolfo's father.
Michael Redolfo—Brooklyn cab driver.

Earth, 1944

Gertruda—Czechoslovakian safe house owner. Wife
of Ignác.
Reuben Hecht—Jewish paramilitary *(Irgun)* activist.
Historic figure.
Heinrich Himmler—SS-Reichsführer and General
Plenipotentiary of Nazi Germany—Head of
Schutzstaffel (SS) and architect of the Nazi Holocaust.
Historic figure.
Dominic Kominsky—Czechoslovakian accountant.
Lover of Marianna Kravová.
Marianna Kravová —Czechoslovakian Jew. Chemist
and later hairdressing assistant. Lover of Dominic
Kominsky.
Ignác—Czechoslovakian safe house owner. Member
of Communist Party of Czechoslovakia.
Jean-Marie Musy—Swiss diplomat. Historic figure.

Otto—Czechoslovakian Communist resistance group member.

Sara—Factory worker in a Swiss labour camp.

Manfred Schönfelder—SS-Obersturmbannführer. A field grade officer. Historic figure.

Vost

Amitaab—Events organiser. Street fighter.

Banattar—Military vehicle driver for *Vost Intelligence Agency Service* (VIAS).

Bocor, Dozor and Vestbo—Vost criminals.

Cam-Ell—Office worker at *Lucky Day Cabs*.

Caryalla—Trinket designer. Street fighter.

Cernunnos—Celtic woodland god. Mythological figure.

Danysus—Street fighter.

Diselda—Office worker at *Lucky Day Cabs*.

Gethsemona—Schoolgirl.

H'droma—a kitchawan. A frequenter of the *Opprobrium Bar.*

General Hostian—Chief of Staff of *Department of Vost Investigative Civilian Enforcement (DEVICE)* and CIC Vost military forces.

Leiath Dowola—Vernikell's second-in-command at *Vost Intelligence Agency Service* (VIAS).

John Moorshead—Owner of *Opprobrium Bar*. Human.

Febryalla Ner-all (Baroness)—VIAS Central Species Anthropological Research and Equalities Board.

Capell Parchi—Vost government chief scientist and chair of several scientific steering groups.

Senesul Rimikk—VIAS field agent.

Sarokis—Mercenary.

Talamat Schneider—Scientist and founder of the *Schneiderian Defence Agency* (SDA).

Temeria Schneider—Director of the *Schneiderian Defence Agency (*SDA*)* and inventor of the 3D anti-gravity Temeria engine. Daughter of Talamat Schneider.

Baranak Squintt—Owner of *Lucky Day Cabs*.

Glyrian Squintt—Mechanic for *Lucky Day Cabs*. Brother of Baranak Squintt.

Sellibot Spaan, *Chief Protector of Faith*, and President of the *United Faiths of Vost*.

Cern Tannis—Antlered, powerful fighter. Vost malefactor.

Ariael Vernikell—Deputy Chief of Staff at *Vost Intelligence Agency Service (*VIAS*)*.

Cashall Zanusso—Chief science officer of the *Schneiderian Defence Agency (*SDA*)* and inventor of the *Neuron 86G Synaptic* mind control weapon.

Epilogue (see online at **www.AdamFroshAuthor.com**)

Father Elenkus—Religious leader.

Parantis—male quadruped. Friend of Scaralia.

Scaralia—female quadruped. Friend of Parantis.

ABOUT THE AUTHORS

Adam wasted much of his youth watching Star Trek on the TV and films like Planet of the Apes and Alien on the big screen. He redeemed himself by becoming a surgeon but has since graduated from writing articles for science journals into writing his own Sci Fi and Alternate History stories. As a writer he is dedicated to giving his readers a great story laced with strong, fun and scary characters.

Descended from Jewish refugees who escaped from the pogroms, he is haunted by the stories of the Holocaust but inspired by heroes who put themselves at risk to save others.

Adam likes to hear from his readers. You can find him at http://adamfroshauthor.com or on his Facebook page:

https://www.facebook.com/AdamFroshAuthor

Harriet will never be able to let go of Greek gods. No, not the sculpted Adonis-like figures on the beach, but the ancient ones.

Loving all things mythological, her writing incorporates myths and legends from around the world. Her other fascination is with the criminal mind, and you can expect to see a blend of these two interests in her writing.

As a student of English, she spends her day critiquing literature and her evenings creating exciting characters and fun stories.

Harriet is also an artist, and she would like to hear from her readers and those interested in her art. You can get in contact at http://harrietfrosh.com/

More **Burton Mayers Books** titles:

Complete Darkness

For centuries many have pondered the prospect of an afterlife and feared what came to be known as 'hell'. One day soon we accidentally 'map' it whilst investigating 'dark matter'.

Complete Darkness is an action-packed literary shock to the senses that mixes flights of comic fantasy with bouts of brutal violence.

**October 2019 - £7.99 UK
ISBN 0957338775**

#StoptheGlitch

In a post-pandemic world, the nation is healing itself and trying to get back to a new normal, but the threat of a second wave looms.

When a second cyber attack disables all digital communications and power networks, Robin is pulled back into a world of conspiracies and competing gangs.

Does Robin hold the key to help stop the glitch?

**October 2020 £7.99 UK
ISBN 1916212657**

Lightning Source UK Ltd.
Milton Keynes UK
UKHW012321071020
371175UK00003B/74